Prince of Hearts

Nicco & Arianne's Duet
Book #1

L A Cotton

Copyright © 2020 L A Cotton

All rights reserved

The characters and events portrayed in this book are fictitious. Any similarity to real persons, living or dead, is coincidental and not intended by the author.

No part of this book may be reproduced, or stored in a retrieval system, or transmitted in any form or by any means, electronic, mechanical, photocopying, recording, or otherwise, without express written permission of the publisher.

Editing by: Andie M Long
Cover Image: Michelle Lancaster Photography

Verona Legacy

Prince of Hearts
King of Souls

For never was a story of more woe than
this of Juliet and her Romeo

                      WILLIAM SHAKESPEARE

Chapter 1

Arianne

"Oh my god, can you believe it?" Nora sighed as she flopped back onto her bed, the one she'd claimed within two seconds of arriving in our dorm room. "We're here. We're really here. I never dreamed your father would actually go through with it."

"Don't jinx it," I said, half-teasing as I began unpacking my small suitcase. "There's still time for him to change his mind."

My best friend shot up, glaring at me. "Why would you say such a thing?"

"Chill, Nor, I'm just kidding. Mom made him promise he wouldn't do anything stupid. Besides, orientation is almost over. If he was going to rescind his offer, he'd have done it by now."

I did another sweep of the room. It wasn't much. Two single beds pushed up against opposite beige walls, matching nightstands separating them. Two desks, one closet, and a small bathroom with a shower. It was clean and tidy and in one of the two girls only dorms on campus. It could have been a hovel for all I cared.

Because to me, it was freedom.

"Have you decided what you're going to wear?"

"Huh?" I blinked over at Nora and she blew out an exasperated breath.

"Please tell me you haven't forgotten. Your date with Scott?" Her eyes grew to saucers as she watched me.

"Ugh. That." I melted back into the pillows, pulling one free and burying my face in the soft feathers.

"One of the hottest guys at MU asks you out and you're acting like it's a chore?"

I mumbled some incoherent response, but then my bed dipped and Nora's fingers were prying the pillow away from my face. "Ari, talk to me."

"I..." The words dried on the tip of my tongue.

She was right. All I'd wanted was my freedom. A chance to be a normal eighteen-year-old girl. To experience all the things other girls my age got to experience. "I don't feel anything with Scott."

"And?" She looked like I'd just spoken in the mother tongue to her.

"Nor, come on, you know what I mean. There's nothing there. No spark or butterflies. Scott looks at me and I feel... nothing." Even with my virtually non-existent experience with guys, I knew that's not how it was supposed to be.

Her eyes rolled dramatically. "You have spent far too much time reading those romance books of yours. Real life isn't like that. It's messy and ugly and most of the time it hurts like a bitch. No one is saying you have to marry the guy; it's a date. Go, have fun, make out in the back of his car. Be a *normal* teenager."

But that was just it; I wasn't a normal teenager. Not even close. I was daughter of Roberto Capizola, Verona County's most successful businessmen. Heir to the Capizola fortune. Up until starting Montague University, I had spent the last five years living under lock and key at my father's orders. If it wasn't for the fact my older—and overprotective—cousin Tristan was a senior here; and Nora, my best friend since forever, had agreed to room with me; I would be stuck studying online courses from the safety—or as I liked to call it, prison—of my bedroom.

"Look." She shifted further onto my bed, crossing her legs in front of her. "Scott is Tristan's best friend, right? He's practically Capizola certified. He's safe. You need to see this for what it is."

"And what would that be?" I raised my eyebrow and she giggled.

"A practice date. A test drive. You're eighteen, Ari, and you've never even been kissed."

"I've kissed a guy before."

She frowned. "Your father or Tristan does not count."

"I..." My mouth hung open, but I had nothing. She was right. I didn't make a habit of kissing guys for the sake of it. And when the only guys you ever got to be around were all family friends, it was kind of a non-starter.

"This is a good thing," she smiled, "I promise."

"Okay, fine." It was just one date.

What could possibly go wrong?

∞∞∞

"Problem with your chicken?" Scott asked before shoveling another spoonful of spaghetti into his mouth.

"No, I'm good," I said, glancing around Amalfi's, a cute little Italian place in the city overlooking the river. It was one of my favorite restaurants despite not seeing the inside of the place for almost five years.

"You must be relieved to finally be at MU."

"What's that supposed to mean?" The defensive edge to my voice surprised me. Scott was no stranger to how sheltered I'd been growing up. But there was something in his tone I didn't like.

"Lighten up, A—"

"Lina," I hissed, my eyes darting wildly around the restaurant.

"Geez, relax. We're in the city. No one is—"

"Scott..." I warned.

"Fine, fine. I didn't mean anything." He held up his hands. "I'm just saying, it must be a relief to finally have some freedom."

"It's only been a day." A strangled laugh spilled from my lips as I placed my silverware down gently on the plate. I'd barely touched the food, but my stomach was a giant ball of nerves.

Scott had been nothing but a gentleman, opening doors and helping me into my chair, complimenting me on how pretty I looked, but his touch was a little overfamiliar, his gaze a little too intense.

It didn't feel like a test run, it felt like something else entirely.

"You know," he said, his voice dropping an octave, "I've been trying to get your father to let me take you out for almost two years."

"You have?" I blurted out, feeling heat creep into my cheeks.

"Lina, come on." He gave me an easy smile, relaxing back in his chair. "How long have we known each other? If you failed to read between the lines all those times I hung out at the house, I seriously need to brush up on my charm."

"I..." Nothing. I had nothing.

Scott was one of the few people allowed over to the house, usually accompanied by my cousin. There had been family parties and gatherings, or sometimes they came over to get away from campus and hang out at the pool or use the fully equipped gym. Of course, I'd caught him watching me, I wasn't blind. Too often his baby blue eyes would linger in my direction. But I'd never acknowledged it because it was Scott. He might not have been family but he sure felt like it.

My eyes darted around the restaurant again. I was so used to being kept at home, walking around the city freely was... disarming. No one paid me any attention though, probably because they had no idea who I was. Father had made every effort to keep me out of the public eye since I was thirteen.

I suppressed a shudder.

"You're safe here with me," Scott added, as if he could hear my thoughts. "You know that, right? He leaned over and covered my hand with his. "I would never let anything hurt you, Lina."

Nodding, I offered him a polite smile. His words, meant to comfort, only served as a reminder that my life would never be normal. I could attend college and try to blend in, but I would always be Arianne Carmen Lina Capizola.

I would always be my father's daughter.

∞∞∞

"It's getting late and I'm kind of tired." I yelled over the music. Scott leaned closer and my back hit the wall.

"What'd you say?" His mouth almost brushed my ear.

"It's late, and I'm tired." I said, but he only grinned back, closing the distance, skimming his lips over mine. Pressing further into the wall I tried to avoid his advances, using my hands to gently push him away.

"I want to leave, now, Scott."

He had been bearable at the restaurant, gentlemanly even if a little smarmy, but since we arrived at the party, something had changed. He was still attentive, making sure I had a drink, hovering at my side. But his attention was elsewhere.

"Already?" He pouted, big blue eyes glittering at me.

I rolled back my shoulders and nodded. "I'm really tired."

For a second, a flash of irritation twisted his features, but it melted away as he took my hand and led me through the sea of bodies. Guys hollered at him and girls watched us. But I was used to it. Occasionally, Papá had allowed me to visit Tristan at college, and a couple of times he'd brought me and Nora to a campus party. In secret, of course, and with the promise that we were nothing more than family friends. Tristan was kind of a big deal. A Capizola *and* the star quarterback for the Montague Knights. And Scott was his second. His best friend and teammate; his brother in all the ways that counted.

I knew most girls would have felt special; walking hand-in-hand with Scott Fascini, but there was nothing there. Not even the flicker of possibility. I just wasn't attracted to him. He was a good-looking guy in that All-American way, inheriting his mother's genes instead of his father's Italian coloring. But I didn't want to settle. I wanted to hold out for someone special. Maybe that made me naïve or a dreamer, but my life had never been my own. So this—my kisses, my body, my first time—it would be mine.

On my terms.

"Where to, bellissima?" Scott said as we reached his Porsche, and I glanced up, narrowing my eyes at him.

"Are you drunk?" I started mentally recalling how many drinks I'd seen him with. One at dinner, two maybe. But he'd drunk water at the party, or so he'd told me.

"Worried about me? That's cute." He hugged me into his side but I shucked out of his hold.

"Maybe I should drive?"

"No fucking chance. Do you have any idea how much this car is worth?" He smirked and something about the glint in his eye had me on high alert.

"Fine. I'll call Tristan to come—"

"Fine, you can drive. No need to bust my balls, *Lina*," he grumbled as he slipped the keys into my hand. This date was rapidly going downhill and I made a mental note to remind Nora never to railroad me into this again.

Inside his car, the air was thick, hostile, and from Scott's clumsy movements, I knew he was more than a little buzzed. But it was only a ten-minute drive to the other side of campus where I planned to leave his car and let him walk his sorry ass back to the frat house on the edge of campus that he shared with Tristan and their football player friends.

Silence lingered between us until his hand slid over my knee and up my thigh. I froze, my fingers clenching around the wheel. "Scott," I warned. "What are you doing?"

He laughed. Deep and smooth. The kind of laugh most girls would melt into a puddle to have aimed in their direction. But I was cranky and so over this date.

"Come on, Ari, don't be such a tease. I've been waiting for this a long time."

My eyes flashed to his as I turned for my dorm building, relief flooding me when it came into sight. "I'm going to park at my dorm," I said, ignoring his hand still smoothing over my thigh. Thank God for pantyhose. "You can get it tomorrow or something."

"Yeah," he slurred. "Whatever you want, babe."

I found a spot and parked up. The building was bathed in shadows with no signs of anyone coming or going. Slowly, I turned to him and smiled. "Thank you for a lovely evening. I'll see you—"

"Whoa, so eager to leave?" Scott's brows quirked up as his hand continued his exploration of my leg. I slid my hand over his and encircled his wrist.

"Scott, I said stop."

Confusion creased his face but then he was smirking, leaning in closer. Forcing me to wiggle closer to the door. "Come on, dolcezza." His fingers grazed my chin, tilting my face up. "I'll make it good for you."

"Make what good—" His mouth crashed down on mine, stealing my words, and the air from my lungs. Fear bolted through me as I struggled to understand what was happening. I mean, I knew what was happening, but why?

Why was Scott, my cousin's best friend and a guy my father adored, doing this?

"Scott," I breathed out, but it was a mistake. His tongue slipped past my lips, invading my mouth until I gagged. I curled my hands into fists, slamming them into his chest, trying to stop him. But he was big. All broad shoulders and thick muscle. And I was small. Slender and delicate and weak.

He fumbled between us and the seat swung back. I shrieked into his mouth but then he was there, covering my body, clawing at my hose. My skirt. My thighs.

"I'm going to make you feel so good, Arianne," he whispered, grinding into me. Bile rushed up my throat when I felt his erection pressing into my thigh.

Oh God.

This was happening.

Scott Fascini, a guy I'd known for most of my life, was going to steal the one thing I'd promised I would never give without giving my heart first.

"Shit, babe, you taste so good." He dragged his tongue over my jaw. My neck. The curve of my chest. His fingers ripped through the crotch of my hose, finding the soft material of my panties. *No, no, no*, the silent plea got stuck in my throat as he hooked the material aside and began touching me. I grappled desperately with his shirt, trying to get leverage, something, *anything*, to get him off me. My hand traced the door and I found the handle, yanking.

The door swung open, fresh air blasting my face. Scott started pulling away, muttering under his breath, but I didn't wait around to hear his pleas. Using all my might, I rammed my knee into his dick. He recoiled in pain, grunting and cussing. It was enough for me to clamber out from beneath him and haul myself out of the car. I landed with a thud, the asphalt scraping my hands and knees, pain shooting through me. But there was no time to see the damage. I took off, sprinting across the lawn, tears streaming down my face, skirt hitched up around my waist, torn hose clinging around my legs.

The dorm was right there. But I cut left, running away from the building.

Away from Scott.

"Cazzo!" he yelled, although it was more like a roar. I didn't look back though. I just kept running, feet pounding the sidewalk, heart hammering in my chest. The feel of his fingers still on my skin.

The sound of laughter made me pause, my eyes darting around for somewhere to hide. I ducked around a building—the library, I think—and dropped to my hands and knees, dragging desperate breaths into my burning lungs.

"What the...?" My eyes snapped over in the direction of the voice. Two guys were hidden in the shadows at the end of the alley. "Hey, are you okay?" One slowly approached me and I threw up my hands, scrambling away.

"Whoa," he said, holding out his hands. "I'm not going to hurt you. I just want to check..." He stepped into the light. "Oh shit, Nicco, I think she's hurt."

"Please, I just need..." The words stuck in my throat as the other guy came fully into view. His hard eyes swept down my tattered form and flashed with an indecipherable emotion.

"Do we need to call campus security?"

"No, no," I cried, my hand still warning them not to come any closer. "I just need..."

What?

What did I need?

I couldn't go back to the dorm. Not with Scott still there. And Nora. Oh God, she'd lose her shit if she ever found out about this. But it was Scott Fascini for Christ's sake. His family was almost as powerful as my father. And it was my word against his.

"What should we do?" It was the younger guy who spoke and the other guy—Nicco, he'd called him—dragged a hand over his jaw, his eyes still set firmly on me.

"A guy do this to you?" He flicked his head to my skirt and I tried to smooth it out.

"It doesn't matter. I just need..."

"What? What do you need?" He inched closer and I sucked in a sharp breath. I was one second from falling apart in front of two complete strangers; the weight of what happened—what *almost* happened—sinking into my bones, but something in his voice grounded me.

And I clung to it.

"I need to get out of here. Just until I can figure things out."

"Bailey, I need your car."

"Come on, Nicco, shouldn't we at least call someone? She's pretty messed up."

"Bailey," he ground out and the younger guy relented, handing him his keys. "You good to ride my bike back?"

"For real?" The kid's eyes sparkled and Nicco smirked.

"If there's even so much as a scratch on her..." He let the warning hang in the air.

"You have my word." Bailey turned to me and offered me a weak smile. And then he was gone, swallowed by the shadows.

"Are you sure there isn't someone you want me to call?"

My eyes went wide as realization dawned on me. "My purse," I gasped. "It must have..." I swallowed the words, panic filling me.

"Must have what?"

"When I... ran... I must have dropped it somewhere. My cell phone was in there." Tears began streaming down my face again.

"Come on." Nicco ran a hand down his face. "Let's get you out of here and then we'll figure out the rest."

Chapter 2

Nicco

"What's your name?" I asked the girl curled up on Bailey's seat. She hadn't uttered a word since I led her to his Camaro. Or when I'd asked her if there was somewhere she wanted to go. She had completely closed down on me and I didn't know what the fuck to do with that.

The silence was deafening. Then, after what felt like an eternity, a whisper of a voice said, "Lina."

"I'm Nicco." I gave her a sideways glance. "The young guy you met back there, he's my cousin Bailey. Good kid."

"He seemed nice." She shifted, rolling her scraped knees toward me. "Thank you, for doing this. I- I didn't know what else to do."

I gave her a tight nod and settled my eyes back on the road, but I couldn't fight the urge to keep glancing over at her. The rips in her hose. The grazes on her knees. It had taken everything in me not to grab her by the shoulders and demand she tell me who did this to her. But she'd been like a skittish animal. All wild eyes and uncontrollable sobs. I didn't want to scare her any more than she already was.

"Where are we going?" Lina stretched her legs out, hissing with pain, and sat straighter.

"Is there somewhere I can take you?"

"No, I just... I'm not ready to go back yet."

"You live on campus?"

"Yes. I just moved into Donatello House. I'm a freshman."

Jesus. She'd been in MU less than a week. She didn't look the type to draw unwanted attention, and my blood boiled at the idea of someone hurting her. But I couldn't babysit her all night.

"Are you sure there isn't someone I can call?" My eyes slid to hers and she gave me a weak smile, shaking her head.

"I just need a minute." Her body was trembling, mascara streaked down her cheeks.

Rapping my fingers gently against the wheel, I waited. Nervous energy rippled off her, filling the car. I knew I was in way over my head, but I couldn't leave her now. "I can walk you back to your dorm, make sure—"

"N- no," she rushed out. "I can't go back there... Not yet."

"Listen, I'll make you a deal. I know a place we can get you cleaned up and then I'll drive you to wherever you want to go, okay?"

Her eyes grew wild, her whole demeanor jumpy, so I added, "No strings, I promise."

A beat passed.

And another.

Then eventually, she choked out, "Okay."

∞∞∞

I breathed a sigh of relief when I finally pulled into the empty driveway. Even when I didn't intend on going into the main house, Aunt Francesca liked to venture out to my apartment above the garage to fuss over me.

"Where are we?" Lina sat forward, rubbing her eyes and I stole another quick glance at her. It was impossible not to.

"My place."

The air shifted as she sucked in a sharp breath. "Your place? Just how old are you?"

"Nineteen. Relax. I live in the apartment above my uncle's garage."

"When you said you knew a place, I assumed you meant a Wendy's or something." She flashed me an uncertain smile and my chest tightened.

"We don't have to..." My eyes flicked to the stairs around the side of the building.

"I could really use a drink and somewhere to clean up." My pinched brows must have said it all because she quickly added, "Water, I could use a glass of water."

Quiet laughter rumbled in my chest. "Come on." I climbed out and went around to the passenger side, opening the door for her. She mistook my action for an offer of chivalry and reached out for me, her slim fingers finding my hand.

Fuck.

What the fuck was I doing?

"I... uh..." Jerking away, I thrust my hands in my pocket. "We should go inside." My eyes darted around the place, met with nothing but the shadowy figures of the surrounding red leaf Maple trees. Lina hesitated, folding in on herself. I hadn't noticed how small she was before, but now we stood here, me looming over her, my six-foot-one stature seemed almost giant like.

Lina stuck close behind me as we walked to my apartment. Last year, I'd had a place on campus but it was bad enough being in class, let alone being in dorms. And since my family's place was across the river, it had been the excuse I needed to move into the apartment above my uncle's shop.

"It isn't much," I said, pushing the door open and flipping the switch. The dim lighting cast shadows off the walls as we stepped inside. "There's a bathroom back there," I flicked my head to the hall toward the rear of the apartment, "if you want to clean up?"

Lina's eyes swept around the place. It wasn't much: an open-plan kitchen and living area with a small hall off it, leading to the bathroom and bedroom. There was a charcoal sectional pushed up against one wall, facing a modest flat screen. The refrigerator usually housed an assortment of leftovers, courtesy of my aunt. It wasn't a warm and inviting space, but it was mine, which was more than enough.

"Thank you," her soft voice cut through the silence like a blade, and Lina took off toward the hall.

The vibration of my cell startled me, and I dug it out of my pocket.

Is she okay?

I smiled. Bailey was too fucking good for this life.

I'm way out of my league here.

I should have never brought her here. But the desperation in her eyes had called to something deep inside me—

something I thought I'd buried a long time ago.

Want me to come over?

No, I don't think we should crowd her.

What do you think happened to her?

My fist clenched until my knuckles whitened.

Nothing good.

I wasn't a saint. I'd done some god-awful things in my short lifetime. Things no kid should ever see. But if my less than conventional upbringing had taught me one thing, it was that even in the bowels of hell there still existed a thin line of what a person was or wasn't willing to do.

And I'd promised myself a long time ago, never to lay an unwanted hand on a woman.

Movement caught my attention and I turned to find Lina standing there, arms still wrapped around herself like a protective shield. My gaze immediately went to her legs. She'd taken off her hose and cleaned up her scraped knees, but I barely saw the cuts; all I saw was inches upon inches of smooth olive skin.

Get a grip, Marchetti. She isn't a plaything, she's a damsel.

"Want to talk about it?" I found myself asking. Mainly because if I knew who was responsible for the skittish look in her eyes, I could make the piece of shit pay.

"N- no," she croaked out.

"If someone hurt you, Lina, I—" I stopped myself. This wasn't my mess to fix, not this time. I had enough problems circling me, like piranhas waiting for the perfect moment to strike.

"I'm fine. I just needed to get away."

"Here." Grabbing a bottle of water from the refrigerator, I slowly approached her. Lina took it from me, our fingers brushing. My brows drew together as sparks shot up my arm.

What the fuck?

I inched back, dragging a hand through my hair. My blood boiled and my skin itched, and I knew sleep wouldn't come easy tonight.

It rarely did.

Not unless I found a way to expend some of the tension currently radiating through me.

"Are you okay?" Lina stared up at me and I fought a chuckle. As I suspected, she had no idea, no fucking clue who I was and what I was capable of. It was probably a good thing too. She'd already suffered enough trauma for one night without discovering her knight-in-shining-armor was in fact nothing more than the devil in sheep's clothing.

"I'm good. Are you sure I can't take you somewhere?"

"I don't have anywhere else to go." There was something so fucking sad about the way she said the words, I found myself wanting to know more.

Who was she?

What had happened tonight?

Why did she come with me, a stranger, instead of seeking help elsewhere?

"Then you should call someone. A friend? Roommate?"

"I lost my cell, remember." Sadness edged into her

dark-brown eyes. "When he..." Lina trembled as she pressed her lips together.

Anger zipped up my spine. Some fucker had done this to her. Hurt her. Put his hands on her. Scared her enough to run.

It seemed fucking ironic that she'd ended up where me and Bailey just happened to be meeting.

"Here, you can borrow mine." I held it out, but she just stared at it like it was contagious.

"I'm fine, really. Besides, it's late." She stood taller, letting one hand glide to her neck. "If it's not too much trouble, I should be getting back. My roommate will be worried about me."

Lina wasn't looking at me. In fact, she was looking anywhere but at me.

"Reality finally crashing down around you?"

"Excuse me?" Her eyes flashed to mine.

"It's sinking in?" I asked. "Whatever happened to make you run? The fact you agreed to get in a car with a total stranger and are now standing in his apartment with no cell phone or no way out." I was being a dick, but her sudden change of heart had caught me off guard.

"You're right, I'm being rude." She pulled herself taller, eyes fierce on mine. "I really do appreciate everything you've done for me, Nicco. It's just late and I'm tired. I want to go back to my dorm and forget this whole night ever happened."

She was too calm, too fucking composed for someone who was almost nearly... shit. I didn't have any idea about what had gone down. I'd just taken one look at the girl with holes in her hose and tears in her eyes and acted.

But Lina was giving me a get out of jail free card, and I

needed to take it. I wasn't the savior she wanted or needed. Even if I did want to find whoever was responsible for hurting her and make him bleed.

"Come on," I grabbed my keys, "I'll take you back."

"Thank you, Nicco, truly." She smiled, a real honest-to-God smile that hit me right in the chest. Jesus, I needed to get laid. Or fight.

Maybe even both.

∞∞∞

By the time we pulled up outside Donatello House, it was almost one thirty. I cut the engine and ran my hands around the wheel. I didn't mind driving Bailey's car, but I preferred my bike. The feel of the wind whipping around my face, the rumble of the engine beneath me.

The freedom.

Lina had been quiet on the ride over, her head pressed against the glass, the rise and fall of her chest gentle. Not that I'd been watching her or anything. At one point, I'd even wondered if she had fallen asleep, but the second we turned into campus, her body tensed, her hands wringing in her lap.

"You okay?" I asked.

"I will be." She gave a little sigh, hesitating.

"I can walk you to the door, make sure you get in okay?"

"No, really, it's fine. I just... I didn't ever imagine the night would end up here."

"You should talk to someone."

"It's complicated," she whispered, her gaze darting

away from me. Silence crackled between us. The urge to demand she tell me what happened burning through me.

"Lina, look at me." My tone was hard; harder than I meant it to be. But she responded, lifting her face slowly to mine. "No one has the right to put their hands on you, not if you don't want it. Remember that."

"You're a good guy, Nicco." She leaned over, pressing a soft kiss to my cheek. I went rigid.

I didn't move.

Didn't breathe as her lips lingered there, just for a second.

"I, uh..." Lina finally pulled away, "I should go. Thanks again."

Nodding, I watched her climb out of the car. I could still feel her lips on my skin, the warmth of her breath. There was either something very wrong with me or she had magical voodoo powers because I wanted nothing more than to run from the car, pull her into my arms, and kiss her the way a girl like her deserved to be kissed.

But what the fuck did I know about girls like her? Girls so sweet and pure and innocent that when they looked at you, you wanted to drown in their light.

Nothing.

I knew nothing.

It's why I didn't get out of the car. Why I watched, like a creeper in the shadows, as she slipped into her dorm building.

It's why five minutes later, when she had disappeared and everything had gone quiet again, I was still sitting there.

A strangled laugh spilled from my lips, yanking me back to reality with an almighty *thud*. I was losing my fucking mind, and all over some girl. A girl who didn't belong with a guy like me.

Putting the car into reverse, I spun a U-turn and took off. It was late but the night was still young.

And I needed to burn off some energy.

∞∞∞

"Didn't expect to see you here tonight." My cousin and one of my best friends, Enzo, stalked toward me.

"It's been a weird-ass night. Figured I'd drop by and see who's on the roster." My eyes flicked to the ring where two guys were pounding the crap out of each other. People hollered and whooped with every crunch of bone, every grunt of pain. The smell of blood and sweat lingered heavy in the air, calling to the restlessness inside me.

Enzo's brows knitted. "Bailey causing you shit again?"

"Bailey's a good kid."

"He's a fucking liability." My cousin took a pull on his beer, staring out at the crowd.

"He's family."

"I'm fucking family, and yet I don't see you running to fix my problems every five seconds."

"You know I've got your back." My eyes slid to his, narrowing.

"So what's his issue this time?"

"It wasn't Bailey, it was..."

Enzo inclined his head, studying me in that cold, calculated way of his. "What the fuck is up with you?"

"There was this girl." I blew out a long breath, scrubbing a hand over my jaw.

"A girl? What girl?" he hissed the words.

"Hey, Nicco, you weren't—"

Enzo cut off our other cousin, Matteo, who wore an easy just-got-fucked smile as he breezed up to us. "Nicco was just telling me all about the girl that has him twisted up in knots."

"She doesn't..." I glowered at Enzo. "It wasn't like that. She was running from someone. Me and Bailey just happened to be there."

"Running from someone?" Matteo clarified.

"Fuck, I don't know. Her hose were all ripped and her knees were scraped."

"Didn't you call campus security?"

"She didn't want us to, asked us to get her out of there."

"Don't tell me you did it?" Enzo clucked his tongue.

"What was I supposed to do, leave her there? She was terrified. She's a freshman."

"Not your fucking problem." He shrugged.

"You're a heartless bastard, E," Matteo said, his lips thinned with disapproval. "Where d'you take her?"

"To my place."

Matteo nodded. He was the best of us. Enzo was cold and cruel. He used girls for sex and then cast them aside like they were nothing. Sometimes I wondered if the guy even had a heart. But he was loyal. So fucking loyal. The kind of guy you wanted by your side when things went to shit. Matteo was different. There was still some good left inside him. Maybe it was his mother and sister's influence. He had people to remind him how to be kind and compassionate. He had people who loved him.

Enzo was dark as night and Matteo was a hint of sunshine on a rainy day.

And me?

I was fucking numb.

Stuck in purgatory, awaiting the day fate finally claimed my soul.

"Have you lost your fucking mind?" Enzo glared over at me. "You took a complete stranger back to your apartment?"

"I didn't know what else to do." The lie soured on my tongue. The truth a huge knot in my stomach.

Because my cousin was right.

There were a hundred other things I could have done with Lina. I could have dragged her ass to campus security or let Bailey take her somewhere. I could have taken her to to a late-night drive thru and gotten her a soda and something to eat and then washed my hands of her.

But I hadn't.

I'd taken one look into those terrified pools of dark honey and wanted to comfort her.

It was disarming, the way she had completely bewitched me.

Not to mention completely out of character.

"Nicco, my man." Jimmy, the owner of L'Anello's, strolled over to us.

"Hey, Jimmy." I shook his hand. "How's the roster looking?"

A slow smirk tugged at his lips. "Better now you're here. Want me to find you a spot?"

"Nicco, this isn't a good idea," Matteo whispered.

"Yeah." I stepped forward, stretching my neck from side to side, a blast of adrenaline shooting through me. "Set it up."

I swear dollar signs flashed in his eyes. "The regulars have been asking when the Prince of Hearts is going to make an appearance again."

"Not that bullshit again," I mumbled.

"Heartless Prince didn't have the same ring to it." Deep laughter rumbled in Jimmy's chest.

"Fuck off, old man," I growled. "Before I change my mind."

Jimmy winked before disappearing into the crowd.

"Prince of fucking Hearts my ass." Enzo slammed his beer down.

"You're just jealous you didn't get a stage name." Matteo smothered a grin.

"It's bullshit," our cousin grumbled.

"It's just a nickname." A stupid nickname Jimmy had given me the first time I'd ever stepped into the ring when I was a cocky sixteen-year-old. I didn't need a name; everyone already knew who I was. But the people liked a show and Jimmy liked busting my balls.

He caught my eye across the basement and gave me a thumbs up. "That's my cue," I said to my friends. My brothers in all the ways that counted.

"You have nothing to prove," Matteo said. "Tell him, Enzo. Tell him he doesn't need to do this."

"Like he'll listen."

"It's cute you care." I flashed Matteo a smug smirk. "But I need to do this."

"You could just call up Rayna and get her to come

over." Enzo suggested.

And on any other night I would have.

But not tonight.

Tonight I needed to hurt.

I needed to hurt until it all went away.

Until *she* went away.

Chapter 3

Arianne

"Holy crap." My eyes widened at the sight of Nora staring down at me. "Creeper much?"

"Sorry, it's just I have a meeting at ten and you were out for the count. Since you didn't get home before I was asleep, I wanted to..." She let the words hang between us.

"You wanted to know all the gory details." I sucked in a shaky breath, my fingers curling around the sheet.

"Ari, what is it?" Concern flooded her expression. "What happened?"

I sat up, pressing my back into the pillows. "Everything was fine. I mean, I didn't feel the spark or anything, but Scott was polite. After dinner he took me to this party and things went downhill from there."

"Downhill how?" She frowned.

"I wanted to leave. He was buzzed, so I drove his car and then he..." The words lodged in my throat as I remembered his fingers clawing at my thighs, his hot breath on my face.

"Ari?" Nora's voice cracked. "What did he do?"

"N- nothing," I breathed, forcing down the memories of his fingers clawing at my skin. "I managed to get out before he could..."

"I'll kill him." She leaped up. "I'll fucking kill him."

"Nora, calm down."

"Calm down?" Her eyes almost bugged out. "Oh, I'll calm down. After I've called your dad and told—"

"No." I shot to my knees, wincing as my tender skin brushed the sheet, and scrambled off the bed. "You can't call my father."

"I most certainly can," she seethed.

"Nora, think about it. Scott is as good as family. He's Tristan's best friend. And I'm nobody."

Her brow quirked up at that. "You're not nobody."

"I know that and you know that, but to everyone here I'm just another freshman at Montague. Besides, if my father thinks for a second that I'm in danger he'll yank me out of here quicker than I can say no." If he even believed me. In his eyes, Scott was a good man. An upstanding member of society.

"So what did you do?"

"I... I managed to get away and came straight here." I flinched. The lies were stacking up around me.

I don't know why I felt so guilting lying to Nicco about my name last night. After all, it was only what everyone else believed. I was here under false pretenses, a condition to my father agreeing my enrolment at MU. I was too precious, too important, to be here under my true identity. So for all intents and purposes, I was Lina Rossi, a friend of the Capizola.

I didn't want to lie. It wasn't in my nature. But some lies were worth it.

Some lies meant my freedom.

I'd spent so long locked away on my family's estate. Lonely days spent watching the world beyond from the window seat in my bedroom. When I was a young girl, I'd often dreamed of a handsome prince coming to rescue me; to steal me away from my prison. Nora said it was the romantic in me, but when you had so much time to daydream, reading became an escape. I was no longer a prisoner though. I finally had some freedom and I was not about to let Scott Fascini, or anyone else for that matter, ruin it for me.

Nora regarded me, some of her anger ebbing away. "You're right, it'll be the excuse he needs to end your college experience before it's even started." She flopped down on her bed defeated. "But what are you going to do about Scott?"

"Nothing." I swallowed the bile rushing up my throat. "I'm going to do nothing. Tristan and Scott are seniors. They're going to be busy with the football team and classes. I can avoid him easily enough."

"I still don't like it, Ari. He tried to..." Guilt flashed in her eyes.

"This is not your fault. Hopefully Scott will realize I'm not the kind of girl who wants to fool around in the back of his car and turn his attention elsewhere."

"I heard he was hooking up with Carmen Medina over the summer."

"See, maybe they'll start up again." I could hope. Carmen and Scott had history. Messy, colorful history. She was also a family friend, but I'd never really gotten to know her. Like most of the people in my life, I knew them. I knew all about their lives and their families, but they didn't really know me.

They weren't allowed to know me.

I was the girl looking in, always on the periphery but never in the spotlight.

Just then, a knock at the door startled us. Nora frowned, glancing back at it. "Expecting someone?" I shook my head, and she went over to it, peering through the peephole. "You have got to be freakin' kidding me."

"Who is it?"

"Scott," she half-whispered, half-snarled.

"Let me." I steeled myself, grabbing a hoodie and slipping it over my thin pajama top.

"Are you sure? I don't like this." My best friend gnawed her thumb while glancing between me and the door.

"It's fine. Maybe he came to apologize."

Taking a deep breath, I opened the door and stared right at the guy I'd known almost as long as Nora. "Scott," I said flatly.

"Hey, Lina. I just wanted to bring this by, you left it in my car last night." He thrust my purse at me, and my eyes narrowed.

"That's all you came by for?" Anger rippled up my spine. He was acting as if nothing had happened. Smiling at me in that easy way of his.

"Did you need something else?" He turned the tables on me, the faintest smirk lifting the corner of his mouth.

"Nope, I think I'm good."

His eyes went to my chest and I yanked the zipper up higher, suppressing a shudder.

"I guess I'll see you around then. Welcome to MU." He gave me wicked smirk before spinning on his heel and walking away as if he hadn't tried to force himself on me last night.

As if it had all been a dream.

But I was wide awake and I had the scraped knees to prove it.

"What the hell was that?" Nora asked as I closed the door, clutching the purse to my chest, anger radiating through every inch of me.

How dare he.

How dare he act as if nothing had happened.

"He knows I won't say anything."

Nora made a hacking sound low in her throat. "Tristan would—"

"Would he?" I arched a brow. "You know as well as I do, the two of them are practically Montague royalty." Scott didn't apologize because he didn't need to apologize. He was used to girls falling at his feet. Acknowledging my rejection would be a huge dent in his reputation. Besides, nobody would ever believe I turned him down.

"This is bullshit, you know that, right?" God, I loved Nora. She was exactly the girl I needed in my corner if I was going to survive MU. I'd been so excited about coming here, about escaping my four-walled prison. I'd underestimated just how difficult it would be being no one.

"Don't worry about me," I gave her a weak smile, "I can handle it."

I had to.

Because the alternative, telling my father, was not an option. Not now. Not ever.

A look of pride washed over her. "Damn right, you can. Just wait, Ari, you'll see. This year is going to be epic. Starting with the party tonight."

"Party?" My stomach dipped. "I'm not sure—"

"Oh, hell no," she grinned, "We missed all of orientation. So no excuses. We are doing this and we are going to have fun. It's long overdue."

Fun.

I rolled the word around on my tongue. It was unfamiliar. Full of possibilities and promise.

It was my life now.

And Nora was right, it was long overdue.

∞∞∞

Montague campus was beautiful. A mishmash of Gothic architecture and limestone buildings were scattered among a canvas of red leaf Maple and Oak trees. Perfectly tended lawns and evergreens filled the open spaces. But the showstopper was the Saint Lawrence Chapel, standing proud at the heart of the campus, with its pointed arches and intricate bell tower.

"Seeing it never gets old." Nora let out a little sigh of contentment. Being here was as much a blessing for her as it was me. Nora's family, the Abato, had served my family for generations. Her father was my father's driver, and her mother was our housekeeper. They lived in the cottage on our estate. Outside of immediate family, Nora and her brother, Giovanni, had been my only playmates growing up. We'd spent our summers exploring the grounds, discovering new ways to sneak beyond the perimeters. It helped there was a stream at the back of our property that flowed into the Blackstone River. We used to go down there and try to catch fish or dip our toes into the icy cold water.

I never saw Nora as anything less than me and she never looked at me as anything more than her. We were best friends. And when my mother finally convinced my father to let me attend Montague University, I think they were both relieved I wanted Nora by my side.

Of course, as a benefactor of the college, Roberto Capizola was able to pull enough strings to not only secure Nora's place at MU, but to make sure his daughter and her best friend were allocated a shared dorm room.

"Are you hungry?" Nora turned to me.

"I could eat. Maybe we can try out the coffee shop?"

"You read my mind." She hooked her arm through mine as we walked toward the Student Union. "How are you feeling about classes?"

"Nervous. I haven't sat in a class for a long time."

"Like I've told you a hundred times before, you really didn't miss much." Nora flashed me a smile. "I can't believe we only have one class together." She tucked her head onto my shoulder.

"You'll live," I chuckled. "I can't wait for Introduction to Philosophy with Professor Mandrake. He's one of the best in his field."

"And this is why we only have one class together. I like answers to my questions."

"Because the Sociology of Fame is so much better." I rolled my eyes.

"To each their own."

"Indeed." Our laughter filled the air and I took a moment to appreciate this moment. Me. Nora. A wealth of possibilities before us. So maybe I couldn't truly be myself here, but I could still soak up the fresh air; the knowledge that, for the first time in my life, I was free.

"What?" Nora pulled away to look at me, her brows knitting together.

"Nothing." My lip quirked.

"You're finally getting it, huh?"

I gave her a small nod, understanding passing between us.

"Come on," she said, taking my hand. "I might be your much poorer friend but I think I can afford to buy you coffee."

We entered the coffee shop only to be met with a sea of students. "Wow," Nora breathed. "It's... busy."

"It's fine." My eyes scanned the room for a table. "I'll find a seat while you order?"

"Sure." She joined the line while I stood there, rooted to the spot. There were so many people. Friends talking over one another, trying to hold court. Couples kissing over pastries and lattes.

Taking a deep breath, I focused on the task at hand when a deep voice said, "Lina, is that you?"

I found Tristan across the room, sitting in among a group of people. Football players, if their jerseys were anything to go by. He waved me over and I jolted into action.

"It *is* you." He stood up, waiting for me to reach their table. "Everyone, this is my friend Lina Rossi. Lina, this is everyone."

God he was good at this. The lies. The façade.

A grumble of hellos rang out around me while I lifted my hand in a small wave. I recognized a few of the guys—Tristan's teammates—the girls not so much. One eyed me up and down as she pulled my cousin back down beside her.

"I'm Sofia."

"Lina."

Her eyes narrowed. "Freshman?"

I nodded, aware everyone was watching our icy exchange. "Oh you might know Emilia," she tipped her head to the pretty girl beside her, "She's a freshman too."

"Are you the same Lina, Scott took out last night?" Emilia asked, jealousy glittering in her eyes.

Heat flooded my cheeks. "I..."

"Put your claws away, Em." Scott appeared, slightly breathless. He ran a hand through his dirty blond hair and flashed me an easy smile. "Lina is a friend," he said without missing a beat, "I wanted to help her settle in."

"I bet you did." Sofia and her friends snickered.

"Back off, babe." Tristan glared at her. "Lina's family are good people." He shot me a knowing wink.

No one else spoke. But I was hardly surprised. It wasn't the first time I'd seen my cousin exert his position as my father's favorite eldest nephew.

"Let me get you something to drink?" he asked, his eyes silently asking me more.

Was I okay?

Did I need anything?

"Nora's in line."

"Nora and Lina?" Sofia's perfectly plucked brow mocked me. "Cute."

Emilia smothered a snicker, and I wanted the ground to open up and swallow me whole.

"Don't be a bitch, babe."

Sofia ignored Tristan's warning though, pressing herself closer to his side to whisper something in his ear. My cousin released a strained breath, desire clouding his eyes.

I'd watched enough men to know when they were drunk, angry, or in this case, turned on. I already disliked the beautiful girl at his side, but I couldn't deny I envied the way she handled my cousin. How she used her female prowess to command his attention and distract him from the situation at hand.

Me.

"I'll catch up with you later," I said, excusing myself before Tristan could argue. Scott caught my eye as I turned to find a table but I didn't linger.

I had nothing to say to him.

Nothing good, anyway.

A couple got up, leaving an empty table. I slid onto the soft leather couch and searched for Nora in the line. She was finally being served, thank goodness. Seeing Tristan and Scott had set me on edge. Or maybe it was Sofia and Emilia's reaction to me. Whatever it was, my good mood was slowly dissipating.

"Here we go, one caramel latte, extra cream."

"You're the best." I gave her a warm smile as she placed the tall glass down in front of me.

"I see shitface is here."

"Nora!" I almost choked on my latte.

"What? He deserves it. Who's the girl?" She discreetly glanced over in their direction.

"That would be Sofia, Tristan's latest fling." My cousin was a playboy. But it was okay for him. He wasn't the heir to the Capizola empire.

I was.

He got to play football and attend college. To date pretty girls and get drunk at parties. He got to have the life that should have been mine. And while I loved him like a brother; a small part of me also hated him for it.

"If she thinks he'll keep her around, she's sorely mistaken."

I shrugged. "They want to tame him." And they always failed.

"I don't get it," Nora mumbled, "the whole taming a bad boy thing."

"That's because you don't read romance." My brows waggled.

"Oh, please. Don't tell me you buy into the whole notion?"

"I don't know." Sitting back, I ran my finger around the glass. "There's something poetic about the tortured hero and the girl who saves his soul." Dark intense eyes filled my head.

Nicco's eyes.

He was brooding and mysterious enough to rival any of the heroes of my favorite romance novels.

"You need to get out more."

"Hey!" I protested and Nora poked her tongue out, laughter shaking her shoulders.

"It'd be one way to stick it to your dad. Can you imagine if you went home with someone like..." Her eyes roved the coffee shop, landing on two guys over by the display counter. "Him."

As if he heard her, one of the guys glanced our way, his cold stare sending a shiver up my spine.

"Sweet baby Jesus, he's looking over here."

That was one way to describe it. He wasn't looking at us. He was glaring with such intensity, the air left my lungs.

"Too dark and broody for me." Nora broke the strange stand-off between us and the stranger.

I blinked at her. "Yeah, he's a whole other level. Anyway, it's not like I can actually date," I grumbled. Letting me come to MU was one thing but if my father found out I was dating, I shuddered to think.

"You can do anything now," Nora said around a mischievous smirk. "You just have to get creative."

"Like the party tonight?"

"Exactly. Now, you keep out of trouble while I go to this meeting. I'll catch you later, and then we can let loose." Her smirk morphed into a grin, and I couldn't help but wonder what I was getting myself into.

∞∞∞

"It's loud," I yelled over the music. The beat pulsed through me, making me feel a little dizzy. Or maybe it was the drink Nora had insisted we have. Clutching the red cup like it was an anchor, I followed her through the sea of bodies.

"Of course it's loud, it's a party." Nora swayed her hips. My best friend was amped, looking every bit the college freshman out for a good time. I'd raised a brow earlier, when she'd stepped out of our shared bathroom wearing the skin-tight dress that dipped low in the back and sculpted to her ample curves. But then I'd checked myself, remembering this wasn't only my college experience, it was Nora's too. One she never thought she'd get to have. It didn't stop me reaching for something more modest though. After my altercation with Scott last night, the idea of wearing anything less than jeans and a sheer blouse was simply not an option. I'd let Nora curl my hair though. It hung around my face in soft waves, barely touching the nape of my neck.

I loved it.

"Oh, I love this song." Nora grabbed my hand, pulling me toward the makeshift dance floor. Downing the rest of her drink, she discarded the cup and began shaking and rolling her hips, hands weaving patterns in the air. "Come on," she mouthed, as I stood there. A fish out of water.

It was a just a party.

I'd been to them before. But then Tristan had kept us in his sights. He hadn't let us drink, or dance with guys.

But Tristan wasn't here now.

"Come on, please." My best friend crooked her finger.

"Fine," I mouthed, looking for a place to dispose of my drink. Spotting a table, I made a beeline for it only to be cut off by two guys. They didn't see me, too busy looking at something on one of their cell phones.

"Hmm, excuse me..." I croaked, trying to move around them.

"Hold up, pretty thing," a gravelly voice said, and I looked up to find two vaguely familiar eyes pinning me to the spot.

"Leave it, Enzo," the other one said, pocketing his phone and finally giving me his attention. "Lina?" A strange expression passed over his face.

It was him.

The guy from last night.

"Hello, Nicco." I smiled, a strange sensation taking root in my chest.

"You two know each other?" Disbelief dripped from the other guy's words.

"We, uh... we have a mutual friend."

We did?

I gave him a questioning look, but Nicco averted his eyes. "Come on, man," he grumbled, "this party sucks. Let's go hang out at L'Anello's."

"Fuck yeah, the pussy is better there anyway."

My lips parted on a gasp as my hand drifted to my neck. Nicco lifted his eyes to mine, and I was ensnared. A beat passed, the air crackling between us.

"It's nice to—" I started, but Enzo roped an arm around Nicco's shoulder and led him away.

No goodbye.

No, how are you.

Nothing.

Dejection pulsed through me.

"Hey, what's up?" Nora nudged my shoulder. "Was that the guy from the coffee shop earlier?" She flicked her head to where Nicco and his friend had disappeared into the stream of people coming and going.

"I... was it?"

"It looked like him. Hard to forget that face. Mind, his friend wasn't too bad either."

"Hussy," I replied, trying to deflect her question, and give myself chance to catch my breath.

To try to understand what the hell had just happened.

"Hey, it's college and I am more than ready to experiment."

"Weren't you the one telling me earlier dark and broody wasn't your thing?"

"It's not, but that doesn't mean I don't want to sample the goods before I make a final decision."

"Who are you and what have you done with Nora Abato?"

"I'm young, free, and single, and ready to mingle." Her laughter was infectious, her mood like sunshine on a summer's day. I wanted to bask in it. To let her happiness blot out the dark corners of my mind.

I wanted to forget.

About Scott.

About my father's expectations and the future that awaited me.

About the weird connection I felt between me and Nicco.

Who was I kidding? There was nothing between me and Nicco. He was just in the right place at the right time.

So why had he lied to his friend about me?

And why every time I closed my eyes, did I see his face?

Chapter 4

Nicco

She was there.
Lina.
I had been so surprised to see her at the party, I'd totally froze. Well, that and I didn't want Enzo to figure out she was the girl from last night.

"Hey, what's gotten into you? You seem jumpy?"

I glanced back at the house. "Maybe we should stick around. Just in case trouble blows up."

What the fuck was I saying?

"Trouble? It's a college party. Those guys couldn't find trouble if it yanked down their pants and attached itself to their dicks."

My eyes narrowed.

She was still in there.

Why the fuck was she in there after what happened last night?

"You sure you're okay? You're acting weird."

"Just restless."

"Still? I would have thought taking it out on Domenico last night would have loosened you up. He was a mess."

I inspected my knuckles, relishing the sting of pain as I clenched and unclenched them, watching the tender skin stretch and contract over bruised bone. Enzo was right. I had gone to town on Dom, and it had helped. Until I'd found myself staring into dark honey eyes again.

The bleep of Enzo's cell phone cut through my thoughts. "It's Matteo," he said. "He's going to meet us at L'Anello's."

My expression fell and Enzo scoffed. "You're not coming to L'Anello's, are you?" His icy glare burned through me.

"You go. Tell Matt I said hey. I'll catch you tomorrow."

"You're going back in there?" He flicked his head to the house.

"Nah, man." I gave him an easy smile, playing down my strange mood. "I'm going to ride, clear my head."

"Yeah, okay, whatever." Enzo shrugged, letting out an exasperated breath. "Don't do anything I wouldn't," were his parting words as he cut across the street to his car.

He never parked his car with the rest of the cars. It was his most prized possession, that and an 1886 original Saw Handle Derringer. Enzo had three great loves in his life: restored cars, hot women, and collector's edition weapons.

I headed for my bike and waited. When the taillights of his GTO disappeared in the distance, I circled back to the house, pulled up the hood on my jacket, and slipped inside. The place was crammed full of drunken students looking to let loose and get it on. Bodies writhed together in the middle of the room, touching and kissing. The air was thick with lust and longing.

It didn't take me long to find her.

Lina and her friend were right where I'd left her only minutes earlier. Only now, they had a group of guys circling, like a pack of wolves moving in for the kill. I lingered near the wall, in the shadows, watching as Lina tried to evade some asshole with bad taste in clothes and even worse taste in hairstyles. Her friend wasn't playing so hard to get, letting one of the guys pull her in for a dance. Next thing you know, he had his tongue down her throat. Lina's eyes went wide as she stood there completely out of her depth. Douchebag attempted to move in on her again, crowding her into a darkened corner of the room.

Before I could stop myself, I stalked over to them, roughly fisting the back of his shirt. "You need to leave, now," I growled.

He swung around, indignation burning in his eyes. "Who the fuck do you..." he choked over the words, the blood draining from his face as I cut him with a deadly look. "Yeah, I... uh... sorry, man." He almost tripped over himself trying to get out of there, not sparing Lina a backward glance.

"What was that?" Lina was in my face, glaring at me.

"That was me saving your ass, again."

She rolled her eyes. "I had it handled."

"Looks like you did, Bambolina," the word spilled from my lips without warning.

"Doll?" Her eyes flashed with irritation. "You can't call me that."

"Just did." I shrugged. It wasn't a word I'd ever really used before, but it fitted her to perfection. She was small and dainty, with perfect skin and lips, and eyes that were too big for her face.

The fact she was pissed at my impromptu nickname only made it sweeter.

"What do you want, Nicco?" She let out a heavy sigh,

looking over my shoulder to check on her friend.

"You need to be more careful," I said, a strange sense of possessiveness snaking through me.

"I need to be more... wow. So you think what happened last night was my fault?" Disappointment edged into her expression and my chest tightened.

"That's not what I meant." What the fuck did I mean? She wasn't mine. I had no right to charge in here like a bull and tell her how to live her life.

A couple of guys barreled past us, forcing me closer to Lina. Her breath caught as my hand shot out to the wall beside her head.

"Why didn't you tell your friend how we know each other?" she asked.

"Did you tell your friend about me?"

Lina's lips pressed into a flat line as she gave me a little shake of her head.

Yeah, Bambolina, didn't think so.

"So I'm your dirty little secret too?"

"Don't do that." Disapproval clouded her eyes.

"Do what?" I leaned in, unable to resist the way she smelled. Like cotton-candy with a hint of vanilla. "What am I doing, Bambolina?"

She craned her neck to look at me. "Playing with me. I'm not a toy."

"No, you're not." *You're so much more than that.*

I felt it in my soul.

Lina was trouble.

A distraction I didn't want... *or need.*

Yet, here I was, in the middle of a college party, caging

her against the wall, lecturing her on staying safe, as if it was my God given right to protect her.

Squeezing my eyes shut, I inhaled a shaky breath, trying to get some clarity on the situation. Only to open them and find Lina staring back at me. Jesus, the way she looked at me... it completely disarmed me. Made me want things.

Things I could never have.

"I need to go," I said.

"Go?" she balked, looking at me like I'd lost my fucking mind.

It occurred to me that maybe I had.

"This, us, it's a bad idea."

Her eyes grew to saucers. "There's an us now?"

"I... fuck, no... I just meant..."

"Nicco." She smiled, tucking a loose curl behind her ears. "It's okay, I like you too."

"You shouldn't."

Her expression fell. "I see."

"I'm not the good guy here, Lina, I'm..." I rubbed a hand over my face. "Complicated."

"Said every guy ever." Her soft laughter was like a bolt of lightning straight to my hardened heart.

"If I ask you to go back to your dorm, will you?"

"And leave Nora?" She grimaced. "Not going to happen."

"Please?" The corner of my mouth lifted.

"It's just a party. I think I can handle it."

I let my gaze fall down her body. If her outfit was an attempt at demure, she'd failed. The denim molded to her hips like a second skin, and her blouse, while long-sleeved, was sheer enough to draw my eyes to the outline of her bra. When I finally finished my perusal, and lazily dragged my eyes back to her face, she was flushed and I was sporting a semi.

"Do you have any idea how fucking good you look?"

"I..." Lina swallowed. Something told me she didn't. She wasn't here to catch some guy's attention. If I had to put my money on it, the only reason she was here was for her friend.

"I'm taking you home," I said.

"W- what?"

"You can go get your friend or I can pick you up and throw you over my shoulder. Your choice, Bambolina, but we are leaving." I had no plans to make her leave with me, but it was impossible to resist playing with her. Earning me another one of her starry-eyed expressions.

My brow rose. "I'm waiting."

She gave a little huff, rolling her eyes, before slipping around me and making a beeline for her friend. Lina didn't mess around, yanking the girl's arm, causing her to break the kiss. They had a heated conversation, both their gazes flicking to me on more than one occasion. Then Lina walked back to me.

"She doesn't want to leave; apparently Kaiden plans to show her a very good time later." Her eyes rolled.

I smirked. I couldn't help it.

"Is that so?" I scratched my jaw. "Okay, come on." Grabbing Lina's hand, ignoring the jolt of electricity, I went straight over to her friend.

"I'm taking her home," I said. "You should come with us."

"But Kaiden wants to—"

"Yeah," I cut her off, glaring hard at the guy plastered to her side. "What *does* Kaiden want?"

His eyes narrowed and then widened with realization. "Shit, man, I didn't know you knew Nora."

"I don't. But she's my... she's Lina's friend, and I know Lina. So listen up and listen good. You get her home in one piece. If I hear you put so much as a finger wrong, I will—"

"Whoa." He threw his hands up. "I'm not a total dick. I'll look out for her."

"You'd better." My jaw clenched.

"You're going with him?" Nora asked Lina, who stood beside me, her eyes dancing between the three of us.

"I think so. The party isn't really my thing. But stay, have fun with Kaiden." She settled her eyes on him. "Hurt her and I'll kill you."

"Fuck," he breathed through a strained smile. "The three of you are intense."

"Relax, I have a can of mace in my purse. We're all good here. Go." Nora wasn't looking at me, she had her eyes fixed right on her friend and they said, 'don't do anything I wouldn't'.

"I'll see you later." Lina said, leaning over to give her friend a hug.

"Tomorrow." Nora chuckled. "I'll see you tomorrow. Don't wait up."

Fuck, what the hell had I gotten myself into? Lina was hard to get a read on, but her friend was something else entirely.

"I'm watching you, Kai." I jabbed my finger in the guy's face.

"It's Kaiden," he stuttered.

"Whatever, we're out." My hand tightened around Lina's as I led her through the crush of bodies. I knew I'd just made a statement, at least in front of Nora and Kaiden. But the semester hadn't officially started and everyone else was too wasted or high to pay us any real attention.

I could take her home, make sure she was safe, and then move on with my life.

"I can't believe she's staying with that guy," Lina said as soon as we stepped outside.

"Why did you come tonight?"

"Nora wanted to. She wants us to have all these college experiences."

"Is it so surprising she's in there with him then?"

"I guess not, no." Lina dropped her gaze. And something inside me twisted. She wasn't supposed to cower, she was supposed to stand tall.

I didn't know her, not really. But I knew enough to know she wasn't like most girls at the party. She had class. An alluring naïveté that was a rare find these days.

Bottom line, Lina was special.

I felt it.

I didn't want to, but I did.

"What?" she asked, and I realized she was looking at me again and I was staring at her like a fucking idiot.

"Nothing, come on." Taking Lina's hand again, I guided her to where my bike was parked. Releasing her, I grabbed the helmet and held it out.

"You want me to ride on that death trap?"

My mouth twisted. "I'll go slow."

"No. No way."

"You want the full college experience, right? Well hop

on, Bambolina."

"Nicco, I'm not sure—"

"Look," I ran a hand through my hair. "It's almost a mile walk back to your dorm or we can ride my bike."

Her eyes drank it in, running over the polished frame up to the handlebars. I'd restored every inch of her in my uncle's shop; she was my pride and joy.

And I'd never had a girl on the back.

"Okay." She took a deep breath, a small twinkle in her eye. "But promise not to go too fast."

"I promise. Here." I helped Lina get the helmet on. "It suits you." *A little too much,* I swallowed the words.

Swinging a leg over my bike, I got situated and glanced back at Lina. "Slide on behind me."

She looked so fucking adorable, standing there, gawking at me.

"Any day now," I teased, fighting a smirk.

Gingerly, Lina climbed on, careful not to press too closely to me. But I hooked an arm behind me and snagged her hip, pulling her as close as possible. Her breath hitched, and my heart did a somersault. Okay, so maybe this was a bad idea. She felt too good; her thighs hugging me... her hands pressed flat against my stomach.

Fuck.

I hadn't expected her to fist my t-shirt. To hold on as if she never intended to let go.

And I really didn't expect to like it so damn much.

I kicked the starter and the bike rumbled to life beneath us. Lina let out a little shriek of excitement as I took off down the road. I wasn't lying earlier when I'd told Enzo I wanted to ride, to clear my head. But now I had Lina on the back of my bike, I imagined taking the road out of town and hitting the highway. Miles and miles of open road. Just me. My bike.

And my girl.

Lina wasn't mine though, even if part of me wanted her to be. Something deep inside me already felt tethered to her. Protective and possessive. It didn't make any sense. None of it. And it wasn't like I could act on it. She was too good for a guy like me.

Somewhere around halfway to her dorm, she pressed her cheek against my back, gripping me tighter. I almost felt disappointed when we finally rolled into the small parking lot behind Donatello House. I hadn't gone around front to avoid drawing any unnecessary attention. I cut the engine and heavy silence filled the space between us.

"Wow, that was... wow." Lina climbed off the bike and pulled off the helmet, shaking out her curls. "I had no idea it could be so invigorating." A slow smile broke over her face. "You'll have to take me on a proper ride sometime. I mean... if you want." Embarrassment stained her cheeks, and I chuckled. I was pretty sure there was a joke in there somewhere, but I didn't want to ruin the moment.

"You look good on my bike," I said.

And that I fucking meant.

"Thanks for the ride."

I tucked the helmet into my chest and gave her a small nod. "You should go inside." My eyes flicked beyond her to the door.

"I think I'll have to go around front."

"Your key operates both doors."

"Oh, okay." Lina rocked on her kitten heeled boots. I couldn't resist letting my eyes sweep down her body again.

She was everything I could never have.

Everything I'd never wanted.

Until now.

I swallowed, lifting my gaze to hers. "Go on."

"Goodnight, Nicco." Lina smiled.

"Goodnight."

She didn't move. Her eyes didn't leave me even for a second. Slowly, she walked over to me and slid her hand against my face. "Thank you, for coming to my rescue again." There was a playful lilt in her voice.

"Anytime, Bambolina." I smirked but it was wiped away when Lina leaned in, her lips brushing my cheek. She hesitated just for a second, but it was enough for me to turn my head and let my lips slide against hers.

Rookie. Fucking. Mistake.

The moment I tasted her, everything shifted. All I could think about now was pulling her down on my bike and devouring her. She tasted too good. Too tempting.

She tasted like my fucking downfall.

"Nicco." My name was a whisper against my lips as I ran my tongue against the seam of her mouth. My hand slid into Lina's hair, anchoring her to me as I kissed her deeper, harder. Her body shuddered, a soft sigh getting lost between us. I wanted to paint her skin with my lips, brand every inch of her. This wasn't even a real kiss. It was fleeting and cautious. But I already knew I wanted more.

I wanted everything this girl—this *stranger*—had to give.

"What are you doing?" she whispered when I paused, my lips hovering over the corner of her mouth. "Nicco, what are—"

I jerked back as if I'd been struck by lightning. "You should go, Lina. I'll wait until you're inside."

"I see." Her lips thinned as she stepped back, putting a thousand miles between us, the invisible tether between us almost snapping. "Well, I guess I'll be going then." She didn't hesitate this time. Lina walked away from me with her head held high, without so much as a backward glance.

It was no less than I deserved, but it hurt all the same.

I wanted her.

I wanted Lina the way I'd never wanted another girl before. But I couldn't be that guy. I couldn't give her hearts and flowers and romance.

I couldn't be the prince she deserved, because my life wasn't a fairytale.

It was the stuff nightmares were made of.

Chapter 5

Arianne

"Good night?" I peeked over at Nora as she slipped into our dorm room wearing an oversized MU hoodie and her shoes from the night before.

"Oh. My. God. The best." She flopped down on the bed, arms stretched out by her sides, a dreamy expression plastered on her face. "I think I'm in love."

"With Kaiden?"

"With his tongue. Seriously, Ari, he did this thing—"

"Whoa, too much information." My cheeks heated, my stomach clenching. "You stayed over?"

"He brought me breakfast in bed. Can you believe that?"

"That's... nice." At least, it seemed like a nice thing to do. It wasn't like I had experience. I'd barely even been kissed.

Nicco kissed you.

Technically, I'd kissed him first, but still, I could vividly remember the way his lips felt against mine. The roughness of his day-old stubble against my soft skin. The way tingles had zipped through me, firing off in all directions. It was imprinted on my mind.

He was imprinted on my mind.

Unfortunately, the look of regret as he'd jerked away from me was also imprinted there.

One thing was certain though, Nicco gave me whiplash.

"Ari?"

"Sorry, what?"

"I was telling you all about Kaiden and you're over there, lost in your own thoughts. Wouldn't happen to be thinking about a certain brooding hotty who practically dragged you out of the party, would you?" Nora pushed up on her elbows, grinning at me.

"Who, Nicco?"

"Oh, he has a name. Nicco, you say? Funny because the two of you looked far too close to be new acquaintances, and yet I've heard nothing about a guy called Nicco. Spill."

"There's nothing to spill, not really. He helped me out... the other night."

"The other night?" Her brows pinched. "But we've only been here two nights... no," she gasped. "He helped you out with the Scott situation? But you said you came straight here."

"It was confusing."

"I can see why you'd be confused over a guy who looks like he does."

"Nora!"

"What? The guy was hot. If tall, dark, and brooding is your thing, which it obviously is."

"He's very bossy."

"So what happened after you left the party?"

"He gave me a ride... on his motorcycle."

"Sweet baby Jesus, he's got a bike? That just upped his hotness by at least ten."

"You have a scale of hotness?"

"Not important." Nora rolled her eyes, sitting up fully. "So did anything else happen?"

Everything and nothing, I wanted to say.

The kiss had been unlike anything I'd ever experienced. But then, Nicco had pulled away like a bucket of ice-cold water had been dumped all over him. It left a sour taste in my mouth. He felt the chemistry between us, I was almost certain he did. But he was hesitant. And I couldn't help but wonder if I was the problem.

"Ari..." Her brow rose.

"We kissed."

"Thank God," she shrieked with delight.

"Seriously?"

"Oh, come on. Nicco is totally into you and you'd be a fool to not want to sample the goods."

"You make it sound so crass."

"It's only sex, Ari. Everyone does it."

"Yeah, but I want my first time to be right."

"I hate to disappoint you, but first times are usually a huge let down. All the fumbling and awkward condom conversation, not to mention it's usually over in less than five minutes."

"At least you've had sex." She'd gotten all the teenage rites of passage stolen from me: homecoming, first kisses, first base, prom, the party after prom... *sex* at the party after prom.

"It'll happen. We're in college now, the world is your oyster." She gave me a warm smile. "Hey, who knows, maybe

Nicco will be willing to pop your cherry."

"Stop, just stop." I picked up a pillow and threw it at her. Nora caught it, falling back onto the mattress in a fit of laughter.

"Okay, I'm sorry," she finally calmed down. "So what do we know about him?"

"He's a sophomore."

"And?"

"He rides a motorcycle and has a cousin named Bailey. Oh, and his best friend is the guy from the coffee shop."

"The guy from earlier, with the intense eyes and tats? No freaking way."

I nodded.

"What is he studying?"

"I don't know." Okay, so maybe I didn't know much about Nicco at all.

"Well, he's someone. Didn't you see the way Kaiden almost peed his pants when Nicco warned him to behave?"

"You didn't ask?"

"We didn't exactly talk much." Nora smirked.

"Will you see him again?"

"Who, Kaiden? Maybe." She shrugged. "The sex was good, but I don't want to tie myself down. It's only fall semester. What about you? Will *you* see *Nicco* again?"

That was the million-dollar question. After his strange dismissal last night, I wasn't sure he'd seek me out again. But something deep inside me felt like our paths would cross again eventually.

And I couldn't deny part of me hoped they did sooner rather than later.

∞∞∞

By the time Monday morning rolled around, I'd almost forgotten about the kiss with Nicco.

Almost.

I found myself looking for him, hoping to catch a glimpse as I walked from building to building, class to class. Nora teased me about him constantly over text. She even asked me if I wanted her to text Kaiden and snoop, but I told her if she dared, I'd call Gio and tell him all about his baby sister's freshman *activities*. He might have been off pursuing his dream of becoming the next great football player, on an all-expenses paid scholarship to the University of Pennsylvania, but he was fiercely protective of Nora. Protective enough that he wouldn't hesitate to drop everything and drive back to Verona County if he thought Nora was in trouble.

It was lunchtime when I finally saw him. I'd arranged to meet Nora in the food court, where I found her flirting with yet another guy.

"There you are," I said, approaching them. "I almost didn't see you for all the *people*." I shot her a knowing look before sliding my eyes to the guy. "Hi, I'm Lina."

"Dan. I'll catch you tomorrow?" he asked Nora and she nodded. "See ya."

He left and I turned to her. "Another guy? You work fast."

"Oh stop, we were talking."

"I heard you can catch all kinds of disgusting things from *talking*."

"So you didn't spot hotty the second you got here?"

"I..." My eyes flicked over to where he sat with Enzo and some other people, my brows crinkling when I noticed the girl sitting a little too closely to him.

My stomach sank.

"They look friendly." Nora linked her arm through mine, guiding me toward the pasta counter.

"He can talk to whoever he likes."

"Mmm-hmm." My best friend was too busy eyeing today's selection.

I risked peeking over at him again, only this time, he was looking right back. His intense gaze pinned me to the spot. Our connection was severed though when Enzo nudged his ribs. He cast a dark look in my direction before commanding the attention of everyone at their table.

Releasing a heavy sigh, I picked some lunch and followed Nora to the service counter. Once we had paid, we found an empty table. Montague had an impressive food court; something more fitting for a shopping mall. But it was no surprise really, given the college's very private, very elite status. Montague University was built with old money.

Old Italian money.

Founded by the original settlers during the first wave of Italian immigrants who arrived in New England during the late eighteen hundreds, MU was on the cusp of celebrating its Centennial.

Celebrations my father and mother had a personal hand in planning.

"You're sitting at the wrong table." Sofia, the girl from the coffee shop, glared down at us.

"Excuse me?" Nora rolled back her shoulders. "I didn't see a sign that said it was taken."

"Well," Sofia flicked her hair off her shoulder, shooting her girlfriends a smug look. I noticed Emilia glaring at me as if I'd stolen her favorite toy. "I'm telling you now, we sit here."

"Come on, Nora, it isn't worth it." I grabbed my tray to get up, but Nora slammed her hand down on top of it.

"We're not moving, Lina. If they want to sit here, there's plenty of room." Her eyes went to the empty chairs.

I might have spent the last few years locked away from the world, but I knew girls like Sofia and Emilia. They were self-absorbed and spoiled and had claws sharper than any lion.

"Nora," I whisper-hissed, shrinking into my seat as people around us began to stare.

"Ladies," Tristan appeared out of nowhere, slinging his arm over Sofia's shoulder. "What did we miss?"

"Oh, nothing." Sofia smiled sweetly. "We were just telling Lina and her friend that this is our table."

He snorted. "Seriously, babe?"

"What?" She pouted. "We always sit here. Everyone knows that."

"So let's all sit then," he shrugged, "there's enough space." Chairs scraped and people stared as Tristan and his friends began to sit down. Emilia shot around the table to take the seat at Scott's side, smirking at me as if she'd won this round.

"What do you possibly see in her?" Nora grumbled beneath her breath.

"She gives great head." Tristan grinned, leaning over to high five Scott and their friend. Sofia acted mildly offended, swatting his chest. But her anger quickly melted away as my cousin began kissing her.

"Disgusting," Nora said what we were both thinking.

"So, Lina, how is your first day of classes going?" Sofia asked me, her voice saccharine sweet. The table fell quiet, watching the two us."

"Babe, lay off—"

"It's just a question, Tristan, lighten up."

He threw me an apologetic glance. If Tristan made a big deal out of standing up for me, it would look suspect, something I couldn't afford.

"It's fine," I said. "Classes are good, thank you."

I felt Scott staring at me, and I hated that Tristan wasn't the only one who knew the truth. It wasn't like I wanted to deceive people about who I was, but my parents agreed that it was for the best initially. At least, until I'd settled in. If people knew I was Roberto Capizola's daughter, heir to the Capizola empire, things could turn sour for me pretty quickly. Even with Tristan's protection.

"What about you, Nora? How is your college experience shaping up so far?"

"What the hell is that supposed to mean?" Nora stiffened.

"I heard you've been making yourself at home, if you know what I mean." Sofia snickered, and Scott and his friend followed suit.

"Something you want to say?"

"Guys talk, especially in the locker room."

"You mean Kaiden..." Her teeth ground together. "What an asshole."

"Watch your back with that one," Scott added, "he's known to get a little handsy. If you know what I'm saying." His gaze found mine again, a smug expression on his face.

A deep shudder worked through me as I averted my gaze. Thankfully, Sofia chose that moment to steal the limelight. "Oh, is that the time," she said. "I need to go. Girls." They got up, lingering while she made moon eyes at my cousin.

"See you after practice?" Tristan asked her.

"Maybe, if you're lucky."

"Will I see you after practice, Scott?" Emilia made no attempt at hiding the lust in her eyes as she flipped long golden hair off her shoulder.

"I... uh... sure, maybe." His eyes found mine as he stumbled over the words.

She gave him a placated smile and took off after her friends.

"Sorry about them," Tristan said the second they were out of earshot. "I can talk to Sofia, maybe explain—"

"Please," it came out a low groan, "don't make things any harder for me than they need to be."

"Yeah, you're right." He let out an exasperated breath. "I think you made a good impression the other night," Tristan whispered out the corner of his mouth. "He hasn't stopped talking about you."

I went rigid, curling my hand around the chair. "We're just friends."

He chuckled. "You know he wants to be more than friends, right? It's time to grow up and live in the real world."

A frown crossed my expression. "What is that supposed to mean?"

"Nothing." He let out an exasperated breath. "It means nothing. Just give Scott a chance, yeah? Who knows, the two of you could become the golden couple of MU before the year's out."

"How about you lay off my girl, Capizola?" Nora arched a brow at him. "We've barely been here three days."

"I'm done," I announced, breaking the strange tension that had descended over the five of us. "Nora?"

"Yeah." She got up. "It's a little too crowded."

"Watch your back, Rossi," Tristan called after me. He was joking, I knew that, but after what happened with Scott, and the fact my cousin knew nothing about it, things between us felt wrong.

"Who the hell do they think they are?" Nora hissed as we emptied our trays and headed out of the food court.

"The elite of MU." I rolled my eyes.

"Did you see Sofia's friend practically drooling over Scott? If only she knew…"

"Whatever. If she wants him, she's welcome to him." Because one thing was for sure, I had no intention of going out with Scott Fascini ever again.

We reached the doors, but I hesitated, glancing over my shoulder to where Nicco and his friends were sitting. Enzo was staring right at me, his eyes sharp and cold.

But Nicco was gone.

∞∞∞

"Welcome to Introduction to Philosophy, I'm Professor Mandrake. If you're in the wrong class, please leave now."

A chorus of snickers rang out around me. After a quick trip to the restrooms, I'd arrived with seconds to spare, sliding into an empty seat in the back row. It was the perfect spot to blend in. The professor got straight to it, scrawling the topics for this semester on the whiteboard while students tapped out notes on their iPads and phones. I preferred the old-fashioned method, decorating a fresh page in my notepad with words like philosophy of mind, moral philosophy, metaphysics, and epistemology.

"For the next couple of weeks, we'll be looking in depth at free will. Reading is chapters one and two of your textbooks." Someone slid onto the seat beside me. I peeked over at them, my heart skipping a beat when I realized it was Nicco.

"Hi," he mouthed.

"Hmm hi," I whispered, feeling myself get hot all over.

He gave the professor his full attention, but I caught a hint of a smirk tugging the corner of his mouth.

For the next twenty minutes, I sat there, barely breathing, trying to think about anything other than the feel of Nicco's lips ghosting over mine. By the time the professor asked us to introduce ourselves to the person on our right, I felt ready to combust.

"I guess we're partners," Nicco said, giving nothing away. He twisted his broad shoulders to mine, leaning in slightly. The black t-shirt he wore displayed his muscular arms

My breath caught again.

"Intro to Philosophy? I thought you were a sophomore?" And this was a freshman class.

He regarded me long and hard, inching closer. "How do you know Capizola?"

"Excuse me?"

"Tristan Capizola. How. Do. You. Know. Him?"

"Are you kidding me? Who *doesn't* know him?" I

schooled my expression, ignoring the storm sweeping through me.

"I saw you today, at lunch."

"Then you saw his girlfriend giving us crap over *their* table. I guess he felt bad or something because we were already sitting there and she was making a scene."

"So you don't know him?"

"Sure I do. My parents know his mom. But we're hardly friends, if that's what you're asking." The lie rolled off my tongue too easily.

"And Fascini, is he a friend too?"

"Are you jealous?" I deflected his question, a funny sensation washing over me.

"Jealous?" Nicco said through gritted teeth. "Of Capizola and Fascini, please."

The air had turned thick making it hard to breathe. "We should answer the questions." I tried to steer the conversation to safer shores, but Nicco was staring at me with such intensity I couldn't think straight. His gaze darkened as his eyes dropped to my mouth, lingering there.

I felt lightheaded; disarmed by his proximity. I'd never felt such a strong reaction to anything or *anyone* before. It was like I could feel him. Feel him undressing me with his eyes. Touching me with his fingertips.

Professor Mandrake's voice cut through the air, startling me. Nicco let out a quiet chuckle, shifting his attention back upfront. It was my first philosophy class, and I'd already failed the first task. If I had any hopes of staying on course, I couldn't partner with Nicco. He was too distracting.

Too intense.

Too *everything*.

"This week I want you to ponder this, 'men make their own history, but they do not make it as they please'." I scribbled down the famous Marx quote. "I expect you to come to our next class armed with ideas, people. This is, after all, philosophy." Professor Mandrake excused the class, and everyone began to gather their things. It was only then I noticed Nicco had nothing with him. No notebook, no phone or iPad... not even a bag.

"Do you have a photographic memory or something?" I asked him, standing up and slinging my backpack over my shoulder.

"Or something." He tapped a finger to his temple. "See you around, Bambolina." Nicco ducked into the aisle and disappeared into the stream of bodies filing out of the room before I could even form a reply.

It was that moment I realized Nicco was like a storm. He swept in without warning and disappeared just as quickly, with no regard for the wreckage left behind.

I didn't want to be wrecked by him. But much like the storm, sometimes it was impossible to escape. You just had to batten down the hatches and hope you survived.

∞∞∞

I was walking back to Donatello House when my cell phone rang. "Hello, Mamma."

"Ciao, cucciola," she replied. "So how is it? Tell me everything."

"It's... college, Mamma." I chuckled. "I just got done with classes."

"My baby at college, I can hardly believe it. The house isn't the same without you."

"I'm sure you're finding ways to keep busy." Gabriella Capizola was a force to be reckoned with. Strong and opinionated, there was never any doubt she wasn't cut out to be a trophy wife. Of course, my father humored her, and together they had become one of Verona County's most influential couples. It was hardly surprising, considering the Capizola were one of the founding families of our small slice of Rhode Island.

My father's grandfather and his father before that, had worked tirelessly to build a life for themselves after emigrating from Italy in the late eighteen-hundreds. Through hard work and a lot of blood, sweat, and tears, they had laid the foundations to pave the way for my grandfather to become one of the most successful men in the State. Property development, real estate, business, he had held a broad portfolio. A portfolio that all got handed down to my father when my grandfather died.

Capizola was a name people revered. A name that commanded respect.

For me though, it was a life sentence.

"How is he holding up?" I asked.

"Billy has only had to refuse to drive him out there twice. I'd call that a success."

"It's been three days."

"A lifetime to your father," Mamma said. "You're his most precious possession, Arianne."

Possession.

It sounded sweet rolling off my mother's tongue, but it felt wrong; reducing me to a thing rather than a person with feelings and hopes and dreams of her own.

I knew he meant well.

They both did.

It was just too heavy a burden to shoulder at times.

"Tristan is here. Scott too." I suppressed a shudder. "And Nora is extra sassy since we arrived. I'm fine, Mamma. I promise."

"Oh, I know, Principessa. Just promise me you'll keep your wits about you."

"I promise."

"Good. Will you be home over the weekend?"

"I'm not sure yet. Nora is taking our freshman experience quite serious."

"I'm glad she's there with you."

"Me too."

"Oh, silly me, I forgot to ask how your date with Scott went?"

"You know about that?" Incredulity lingered in my voice.

"Of course we know. Scott asked your father's permission."

"To take me out? That seems a little much, Mamma." My eyes rolled.

"He's a traditionalist like your father. I think it's sweet."

"I'm not sure we're compatible."

Her soft laughter filled the line. "It was one date, Arianne. These things take time. Give it a chance."

"I don't want to give it a chance." I stopped outside my building.

"Your father approves of Scott, he's practically family. The Fascini are good people."

"Okay, Mamma, what's going on? First Tristan, now you.

Why the sudden interest in mine and Scott's relationship?" Or lack thereof.

"You know, I was talking to Suzanna just the other day about the Centennial Gala. It's set to be a big affair." She launched into a blow by blow account of the planning, of which my mother and Scott's mother were both on the committee. Eventually, Nora caught up with me and I made my excuses to end the conversation.

It wasn't until we said goodbye and I hung up, I realized she never answered my question.

Chapter 6

Nicco

"Nicco, my man, what's up?"

"Hey, Darius." I tipped my head at the short stocky guy behind the counter, while Enzo and Matteo checked out the place.

"Is it that time of the month already?" he gave me a toothy smile.

"Sure is. You good for it?"

"Ain't missed a payment yet. I'll be right back." He disappeared through the door.

"What is all this shit?" Enzo grunted, holding up some weird-ass dish.

"It's a pawn shop, cous. One man's trash is another man's treasure."

"Wrong kind of pawn if you ask me." Enzo smirked over at Matteo. "Is it me, or does this take longer every month?"

"Relax, E," I said. "You know Capizola is applying pressure."

"Right, boys." Darius reappeared with a brown envelope. "I'm good for most of it but I need a little time—"

"Darius," I let out an exasperated breath. "You know

the deal. My father lets you trade your harder to find items out of the store, and in return he expects a cut of the profits."

"I know, Nicco, I know. It's just Capizola is turning up the heat. Had his Suits come around the place again the other day, offering to help me shift some of my stock. Said I could move to one of his fancy stores over in the city."

"You really think they're going to let you sell this shit over there?"

"Enzo," I warned. Darius was a proud man. The last thing we needed was Enzo showing disrespect to his business; his legitimate one, anyway.

"Yeah, yeah." My cousin waved me off, stalking out of the store.

"It's got to be the full amount, Darius. I can't be going back to the boss short."

"Just a couple of days, Nicco. Please. Trade ain't what it used to be around here."

Matteo caught my eye, shaking his head. He knew the deal. We both did. If you gave an inch, people like Darius would take a mile. His pawn shop might have fallen on hard times but his side business dealing in counterfeit goods and providing high-interest loans to people in and around La Riva and Romany Square was booming.

"Go check the safe again, D." I peeled back one side of my jacket, flashing him my pistol. "You're only what? Two or three hundred short? I'm sure you can dig deep and find it."

Panic flooded his expression. "Come on, Nicco, we're friends, aren't we? I just need a—"

"Don't make this any harder than it needs to be, D." My hand slid into my jacket. "Go get the cash or I can make you get it."

"Shit, yeah. Okay." He ran a hand through his thinning hair.

"What's his deal?" Matteo drummed his fingers on the counter as we waited.

"Fuck knows." I didn't doubt Capizola had sent his guys to rattle local business owners. He wanted people scared, ready to offer them false promises and pipe dreams about a better life across the river.

But guys like Darius would use any excuse to try and shirk from paying up.

He reappeared a couple minutes later and slapped the envelope down. "It's all there, you can count it."

"I trust you, D." I shoved it into my inside pocket. "Same time next month."

"Yeah, yeah. Maybe ask your old man what he plans to do about Capizola. This shit is getting out of control, Nicco. I heard Horatio's place got torched, destroyed half his stock. There are rumors circulating Capizola is prepared to use any means necessary to get people to sell up."

"Is that so?" I raised a brow. "Well you can spread the word that La Riva, Romany Square, and everything west of the river still belongs to Antonio Marchetti."

"So why the fuck isn't the boss doing anything about it?" Darius glared at me.

"Nice doing business with you, D," I said, cutting the conversation short before shit got out of control. "See you next month."

Matteo followed me out of the store. "It's like they think Uncle Toni can just have him taken out. It's Roberto Capizola for fuck's sake. A hit like that would bring all kinds of heat."

"Exactly," I snapped. "But Capizola knows that. It's why

he's putting pressure on local businesses because he knows my father's hands are tied."

"It's bullshit, is what it is." Enzo strolled over to us.

"Yeah, well, it's only going to get a whole lot worse before it gets better." The vibration of my cell phone caught my attention. I pulled it out and scanned the incoming text.

"We're needed at the house," I said.

"Uncle Toni?" Matteo asked, and I nodded.

"Who else."

"What do you think he wants?"

"Beats me," I said to Enzo as we piled into his fully restored Pontiac GTO. "You know how it is. When the boss calls, we come running."

Matteo ducked into the backseat, his knees digging into my back. "You need to get a bigger car." I eyed Enzo and he smirked. It was his international language for fuck you.

"Maybe he's got another job for us."

"We don't know what he wants yet," I grumbled.

But gut instinct told me it wouldn't be anything good.

The ride back to our neighborhood was about fifteen minutes, enough time for Enzo to tell us about the three-way he'd had the other night.

"I'm surprised your dick hasn't fallen off," I said. "Too much fucking use."

"More like too many diseases."

"Fuck you, Bellatoni, I wrap that shit every time."

"That's what she said."

"What's up with you, Nicco? I heard you snuck into Mandrake's class today?"

"Philosophy?" Enzo balked, his questioning gaze burning into the side of my face.

Fuck.

I ran a brisk hand over my head, hoping to deflect Matteo's question, but he was like a dog with a bone.

They both were.

"Just wanted to remind him we're here, watching."

"I thought he settled things with Uncle Toni?"

"He did." I shrugged, trying to act indifferent. Mandrake had paid the debt he'd run up at one of my father's gambling circuits fair and square, but it wasn't the first time we'd watched someone to make sure they didn't become a persistent problem.

"Going against the old man's orders?" Enzo chuckled. "It's like you have a death wish or something."

"Lay off it, Enzo. Those business classes are as boring as fuck."

"And philosophy is better? That shit is senseless."

"Full of hot booksmart girls though, am I right?" Matteo grinned at me through the rear-view mirror, pushing his messy dirty-blond hair out of his eyes. "Maybe I'll come next time, scope out the potential pus—"

"Do you two think with anything other than your dicks?"

"Since when *didn't* you think with yours?" Enzo's brow rose.

"I just... fuck, I don't know."

I did know, and she had eyes the color of honey.

"You've been tense the whole weekend. You need to either fight it out of you or fuck it out. And you already kicked Dom's ass, so I guess we all know the answer you're looking for. Just call up Rayna and make it right." His hand tightened around the wheel as we crossed the bridge separating Verona City with La Riva.

"Just drive, yeah. I've heard enough of your bullshit for today." I leaned back against the leather headrest, watching the city roll by. The landscape changed the further you moved out toward La Riva. The houses were smaller, with worn paintwork and overgrown lawns. Tired and forgotten, it wasn't a bad neighborhood, but it wasn't in the same league as its flashier more upmarket counterpart over the river.

Enzo navigated the streets with ease. We grew up here. Played on the very blocks we passed. La Riva was our home. Every childhood memory, the good and bad and sometimes the downright ugly. It was in our blood.

And it was my legacy.

While Roberto Capizola and his holier than thou Suits in the city controlled the three biggest towns in Verona County—Roccaforte, University Hill, and Verona City—my father owned the streets of La Riva, and Romany Square, and refused to give them up to the man he hated more than anything.

It was fucking ironic that Capizola was trying to make life difficult for my father because of his *associations*, when the very money that got old Rob to where he was today was stained with the blood of his enemies.

That's partly why I'd been so taken aback to see Tristan Capizola, Roberto's eldest nephew, hanging around Lina. He was a sneaky sonofabitch who enjoyed flashing his family's name around. Everyone knew he wanted to fill his uncle's shoes one day, to take over the family business; but unlucky for him, Roberto already had an heir.

A daughter.

Not that anyone had seen her in years. Roberto apparently kept her locked away on their estate in Roccaforte. There were even rumors circulating she was dead. I didn't believe that. I believed Capizola was a smart man. A man who, just because he'd renounced his family's tainted history, hadn't forgotten what it meant to have enemies. A man like Roberto Capizola was untouchable; he had too many friends in high places, was in the public eye too much. But his family, his daughter wasn't.

The sight of my childhood home silenced my thoughts. I always had mixed feelings about coming back here. Ever since my mother left five years ago, it felt empty. It was one of the reasons I'd so easily agreed to go to MU. College wasn't my choice, not when my life was already mapped out before me. But if it meant being out of this house, of pretending just for a little while that my life was my own, then I'd take it.

The other thing tethering me here, besides obligation and loyalty, was currently running down the driveway in a blur of wild curls and soft laughter.

"Jesus, you're going to have to beat them off with a stick when she's older."

"She's almost seventeen," I reminded Matteo.

"Still, that girl has trouble written all over her."

"You're not actually checking out my sister—my *baby* sister?"

"The fuck I am, she's my cousin," he ground out. "I'm just saying, I have eyes, and she's a looker. Takes after your mom."

"Way to go, man," Enzo snickered. "First Alessia and now his mom."

"You know that's not what I mean. Shit, Nicco, you know I wouldn't—"

"Relax, I know. Just don't go talking about my sister like that again, okay?" The thought of my sister ending up with someone like Matteo or Enzo made me want to tear my fucking hair out. She was too good. Too fucking pure. She was all my mom while I was every bit my father. It was a burden I would gladly carry if it meant I could shelter her from this life.

Enzo killed the engine and we climbed out. I'd barely even gotten my feet on the ground when Alessia leaped into my arms. "Nicco," she breathed, "I missed you."

"Nice to see you too, Sia." Enzo chuckled, kicking the gravel with his boot. "Is my dad here?"

"Yeah, he's inside. Uncle Michele too."

He shot me a serious look. If Uncle Vincenzo and Matteo's father, Michele, were here too then it was as a good as a family meeting.

"How's school?" I asked Alessia, tucking her into my side as we approached the house.

"It's okay, I guess." She gave a small shrug.

"Sia, it's junior year. You need to learn to let loose and have fun. But not too much fun," I quickly added. "No guys. Definitely no guys until you're eighteen."

Or never, if I had anything to say about it.

"Relax, big brother, it's not like anyone wants to date me anyway."

"What the fuck does that mean?" I pulled Alessia in front of me, holding her at arm's length. "Any guy would be lucky to have you."

Her eyes darted to the ground.

"Sia, talk to me," I said softly.

She slowly lifted her face to mine and what I saw there gutted me. "I'm a Marchetti, Nicco.

"So?" Being a Marchetti in high school had never been a problem for me. Guys looked the other way and girls all wanted a piece of me. The three of us—me, Enzo, and Matteo—had ruled the halls at high school.

"It was different for you. You're a guy. It earns you a certain level of respect. Not for me though, it makes me untouchable," her voice trailed off.

"Someone said something to you, Sia?" Matteo inched closer. "Because if they have—"

"*That*, that's the problem." She didn't sound angry, just resigned, and it was like a vice around my heart. "No guy will even look twice at me because of who my brother is. Who my family is."

"Screw them," Matteo said, and I frowned at him. That was supposed to be my line. But then, he had a younger sister too, so I guess he knew how to handle this kind of thing. "If a guy is intimidated by the fact you're a Marchetti then he doesn't deserve you."

"Thanks, Matt." Alessia gave him a coy smile. "Maybe I need to find someone older. A college—"

"*Do not* finish that sentence," I growled.

Enzo chuckled darkly from the porch. "Told ya." He motioned swinging a bat. I flipped him off.

"Come on, we don't want to keep daddy dearest waiting." He didn't like tardiness.

And I had a feeling the day was already about take a turn without getting berated by my old man for being late.

"Hang out with me for a little while later?" Alessia asked.

"You know it." I gave her a warm smile before following my friends into the house to find out whatever awaited us.

∞∞∞

We found my father and uncles in the den. It was my father's office/meeting room/room where he liked to entertain. And until a little over a year ago, it had been strictly off limits to me and my cousins. But ever since graduating high school, we'd been officially initiated into the family. A deep shudder worked down my spine, remembering exactly what we'd done that night. But it what was it was. The world was a dog eat dog place, and we all had our parts to play.

Mine just so happened to be the only son to Antonio Marchetti, boss of Dominion, or as it was called among outsiders: The New England Mafia. With his cousin, Alonso Marchetti, running the Boston faction, my father, with my uncles at his side, and a string of cousins, extended family, and associates in the ranks, owned and controlled various businesses in and around Verona County. Most were legitimate, providing a smokescreen for racketeering, money laundering, and gambling.

Verona County was built and founded on mafia money. The very foundations it stood on were tainted with blood and deceit. But people were happy to turn a blind eye to what went on around them, to forget their less than holy roots, if it meant they got to drive around in their posh cars, wearing their expensive fucking suits and clothes, eating rich people's food and sipping bottles of champagne that cost enough to feed a third world country.

"Niccolò, boys, get in here. Have a drink." My father motioned to Genevieve, the housekeeper, although I was pretty sure her duties far extended servicing just the household chores.

I sucked in a harsh breath. My father had aged well. His eyes still sparkled with the Marchetti charm and he still had a head full of dark unruly hair. He also kept physically fit thanks to many hours spent at my uncle Mario's gym. But he was my father, and I knew him better than anyone. I saw what others didn't see—the extra crows feet around his eyes, the dark cloud circling him.

My father was tired. Worn down by life. And although I knew he would never admit it, I suspected he still suffered with a broken heart. Which was fucking ironic since he was the reason my mother fled.

Enzo and Matteo accepted a glass of whisky each, but I refrained, opting for water instead, preferring to keep my wits about me. "What's going on?" I asked, pulling out the various envelopes of cash and throwing them down on the table. Michele got up to collect them, depositing them in my father's safe. They'd count the cash later before cleaning it.

All I wanted to do was get down to business. The sooner we were done, the sooner I could spend some time with Alessia and then get the hell out of here.

"How is college?" Uncle Vincenzo asked, relaxing back in the big leather chair. "Plenty of fresh pussy?" One of his thick brows rose suggestively.

"Really, old man?" Enzo scowled. "If Nonna heard you—"

"You should know by now, son, what happens inside these four walls, stays inside these four walls." He chuckled as if we didn't all know just how important the code of silence was. "So, how is it, really? Have you managed to bed any—"

"Enzo," my father scolded his younger brother. "We haven't come here to talk about your son's sex life. Although, kid, I gotta say it, remember to wrap that shit. The last thing we need is some girl getting knocked up with Marchetti seed."

"Jesus," I muttered under my breath.

"A-fucking-men to that." Uncle Vincenzo lifted his glass before necking the contents.

"Thanks, Gen, you're excused. If we need anything, I'll be sure to call."

The housekeeper nodded, before scurrying out of the room. She couldn't have been much older than me. Far too young to be underneath my father but he wasn't exactly the type of man you told no.

"How's things in that department?" Uncle Michele flicked his head to the door.

"It's not serious," my father said quietly, loosening his tie as his eyes slid to mine.

"Don't look at me. Whatever you do in your spare time is your business."

"Niccolò, do you have to be—"

"Are we ever going to get to the point of this meeting?" I grumbled.

"You're right." My father's expression hardened. "There's been an interesting development with Capizola."

"Tommy finally found some dirt on him?"

Tommy, one of our best, most trusted investigators had been watching Roberto for years. Trying to find enough dirt to knock Capizola off his pedestal. But so far, he'd come up with nothing but a few parking tickets and planning regulation violations.

"Not exactly. But we think we might know where his daughter is."

We all sat straighter. "She's alive?" Matteo asked.

"You didn't really believe she was dead?" I asked around a smirk. He was so fucking gullible sometimes.

"No one has seen her for the best part of five years." He shrugged. "I figured perhaps she was pushing up daisies and her old man wanted to keep up pretenses."

He had a point. In a world where money and power were everything, for someone like Capizola, having a living heir was vital.

I knew that first-hand.

"So, where is she?" I turned my focus back to my father.

"We think she's attending Montague University this year."

"What?" I balked. "No way he'd send her there." He had too many enemies watching him, waiting for the opportune moment to strike.

"Obviously we don't think he's sent her there under her true identity."

"Hiding her in plain sight... makes sense." Enzo said. "And it wouldn't be hard. No one has seen her in years. I doubt she still looks like a child."

"You think the intel is good?" I asked my father, and he nodded.

"Tristan will know her. They're cousins, and Roberto treats him like a son. He's the key. Get to him and you'll get to her."

"Yeah, but let's be real here, it's not like he'll be parading her around campus." Enzo snorted. "It won't be someone in his circle, that's way too obvious."

"Get to her to do what exactly?" Matteo asked.

"Son," Michele grumbled, throwing my father an

apologetic look. Matteo straddled the fine line between wanting to embrace the life and wanting more. Unlike Enzo, he wasn't inherently angry, and unlike me, he wasn't permanently numb.

Until her. My mind flickered to Lina. Wondering what she was doing right now this second. I wanted her so fucking much. On the back of my bike. In my bed. Underneath me.

I wanted her any way I could fucking get her, but it wouldn't be fair, to either of us, for me to pull her into this world.

A world where we were talking about using an innocent girl to get to her father.

"If we have to spell it out to you, Matt, then you're not the sons we raised." My father's words lingered in the air, heavy and laced with meaning.

Beside me, Matteo shifted uncomfortably. I narrowed my eyes, hardly surprised my father wanted us to handle this. It was, after all, why we were at MU. Not only did it give the illusion of our family wanting a more legitimate future, it placed us somewhere where we could have our ear to the ground. Kids talked. Especially kids so drunk and high on college life. But a year into college, and our intel was lacking to say the least. My father and our uncles didn't seem too concerned. Taking down Roberto Capizola was the endgame. As long as we kept up pretenses, attended classes, and brought in some cash from our on and off campus ventures, they were happy enough.

"We'll handle it," Enzo said. "When we figure out who she is, how far can we take it?"

The air rippled with dark energy as my father ran his finger around his glass of whisky. "Whatever it takes to make her break. She's the missing piece of the puzzle. Get to her and we'll have the leverage we need to get the upper hand," my father's voice dropped an octave. "I've watched Capizola bleed his redeemed soul bullshit all across Verona. He wants La Riva, then he'd better be prepared to take it from my bloody broken fingers because this is our home and I won't go down without a fight."

The men raised their glasses, toasting their plan. Enzo joined them, always too thirsty, too eager, to get his hands dirty. Matteo was a mask of uncertainty, but he clinked his glass with the others, nonetheless.

Everyone looked at me expectantly. One day, I'd sit here in my father's chair, calling the shots and toasting *my* plan. It was a future I'd never asked for. A future I didn't want. I didn't want the responsibility or the power. Getting my hands dirty, fine. I could do that. I could swallow the orders and see them through. I could even handle being a capo and having my own crew. But I didn't want to be the person making the big decisions.

"Niccolò." Antonio Marchetti didn't like to be kept waiting. His hard, assessing gaze on mine, I lifted my glass and gave him a sharp nod.

I might not have wanted this life.

But it was mine regardless.

Because no one walked away from the family except in a body bag.

Especially not the only son of the boss.

Chapter 7

Arianne

I didn't see Nicco for the rest of the week. It was almost as if he'd disappeared off the face of the earth. He wasn't in Professor Mandrake's class, and I didn't see him and his friends in the food court, or around campus.

If it wasn't for the lingering memory of his lips against mine, I would have thought he was a figment of my imagination. But nothing that good could be made up.

Could it?

"You're looking for him again, aren't you?" Nora asked as we walked back to our dorm building.

"Who?" I played dumb.

"Oh hush, you're so looking for hotty. Not that I blame you."

"I haven't seen him all week. That's weird, right?"

"He's a guy. They're all fucking weird." Nora wore college life well. She'd always been a free spirit but living on my father's estate had clipped her wings to some degree. Since we'd arrived at MU though, I'd watched her blossom.

"Did you decide what to wear to the party tonight?"

"About that..."

She ground to a halt and ducked in front of me, fixing

her eyes right on me. "Oh no, I don't like that tone."

"It's just, I'm not sure parties are my thing." When Nora had mentioned the masquerade party at my cousin's frat house, I'd given her non-committal maybe. I probably should have told her no, but she'd been so excited. I didn't want to drag her down, I wanted Nora to have the full college experience... I just wasn't sure it was what *I* wanted.

No, I was more interested in the flyer I'd gotten from the Student Community Action Committee. They were looking for volunteers to help at the local shelter. I'd spent so long cut off from the real world, locked away in my ivory tower, there was something that called to me about helping others. I'd never wanted for anything in life, I never would. I was born into a life of money and privilege. But it didn't mean I took it for granted. If my father had taught me anything, it was that the higher we found ourselves, the more humbly we should walk. He worked hard, made a lot of money, and yes, he lived a life of privilege, but he also gave to those less fortunate. He donated to charity and contributed his time to non-profits.

I wanted to follow in *those* footsteps, the ones he trod that made a real difference.

"I think I'm going to do it," I said, feeling a sense of rightness wash over me.

"Yeah, you'll come?" Nora's eyes lit up and I immediately felt a pang of guilt.

"No, I... uh, I meant volunteer with the SCA."

"The student action thing?"

I nodded. "They need volunteers to help at the shelter."

"That's great, Lina, but do you need to go right now?"

"Well, no."

"So you'll come? I know shitface will be there but it's a masquerade party, we'll blend. Besides, he'll no doubt have a harem all wanting to get on his dick."

"Nora!"

"What?" She hooked her arm through mine, "you know I'm not wrong."

"No, but you're so..."

"Liberated?" She snuggled close to me. "I feel it, Lina. Like I can really be myself here, you know?"

"I'm happy you're happy," I said. We reached the door and Nora released me to dig out her keycard. I noticed a guy over by the corner of the building, pretending not to watch us. He looked familiar. I'd seen him around campus a few times, always alone, always waiting for something, or someone.

Huh.

Strange.

Nora fumbled with the key, drawing my attention. "I can never get the stupid thing to—"

"Here." I took it from her and gently pressed it against the pad. The door clicked open. "Just needed a magic touch."

She rolled her eyes, pushing open the door and slipping inside. I went to follow her but paused at the last second. There was something else about him, a gentle nagging in the back of my head.

Then it hit me.

It was the guy Nicco had been with the night I'd fled from Scott. His cousin. What was his name? Ba... Bailey! Yes, that was it. He'd been in the alley. It was his car Nicco had driven me in.

My eyes shifted to the corner of the building, but Bailey was gone.

And I was beginning to think I was losing my mind.

∞∞∞

Nora had picked out the gaudiest, most over the top, Columbine Venetian masks she could possibly find. I was almost relieved no one would be able to recognize me; they were that bad. But she assured me it was what everyone would be wearing. Apparently, she'd met a guy who had the inside scoop. I just hoped he wasn't on the football team with Tristan and Scott because that would be all kinds of awkward.

"He's a sophomore so he doesn't exactly hang with them," she clarified. "But he is on the team."

"Seriously? I don't like this. I don't like it at all."

"What would you rather be doing? Reading one of your smutty romance novels in your flannel pajamas, eating your bodyweight in Twizzlers?"

My mouth opened and then snapped shut. "You know I'm right. You blew off going home for the weekend for a reason. So let's make the most of it. If the party sucks, we'll leave. And I promise to stay by your side tonight."

"Until you see the first hot guy and decide he's better company."

"If I recall correctly, you left me with Kaiden when hotty decided to drag you out of there."

The mention of Nicco had my stomach flipping. Maybe I'd see him tonight at the party. Who was I kidding? I couldn't imagine Nicco and his friends at a football team party. He didn't seem to like my cousin much. Not that I blamed him. Tristan didn't just fit into the elite of Montague, he *was* the elite. The king of the kids who walked around flashing their trust funds and family connections. I'd noticed it more and more throughout the week. The cliques and socialite groups versus the outsiders and kids who hovered on the fringe of everyone else. I hadn't realized college would be so much like high school. But then MU wasn't like most colleges. It was very insular; deeply rooted in Italian history and culture. It was no surprise it was the first-choice college for Italian-American families in and around New England to send their kids.

Not to mention, it was extremely expensive. You either got accepted to come here because you had money, and lots of it, or you had an excellent academic standing and received one of the very coveted, very rare scholarships.

"Okay, ready?" Nora asked me as we reached the frat house. It was on the edge of campus, steeped in red leaf Maples and lit up like The White House. Of course, my cousin would live here. It wasn't really a frat house at all, since MU didn't subscribe to the ethos of Greek letter organizations, but the name had stuck. I guess it made a kind of sense considering most of the football team lived here and with the amount of parties they had.

People littered the front lawn, disguised in their own gaudy masks. At least Nora's friend had gotten it right and we didn't stand out like sore thumbs.

"Come on". She grabbed my hand and pulled me toward the door.

"Passphrase?" A guy wearing a red and black Harlequin mask said.

"Passphrase?" I whispered to Nora. But I should have known she'd come prepared. She leaned up, cupping her hands around his ear. A sloppy grin broke over his face and he stepped back, granting us entrance.

"So what was it?" I asked.

"Carpe vinum."

I sifted through my very limited knowledge of Latin. "Seize the wine? How very original."

Nora chuckled. "I guess no one knew the Latin for beer and cheap liquor."

There wasn't a familiar face in sight, but there were plenty of Voltos and Gattos, Pantalones and Scaramouches. We blended in with ease, and I immediately felt some of the tension ebb away from my shoulders.

"See, I told you we wouldn't stand out." Nora pushed her way to the makeshift bar and got us two drinks. I waited for her to sniff the contents. "It's punch." She took a sip. "Sweet with a bitter aftertaste but it isn't bad."

"I think I'll pass," I said, pushing my cup at her.

"Suit yourself."

"At least the football team are wearing their jerseys." I wouldn't have to worry about Scott creeping up on me. He was the last person I wanted to see. But part of me also didn't want to hide, to give him any kind of satisfaction.

"Exactly," Nora nodded, downing the rest of her drink. "It's perfect. We're incognito which means we can dance the night away and not have to worry about Tristan or Scott. The night is ours." She made a sweeping motion with her arm and I smothered a laugh.

"You're crazy."

"Certifiable." Nora grinned. "But you love me."

"I do. I wouldn't be here otherwise."

Just then, one of my favorite songs blasted through the house and even I couldn't deny the hum of excitement coursing through my veins. Nora was right; no one here knew me. I was just another faceless person in the crowd. I could relax and let my hair down.

I could do this.

I could be a normal teenager enjoying a college party.

Moving around Nora, I grabbed a drink and knocked it back in one.

"Whoa, girl." My best friend laughed. "What's gotten into you?"

Grabbing her hand, I smiled. A real genuine smile, and said, "Let's dance."

∞∞∞

We danced and drank and danced some more. After three or four cups of punch, I switched to water. I had a nice buzz, but I didn't want to get drunk; not in a houseful of Tristan and Scott's football player friends. A couple of guys had tried to dance with us, but Nora had quickly sent them on their way. It was loud, the air thick with the cloying smell of sweat and liquor. But it was fun. I was having fun. More fun than I'd had in a really long time.

"I told you this was a good idea," Nora yelled over the music, a sloppy grin plastered on her face. Her mask hid her eyes, but I knew they would be glassy with the effects of all the punch. Unlike me, Nora had opted not to switch to water. But she deserved this, we both did.

"Okay," I conceded. "I can admit it. This is fun."

"I knew it." She fist pumped the air. "I knew you had it in you." Her eyes flicked over to a tall guy wearing a Pierrot mask. There was no mistaking that his eyes, although barely visible, were locked on my best friend. He crooked a finger at her, taking a step forward.

"It's okay," I said, too exhilarated to spoil her fun. "You can go dance with him." She bit her lip, glancing between us. "Nora, it's—"

The words died on my tongue as strong arms looped around my waist. I went rigid, the air evaporating from my lungs. Nora's mouth fell open, then curved into a knowing smile.

"I'll be right over there." She mouthed, tipping her head to where the Pierrot guy was waiting.

"I missed you." Nicco's voice sent shivers rolling up my spine. I wanted to turn around, to look into his eyes to make sure it was really him. But I didn't want to break the spell. His body was hard behind mine, his hands splayed possessively on my hips as he rocked us to the sultry beat.

I rested my head back against his shoulder and asked, "How did you know it was me?"

He also wore a simple Pierrot mask painted with black and golds. His lips ghosted over mine. "I would know you anywhere, Bambolina."

"Where have you been all week?"

"Later," he said cryptically. "For now, come with me."

Nicco took my hand, leading me away from the party. He seemed to know the layout of the house, turning down a long hallway that grew darker and darker, quieter and quieter.

"Where are we going?" I whispered, my heart crashing violently against my ribcage.

I'd missed Nicco. All week I'd searched for him. It made no rational sense, but whenever I had walked into a room, I found myself looking for him. Hoping to catch even a glimpse. I knew people would say I had a crush. A silly schoolgirl crush on the elusive mysterious bad boy who had saved me. But there was more to it. I felt tethered to Nicco. Inexplicably linked to him. Maybe it was because he'd been so gentle with me that night, but I couldn't stop thinking about him. He was under my skin and now he was here, leading me to God only knew where.

It didn't matter though.

I would have gladly followed him into the depths of Hell just to savor the moment.

We reached what I presumed was the back of the house. I could see a large yard beyond the window, a huge pool, and a bunch of chairs situated around a grill. Nicco let go of my hand and tried a door to our left. Sticking his head inside, he whispered, "All clear."

"All clear for—"

He pulled me inside, pushing my body up against the wall. A sliver of moonlight poured in through the window, illuminating the profile of his mask as he stared down at me.

I swallowed hard, the air crackling with anticipation. "Nicco..." My hands reached for him, trembling fingers curling into his black sweater. It molded to his chest, his muscular biceps. My tongue darted out, wetting my lips. I was suddenly so thirsty, my body hot and needy and restless.

Maybe it was the liquor.

Or maybe it's the fact you're in a dark room, alone, with Nicco.

"Jesus, Lina..." He sounded in pain, his words strained and so full of desperation, I wanted to fix it. To ease whatever burden was weighing on him.

"What... what is it?"

He leaned in, brushing his nose across my mine, setting off a hundred butterflies in my tummy, their wings flapping wildly. And then he slowly untied my mask and slipped it off, hanging it on the door handle, before pushing his own up over his head.

"Do you have any idea what you do to me?" His mouth moved to my ear, his voice low and gravelly... and seductive. "I can't get you out of my head. I want to know where you are, what you're doing, who you're with... you're in here." He grabbed one of my hands and pressed it to his temple, his eyes pinning me to the spot.

"Has Bailey been following me? I saw him the other night and I'm sure I've seen him around campus. Did you..." I swallowed the words. What was I saying? Nicco hadn't asked Bailey to follow me. It was ridiculous. And yet, his mouth curved into a wicked smirk.

"He was supposed to be discreet."

"So he is following me?"

"I prefer to think of it as looking out for you."

"But why? I don't understand."

"I feel this irrational need to protect you, Bambolina, and I had to go out of town for a few days to take care of some... personal things."

"So you sent Bailey to watch over me? Isn't he like a kid? Doesn't he have school?" My mind was reeling.

"It doesn't matter. All that matters is that you're safe."

I didn't understand. He was talking like I was in danger. But he didn't know the truth, he couldn't possibly know the truth.

Guilt snaked through me. Something was happening between us. Like a runaway train, it was unstoppable and unpredictable, hurtling toward the unknown.

And nothing could stop it.

Nicco deserved to know the truth. Before we went any

further, he deserved to know who I really was. But when I tried to say the words, they wouldn't form. Because I was scared. Soul achingly scared of losing this—the inexplicable connection between us. I felt it, twisting and tightening, anchoring us together.

Nora had been with guys. She'd dated here and there. Told me all about the butterflies and toe-curling kisses. But she'd never once described anything that came close to what I felt right now, in this second. I looked into Nicco's eyes and I felt... *home*.

Was that even possible?

I'd read enough romance novels, watched enough films, to be familiar with the concept of soul mates; of that one person in the whole world meant for you, and you alone. But it was nothing more than a romantic notion penned by the greats: Shakespeare, Wilde, and Beckett.

It wasn't real life.

"Tell me what you're thinking," he breathed the words against the corner of my mouth.

"Do you believe in fate, Nicco?" I asked.

"Until I met you, I didn't." His finger trailed down my neck, eliciting a soft moan from me. My head dropped against the wall with a gentle *thud*, every inch of my skin vibrating. "What is it that Mandrake said? Men make their own history, but they do not make it as they please."

"What does that mean?"

"It means, I shouldn't kiss you," Nicco whispered, his words a gentle caress over my skin. "It means, I should walk out of this room and never look back. It means, I should do the right thing and walk away from you, Lina. That's what it means."

"But..." my voice quivered, betraying me.

"But I never claimed to be good." He let out a steady breath. "I'm not your prince, Bambolina."

"I see you, Nicco. I see the good in you. And I want—"

I didn't get the rest of my words out. Nicco's mouth crashed down on mine, hard and bruising and demanding. I gasped against his lips, trying to keep up. Trying to stay afloat as I drowned in him. His tongue sliding against mine; his fingers in my hair; his strong, hot body caging me against the wall. My hands ran up his chest, curving over his broad shoulders as he kissed me harder, deeper. Kissing me with a fierce desperation and need that made my knees weak and my body tremble.

"Jesus, Lina, you taste like heaven." He pressed even closer, grinding his hips again at an angle that made me boneless. I could feel him, feel his hard length nudging up against my core as I rocked and writhed, desperate to feel him *there*. Desperate for him to ease the ache building inside me.

Gathering my hair off my face, Nicco pulled away to look at me. My skin was burning, my body a tight bundle of nerves. "You like that?" he asked, and I bit down on my lip, nodding.

"Fuck," he swallowed hard before diving at my mouth again, claiming me. Branding me with every kiss and nibble, stroke and nip. Nicco continued to rock into me, one of his hands dropping to my thigh, hitching my leg around his waist. His pace was slow at first. Teasing and torturous. But he quickly built a rhythm that had me soaring into uncharted heights. I moaned his name, moaned for more.

More.

More.

Nicco cursed: my name, some Italian I couldn't decipher. But he didn't stop. Our bodies were joined in every way possible considering we were both still fully clothed. "Something's happening," I moaned, barely aware of what I was saying. All I knew was it felt good, *too good*, as he ground against me. "More, Nicco, I need..."

His hand dived between us, disappearing underneath my skirt and finding the soft flesh between my thighs. He hooked my panties to one side and thrust a finger up inside me without warning. It stung, but the sharp stab of pain was quickly erased as I bucked against him, riding the waves of pleasure crashing over me.

"Oh God," I chanted over and over as Nicco's finger and thumb found the perfect rhythm, working me into a breathless frenzy. I'd never been touched like this before, not even by myself. It was... everything.

And then it wasn't.

Nicco tore away from me, touching his forehead to mine. "Tell me that wasn't what I think it was?" He ground out, the words raw.

"W- what do you mean?"

"Tell me that wasn't the first time you've been touched... like *that*."

"I... What does it matter?" My breath was ragged, my chest heaving.

"Fuck." His fist slammed against the wall beside my head, the sound reverberating through me, erasing the blissed-out feeling enveloping me.

"Nicco, it's okay." I leaned into him, trying to kiss him. But he jerked back, narrowing his eyes at me.

"I have to go," he said.

"What?" I frowned, my heart beating erratically in my chest. I couldn't think, let alone process what he was saying.

"I wasn't supposed to do that."

"Kiss me?"

"Among other things." The corner of his mouth turned downward as he inched back, leaving me cold and vulnerable. I hiked my skirt down, smoothing out the crinkled material, the icy fingers of reality clawing at my throat as realization dawned on me as to what had just happened.

What was happening right now?

"I wanted you to touch me," I said, trying to fix things. I'd been so happy, and now everything was ruined. "I liked it. You don't need to feel guilty just because I'm a..." I choked over the word. The truth.

His eyes darkened, shame glittering there. And my heart withered in my chest.

"Lina, I'm sorry. I should—"

"Go, you should go." My expression hardened as I forced down the tears threatening to fall. I'd given Nicco something special. Something I'd never given to another, and he couldn't get away from me fast enough.

"It isn't what you think," his voice cracked, "I just..."

"It's fine, I understand," I said, flatly. "You can go now."

"Bambolina, please." He took a step toward me, but I dodged his advance, wrapping my arms tightly around my waist. "Fine," he said through gritted teeth. "But this isn't over."

I stared at him, willing for him to go. I didn't want to fall apart in front of Nicco. Not after what had just happened. He gave me one last lingering look before slipping out of the room.

Taking a piece of my wounded heart with him.

Chapter 8

Nicco

Bailey found me down the hall from where I'd left Lina. I hadn't meant to kiss her, to touch her like that. But she called to me. Her body, her smile, every-fucking-thing about her.

She was my own personal siren's call, and I was too weak to resist.

But a virgin?

Fucking hell.

I realized the second I pressed my finger inside her. She was tight despite how wet she was, and her body had tensed, though only for a split second. But it was enough for me to know the truth.

The fact she'd trusted me enough to touch her so intimately made my heart soar. But I had no right. None. Not when I wasn't here for her.

It had almost killed me not being on campus all week, not seeing her in class or across the food court, but after our family meeting, my old man had gotten a call from Boston. My Uncle Alonso was having problems with his hot-headed son, Dane. He decided to send me, Enzo, and Matteo to deal with it. We'd spent three days babysitting the kid to keep him out of the clutches of a rival gang, while Alonso and his guys took care of the threat.

"We've got a problem," my cousin said, hands jammed deep in his pockets. Bailey was a good kid, loyal and willing. But he was also lost. It's why I'd taken him under my wing.

"Yeah?" I said. "Let me guess. Enzo's struggling to keep his dick in his pants?"

Bailey snickered. "He's with her friend. The wild one." I'd tasked Bailey with watching Lina while I was gone. He was supposed to be in school, but he was going through some stuff. I figured it was better for him to be busy than skipping class and getting into all kinds of trouble he didn't need to be bringing to my aunt and uncle's doorstep.

"Nora? Fuck." When I'd left Enzo dancing with her, I hadn't considered he'd try to fuck her. But then, he didn't know who she really was. He thought I was looking to let off a little steam before we did what we came here to do. Not to mention, the second my eyes found Lina across the room, everything else had faded into the background.

She was the flame and I was the moth who couldn't seem to stay away, even if she burned me to nothing but ash and dust.

"Where are they?"

"Bathroom. First floor."

Shit. He wasn't supposed to be lurking around the house. We could be spotted. Even with our Pierrot disguises.

"And Matt?"

"He's watching the target."

My lip curved. "You've always wanted to say that, haven't you?"

Bailey stood taller, puffing out his chest. "Fuck, yeah. Can I come with you, when you... ya know?"

"Not tonight, kid. You stick with Lina, okay?"

"Nicco, come on. I can help. I can—"

"She's important to me. I need you to stick with her, okay? Text me the second she leaves."

His dejected expression morphed into fierce determination as he gave me a sharp nod. "I won't let anyone touch her."

"I know you won't."

I slid my mask back in place and walked down the hall. I wasn't supposed to know the layout of Capizola's house, but I made it my business to know. The three of us had snuck in here in freshman year and scoped out the place. We knew every entrance, exit, and hidey hole. It's how I knew exactly where to find Enzo.

Taking the stairs two at a time, I knocked on the bathroom door. "Fuck off, we're busy," his growl echoed through the wall.

I could have done the decent thing and told him it was me. I could have pulled rank and told him to get his sorry ass out of there. But I wasn't feeling very decent, not after how I'd ended things with Lina. So I dug my wallet out of my pocket, taking out a credit card and a metal toothpick. In less than thirty seconds, I'd cracked the lock. Quietly opening the door, I peeked inside.

"Oh yeah, just like that." Enzo guided Nora's face to his dick. Her hand was wrapped around the base, stroking him, her lips parted with anticipation. It was one of the weirdest things I'd ever seen, given they were both still wearing their masks.

"We need to go," I said without warning.

"Nicco, fuck," he hissed, jerking his dick away and stuffing it back into his pants. Nora stumbled backward, landing clean on her ass.

"What the hell?" She glared at me. I couldn't see it, but I felt it from behind her mask.

"Sorry to interrupt, but I need to borrow him. And something tells me you'd only regret it in the morning." My hard gaze shifted to Enzo. "Let's go, now."

"Yeah, yeah," he grumbled, raking a hand through his hair as he took one last look at Nora and then followed me outside.

"What the fuck was that?" I asked.

"Like you haven't been balls deep inside that girl. I saw the two of you sneak off. Who is she?"

"Not the point." I ignored his question. "You were supposed to be keeping an eye on the place. Not getting your dick sucked."

"Relax, Matt is—"

"Doing his fucking job." I stomped off down the hall. I needed to get a grip.

"Hey," Enzo caught up to me, grabbing my shoulder, "I'm sorry, okay? She was rubbing her tight little body all over me and I got carried away."

"One day, your dick is going to land you in a whole heap of trouble." My brow rose. "Try to keep it in your pants, we have work to do."

He gave me a wicked smirk, rubbing his hands together. "Ooh, I love it when you talk dirty to me."

"You're a strange fucking guy. You know that, right?"

"Never claimed to be anything else." He ran his hand down his slacks and I knew he was feeling the hunting knife strapped to his thigh.

"Keep a cool head, okay?" I warned him. "This is a recon

mission."

Tonight wasn't about doing any serious damage; it was about sending a message. About getting the confirmation we needed.

I only hoped the guy at my side remembered that.

∞∞∞

We found Matteo downstairs in the open-plan kitchen. It ran the whole width of the house with French doors leading to the yard. There was a big island in the middle with black and chrome stools around it. Stools currently occupied by half-naked girls wearing various masks while they watched Tristan and his closest friends neck shooter after shooter.

Our cousin pushed off the wall and approached us, wearing an identical Pierrot mask to ours. "Football players are pussies," he said, sipping his beer.

"Tell us something we didn't already know," Enzo grumbled, snorting as one of Tristan's friends puked all over himself. Everyone cheered, whooping like the guy hadn't just barfed everywhere. It was fucking embarrassing.

"Your guy know what he needs to do?" I asked Matt and he nodded.

"Just say the word."

I glanced over at Tristan again. His arm was slung around someone, the two of them laughing. He was such a smug fucker. I was itching to knock him off his throne. But that wasn't our order, not yet.

"Now."

Matteo nodded to someone. Three seconds later, the

word 'fight' rang out and all hell broke loose. Bodies jostled past us all trying to get a look at whatever was going down. We moved closer to Tristan who was still laughing and joking with his friends.

"Man, you should come see this," someone yelled, and another couple of guys left him, rushing to the chaos unfolding at the far end of the kitchen.

"Don't fucking trash the house," Tristan slurred, clearly buzzed. He staggered over to the counter and dumped his cup. He was all alone now. We circled him like wolves. Something crashed, glass shattering, and people gasped, grunts of pain following.

"What's with the freaky as fuck mask?" Tristan asked Enzo who was closest to him. "You need something?"

"Yeah, I need something." Enzo roughly grabbed him. Tristan started to protest but Matt was there to silence him. I yanked open the back door, keeping one eye on the crowd, and we herded him out the back door.

We didn't stop, dragging his drunk ass all the way to the workshop at the bottom of the yard. The inky night cloaked us, our dark outfits blending into the shadows.

Inside, Enzo shoved him hard. Tristan stumbled back, his mask slipping off his face. "What the fuck is this?"

"We need to talk," I said.

"Marchetti? Is that you, because when my uncle hears..."

"Do you hear that?" I asked my friends. "The coglione is going run crying to his uncle." Enzo snorted, while Matteo dragged a chair to the middle of the room. "Sit," I commanded.

"Cazzo si—"

Enzo was on him in a second. Fisting him by the shirt,

he maneuvered Tristan onto the chair. His fist clenched at his side, his body shaking with rage.

"Walk away, E."

Enzo hesitated but finally withdrew. We all knew the drill—no names, no prints, no faces. It's why we'd added gloves to our outfits. Tristan knew exactly who we were, but he'd have zero proof and without proof he couldn't come after us.

Not unless he wanted to start an all-out war, and he and his uncle knew we didn't play fair. Unlike their family who, these days, preferred to solve their problems with vast quantities of cash, we had a more hands-on approach.

"My uncle—"

"Your uncle isn't going to do shit." I crouched down to his eye-level while Matteo worked on restraining Tristan's hands behind his back. He barely resisted which told me all I needed to know.

He knew he was outnumbered, and he knew this was one fight he couldn't win.

"You think good old Uncle Roberto wants to bring *this* to his doorstep, to tarnish his perfectly good reputation with the likes of us. Nah," I chuckled darkly, "your uncle is smarter than that. Question is, are you?"

"Fuck you, Marchetti." He seethed, his nostrils flaring.

"You know we would have been on the same side, right? If history had written itself the way it should have, we'd be family right now."

Tristan spat at me, "Vai a farti fottere!"

Before I could stop myself, I backhanded him. His head snapped back, a loud grunt of pain filling the air. I pulled a tissue from my pocket and cleaned myself off.

"You think you're so much better than us. We know

your uncle isn't as squeaky clean as he claims to be. It's only time... But that's not why we're here," I stood up. "We know she's here."

Tristan didn't flinch. He remained perfectly still, perfectly calm.

Too fucking calm.

"Did you hear?" I asked. "We know the Capizola heir is here."

Tristan stared straight ahead, giving nothing away.

"You don't want to help us? Fine." Giving Matt the signal he pulled another chair around to the front of Tristan before untying one of his hands.

"I heard it's a big year for the Knights. You have a real shot at the championship. It would be a shame if their star player finds himself suddenly injured."

Enzo stalked closer, the hammer in his hand slowly coming into view. Tristan's eyes went wide. I grabbed his wrist and flattened his palm against the chair. He was a big guy, ripped from all the hours of conditioning and football drills. But the effects of the liquor were working in our favor. Besides, fear was a powerful motivator.

Enzo handed me the hammer and I stared down at Tristan. "What?" he spat. "You want me to point her out to you? Have you lost your fucking mind?" He laughed bitterly. "Do your worst, Marchetti. I have nothing to say to you. I'm not a rat and I'm not scared of anything you try to do to me." His eyes narrowed but I saw the flicker of fear. "Do your worst. I still won't talk."

A slow smile tugged at my lips. Tristan was deflecting, but what he didn't realize was he'd already given me everything I needed. His silence was an admission of the truth. She was here.

The Capizola heir was here on campus.

All we needed to do was find her.

I lifted the hammer and slammed it down, his cries echoing around us.

"See you around, Capizola," I returned the hammer to its rightful place and left Enzo and Matteo to deal with Tristan while I went to get some air.

∞∞∞

I read Enzo's text before pocketing my cell phone. They had knocked Tristan out, cleaned up the workshop, and dumped his body in the yard. It would be as if we'd never been there. He was going to wake up with one hell of a headache and in a shitload of pain. He was lucky I only smashed his pinky finger.

Bailey appeared at the end of the alley and whistled. I jogged toward him. "She left right after the fight broke out. Her friend wasn't feeling good, so they walked home. I've been watching the building ever since. She's been sitting out there for about ten minutes."

"Any sign of anyone else?"

He shook his head. "It's just her. I know she's the girl from the other night, Nicco, but *who* is she?"

Mine, the word echoed through me.

"Thanks, kid." I ignored his question. "Now go straight home. I'll be calling Aunt Francesca to check you got there, okay?"

"Nic," he started to protest but my stern glare made him swallow the words. "Fine, I'll head straight home. See you Sunday for family dinner?"

"You know it." I clapped him on the shoulder. "Now go."

He ducked out of the alley and melted into the shadows. MU had plenty of lampposts lining the sidewalks and paths, but the overgrown trees provided enough cover that if you didn't want someone to see you, or for campus security to catch you up to no good, you only had to learn the blackspots.

Pulling up my hood, I slipped out from between the two buildings and followed the short path toward Donatello House. Lina was right where Bailey had said she would be, sitting on the bench outside the building, watching the stars.

"It's a beautiful night," I said from the shadows.

"Nicco?" She glanced around, searching for me. When her eyes landed on me standing by the corner of the building, she stood up. "What do you want?"

"Ahh, Bambolina." I let out a weary sigh. "That is a loaded question."

"Humor me." Lina took a step closer. The moonlight danced off the soft features of her face.

Jesus, she was so fucking beautiful.

"I want to kiss you." I inched toward her, unable to resist the magnetic pull I felt whenever I was around her. "I want to finish what we started earlier. I want to feel you beneath me, hear you cry my name."

I want to make you mine.

"You couldn't get away from me fast enough earlier." Her confused gaze cut me like a thousand tiny blades over my skin.

"It's not what you think," I said, moving closer still. Lina mirrored my movements until we were standing in front of each other.

Until she was close enough to touch.

"What's happening to us, Nicco?" she whispered. "Why do I feel like this?"

"What do you feel like?" I brushed the hair off her neck. She had a thick hoodie pulled over her body, but I was still able to stroke the skin beneath her ear. Lina's eyes drifted closed as she inhaled a shaky breath.

"I look for you when you're not there. I feel you when you're close. I can't get you out of my head." Her eyes opened again, fixing on mine. She smiled and it was like a bolt of lightning to my heart.

This girl.

This innocent sweet girl was ruining me.

"Is it always like this?" she asked, leaning into my touch.

"Is what always like this?" I curved my hand around the nape of her neck, pulling us further into the shadows. No one from the main path would be able to see us now.

"When you like someone. Is it always so intense?"

"You like me, Bambolina?" Her confession shouldn't have affected me as much as it did.

"It feels like... *more*." Her cheeks flushed and Lina dropped her gaze.

"Hey." I slid my finger under her chin, tilting her face back to mine. "Don't ever shy away from me."

"You're right, I'm a... virgin." She swallowed. "I have no experience with guys, at all, and you're so... *you*."

The corner of my mouth kicked up. "I think there's a compliment in there somewhere." I leaned in, brushing my mouth over hers. It was only supposed to be a moment of reassurance, but Lina fisted my sweater, anchoring us together as she flicked her tongue over the seam of my mouth.

"Lina, that's not why I came, not tonight." I gently eased away from her.

"I see. Is it not the same for you?" She was so curious about the world, so fucking naïve.

What the fuck was I doing?

Silence stretched out before us, our eyes saying all the things we couldn't. Then she surprised me by leaning in and kissing the corner of my mouth. "I know you feel it, Nicco. You want to protect me, and I get it, I do. It's the chivalrous thing to do. But maybe I don't want protecting; maybe I just want to let go and feel."

I pulled us further into the shadows, pressing her body flush with mine. What I really wanted was to spin her around and cage her against the wall while I showed her exactly what I felt. But I didn't want to scare her, and I didn't want to take more than I deserved. So instead, I kissed her. I let my hand dip underneath her hoodie and tank top and trail up the warm skin of her stomach while our tongues stroked together in slow, lazy licks. Lina's soft moans had a direct line to my dick, already painfully hard inside my pants.

"I feel it," I said, dragging my lips over her jaw and down her neck. "I look for you," I repeated her words back to her. "I feel you when you're close. And I want to make you mine in every way possible. But..."

"No." Lina pulled back, sliding a single finger against my lips. "No buts. We say goodnight here and then tomorrow night, you can pick me up and take me out on a real date, and we can get to know each other."

I hesitated and Lina's hopeful expression fell. "You don't want—"

"Yes," the word rolled off my tongue. "I do. I just need

some time to arrange something."

"Nicco, I don't need anything lavish."

"I know but you deserve it. Give me a few days, please." I knew the perfect place to take her, but it required a favor, and those didn't happen overnight.

"A few days, okay."

"You won't regret it, I promise."

Even if I was going to hell for it.

Chapter 9

Arianne

"You're doing it again," Nora said as she forked some spaghetti into her mouth.

"No, I'm not." I glared at her.

"Yes, you are. If you'd have just gotten his cell phone number like a normal person, I wouldn't have to survive you searching for him every five seconds."

"I'm not... okay, maybe just a little. But there's something romantic about it, don't you think?"

"It's the twenty-first century, Lina. We have cell phones for a reason."

"Why do we have cell phones?" Tristan approached us. My eyes immediately went to the bandage around his hand.

"What happened?"

"Oh, this." He shrugged, cradling it against his body. "Drunken accident. It's nothing."

"Can you still play?" I knew how important the team was to Tristan.

"Yeah, it'll take a little more than an accident to keep me away. I didn't see you Saturday?"

"Oh, we were there," Nora said, smothering a laugh. I stamped my foot down on hers under the table and she swallowed a yelp.

"It was a masquerade party, we were incognito."

Tristan gave us a funny look. "So long as you had fun."

"We did." Nora grinned. "It was very, *very* enlightening, wasn't it, Lina?"

I glared at her, trying to get her to shut up. I didn't want Tristan to know about Nicco, not yet. Not since the two of them seemed to dislike each other. My cousin's frown grew. "Are you sure everything's okay?"

"Why wouldn't it be?" I smiled.

"Just be careful, okay? I've got to go but I'll be watching." His serious expression melted away replaced with mischief. Before I could protest, Tristan left.

"What the hell was that?" I snapped at Nora who exploded into a fit of laughter.

"You should see your face."

"It's not funny. I don't want Tristan to know about this yet. If he does..." My heart sank. Being with Nicco was exhilarating. New and exciting. I felt alive every time he looked at me.

I didn't want to lose that.

"Relax," Nora said. "Tristan thinks you're far too sweet and innocent to be cavorting with the likes of your brooding hotty."

"You make it sound so dirty."

"Lina, you let him—"

"Okay." I clapped a hand over her mouth. "Enough of that." My cheeks burned at the memory of how I'd let him touch me up against that wall in Tristan's house. "It's almost time for class. Nicco might..." I stopped myself. I didn't want to get my hopes up that Nicco would show up in Professor Mandrake's class.

But it was too late.

I was already there—already hoping.

"Just remember," Nora said. "Guys like Nicco are... they're usually experienced and not the settling down type. I don't want you to get hurt."

"I won't," I said with complete conviction.

Because Nicco wouldn't hurt me.

I don't know how I knew; I just did.

Nicco didn't show up to Intro to Philosophy though. I didn't see him the next day either. But when I woke up Wednesday morning, Nora was standing over me, her eyes sparkling.

"Apparently the building isn't as secure as the brochure said." She thrust an envelope at me. "Found this pushed under the door."

I snatched it off her, greedily tearing it open. "Lina," I started, and she shot me a disapproving look. "I'll tell him, I will." I just didn't know when.

"Well, don't keep a girl waiting, what does it say?"

"Tomorrow night at seven. I'll be waiting in the rear parking lot. Wear something warm and comfortable. Nicco."

"That's it? He went to all the trouble of sneaking into the building for *that*."

"I think it's sweet." I read it again, my heart galloping in my chest.

"Those books of yours have a lot to answer for," she grumbled. "Now I have to survive two more days of you swooning over three little sentences."

"You're only jealous." My lips curved, and Nora leaped

onto my bed, letting out a dreamy sigh.

"You're absolutely right. Now give that here so we can dissect every word."

Our laughter filled the room as my best friend launched into a detailed analysis of where he could be possibly taking me. But it didn't matter.

All that mattered was that Nicco had kept his promise.

∞∞∞

"Are you nervous?" Nora asked me. She was sprawled out on her bed, still nursing a hangover from last night. She'd gone out with Dan, her new *friend*. Apparently there had been wine. And sex. Lots and lots of wine-induced sex.

"A little. He's very... intense."

"Yeah, just like his friend," she murmured.

"That's the third time this week you've grumbled something about Enzo." I laid out my outfit choices on my bed and went to her side. "Come on, spill. What happened between the two of you last weekend at the party?"

She'd been tight-lipped about it, and I hadn't wanted to push. But maybe she needed a little nudge after all.

"Ugh." Nora grabbed a pillow and stuffed it over her face. "I don't want to talk about it."

"Hey." I snatched it away and perched on the end of her bed. "You made me talk."

"I almost... you know." Nora's eyes widened.

"Slept with him?"

"In a bathroom in a frat house? Really, Ari, you think

I'm that—"

"No judgment." I held up my hands.

"I almost gave him a blow job, okay?" She slapped a hand over her eyes. "We didn't even talk or make out and I almost..."

"He is kind of hot, in that dark and brooding bad boy way." And completely terrifying, but I didn't add that. Enzo was too intimidating for me. But Nora wasn't like me. She had balls and spirit, and strangely, I could picture the two of them together.

"It's college, freshman year. You're allowed to sow your... well, that."

Nora chuckled. "You're too good to me." She reached for my hand, tangling our fingers together. "Just promise me, whatever happens this year, we won't let any guys come between us."

"Are you kidding me? You're my person, Nora, you always will be."

"Ditto. Now what did you decide to wear for your date?" She beamed.

"Well, he said to dress warmly and comfortably, so I was going to stick with jeans, a sweater, and my boots."

"Hmm, it could work. But I think I might have something..." She sat up, observing the clothes scattered over my bed. "I have an idea." Nora stood up, a mischievous glint in her eye.

"I don't want to be overdressed."

"Oh hush, it's a date; you want to look irresistible. That's the point."

"Right," I grumbled, already half-regretting letting her help.

"Okay. I think I've got it." Nora dumped a pile of clothes

in my arms. "Try them on and we'll go from there."

"Nora..."

"Ari, trust me. Nicco won't be able to keep his hands off you."

Well, when she put it like that... maybe I did need her help.

∞∞∞

At three minutes past seven, Nora finally let me out of the room. She'd insisted I play it cool, saying it was my womanly right to make Nicco wait a couple of minutes. It seemed unnecessary to me, but all my reservations melted away when I reached the back door and saw him sitting there on his motorcycle.

"Sei bellissima," the words formed on Nicco's lips as he approached me. "Hey." He dipped his head, pressing a kiss to my cheek.

"Hi." Wings beat furiously in my stomach. "Are we taking your bike?"

"If that's okay?"

"I'd like that." I gave him a tentative smile.

"Let me." Nicco put his helmet on me, making sure it was secure. His eyes lingered on me, dark and intense and swirling with desire. "You look beautiful, Lina."

Guilt flashed through me, but I forced it down. He didn't know my true identity yet, but I was still me.

I was still the same girl inside.

Nicco swung his leg over the bike and got situated before motioning for me to get on. "Hold on tight," he said over his shoulder as my hands slid around his hard stomach, his leather jacket cool beneath my fingers.

One of his hands slid down my leg, squeezing gently before he kicked the starter making the bike rumble beneath us. We hadn't even moved yet, and anticipation already trickled through me.

"Ready?" Nicco asked and I nodded against his back. He sped off, the *whoosh* of air taking my breath away. He didn't take the main road out of the campus; instead, taking a smaller road behind the administration building. I clung to him, anchoring my body around his as we left campus behind us and whizzed through the streets of University Hill. It was already dusk, the sun disappearing behind a bank of fluffy white clouds. It was beautiful. The soft material of my pantyhose felt warm and snug around my legs, despite the skirt Nora had insisted I wear bunching around my thighs. Seeing the flare in Nicco's eyes when he'd watched me walk out of Donatello House was worth it. He'd looked at me like he wanted to devour me right there in the small parking lot.

A thrill shot through me.

Nicco kept going, taking the road out of town, toward Providence. After another fifteen minutes, he finally eased off the gas, taking a turn down a dark narrow road. I could just make out a fence perimeter, separating the road from perfectly tended lawns. It looked like a golf course, the natural mounds just visible.

Eventually, we rolled to a stop and Nicco cut the engine. I shimmied off the back of the bike, waiting for him. Electricity crackled between us as he removed my helmet and stroked his fingers through my hair, taming the loose curls Nora had taken her time to style.

"I've never had a girl on the back of my bike before."

Warmth spread through me at his words. I didn't doubt there had been other girls in his life, probably lots of them, but I had one of his firsts. And I liked it.

I liked it a whole lot.

"What is this place?"

"Blackstone Country Club, but don't worry we're not heading inside." Nicco smirked as he took my hand and pulled me toward the perimeter fence.

"Are you sure we should be sneaking inside?"

"Don't you trust me?" He closed the space between us, gazing down at me.

"I do." I swallowed.

"Come on."

We walked a little way down the perimeter before Nicco stopped and yanked back a piece of broken fencing. "In you go." His eyes lit up with playfulness.

I slipped through the gap with ease, careful not to snag my hose on any of the brambles on the other side. Nicco followed, wrapping his arm around my waist and pulling me against his solid chest. His warm breath hit my neck before being replaced with his lips, sending shivers rippling through me. "I could spend my life kissing you and it still wouldn't be enough."

Oh my.

Nicco took my hand again, pulling me further around the perimeter. I could just make out the clubhouse in the distance, with people milling around inside. We stayed out of sight, on the other side of the golf course, until we reached a lake surrounded by Maple trees on one side, its vast surface twinkling under the moonlight.

"It's so beautiful," I said, letting out a little sigh.

"Wait here, okay?" Nicco dropped a kiss on my head

and then disappeared into the shadows. Another figure appeared and the two of them talked in hushed voices. The guy's eyes darted to me and he smiled before giving Nicco a knowing look and then handing him a brown bag. He disappeared again and Nicco came back to me, taking my hand once more.

We walked a little further, the trees now surrounding us, until we burst through a clearing to where the trees met the water's edge.

"This is... wow." There was a picnic blanket laid out and a candle lantern flickering, casting golden shadows off the water.

"I wanted you all to myself." His big strong arms wrapped around me from behind again, as we stood there, looking out at the water.

"I can't believe you did all this for me. It's beautiful."

"You're beautiful." He pressed a soft kiss to my neck. "You make me want to be better, Lina. To be more."

Nicco's words hung over us. I didn't know what to say. Everything was so overwhelming.

He was overwhelming.

In the best possible way, and I was already becoming addicted.

"Are you hungry?" he finally broke the silence that had descended.

"I could eat." My stomach grumbled with approval.

Nicco led me to the blanket and we sat down. "Milo is a good friend. He had the chef make my favorite. I hope you like it." He pulled out two containers, two forks, and napkins.

"Is that Bistecca alla Florentina?" The rich smell of meat filled the air.

"You've never tasted it like this." Nicco jammed the fork into the container and brought it to my lips. "Open."

I closed my mouth around the fork, flavor exploding on my tongue. "Mmm," I groaned. "So good."

Nicco's eyes widened, his jaw clenched.

"Sorry." Embarrassment stained my cheeks.

"I'm only jealous," he said quietly.

"Jealous?"

"Yeah, of that fork."

"Oh... *oh!*" I turned a shade darker, the sound of Nicco's laughter sinking into me.

"Come on, eat up. There's dessert too."

"Tiramisu?" I asked, hopeful.

"You'll have to wait and find out." There was a glint in his eyes that made my tummy tighten.

Nicco was right, the food was to die for. The Florentine steak and the pasta, even the bread was delectable.

"This is so good," I mumbled, wiping the corner of my mouth with a napkin. Nicco watched me intently, his eyes dark and sparkling with lust. My tummy clenched. "Tell me about you, your family..."

"What do you want to know?"

Everything. I wanted to know everything. But something told me Nicco kept his cards close to his chest. Something I could empathize with.

"Do you have any siblings?" I asked.

"A sister. Alessia. She's a junior in high school and a total pain in the ass."

"I always wanted a brother or a sister."

"It's just you?"

I nodded. "Although Nora is like a sister to me. I've known her forever. We grew up together."

"How are you liking MU so far? Is it everything you thought it would be?"

Guilt snaked through me, but I forced it down. I didn't want to let anything ruin this. Not even the secrets I kept.

"Classes are fine. I mean, I like learning. But I didn't expect it to be so..." My gaze dropped to the blanket.

"Lina?" Nicco's voice coaxed me to look at him. "What is it?"

"Do you ever feel like you don't fit in?" My eyes widened. I hadn't meant to say the words, but Nicco made it so easy. I wanted to tell him everything—confess my deepest, darkest secrets. I wanted him to know me.

The *real* me.

When he didn't reply, the silence between us thick and heavy, I backtracked. "Ignore me, I'm just nervous, and when I'm nervous, I ramble."

His hand reached out, brushing my jaw, tilting my face to his. "You don't need to be nervous with me, Bambolina. Ever."

I melted at his words, the way he touched me like I was the most precious thing in the world.

"I want to know everything about you," I blurted out.

Nicco chuckled, "We have time," he said. "But first have dessert."

Nicco's eyes darkened, hooded with desire as he pulled out another container. He shucked out of his leather jacket and rolled it up, placing it behind me. My breath caught as his hand ran up my stomach, pressing gently against my breastbone. "Lie down, Lina," he commanded.

I dropped back on my elbows, unable to take my eyes

off him as he straddled my outstretched legs. When his fingers toyed with the buttons on my tight-fitting blouse, I realized now why Nora had been so insistent I wear it. One after one Nicco popped open the buttons revealing my black lacy bra to him. Picking up the last container, he flipped the lid and dipped his finger inside.

"Now where shall we start?" His eyes ran over my body. They lingered on my breasts, trailing ever so slowly up my neck until they locked on my heated gaze. Nicco leaned in, painting my lips with Tiramisu before capturing my mouth and licking them clean. "Hmm, my favorite," he breathed against my skin.

My body trembled beneath him, a coiled spring of nerves. He knew I was inexperienced, and yet, he didn't touch me with hesitation. He touched me with confidence and skill.

Nicco touched me in a way that made me want to give him everything.

His finger dived back into the container but this time he trailed the dessert all over my chest, taking his time to lick it away. "You taste so fucking good," he rasped. My fingers buried deep into his hair, scraping his scalp as he teased the curve of my breast.

"Do I not get to try dessert?" I asked, surprised at the confidence in my voice.

Nicco lifted his head, smiling. "You only have to ask, Bambolina." Sitting up, he dipped his two fingers into the dessert container this time, before bringing them to my lips. My tongue darted out, tasting the sticky sweet goodness, but it wasn't enough. I sucked his fingers into my mouth, imagining it was something else entirely.

"Fuck," he hissed, watching me through hooded eyes. But Nicco didn't watch for long. He pulled his hand away, capturing my lips in a bruising kiss. His body came down hard on top of mine, our hands touching and teasing as he kissed me into submission.

When he finally pulled away, I was high on the taste of him; a quivering ball of nerves.

"Nicco, I want—"

"Ssh, Bambolina, I know what you need." He rolled to one side of me, peppering my lips, my jaw and neck, with tiny kisses while one hand slipped to the hem of my skirt. Nicco carefully inched my hose down my legs, the cool air brushing against my skin. A shiver rolled through me, but then warm fingers were touching me, setting me alight.

"You're so wet for me." Nicco dipped two fingers inside me, stretching me. I couldn't breathe, I felt so good. So... full. It felt even better than the other night. Then he circled my clit with his thumb, and everything grew more intense, the world closing in around me.

"Nicco, I can't..."

"Just feel it," he breathed against my lips. "Feel what I do to you." He hooked his fingers inside me, rubbing deeper. My back arched off the blanket as my body began to quiver.

Nicco kissed me, his tongue mimicking the way his fingers glided in and out of me. It was so erotic, I wanted to watch him. But I could barely keep my eyes open, intense waves of pleasure building deep inside me.

"More," I cried. "More, Nicco."

"Ti voglio," he mumbled before tearing away from me.

"Nicco?" I pushed up onto my elbows, breathless and dizzy. He smirked at me as he kneeled between my legs and inched my hose further down.

Then he was there, flattening his tongue against me and making me cry out his name. He added a finger, licking and sucking, stroking some magical place inside me that set off an explosion of stars behind my eyes.

"I'll never eat tiramisu again without thinking of you like this, sprawled out before me, looking like an angel." Heat burned in his gaze as he stared up at me.

"I don't know many angels who let boys do that to them." Soft laughter bubbled in my chest as I slowly caught my breath. Nicco pressed a final kiss to my inner thigh before straightening my hose.

"Better?"

"Much." I smiled. Nicco made me reckless. Impulsive and uninhibited. But I loved it. He made me feel so special and desired.

I was going to tell him.

When he took me back to my dorm, before we said goodnight, I was going to come clean. Because I was falling for Nicco, and I didn't want to start whatever this was, what I hoped it would become, based on lies.

I only hoped he understood.

"Hey, what is it?" His hand curled around my neck, drawing me close to him. I buried my face in his chest, letting him kiss my head.

"Thank you, for tonight. It was everything."

"You're everything, Lina. Sei più bella di un angelo." He eased back to kiss me. Soft and tender and the perfect end to a perfect first date.

"It's late," he said, "I should get you back before your crazy roommate sends out a search party."

"Hey, Nora isn't crazy, she's just... determined to soak up college life."

"I shouldn't have said that." Nicco held out his hand, helping me up. "She's good for you."

"She is. Although I think she has a thing for your friend, Enzo."

Nicco paled. "That's not a good idea."

"Nora can handle him."

"I love Enzo like a brother, but trust me when I say Nora is better off forgetting all about him, okay?" He sounded so serious all I could do was nod.

"Hey, shouldn't we clean up?" I asked, realizing he was pulling me back toward the hole in the fence.

"Milo will handle it," he said. "He owes me."

Owed him?

I couldn't imagine what kind of debt he possibly had to repay that required him to clean up after us.

When we reached Nicco's bike, I grabbed his hand before he reached for the helmet. If I didn't say this now, I never would.

"When we get back to the dorm, can we talk? It's nothing bad. There's just something I want to tell you before we... well, before this, us," I stumbled over the words. "Before we go any further."

"You can tell me anything." He lifted my hand, kissing my knuckles. "Come on, let's get you back."

Nicco helped me secure the helmet and we got situated on the bike. He didn't need to tell me to hold on this time, my arms locked around his waist and I tucked myself into his leather jacket.

The night hadn't even ended yet and I was already thinking about our next date. And the one after that. Because Nicco wasn't only buried under my skin.

He was imprinting himself on my heart.

Chapter 10

Nicco

I had the biggest grin on my face the whole ride back to MU. Not to mention the taste of Lina still on my tongue. Jesus, watching her come like that had been everything. I'd wanted to take her right there on the picnic blanket, under the stars. But she deserved more. She deserved flowers and a romantic dinner and all that stuff. Stuff I'd never even imagined doing.

But I wanted to do it with her.

My hand covered Lina's as I slowed to a stop behind her dorm building. I already wanted to kiss her again, to slide my tongue against hers and never come up for air. There was so much still left to say though. Things I had to eventually tell her, but I was too lost in the moment with her.

Lina climbed off the back of my bike, slipping the helmet off and hanging it on the bars. I hooked an arm around her waist, pulling her in close. Her hands went around my neck as she leaned down and kissed me. I loved it when she took the lead; the way she peppered tiny kisses over my lips, down my jaw. The soft uncertain flick of her tongue against mine.

"Come on," I said, finally breaking away, knowing that if she carried on, I wouldn't be able to resist taking it further. "I'll walk you to the door."

It was a risk, but she was worth it. Being with Lina made me feel invincible. Like I could take on the world and win.

We walked hand-in-hand to the back door, but there was an out of service notice. "Guess we'll have to go around front," she said, leaning up to kiss me again.

We stumbled against the wall, all teeth and tongue and soft laughter. My heart was a constant drum in my chest, adrenaline coursing through my veins. I felt like an addict flying high off their last hit, and I never wanted it to end.

"What did you want to tell me?" I whispered against her lips, letting my hands drift to her ass and pressing her closer.

"In a minute," she murmured, "I want to make the most of this." Lina curled herself around me as I found the strength to walk us around the side of the building.

"I can barely keep my hands off you."

"So don't." She laughed and it was so fucking pure and real, I wanted to bottle it and keep it for a rainy day.

We kissed and kissed and kissed some more. Until someone cleared their throat. "Arianne?"

Lina went rigid in my arms. "Tristan?" She turned slowly to where Tristan Capizola stood glaring at us.

No, not us.

Me.

My spine stiffened. What the fuck was going on?

"Papá?" Lina croaked.

I hadn't noticed the man at Tristan's side. But I saw him now. Expensive suit. Polished shoes. Smooth beard and sharp, assessing gaze.

"Papá?" I choked out, the truth barreling into me like a runaway train.

"Gosh." Lina stepped out of my hold, smiling up at me with guilt shining in her eyes. "This isn't how I wanted you to find out."

Taking a step back, I motioned a hand at Roberto Capizola and his... *daughter.*

The word lodged in my throat.

Fuck.

How could I have missed it?

"You're... you're Arianne Capizola?"

"Surprise." Lina... no, Arianne said.

"Arianne, please come over here," her father commanded.

"Papá, I know this is probably going to sound crazy, but I want you meet my... Nicco. We've been hanging out and well, I... hmm." She tucked a curl behind her ears, shooting me a coy look. "I like him a lot."

"Niccolò Marchetti, this is a surprise." Roberto enunciated every letter. "How is your father?"

My fist clenched at my side as I stared down at the man who thought he held our future in his hands.

"Papá," Arianne whispered, looking between us. "You know Nicco?"

The hopeful look on her face sliced me open.

"His father is an old friend. You should probably say goodbye to him now, mio tesoro. We have much to discuss."

My cell vibrated in my pocket, but I couldn't move. I couldn't get past the part where Lina, *my Lina*, was Arianne Capizola, daughter of Roberto Capizola, and the girl who was the key to everything.

Arianne bounced over to me, her expression so full of relief I felt gutted. "I take it this was what you want to talk to me about?" My voice was tight.

"I'm sorry I didn't tell you, but Papá thought it would be safer—"

"You should go to him."

Her brows knitted, her expression melting away. "Is everything okay? You look like you've seen a ghost."

"I'm fine." I jammed my hands in my pockets to stop myself from touching her.

I'd known from the second I met her, that Lina didn't belong in my world. But I never anticipated we were enemies on opposite sides of a long and bitter feud between our families. And from the way she was staring up at me starry-eyed and full of lust, she had no idea.

This was a fucking shitshow and there was nothing I could say or do to fix it.

Arianne wasn't mine to have.

She never was.

"Okay," she said hesitantly. "Will I see you tomorrow?"

"Lina ... I mean, Ari—"

"It's one of my middle names, you can still call me Lina. Or Bambolina." She stared up at me with a megawatt smile. "I'll dream of you."

"Arianne," her father said again.

"Coming, I'm coming." Leaning up, she pressed a single kiss to my cheek. I sucked in a harsh breath, my heart cracking clean in two.

I wouldn't ever get to feel this again.

I'd never get to hold her in my arms and kiss her.

Roberto would yank her out of MU and lock her away

where no one could get to her. Where *I* couldn't get to her.

And then he'd come for me.

"Goodbye, Bambolina," I steeled myself, locking away every single thing I felt for her, watching as she walked over to her father and Tristan.

"Let's go inside where we can talk." Roberto roped his arm around Arianne's shoulder and led her toward the dorm building, his eyes fixed on me the whole time. Burning with hatred. "Tristan, see that Niccolò gets off okay. And then join us inside please."

"It would be my pleasure Uncle." The fucker smirked at me.

Arianne glanced back, giving me a small wave. I wanted to go after her; to steal her right out from under him and take her far far away from here.

She was mine.

I felt it deep in my soul.

Lina belonged to me. But Lina wasn't Lina at all, she was Arianne Capizola.

If only you'd paid more attention. But it had been too easy to fall for her. Her smile and innocence. Her beauty and warmth. I'd been so wrapped up in Lina, in the idea of her, I dropped my guard. I'd seen her with Tristan, even asked how she knew him.

But I hadn't wanted to see what was right in front of me.

It was too late though. Arianne had disappeared inside the building. Leaving me outside with Tristan.

"Did you fuck her?" he snarled. "Did you touch my cousin with your dirty fucking Marchetti hands?" He stalked toward me, a splint restraining his pinky finger and the one beside it.

"How's the finger?" I mocked as he drew nearer. My cell vibrated again, but there was no time to check it or text for help. Tristan was coming for me and from the glint in his eye, he was out for blood.

And the worst of it was, I couldn't blame him. If our roles were reserved, I'd want blood too.

"You should have made sure to do both hands. Because I only need one good hand to put you on your ass, Marchetti."

"Take your best shot." I drew to my full height. I could take him. Years of fighting at my uncle's gym and then moving to the underground circuit at L'Anello's meant I could take guys twice my size. But he was Arianne's cousin. Her family.

And even after everything that had just gone down, I didn't want to hurt her.

I couldn't.

"I'm not going to fight you, Tristan," I said keeping my voice even.

"Pussy." He spat, circling me.

"I didn't know. I had no idea who she was. She told me her name was Lina for fuck's sake." I held my hands up in defense.

"You think I believe anything you say?"

"It's the truth." I dragged a hand down my face. "I didn't know."

"You'll pay for this. You know that, right? You'll pay for tainting her. For ever looking twice at her." He was almost on me now.

The fighter in me wanted to attack, to unleash all the anger and surprise and bitterness I felt at the universe for giving me something as good as Lina and then ripping her away from me.

"You don't want to do this, Tristan," I said, flicking my gaze to the dorm building. Arianne was in there, her father no doubt painting me as the devil in disguise.

I rubbed the heel of my palm against my forehead.

"Don't tell me you actually feel something for her?" Tristan laughed bitterly. "Holy shit, you do. You like her." He taunted me. "What did you think, Marchetti? That you and her were going to ride off in the sunset together? She lied to you, and I'd put money on the fact you haven't been entirely honest with her either."

"Fuck you. You don't know anything about us."

"I know she'll never be yours. I know that once she finds out exactly who you are, she'll never want anything else to do with you. Arianne is better than you. She'll always be better than you. You're nothing, Marchetti, nothing but—"

I snapped. My fist flew toward Tristan's face, but he saw it coming, dodging to the side. "Motherfucker," he roared, his fist barreling toward me. I tried to move, tried to duck out of the way. But it was too late. He clipped me right in the chin, sending my head snapping backward. Pain exploded through my jaw as I went down, my head cracking against the pavement.

And then everything went black.

∞∞∞

"Here," Bailey threw a bag of frozen corn at me. "It's the best I could do."

"Gee, thanks." I pressed it to my jaw, hissing at the blast of icy pain.

"He got you good, huh?"

"I wasn't about to fight him." Although I was quickly beginning to regret that. Tristan was a smug fucker. This would only bolster his ego.

"So your girl is the Capizola princess? That's some bad fucking luck."

"Hey, language," I snapped, and heavy silence settled between us.

Bailey had found me a few minutes after Tristan had laid me out. He'd managed to get me up on my feet and onto the back of my bike while he drove us back to my aunt's.

"I keep playing it over in my mind, trying to figure out what I missed..."

"But you only saw her."

"Yeah," I let out a weary sigh. "I only saw her."

The kid was too smart for his own good. But he was right. The second I'd seen her in the alley, scared and disheveled, something shifted inside me. I'd wanted to protect her. To make her smile and keep her safe.

I'd wanted her.

Plain and simple.

And the more time I spent around her, the more I wanted to make her mine.

"Now what happens?"

"Lina..." My heart clenched. "I mean Arianne, will probably be yanked out of college and Roberto will come after me for touching his daughter."

"You really think he'd risk war over her?"

I would.

Deep down, part of me knew I'd risk it all for her. It made no fucking sense, but I felt it.

She was mine.

Even if she wasn't.

"You're falling in love with her?" Bailey asked, but I found no judgment in his eyes.

"Nah, I don't know how to love." A wall slammed down over me. "It's probably better this way. She deserves someone who can give her all the things I'll never be able to." Like safety and security and a normal future.

"Don't sell yourself short, Nicco. You love Alessia, Enzo and Matteo... me. You love my parents too and your other aunts and uncles."

"You're family, of course I fucking love you."

"So fight for her," he said as if it was that simple.

"There are things at play even I don't understand, Bay. The history between our families goes back to the beginning, right back to the birth of Verona County. And me and Arianne are on opposite sides of the line. Nothing will ever change that."

"Maybe this is a chance to fix things," he added. "Maybe this is a chance to reunite the families."

Strangled laughter rumbled in my chest. This wouldn't fix things; it would only make them a hundred times worse. If my father found out I'd been mooning after the Capizola heir, he would cut off my balls and feed them to me.

My feelings for Arianne might have been soul deep, but his hatred for her father, her family, ran deeper. It was ingrained in the very fiber of his being, coursing through his blood.

"You need to keep this to yourself. Can you do that?" I asked my cousin, and he nodded. Until I figured out what the hell to do, no one else could find out the truth.

"Now hand me that bottle of whisky. I need to dull this pain." My jaw stung like a bitch, but it wasn't the only part of me hurting.

I snatched the bottle from him, unscrewed the cap and took a huge gulp. The liquor burned my throat but distracted me from the deep sting every time I opened my mouth. Grabbing my cell, I re-read Enzo's messages. He'd been on Tristan watch when he'd seen Roberto Capizola's black SUV pull up outside of the football team's house.

While I'd been licking tiramisu off Arianne's body, he'd been doing his job just like I'd told him to. He'd followed them as far as the library but then got ruffled by security. He knew something was going down, he just hadn't gotten close enough to learn what.

It was a small mercy, but the universe obviously hadn't completely sided against me.

I typed out a quick reply, letting him know to take it easy for the rest of the night. Enzo was as loyal as they came, but once he found out about my betrayal, I didn't know how he'd react. He hated the Capizola with a fire not even I possessed. So the fact I'd been, albeit unknowingly, fooling around with one would be a giant hurdle in our friendship. Matteo would side with me, his loyalty was unwavering. But Enzo could pick the family over me, and that would be a problem.

What the fuck was I saying?

My loyalty was to my family, it had to be. I had Alessia to think of, her future and safety. Arianne was just a girl. I'd get over her. The fact she was the enemy should have been motivation enough. All I needed to do was call up Rayna or any of the other girls chomping at the bit to get on my dick and fuck her right out of my system.

She's not just a girl, and you know it.

I let out a weary sigh and my fingers tightened around the neck of the bottle as I took another swallow.

"Maybe that's not such a good idea," Bailey said, eying the bottle.

"Do you have a better idea? Because right now it's either get shitfaced on whisky or drive over to her dorm building and..." I mashed my lips together. Going there wouldn't help things, not tonight. I needed to think. I needed to figure out a way forward that didn't end up with Arianne hurt. But first I needed to forget. I needed the gaping hole in my chest to heal. I needed to be so drunk I couldn't do something stupid.

Something I would regret.

Something that would end up with me behind bars, or worse, with a bullet between my eyes.

Chapter 11

Arianne

"Mr. Capizola," Nora rubbed her eyes. "This is a surprise." She glanced from me to him and back again, silently asking me what the hell was going on.

I gave her a little shrug.

"Can we, hmm, get you something to drink?"

"No, that's quite alright. But I would like to speak with Arianne alone, if that's not too much to ask."

"Of course not." She wrung her hands. "I can go hang out downstairs in the common room."

"Nora, you don't need to—"

"Thank you, Nora," my father interjected, "that would be much appreciated."

My brows drew together. He was acting weird, sending tingles zipping up my spine. I'd been so surprised to see my father and Tristan standing there, so embarrassed. No doubt he had questions about Nicco, about the nature of our relationship. But in a strange way, I was also glad the truth was out. Now I didn't have to pretend anymore.

Deep down, I'm sure all my father wanted was for me to be happy.

Safe and happy and loved.

Three words I felt every time Nicco looked at me. Even if it was far too soon to be feeling such things.

So why did I feel like everything was about to change?

"I'd like Nora to stay," I blurted out, suddenly feeling out of my depth, panic swelling in my chest. "Please, Papá."

"Arianne, this does not—"

"*Please*," I said, reaching for Nora's hand. The happiness I'd felt only minutes earlier was rapidly diminishing. Something was wrong, I felt it.

I'd been so blinded by my amazing date with Nicco, I hadn't assumed my father was here for anything besides a social visit. But it was late on a Thursday night and he hadn't called ahead.

It made no sense.

Nora slid her fingers between mine and squeezed, giving me the strength to ask, "What's going on, Papá? Why are you here?"

"Very well, this will affect Nora too. Please," he motioned to our beds. "Let's sit."

Nora and I plopped down on her bed while my father took one of the desk chairs. Just then, the door swung open and Tristan entered the room. He met my father's gaze and gave him a sharp nod.

"Tristan?" I asked, my voice quivering. "What happened? Where's Nicco?"

"He took off." There was something in his voice, but my father cleared his throat, commanding my attention.

"It has come to my attention that you are no longer safe here."

"Safe?" I choked out. "What do you mean, I'm not safe? I haven't even been here two weeks. I don't understand. Did something happen?"

"How long have you been seeing the Marchetti boy?"

"Nicco, Papá, his name is Nicco. And it all happened quite suddenly. He's been—"

"Have you been intimate with him?"

"Wh- what?" Embarrassment stained my cheeks.

"Mr. Capizola," Nora interrupted. "I don't think that's really an appropriate question to ask in front—"

"Answer the question, mio tesoro."

"N- no," I lied, indignation burning through me. What right did he have to ask me that? In front of Nora and Tristan no less.

"No." I collected myself. "I'm still..."

"Good, that's very good indeed." His shoulders visibly relaxed.

What the hell was happening?

My father had always been curt, but he had never been so cold with me before. Everything he'd ever done, although overbearing and over the top, was out of love. I'd never doubted that.

Until now.

"You are no longer to see Niccolò Marchetti."

The words rattled around my head. I didn't understand what he was saying.

"I'm sorry to do this to you, Arianne," he went on. "I am, but you need to pack your things immediately. We leave tonight."

"Leave?" I leaped up, tears streaming down my face. "I'm not leaving. I'm not going to stop seeing Nicco. He makes me happy. He makes me feel... *normal*. You said—"

"I said you could remain here as long as you were safe." My father stood, smoothing a hand through his beard. "You are no longer safe."

"What does that even mean? Does someone want to hurt me? Who?" I cried, tears burning the backs of my eyes. "I've done everything you asked of me. I've barely even talked to anyone except Nora and..."

"Marchetti?" My cousin ground out, a look of disgust washing over him.

"Tristan?" I said softly. "Tell me what's going on. What does Nicco have to do with any of this?"

"She should know," he said to my father, clenching his fist. I noticed it looked sore, the skin around his knuckles red and angry.

"Tristan," he warned. "Now is not the—"

"What did you do?" It came out shrill, the pieces of the puzzle shifting and changing, slowly slotting into place. But I was still missing too many vital parts to make any sense of it. "What did you do to Nicco?"

"Nothing he didn't deserve." Tristan shot up, glaring down at me.

"You bastard," I yelled, fists clenched at my sides, my heart crashing violently against my chest.

"Whoa, there." Nora flanked my side. "I think everyone should just calm down. Mr. Capizola, what is this all about? Is Arianne in immediate danger?"

His eyes clouded with indecision.

"I want to stay here," I said, finally finding my voice. "At least for tonight. This is my life, *my life,* Papá, and I'm not sure I want to go anywhere with either of you until you tell me what the hell is going on."

"Arianne," my father tsked. "Must you be so difficult?"

"Difficult? You think this is me being difficult? You kept me locked away at home for five years. Five. Years. Papá.

I was so excited to come here, to finally be a normal teenage girl, and you want to rip that away from me. Because I'm in danger. But you won't tell me why. Well, I'm sorry, but that doesn't work for me." I ripped my hand from Nora's, planting it on my hip.

He couldn't do this.

He couldn't take away college, my freedom... *Nicco*.

I'd only just found him; I couldn't just forget about him.

I wouldn't.

"You're one of the most powerful men in Verona County, in the State." My eyes narrowed at him. "Surely you can make sure it's safe for me to stay here?"

Tristan's expression softened but it was too late. If he'd even laid so much as a finger on Nicco, we were done. "She has a point, Uncle. I'm here, Scott too. You know we wouldn't let anyone hurt her."

Nora tensed beside me and I quickly shot her a look that said, 'please don't say anything'.

"I'll leave two men."

"Bodyguards?" Disbelief coated my words. "That's not what I—"

"It's this or you can pack a bag and come straight home with me."

"Fine." I folded my arms over my chest, wondering how we'd gotten here. Less than an hour ago, I'd been floating on clouds, wrapped in Nicco's arms, falling so deeply into him I never wanted to come back to reality.

And now... now, they talked about him like he was the enemy and we were at war.

I didn't understand any of it.

All I knew is that my heart was splintering in my chest, and I wasn't going anywhere, not tonight.

"Very well." Father buttoned his jacket. "But Arianne, this isn't permanent. You are my daughter and I will always do whatever it takes to keep you safe. Do you understand that? Take the night to calm down and we'll pick this up again tomorrow."

I didn't trust myself to speak, so I gave him a tight-lipped nod. He came to me, pressing a single kiss to the top of my head. "Mio tesoro, you have grown into such a strong young lady. But don't let yourself be fooled by things as fickle as love. We are Capizola, Principessa. It's time you started to act like one."

Nora's eyes burned into the side of my head as I watched my father walk out of our room as if he hadn't just tipped my world on its axis.

Tristan lingered, his eyes glittering with apology. "Ari, I tried to buy you more time, but I didn't realize you were—"

"Don't 'Ari' me," I sneered. "Look me in the eye and tell me you didn't hurt him, Tristan. Look me in the eye and tell me."

"I'm sorry," he whispered, "But there are things you don't know, cousin. So much history you don't... fuck."

"You need to leave," Nora said, wrapping her arm around me. "Now."

"Yeah, okay." Tristan's gaze lingered on me, but I couldn't look at him. "But you can't hide from this forever, Arianne. This is your destiny. Whether you like it or not."

My cousin stalked out of the room, closing the door behind him.

And I crumpled into my friend's arms, wondering when life had gotten so complicated.

∞∞∞

"Here." Nora handed me a cup of hot cocoa. "How do you feel now?"

"Are the Muscle Twins still standing guard outside my room?"

She went to the peephole and took a look. "Yep."

"Well then, that was all real, and I didn't dream it. So I guess you could say I feel angry, betrayed, confused, disappointed... does that work for you?"

Nora gave me a weak smile. "I'm proud of you."

"Proud of me?"

"Hell yeah. You didn't just pack a bag and dutifully follow your father back home. You stood your ground."

"He told me nothing, Nora. Nothing. All that talk about MU not being safe and forbidding me from seeing Nicco again. What the hell was that? And Tristan..."

"You really think he hurt Nicco?"

"Didn't you see his hand? Something went down." The knot in my stomach tightened.

"Can't you text him?"

"I... I don't have his number..." My voice trailed off.

"You didn't get it tonight? Ari, come on..."

"I realize how stupid it sounds, but he never asked me and I didn't want to... God, Nora, have I been fooling myself this whole time? Is Nicco somehow related to the threat my father was talking about? You should have seen how shocked they were to see me with him. I've seen my father angry plenty of times, but I've never seen him like that."

"What did they say his name is? Marchetti?"

"Yes, why?"

"Marchetti... it sounds familiar. I'm sure I've heard it before. Come on, let's Google him."

"Google him? I don't know if—"

"Ari, they're keeping something from you. And I know hotty came in and swept you off your feet and had you so starry-eyed you failed to get any of the important details from him, like his surname and phone number, but it's time you found out the truth. Don't you think?"

I placed down the mug and let out a heavy sigh. She was right. I'd been too naïve, too wrapped up in how Nicco made me feel to worry about how little I really knew about him.

"Okay." I joined her on her bed. Nora fired up her laptop and we sat back against the headboard.

"Niccolò Marchetti." She entered his name into the search bar and hit enter. "Student at MU, tell us something we don't already know. No hits on social media. No images. Oh wait, what's this?"

She clicked one of the links and the article loaded. "Son of Antonio Marchetti, boss of Dominion, the organized crime syndicate operating out of La Riva, Verona County. The Marchetti have a long and colorful history in Verona that dates back to the original founding families..."

"Crime syndicate?" I whispered. "As in the... *mafia*? But that's—"

"Oh my god," Nora gasped. "That's where I've heard the name before. Giovanni used to tell me these stories about how Verona County was founded. Your great-great-grandfather Tommaso Capizola emigrated here in the late eighteen-hundreds. He and his best friend built a life for themselves. Giovanni made them out to be these larger-than-life characters who built this illegal empire, but I always thought he was exaggerating. Your father is the most law-abiding man I know, but maybe there's more to it?"

I'd heard the stories, knew all about my family's legacy of being the founders of Verona County, but I'd never heard Nora's version. "What are you saying? That my father's great-grandfather's best friend was a Marchetti?"

She nodded slowly. "I think so."

Leaning in, I studied the article. "Dominion," I said, typing the word into the search bar followed by Verona County.

"Holy shit," Nora let out a shaky breath as we poured over article after article linking the Marchetti name to a string of offences. "They're mobsters," she said. "Real life Italian mobsters."

"It's not..." I inhaled sharply. "It can't be true. Nicco is —"

"Prince of Dominion." Nora pointed to the screen. "He's next in line to take over Dominion. At least now we know why your father and Tristan freaked the hell out when they caught you making out with him."

"Nora..." A heavy weight settled over me.

"Sorry, just trying to lighten the mood."

I didn't appreciate her humor, not right now. Not when everything I thought I knew was being obliterated. My family hadn't built their success on the foundations of hard work and determination; they had ridden the coattails of their mobster ancestors. Nicco wasn't just a mysterious bad boy with a good heart; he was the only son of New England's mafia boss.

He was everything I wasn't.

"Ari?" Nora rushed out as I slumped back against the pillows, the air sucked clean from my lungs.

"What am I going to do?" I sobbed, my heart breaking for the boy who had made me feel alive and the girl he'd pulled from her shell.

It made some sense now; Nicco's constant torment over being with me. The way he always referred to himself as being no good for me.

But even though I knew the truth, and I knew there was still a lot more to the story to uncover, I couldn't forget how Nicco made me feel. The way he'd handled me with such love and affection. It wasn't something you could fake, was it?

"I can feel my heart breaking," I cried into my hands, the pain overwhelming. "Was it real? Was any of it real?"

"Ssh," Nora stroked my hair. "We'll figure it out, Ari. I promise we'll figure it out."

But I wasn't sure of anything anymore.

All I'd wanted was a normal life. Then I'd met Nicco, and it was like being in a fairytale. My very own prince to chase away the monsters and protect my heart. But it was all a lie.

The truth was much worse.

The truth was my life had just become a living nightmare.

One I didn't know how I would survive.

∞∞∞

Sleep didn't come easy.

I tossed and turned all night, replaying the events of the night over in my head. At one point, I'd given up hope of falling to sleep and began searching the internet for more information about Nicco's family, hoping, *praying*, that Nora was wrong.

Niccolò Marchetti wasn't the son of a mafia boss.

He couldn't be.

Yet, deep down, I knew the truth. What had he really told me about himself?

Nothing.

And foolishly, I hadn't asked. I'd been so enamored with him, so set on keeping my own secret, I hadn't stopped to consider he was keeping devastating secrets of his own.

"Hey, are you awake?" Nora's voice was thick with sleep. She'd managed to drop off sometime around one, after I'd soaked her pajama top with tears.

"I couldn't sleep," I replied, rolling onto my side and pulling the covers higher. "I wanted it to all be a dream."

"But it's not," she said, sadness heavy in her words.

"It's not."

"So I guess his best friend, Enzo, is also... you know."

"I don't know. I don't know anything anymore."

"You're falling for him, aren't you?"

"I..." The words stuck in my throat. "It's crazy, right? You can't fall for someone you hardly know."

"You can if it's written in the stars."

I chuckled bitterly at that. "Nothing about me and Nicco is written in the stars, Nor. He's a criminal. You read the articles. Murder. Intimidation. Racketeering. Fraud. It all leads back to Dominion."

"Not all people choose to be bad, Ari, some have no

choice. You won't know Nicco's story until you ask him."

"Ask him?" I gawked at her. "You really think he's going to want to speak to me now he knows who I am?" Silence lingered between us, and then I whispered, "I found something..."

"What?" She pushed up onto her elbows.

"I couldn't sleep, so I did some more digging. One of my father's companies is trying to get permission to redevelop La Riva."

"But that's Marchetti territory." We'd learned that during our late-night internet search.

I nodded slowly, my stomach churning. "Antonio Marchetti refuses to give up the land."

"You think that has something to do with the bad blood between them?"

"It's a start." Although I had a feeling it went much deeper than that.

"What are you going to do?"

"I'm going to go and see my father."

She bolted upright. "Ari, I'm not sure that's a good idea. If you antagonize him, he might make you return home."

I swung my legs over the edge of the bed and sat up. "I can't spend my life being his dutiful, docile daughter. I spent my entire teenage years locked away in the house. I want to know why."

Nora mirrored my position, pushing her feet into fluffy gray slippers. "So I guess we're going home this weekend after all?"

"You'll come with me?"

"As if you even need to ask."

"Thank you." I smiled.

"You think the Muscle Twins will drive us there?"

"There's only one way to find out. But before I face my father, I need breakfast."

"Are you sure?" Her brow rose. "Maybe we should—"

"It's college, Nora. What could possibly happen to me here? Besides, it's not like we'll be alone." My gaze flicked to the door. I was used to seeing my mother and father being flanked by bodyguards. Even Nora's dad, Billy, was trained in close protection. It was all part and parcel of working for Verona County's wealthiest family.

"I think we should get drive-thru on route."

"Nor, come on. It's just breakfast."

"I get it." She gave me a weak smile. "You're feeling defiant and you want to fight back. I would too. But we still don't know all the facts."

"Fine," I conceded. "We can get drive-thru."

She was right. I did feel defiant. It burned through me, swirling with anger and frustration. I wanted answers.

I wanted the truth.

Even if I didn't like it.

∞∞∞

In less than half an hour, we were both washed and dressed, staring at the door as if it led to some unknown world. "Are you sure about this?" Nora asked me.

"It's the only way. I want answers. I deserve answers, Nor. And my father has them."

"I like you like this." She smiled. "All feisty and strong."

"Oh, I don't know about that." Inside, my heart was battered and bruised. But my father was a formidable man and I didn't want to give him even an ounce of ammunition. He needed to see I was an adult now. A young woman capable of handling the truth.

"You've got this, Ari. *We've* got this. Come on." She yanked the door open and stepped out into the hall. The two bodyguards stood to attention, focusing their narrowed gazes on me.

"Miss Capizola. Your father has requested—"

"I need you to drive me home," I said.

They shared a glance. "Mr. Capizola would prefer it if —"

Clearing my throat, I took a deep breath and said, "What are your names?"

"I'm Luis, and my partner here is Nixon."

"Well, Luis, you can either drive me home or we'll make our own way."

"Very well," he said. "The car is out front."

Of course it was. I rolled my eyes at Nora who chuckled. A couple of girls were walking down the hall toward us, their eyes widening at the sight of me and Nora being escorted by Luis and Nixon. But I let their whispers of curiosity roll off my shoulders. They were the least of my problems right now.

"I know things are a mess right now." Nora leaned in close. "But you can't deny there's something kind of cool about this." She motioned to Luis.

Trust her to find this exciting. Giving her a little shake of my head, we followed our escorts out of the dorm building and toward the sleek black SUV.

"At least everyone already left for class and we don't have an audience," Nora murmured.

151

She was right, there was no one around. No one except...

"Bailey," I breathed, spotting him at the corner of the building, hiding between the wall and a huge Maple tree.

"Bailey?" Nora whispered.

"Yeah, Nicco's cousin." Hope blossomed in my chest. "I have to go talk to him."

"Hmm, hate to break it to you, but they're never going to let you go over there. Let me handle this, okay?"

My brows pinched as I glanced over at Bailey again. I needed to talk to him. I needed to know Nicco was okay.

"Okay, but what are you going to—"

"Oh, crap," Nora announced, jerking to a stop. "I need to go grab something from the apartment."

"Miss Abato, we really need to be going."

"You stay with Ari in the car. I'll be two minutes."

"Nixon." Luis motioned to him. "Go with her."

"No, *no!* It's... girl's stuff. Highly embarrassing. As if being escorted out of the building by two burly bodyguards isn't embarrassing enough," she grumbled. "I'll be two minutes. In and out, you'll see. Go get Ari in the car, she's the important one here."

Luis yanked open the door and motioned for me to get inside.

"Hurry," I called after Nora as she hurried back toward the building. I had no idea how she planned on getting Bailey's attention without alerting Luis and Nixon, but my best friend was full of surprises.

The atmosphere inside the SUV was tense. Luis discreetly talked over his radio while Nixon kept his eye trained on the building. Bailey was right there, and it killed me not being able to go to him.

A minute passed, and another. Nixon started to grumble. "It's been long enough, I'm going to—"

"She got her period," I blurted out.

"I... uh, right." He ran a hand down his face while I fought a smile.

Another five minutes passed, and even I was starting to get worried. But then I saw her jogging toward the SUV. The door swung open and she climbed inside. "All better, sorry it took me so long."

"Please buckle up," Luis said, putting the car into drive.

"What did he say?" I whispered, keeping one eye on the rear-view mirror.

"Not here." Nora shook her head.

"Nor, please..."

I needed to know something, *anything*.

She reached out and grabbed my hand, keeping her face upfront. "He's okay," she mouthed, anger flaring in her eyes. "But you were right, Tristan did hurt him."

My heart sank. "Oh God." Tears welled in my eyes and I desperately tried to blink them away.

"Ssh, it's going to be okay, Ari."

But nothing about this was okay.

Not a single thing.

Chapter 12

Nicco

"Niccolò, what on earth happened to your face?" Aunt Francesca reached for me, cooing as she smoothed her fingers over my jaw.

"Leave the boy alone, amore mio." Uncle Joe ushered her away from me, narrowing his eyes on my bruised face.

"Should I be worried?"

"Nicco met a girl. Isn't that right, cous?" Bailey breezed into the room, smirking in my direction.

"Fuck you," I mouthed over my uncle's shoulder. He flipped me off, earning him a slap upside the head.

"No swearing at my table. Now get washed up and sit. This food isn't going to eat itself."

"Smells good, Auntie," I said, dropping into one of the chairs. My head hurt like a motherfucker and my stomach was tender, but I knew if I missed breakfast, my aunt would come looking for me. Besides, there wasn't much her eggs and bacon couldn't fix.

"So, tell me about this girl." She placed their final bowl down on the table and took her seat. "What's her name? Does she go to Montague?"

"There is no girl. Bailey is just busting my balls." I levelled him with a hard look.

"Well, it wouldn't hurt you to think about settling down. You're almost twenty, and with so much... responsibility on your shoulders."

"Fran," my uncle warned. "Let the boy be. He's here to get away from all that nonsense."

Heavy silence settled over us. Unlike Matteo's father who had worked his way up the ranks before marrying into the family and becoming one of my father's captains, Uncle Joe had wanted nothing to do with it. Aunt Francesca's mother had been my grandfather Francesco's sister, and like her daughter, she had been allowed to marry a man with no ties to the family.

The Romano weren't really my aunt and uncle in the traditional sense of the word, but they were family in all the ways that mattered.

"Bailey, would you like to say grace?"

My cousin grumbled but nodded all the same. We all linked hands and waited while he said thanks. When he was done, Uncle Joe served for my aunt and then himself, handing me the spoon.

"How are classes?" he asked.

"Dull." I admitted. "I'd rather be in the workshop helping you or down at the gym."

"An education will serve you well, Niccolò." He gave me a knowing look. We all knew why I was attending MU; we just didn't talk about it. It was the way of the life—the code of silence, or as we called it omertá.

"You need to hurry if you're going to make your classes today," she said.

"Actually, I'm heading down to the gym," I said, wiping my mouth with the napkin. "I need to burn off some steam."

And beat the shit out of something, or someone.

"I'm going to tag along," Bailey said, "if that's okay?"

"What about school?" His mom shrieked. "You need to make an effort, Son. Please."

"I can't be there, not right now." He slid his fingers into his hair, tugging the ends. "I'll go Monday, I promise."

Aunt Francesca let out an exasperated breath. "Okay, you stay out of that ring, ragazzo mio."

"Yes, Mamma."

"I'll keep an eye on him."

"Such a good boy," she crooned, leaning over to pat my hand. "Now eat. You know I like a clean plate."

∞∞∞

"I have something for you," my cousin said the second we climbed into his car.

"Is it a magical wand to fix this fucking shitshow?"

"It's better."

That piqued my interest as I glanced over at him. "Here." He rummaged in his pocket and pulled out a scrap of paper, pressing it into my hand.

I smoothed it out. "It's a phone number."

"Not just any number, *her* number."

My muscles tensed. All night I'd thought about Arianne, and if I hadn't been thinking about her, I'd dreamed of her.

She was the Capizola heir.

The girl my father wanted to use as leverage against Roberto.

But she was also the girl who had reached into my chest and ripped out my heart, holding it in the palm of her hands.

"How did you get this?" My teeth ground together.

"I went back over there last night."

"You what?" I barked.

"Relax, nobody saw me. Anyway, they never left. Roberto posted two of his men at her dorm, but she stayed. I went back this morning to case the joint. And guess who I saw just before they were about leave?"

"Arianne," I breathed. Just saying her name hurt. Tore my chest open that little bit more until I was sure I was bleeding out all over Bailey's car.

"You spoke to her?" I asked.

"No, her roommate managed to shake Capizola's guys. She told me to give you this and I quote, 'tell him if he meant any of it to fucking call her'. She's feisty that one."

I stared down at the digits. This was my link to her. All I had to do was dig out my cell and call her.

"What are you waiting for?" Bailey asked after a few seconds.

"I need to figure shit out first."

"Nic, just call her, man. You want to. I know you do."

Dragging a hand through my hair, I let out a long breath. "You don't know anything, kid. Just drive."

He cussed me out in Italian but didn't say any more. What was there to say? No amount of his mom's home-cooking was going to fix this.

We pulled into the dusty parking lot of Uncle Mario's gym ten minutes later. He was my father's second cousin, but it was tradition to call our elder relatives uncle. It was in the heart of La Riva on the corner of one of the commercial blocks.

I spotted Enzo's Pontiac immediately. He'd been blowing up my cell about Roberto Capizola being on campus last night, but I hadn't had the energy to get into it with him.

Besides, I still hadn't decided what to tell him.

We climbed out of Bailey's car, and I grabbed my bag out of the trunk.

"Nicco," a couple of guys greeted us as we entered the building.

Hard Knocks smelled like a sweat pit, but there was something comforting about the stale air, and the grunts and groans echoing off the walls.

"We need to talk," Enzo stalked over to me the second he noticed me.

"Not now." I dumped my bag down on a bench and peeled the t-shirt off my body. "Tape," I said to no one in particular and Bailey handed me a roll of tape. I began fixing it around my knuckles, pulling it tight enough to protect my skin but not enough to prevent movement.

"Yo, Russo," I yelled over to the trainer working the ring. "I want in."

"Killian's paid for a full hour." He motioned to the guy jabbing the air in the center.

"I'll fight him," the beefed-up guy said, slowing his movements and walking over to the ropes.

"You don't want to do that, my man." Russo let out a low whistle. "That there is Niccolò Marchetti."

Recognition flared in the guy's eyes. "I'm in, if he is."

"It's your funeral." Russo mumbled, pulling up one of the ropes and beckoning me over. I kicked off my sneakers and climbed barefoot into the ring. I liked to feel the canvas beneath my feet, the vibrations through my body.

"I've heard of you, kid." The guy smirked. "I gotta say, I'm not impressed so far." His scrutinizing gaze looked me over.

Stretching my neck from side to side, I rolled my shoulders, bouncing on the balls of my feet. Usually, I warmed up before getting in the ring with someone. But I didn't want to go easy today. I wanted to hit. To hurt. I wanted to feel every-fucking-thing.

"Kick his sorry ass, cous," Bailey called out. The rest of the guys in the gym had stopped their workouts and moved closer, all ready to watch me go head to head with Killian.

"I'm going to put you on your ass, kid."

"Bring it on." I banged my fists together. The air crackled around us, thick with anticipation.

"You sure about this, Nicco?" Russo gritted through his teeth as he got into position.

"Just call it," I said.

"Okay then." He shoved his arm between us. "Keep it clean. No shots below the waist, no holding, tripping, or kicking. If I see any teeth or cheap shots, you're out, got it?"

I nodded, my hard eyes fixed on Killian. I'd never seen him around before. Didn't know his strengths or weaknesses, but I didn't need to know. All I saw was a target. Someone to take out all my frustration and anger on. Adrenaline pumped through me.

"You're mine, pretty boy," he taunted, dancing on his feet.

I raised a brow. "We'll see."

"Fight," Russo's voice rang out like a shotgun firing. I dropped back, anticipating his move. Sure enough, he came at me like a bull out of a gate, fists swinging.

Staying light on my feet, I dodged a right hook and came up ready with a counter upper cut. My fist made contact, Killian's head snapping back as his pained grunts filled the air. He staggered back, but I didn't give him time to shake it off. I was on him. Fast and hard, hitting him blow after blow.

"Get him good, Nicco," someone yelled, their words drowned out by the roar of blood in between my ears.

"Easy, Marchetti." Russo forced himself between us, letting Killian catch his breath. His brow was split open, a trickle of blood snaking down his face.

"Still ready to put me on my ass?" Now I was taunting him. But I felt pumped, molten lava running through my veins, spurring me on. I wasn't even close to soothing the beast raging inside me.

"Let's go, brutto stronzo." I chuckled darkly, bouncing on the balls of my feet.

He barged Russo out of the way and lunged for me, his clumsy punch colliding with my shoulder. A sharp blast of pain ricocheted through me but it barely registered. Pain was good. Pain reminded me I was alive. It drowned out all the other shit weighing me down.

"Figlio di puttana," Killian grumbled, diving for me again as I ducked and dodged his advances. His wrapped knuckles grazed my cheek a couple of times, crushing into the soft tissue between my ribs. But it was nothing I couldn't handle.

"Finish him, Nicco," Enzo yelled.

But I had no plans to end it too quickly. I was still too wound up.

I advanced, crowding Killian against the ropes, landing punch after punch. Face, chest, ribs, it didn't matter. So long as my fist kept finding body parts, there was no stopping me. He went down on his knee, desperately trying to block his face.

"Nicco, relax," someone shouted. But I couldn't stop. My knuckles rained down hellfire on him until I could see nothing but mangled skin, blood, and fresh bruises.

"Easy boy." Strong arms grabbed me from behind, tearing me away from Killian. "Go walk it off." Russo gave me a hard shove to the opposite side of the ring where Enzo and Bailey were watching me, concern etched deep into their frowns.

"What?" I snapped, climbing out of the ring and grabbing a bottle of water. I drank it down, pouring the rest over my head. Icy cold water ran in rivulets down my chest, cooling my temperature and my mood.

Glancing back, I took in the state of Killian. He looked like he'd been jumped by four or five men.

"Fuck," I cussed under my breath. Guilt flashed through me, but I shook it off. He'd challenged me, acting like he could take me. It wasn't my fault if he caught me at a bad fucking time.

"If you wanted to kill the guy," Enzo said, falling in step beside me as I headed for the locker room. "You almost succeeded."

"He knew what he was getting into."

"Did he?" My best friend's eyes burned into the side of my face. "What the fuck has gotten into you? Is this about Capizola because we need to—"

"Not now, yeah." I brushed him off. "I need to get cleaned up."

Enzo slammed his hand against the lockers, cutting me off. "Talk to me, cous. What's going on with you?"

I finally met his questioning glare. "Let me shower and

then we'll talk, okay?"

He gave me a sharp nod, removing his hand. "I'll call Matteo."

"It's Friday. You know he drives Arabella to school today and takes his mom for breakfast."

"Business comes first."

And that was the problem. Enzo was too devoted to the life. It gave him purpose, made him feel like he belonged. I wanted to believe it was because he'd never had a mom growing up, but part of me thought it might just be the way he was wired.

"Okay," I conceded. "Tell him to meet us at Carluccio's in an hour."

"An hour?" Enzo balked.

"Family is important too. Let him eat with his mother and then he can come meet us. I need some time under the hot jets anyway."

"You mean you need a post-fight release." He smirked and I flipped him off. "I'm sure Rayna would come over and help you with that."

"Me and Rayna are done." I grabbed my shit and started toward the shower blocks.

"Does she know that?" he called after me and I flipped him off again over my shoulder. Rayna hadn't been on my radar ever since I met Arianne.

I stripped out of my sweats and stepped in the shower, turning on the jets. The hot water soothed my tender muscles. It wasn't long before my hand slipped down to my rock-hard dick. Enzo was right; usually after a fight I needed another kind of release. But the only person I wanted was the one person I couldn't have.

My hand gripped the base of my shaft, stroking up and

down as I pictured Arianne's face, her big honey eyes staring up at me as she came all over my tongue.

Fuck. How was I just supposed to walk away? It wasn't just a physical attraction I felt toward her, it was deep inside me.

She was inside me.

My palm flattened against the tiles, keeping me upright as I worked my hand harder, faster, chasing the release I so desperately needed. I imagined her on knees before me. Teasing me with her tongue, looking up at me through her thick lashes. Giving me another one of her firsts.

Jesus.

I couldn't let her go. There was too much I wanted to show her, to experience with her. I wanted to make her mine in every way possible until we were bound together in a way nothing and no one could sever.

Bailey was right all along.

I had to fight for her.

I had to.

Because not fighting for her felt like giving up on part of my soul. A part I'd never get back.

The bottom line was, meeting Arianne had changed me, and I wasn't sure I could go back to before.

I just had to figure out how the hell to balance what I wanted to do with what I should, while keeping everyone I cared about safe.

∞∞∞

Matteo was waiting for us when we got to Carluccio's diner. He looked up from the booth and saluted. "What's up?" he asked the second he slid in opposite us.

"Nicco broke a guy's face at Hard Knocks."

"What's new?" Matteo gave me a wolfish grin.

"This was different," Enzo replied coolly. "He was out to ki—"

"So maybe I got a little carried away." I shrugged, grabbing a menu. "The guy will live."

I'd stuck around after my shower to make sure he was okay. Russo wanted to take him to the local medical center to get one of the cuts above his eye looked at, but Killian didn't want the fuss. Probably didn't want to admit a nineteen-year-old guy had kicked his ass.

"Where were you last night? I thought this one,"—Matteo flicked his head toward Enzo—"was going to lose his shit when we spotted Capizola's SUV on campus."

"I was busy." I signaled for the server.

"Usual?" she asked.

"I'll just take a basket of fries and a chocolate shake, please. Enzo?"

"Yeah, usual please, Trina." He leaned forward. "I almost had her. You said he'd lead us right to her and he would have if it wasn't for that fucker Johnny getting in the way."

"Security Johnny?"

"Yeah, he thought I was acting suspiciously. Well, I guess I was, but he didn't realize it was me until it was too late. He'd already called for backup. I lost Capizola heading toward the library. That road only leads to three other buildings."

"The Administration Building or the girls only dorms,"

Matteo added. "So she most likely lives in either Donatello or Bembo House?"

"It doesn't matter, he knows we know," I said, sinking back against the leather bench. "Tristan must have tipped him off."

Fuck.

I needed to tell them.

I needed to just come clean and tell them.

But I couldn't get the words out over the giant lump in my throat. If I told them, there was no going back.

The scrap of paper Bailey had given me burned in my pocket. I needed to hear her voice, to know she was okay. Maybe Arianne had some idea about how we minimized the impact of this bomb that had been dropped on us.

Unlikely. I smothered an exasperated breath. She'd been in the dark as much as I had. I'd seen the flash of surprise in her eyes when her father indicated he knew me.

We were both pawns. Her unknowing. Me unwilling. Both of us bound by our family's legacies.

"What the fuck are we supposed to do now?" Enzo grumbled, clearly pissed about the turn of events. "He's probably already whisked her back to Castle Capizola and locked her away in the tower."

"Maybe, maybe not. There's a reason he sent her here in the first place, a piece of the puzzle we haven't figured out. Why now? After all these years? Roberto is no fool." I went on, trying to keep the focus on Roberto and not his daughter. "He must have known we would find out eventually, so what changed? That's what we need to figure out."

"You know your old man is going to lose his shit when he hears about this?"

I levelled Enzo with a hard look. "Which is why we

won't tell him anything until we have more information. We know she's enrolled at MU; we know she's staying in either Donatella or Bembo House; and we know Roberto paid her a visit last night. Now we just have to see how it plays out."

"It's a big risk," Enzo said. "We could have let her slip through our fingers before we—"

The server appeared with our drinks. "Here you go." She placed them down. "Your food will be along shortly. Anything else I can get you?" Her eyes raked over Matteo, lingering on the tattoos snaking down his neck and disappearing under his tight black t-shirt.

"We're good," Enzo grunted, and she scurried off.

"Do you have to be such an asshole?" Matteo rolled his eyes.

"She was practically foaming at the mouth."

"Just because she wasn't ready to climb on your dick." He clapped Enzo on the back. "You're losing your touch, cous."

"Oh yeah? You don't think I could get her to follow me into the restroom and drop to her knees?"

"Seriously," Matteo balked. "What the fuck is wrong with you? It's Trina, we've known her for years."

"And yet, you still haven't done shit about it."

He shrugged. "She's not my type."

"They never are."

"Enzo," I warned.

"Yeah, yeah." The air cooled between the three of us.

"Let's eat and then figure shit out."

"Fine by me," Enzo muttered.

"Yeah, whatever, Nic, it isn't like I just ate a big meal or anything."

"Porca puttana!" My hand slammed down on the table, rattling the salt and pepper shakers. "You two are driving me in-fucking-sane. Knock it off, capito?"

They both stared at me as if I'd lost my mind.

And I was beginning to think that maybe they were right.

Chapter 13

Arianne

"Breathe," Nora whispered as we sat in the kitchen, waiting for my father.

We'd arrived at the house almost an hour ago, only to discover he was unavailable, and my mother was in the city at her appointment with her personal trainer.

So we waited.

Nora's mother, Sara, prepared a spread of breakfast items for us, despite us both telling her we weren't hungry. But it was Mrs. Abato's way of smothering the tension. She'd taken one look at my tight expression and decided to start cooking.

After all, food fixed everything.

"I'm sure he will be along soon," she said, cleaning away the dishes.

"Mamma, let me help." Nora stood up and began helping, but her mother waved her off. Mrs. Abato served our family proudly, she always had, but she wanted more for her daughter. It was the thing I admired most about her. She raised Nora to be limitless, to want more than a life of servitude, despite their family's ties to my family. My father agreeing to finance Nora's time at MU with me was like a dream come true. She would get a first-rate education, life experience outside of my family's estate and connections, and the opportunity to make a future of her own.

I loved my best friend, but I also envied her.

Her wings would only continue to grow, to beat harder, taking her to unknown heights.

My wings were clipped.

My future decided.

One day the Capizola empire would be mine, whether I wanted it or not.

The air shifted and I glanced over my shoulder to see Luis and Nixon step into the room, followed by my father. "Arianne," he said around a smile. "This is a surprise."

"Papá." I stood up and went to him, letting him wrap me in his arms.

"Thank you, Luis, Nixon. You may leave us."

"Can I get you anything, Mr. Capizola?" Nora's mother asked, wiping her hands down her apron.

"No, thank you, Sara, all I request is some privacy with my daughter."

"Of course. Nora, come, cucciola."

Nora shot me a questioning look, but I nodded. "I'll see you in a little while, okay?"

She offered me a tight-lipped smile before following her mother out of the kitchen.

"We should go into my study," my father motioned for me to go ahead.

"Very well." We walked down the long hall in silence. We lived in a Victorian style house, nestled among three acres of land in the most easterly point of Verona County, where the boundary line met Providence County. It was full of character with its steep gabled roof, asymmetrical windows, and wraparound porch. I had fond memories of playing in and around the house, exploring the vast grounds. What I hadn't realized back then, when I was just a child, was that it would one day become my prison. A beautiful, sprawling prison with a huge library and many sitting rooms. We even had a sizeable indoor pool. Then there was the kitchen, one of my favorite rooms in the entire house. It was warm and homely, and overlooked the luscious green lawns and many Maple trees, and it smelled constantly of Mrs. Abato's home cooking.

It was home and I'd loved it. But somewhere along the way, I began to resent it too.

We entered my father's study and he closed the door. I hovered, my stomach a tight ball of nerves. I'd felt so determined to demand answers earlier, but now I was here, staring at the man who had only ever done everything in his power to protect me and provide for me, and words failed me.

"Is there something you want to say, Arianne?" He sat down in his leather chair.

I'd spent so many hours in here as a child. Sitting at his feet playing while he worked. He would lift me onto his knee and tell me all about his projects. Plans to make Verona County thrive. I'd listen raptly as my father talked so passionately about making a future for the younger generation.

For *me*.

But now I looked at him and no longer saw that man.

I saw a liar.

"Arianne, mio tesoro, sit, please." He gave me a warm smile.

"How do you know Nicco's father?" I blurted out.

"Antonio Marchetti is a businessman much like myself." Father loosened his tie but didn't flinch.

"Businessman? What kind of business? The legitimate kind, like you?" My brow rose.

"He's not entirely legitimate, no."

"Is it true you want to redevelop La Riva? The Marchetti neighborhood?"

He stroked his beard, a flash of surprise in his eyes.

"Is that how you know him? Or is it because our families used to be friends?"

Now his brows furrowed. "How did you—"

"It's called the internet, Papá."

"There is so much you don't understand."

"A lot you've kept from me, you mean."

"Principessa," he sighed. "Don't you trust me?"

"Why don't you want me to see Nicco anymore?"

I wanted to hear him say the words.

I *needed* him to say them.

"Arianne, mio tesoro." His eyes pleaded with me.

"Tell me." I inhaled a shaky breath. "Tell me the truth, Papá. I need you to tell me the truth."

He pinched the bridge of his nose, letting out a long sigh. When his resigned gaze met mine, I steeled myself for whatever bomb he was about to drop.

"You know our family moved here in the late eighteen-hundreds. Well, my father's great grandfather, Tommaso Capizola, was one of the first men to arrive here with his best friend, Luca Marchetti. They wanted to escape the oppression in Italy and make a better life for themselves, but it wasn't easy. Settling in La Riva, although it was called something different back then, they turned their hand to anything that could make them a dollar or two. The Marchetti had ties to the mafia, and with the introduction of the statewide Prohibition Law, it wasn't long before Luca saw an opportunity to make a quick buck bootlegging.

"By the late twenties, the population of La Riva had grown, spilling into new townships: Romany Square and Roccaforte. Luca and Tommaso were a force to be reckoned with, and many of the Italian families arriving in New England gravitated to them. In order to expand their control, Tommaso moved across the river and Luca remained in La Riva. Then in the early thirties, they petitioned the State for secession from Providence County to form a new county."

My brows furrowed. He was giving me an in-depth history lesson but still omitting crucial facts.

Releasing a frustrated breath, I finally asked the question on the tip of my tongue. "Was Tommaso Capizola a mobster, Papá?"

The blood drained from his face, his fist curling against his polished mahogany desk. "Just how much did you research?" His brow rose.

"Enough."

The temperature cooled as he inhaled a long-ragged breath.

"Papá, I deserve the truth."

"The truth." It came out bitter. "I have spent my entire life trying to protect you from the truth, Arianne. Things you didn't need to know, that you still don't need to know."

"What really happened when I was thirteen?"

I remembered the day like it was yesterday. It was the

end of the school day and Nora and I were walking to the car when suddenly, we were surrounded by my father's men. They ushered us into a different vehicle and took off at lightning speed. I'd been too scared to even ask what was happening, but Nora had kicked up a storm, demanding they tell us. Of course, they hadn't. They had simply delivered us into the awaiting arms of my parents, and Nora's mother. Father told me that my school was no longer safe, that there had been some kind of security breach. A fellow student had threatened to hurt me, and my father didn't want to risk my safety.

It was the last day I ever stepped foot into school.

Nora was transferred to the public high school in Roccaforte, and we never spoke about it again. My parents just wanted to keep me safe. I still had the best education, the best teachers and classes; I just had them all from the safety of our home.

"An attempt was made on your life." He said every word with precision, as if he couldn't take any chance of me misinterpreting them.

"An attempt on my life?" A shiver zipped down my spine. "You mean someone tried to... *kill* me?"

He nodded, a grim expression washing over him. "I thought you were safe at that out of county private school. It was off the radar. I didn't think he'd find you."

"Antonio Marchetti?" I staggered back, crumpling into the chair. "Antonio Marchetti tried to kill me?"

"We think he gave the order, yes."

"So you don't know for certain it was him?" A tiny seed of hope took root in my chest. Maybe this was all some big misunderstanding. Nicco's father didn't want me dead. It made zero sense. "It could have been—"

"The likelihood is that Antonio Marchetti called in the

hit."

"H-hit?"

I'd seen all shades of my father's expressions, but I'd never seen him look so devastated as he did now.

"I'm sorry, mio tesoro. All I ever wanted was to protect you. You were safe here. Nothing could touch you."

He wasn't wrong there; our estate was like Fort Knox. But there was still something I didn't understand.

"What happened, Papá, between our family and the Marchetti?"

"That is a whole other story entirely," he said with an air of sadness.

"I have time. Besides, I think I've earned it."

"Figlia mia, so much like your mother." He ran a brisk hand over his face. "I guess you might as well know the full story. It all started with a woman, Arianne. My father's great-aunt, Josefina..."

∞∞∞

Nora found me in my bedroom. I was sitting in the window, lost in my thoughts, looking out over the lawns that led down to the stream. "Ari," she said quietly. "Can I come in?"

"Sure."

"Your father said I might find you up here. Is everything—"

"He told me." My heart clenched. "He told me everything."

My best friend joined me on the seat. "It's true? About

Nicco's family?"

I nodded. "My grandfather's aunt, Josefina, was promised to Nicco's grandfather's uncle, Emilio. They were to be married, but Emilio loved another, Josefina's brother's fiancée Elena. They ran off together. Josefina was devastated. My great-great-grandfather, Tommaso, too. But where her brother's pain turned to hatred, Josefina's turned to grief, and, eventually, she took her own life. Tommaso never recovered. It caused a huge rift between him and Luca Marchetti that spilled down the families. But it all came to a head when he finally tracked down Emilio and ordered his son to avenge Josefina and kill him."

"Holy crap," Nora breathed, her eyes alight with a strange mix of intrigue and horror. "What happened then?"

"Emilio's brother wanted vengeance, but Luca and Tommaso came to a truce. They knew any further bloodshed would greatly diminish their power. So they agreed to split the county. Tommaso Capizola would take the east side of the river: Roccaforte, the city, and what we now know as University Hill. And Luca took everything west of the river: Romany Square and La Riva.

"Tommaso died shortly after that, and Alfredo became head of the family. He carried so many demons over losing the love of his life and killing his best friend, that he wanted out of the life. Gradually, he started to clean up the family businesses, moving into legitimate ventures. His empire went from strength to strength while Luca's remaining son, Marco Marchetti, and his son, Francesco, Nicco's grandfather, positioned themselves as the mafia stronghold of Rhode Island."

It was strange. I'd been so shocked hearing my father recount the story, the real truth behind my family, and Nicco's. But telling Nora, I felt like a weight had been lifted.

"So your hotty really is a mafia prince?"

"It should matter, shouldn't it? Our history is painted with so much blood and hatred. I should run from Nicco and never look back. But..."

"But you can't." Nora smiled sadly.

"I don't think I can," I admitted. "It's like I feel him, in here." I touched a hand to my heart.

Just then, my cell phone vibrated, cutting the tension like a knife. I snatched it off the desk and scanned the message.

I shouldn't be writing this. I shouldn't even be thinking about texting you, and yet, here I am. Tell me what I'm supposed to do here, Bambolina. Tell me how I'm supposed to fix this?

I stared at Nicco's text, tears welling in my eyes. Nora tried to peek, but I covered my phone, holding it against my chest.

"That bad, huh?" Nora moved in closer, resting a hand on my arm.

"Tell me we're not doomed," I said. "Tell me there's a way for us to figure this out?"

"You're not doomed." Her voice was full of fake enthusiasm. "Feel better?"

"Not even a little." A fat tear rolled down my cheek.

"Hey, hey, no tears. He texted you. That's a good sign, Ari."

"Is it?" A weary sigh spilled from my lips. "Maybe we should make a clean break. My father will never let me see him again and his father wants me—" I swallowed the words.

"Wants what, Ari? What aren't you telling me?"

"My father thinks Antonio Marchetti tried to have me killed five years ago."

"HE WHAT?" She leaped up. "*That's* why you had to leave school? Sonofabi—"

"Nora..."

She held up a finger. "Let me have my moment, I deserve that much. I knew there was a whole history book's worth of bad blood between your families, but I didn't realize... dead." Her eyes grew to saucers. "He wants you *dead*."

"Maybe. Maybe not. But at least now I know my father wasn't irrationally overprotective." A weak smile tugged at my lips.

"This changes things, Ari. You have to know that? What if..." She mashed her lips together, but it was too late, I saw the guilt in my best friend's eyes. "What if this is all part of his father's master plan?"

My eyes fluttered closed as pain washed over me. "No," I whispered. "It's not possible."

It couldn't be.

What I felt was real. Every stolen glance and secret touch. Every kiss and fleeting moment. The connection between us wasn't a trick or game. Some cruel scheme to lure me into his father's claws. Nicco would never do that to me.

He wouldn't.

What do you really know about him, an unwelcome voice whispered.

"He wouldn't," I said, reading his text over again.

Before I could stop myself, my fingers flew over the screen.

I need to see you.

"What the hell, Ari?" Nora peered over, this time seeing every letter.

"I need to see him. I need to look him in the eye and see the truth."

"Hmm, in case you haven't noticed, we're in your house in the middle of your very fortified, very well protected estate. It's not like he can just stroll up and knock on the door. Besides, maybe you should give this some more thought. I'm worried about you." The panic in her expression faded.

"I can't explain it, Nora, but what I feel toward Nicco is..."

"He's your first crush, not to mention the fact he helped you that night. It's no surprise you feel a strong attachment to him. But everything is different now."

Everything was different.

I knew the soft brush of his lips, the gentle caress of his fingers. I knew the taste of his tongue and the way his heart beat like thousands of wild horses galloping across open fields. But it was all the little things too. Not to mention the tether I felt every time he was around.

Nicco and I were bound.

It defied all logic, disregarded all rational thought, and made me sound like a lovesick puppy. But I knew.

Deep in my soul, I knew Nicco was mine.

As much as I was his.

"I need to go back to Montague," I said with complete conviction.

"Have you lost your goddamn mind? Your father is never going to allow it, not now."

"Have you lost your balls?" I clapped a hand over my

mouth, surprised by my words.

Nora stared at me in complete shock; her wide eyed at me, and me wide eyed at her. Then slowly, her mask cracked as laughter bubbled from her chest. She flung her arms around my neck, her hysteria wrapping me up in nothing but love and comfort. "You're right," she said. "You're totally right. What do you need from me?"

I pulled back to look at her and said without hesitation, "I need you to help me convince my father to let me go back to MU."

Chapter 14

Nicco

"Spill," Matteo said as he drove us back to my aunt's. My cell phone rested against my thigh; my fingers curled so tightly around the damn thing that I was surprised the screen didn't crack.

"Huh?"

"Whatever's on your mind, spill."

Where did I even begin?

I shouldn't have texted Arianne, but I had, and now she wanted to see me. She knew we were enemies, pitted on different sides, and yet, she *still* wanted to see me.

For all I knew, it could have been a trap. Some mind-fuck scheme laid down by her father to teach me a lesson.

"It's her, isn't it? The girl you saved that night."

"I didn't save—"

"You know what I mean." He gave me some serious side-eye. "I know you, cous, and you haven't been the same since that night. All this anger and frustration, it's her."

"When the fuck did you get so intuitive?"

Matteo shrugged. "I pay attention."

I nodded, bending my leg to rest my foot against the glove compartment.

"So spill," he repeated. "I'm not going to give you shit like Enzo or tease you like our uncles. I'm here, Nicco, one hundred percent."

"You wouldn't believe me if I told you."

"Try me."

"Something happened that first night, Matt. I can't even... fuck, I feel like such a pussy saying this."

"You fell hard."

"Yeah, cous, I did. It's like I took one look into her scared honey brown eyes and drowned. I wanted to hunt down the motherfucker who hurt her and make him pay, but more than that, I wanted to protect her and make sure it never happened again."

"You think it made all the shit with your mom come back to the surface?"

I inhaled a sharp breath. "Maybe. I don't know. But there was something about her... something I couldn't forget."

"So... what happened?"

"I followed her."

"Let me guess, Intro to Philosophy?" The corner of his mouth kicked up.

"Yeah."

"Jesus, cous, she must have you tied up in knots to get you to sit through one of Mandrake's classes."

It had been worth it, though.

So fucking worth it to watch her eyes sparkle as the professor talked about free will and determinism. Watch how her breath had caught every time I inched closer, our legs brushing underneath the desks. I loved seeing how I affected her. Because, dammit, if she didn't affect me too.

"I took her to Blackstone Country Club; we made out under the fucking stars."

"You really are the Prince of Hearts." He punched my shoulder, chuckling.

"Fuck off with that bullshit."

"Relax, I'm only busting your balls. You really like her, don't you? So what's the problem?"

"She's..." The words stuck in my throat.

"Nicco, come on, cous." Matteo shifted, easing off the gas as he turned onto my aunt's street. "It can't be that bad."

"Oh, it's about as bad as it can get... She's... fuck. She's Arianne Capizola."

His foot slammed on the brake, sending me flying forward. My hand shot out just in time to break my fall against the dash. "Jesus, Matteo," I gritted out.

"Sorry, I just... Capizola. She's the *Capizola* princess?"

I jammed my fingers into my hair, scraping my scalp, and nodded slowly.

"Fuck," he exhaled.

Fuck, indeed.

∞∞∞

Before I went into any more detail, I gave Matteo a chance to pick his jaw up off the floor. Bailey joined us in my apartment, and the three of us sat around, drinking beer, avoiding the huge fucking honey-eyed elephant in the room.

"Arianne Capizola, that's some bad fucking luck," Matteo said. "It's like fate thought you deserved to be dry-fucked in the ass."

"Whoa, dude," Bailey fake retched. "Bad fucking visual."

"Language," we both yelled at him.

"Just exactly how far have you two..." Matteo's brow lifted. "You know."

"Not *that* far."

"So Roberto Capizola won't be coming around to chop off your dick just yet."

"Oh, I wouldn't be so sure about that." I tipped my head back, letting my eyes drift closed, trying my best not to picture her. "What the fuck am I supposed to do here?"

"Have you spoken to her since?" Bailey asked.

I met his knowing gaze. "I texted her."

"And?" His eyes lit up. I knew the kid was rooting for us. I didn't get it. Hell, I didn't get any of this, but it was nice having him in my corner.

"She wants to see me."

"Of course she wants to fucking see you. It's probably a trap."

My eyes shifted to Matteo. "You think I don't know that."

"So what will you do?"

"I don't know yet."

"Enzo can't know," Matteo added. "Not yet, not until you've figured shit out."

"I know." The thought of lying to my best friend, a guy I trusted with my life, didn't sit well with me. But while I knew he'd take a bullet for me; I also knew he'd try to protect me from myself if that's what it took to make sure the family came out unscathed.

"Well, whatever you need from me, just say the word."

"Just like that?"

"Just like that." Matteo shifted forward, clasping his hands between his legs. "I'm loyal to *you*, Nicco, you should know that by now. I trust you and I trust your judgment. And if Arianne is the girl for you, then that extends to her. Besides, the idea of hurting an innocent... it doesn't sit right with me."

"Thanks, cous, I appreciate that. More than you know."

"Hey, me too," Bailey added. "I trust you too. And I've already been looking out for her."

"I know you have, kid. And I appreciate it."

"So you're going to meet her?"

"Yeah, I am."

Because I had to know. I had to know if everything I'd felt with Arianne was real.

I had to know if she wanted to fight for us too.

∞∞∞

Turns out, I didn't have to figure out how to get to her. About thirty minutes after arriving at my place, Arianne had texted me. She was coming back to MU and she wanted to meet me. Tonight. That's how I found myself, hiding in the shadows, staring up at Arianne's window.

"Are you sure about this?" Bailey whispered.

"Nope, but do you have a better plan?"

"Okay," Matteo jogged beside us and inhaled a ragged breath. "The guy is all set."

"And he won't talk?"

"He's trustworthy."

"How much did you pay him?" I asked.

"Enough. Tell me the plan again."

"Your guy will turn up out front, demanding to see Nora. She'll come down and the two of them will get into it, keeping Capizola's guys on her. I'll climb the fire escape and slip into Ari's room."

"And if there's a bodyguard in there with her?"

"There isn't." I checked my cell phone again. Arianne and Nora had persuaded Roberto to let them return to MU under the watchful eye of her cousin, and a small army of his men. She'd concocted the entire plan. All I had to do was provide the distraction, in the form of Matteo's guy, and scale the fifteen-foot wall to her window balcony.

"You heavy?" Matteo asked me, and I nodded, feeling the weight of my pistol beneath my hoodie. "You get so much as a whiff of it being a set up and you give the signal, okay? I mean it, Nicco. I know you're in deep with her, but she's not worth getting sent down."

Another nod and I inched out of the shadows, waiting for her text. Two seconds later, my cell vibrated. I quickly scanned the message and jogged over to the wall. The building was fitted with fire escape ladders that made climbing to Arianne's window easy. Within a couple of minutes, I'd pulled myself over her small balcony. My knuckle rapped gently against the glass. She appeared, relief sparkling in her eyes as she opened the window and waited for me to climb inside. I immediately did a quick sweep of the room.

"You really thought I'd set you up?" There was a trace of hurt in her voice.

"Not you, your father."

"I am not my father, Nicco," she said, defiance burning in her eyes. "Just like you're not yours."

"But I'm not good, Arianne. I might not be my father, but I'm no saint either."

"Have you ever... killed anyone?" The words spilled from her lips. Before I could answer, she added, "Wait, I don't want to know."

"Bambolina..." I drew in a harsh breath as I stepped forward, drawn to her light. Her beauty.

"Oh my god, your face." Guilt swirled in her eyes. "I'm so sorry—"

"Don't you dare apologize for him."

"Does it hurt?" Arianne winced, reaching for me.

"I've had worse."

"Still, I hate that he did that to you. I had an interesting conversation with my father yesterday. He told me things... things about my family I didn't know. Things about you and your family. I keep telling myself it should matter...." She stared up at me, her eyes glittering with so much emotion I felt winded.

"But?" I whispered, stepping closer still.

"But I'm not sure it does. Everything I thought I knew about my family, my life... my legacy, it's all a lie."

"Some lies protect us."

"You're right." Arianne's lips curved into a sad smile. "Sometimes the truth is too much to bear."

"I would never hurt you." I reached out, tucking a strand of hair behind her ears.

"But you hurt other people? Men? Your enemies?"

"Men make their own history, but they do not make it as they please," I repeated the quote Mandrake had spoken in his first class. "I was born into this life, Ari, just as you were born into yours. It doesn't mean I like the hand I've been dealt, but it is mine nonetheless."

She slid her hands up my chest, pressing her head to them, and breathed in a gentle sigh. Everything else faded away. My arms hooked around her waist, anchoring us together.

This wasn't a trap.

Arianne was here with me because she felt it too.

Because she couldn't forget either.

"Our fathers will never agree to this," she whispered, finally giving me her eyes again.

"I can't give you up," I leaned down, brushing my lips over hers. "I won't."

Arianne's fingers curled into my hoodie, clawing at me with the same desperation I felt coursing through my veins. "He wants me dead."

The words echoed through my skull, and I jerked away, staring down at her. "What did you say?"

"Five years ago, I was at school; a private school out of state. It was just a normal day, until it wasn't. My father told me there had been a security breach, that another student had wanted to hurt me. That was the last day I ever set foot in school."

"I don't understand… What does that have to do with my father?"

Arianne looked at me with so much pain and regret, I felt my chest crack wide open. It hurt worse than any man's fist crunching against my ribs. "He ordered a hit on me, Nicco."

"No..." It rolled off my lips, piercing the air like a gunshot.

My father was many things. Cold. Calculating. Callous. But he would never—

"Five years ago?" Realization slammed into me. "When exactly?" I grabbed her shoulders. "When did it happen?"

"I..." Sadness washed over Arianne. "It was right before the holidays. I remember because we'd been practicing for the annual talent contest and I didn't get to perform."

I tore away from her, trying to do the math as I paced the room. But I already knew the answer, the truth rattling around my head.

"Nicco?" Arianne watched me as I slowed to a stop, dragging a hand over my face. "What is it? What's wrong?"

"My mother walked out five years ago. Gone, just like that. She left a note that she couldn't do it anymore. She could no longer stand at my father's side. She left us... and I think it might have something to do with you."

Nothing about my mother's disappearance made sense. Like most wives in the family, she'd stood by my father through thick and thin, through the good and bad, the endless string of goomars. But through it all she'd kept her dignity. And above all, she'd been a doting mother to me and Alessia.

Growing up, my father had a short fuse and a quick backhand. I'd watched countless times as he took his frustrations and anger out on her. As I got older, I defended her with my growing body. But she never once wavered in her loyalty, her vows, remaining steadfast at his side.

Until one day, she didn't.

It came out of the blue for my father. He had mellowed somewhat over time as Alessia and I got older. He was more attentive to her, showering her with gifts and affection. But when he sat us down, and told us she was gone, part of me wasn't surprised. I was relieved. Watching your father beat your mother until her pained cries filled the house was something I never wanted to witness again. It was ironic that a man of so much honor could be so cruel and violent.

"I- I don't understand." Arianne reached for me, the brush of her slim fingers sending shocks zipping through me. My head hung low and I looked at her, strands of my hair falling over my eyes. I'd never really talked to anyone about that day. About being a fourteen-year-old boy being told that your mother was gone. Alessia took it the hardest. She was only eleven and our mamma had been her world. She felt betrayed. Unable to understand how any mother could abandon her children like that.

"I want to tell you everything," I confessed, inching closer. Close enough that I could drop my chin on Arianne's head and tuck her into the hard lines of my body. "I can't explain it, but I want to bare my soul to you, Bambolina. But it's unfair of me to ask you to walk this life with me. A life where our families will never agree to us being together. A life filled with darkness when you deserve nothing but light."

She craned her neck to look at me. "Nicco." My name was a prayer on her lips. "I have spent the last five years bending to the will of others, to the will of my father. But I am no longer a child." Her palm rested against my face. "I choose you, Niccolò Marchetti. I choose us."

Leaning down, I fixed my mouth over hers. The second our lips touched, I felt it. Felt a sense of peace wash over me. Arianne was my sanctuary. She was the other half of my soul. Even if I walked away from her, I knew we would always find a way back together.

But I wasn't walking away.

Not now.

Not ever.

It would only be a matter of time before Arianne's identity was discovered, and then she wouldn't be safe, with or without me by her side. I'd stood by so many times when my father hurt my mother, I'd promised myself I would never do it again.

I'd promised *her* I would never do it again.

Maybe Arianne was my redemption? My shot at righting all my wrongs. I would never be a good guy. My soul was too black and dirty for that.

But I could be good... for her.

Arianne pushed up on her tiptoes, pressing her body closer to mine. My hands slipped down to the backs of her thighs, hoisting her against me. Her legs wrapped around my waist.

"I want you," she whispered. "More than I have ever wanted anything in my life."

"I am yours, Bambolina." I touched my head to hers, barely breaking the kiss. "I am yours and I will do whatever it takes to keep you safe, okay? But you have to trust me. You have to trust me, Arianne. No matter what happens, what you hear or see, you have to trust that whatever I do, whatever I say, it's to protect you. To keep you safe."

She nodded, tears spilling down her cheeks. "I trust you, I do. Just promise me we'll get through this. Promise me, we'll find a way to be together."

"I promise." I kissed her hard, pushing my tongue deep into her mouth, stroking it against hers. I wanted more. I wanted to lie her down on her bed and worship every inch of her skin. I wanted to take each one of her firsts and make them mine.

I wanted it all.

Her heart.

Her body.

Her soul.

But Capizola's men were right on the other side of the door. And I couldn't protect her if I was locked up behind bars, or worse, dead.

"I have to go now," I said, slowly lowering her to the floor. Arianne resisted, hugging me tighter. Her quiet sobs cutting me to the bone. "Ssh, Bambolina, don't cry." Cupping her face, I swiped the tears away with my thumb. "I'll figure this out, I promise. I just need time."

"Time." She nodded, swallowing her tears like the strong brave girl I knew she could be. "When will I see you again?"

"Soon. I'll text you." I started moving toward the window, but Arianne caught my wrist, leaping into my arms and kissing me again. My laughter was lost in the taste of her lips, her tongue moving against mine.

"This, us, it's real," she said against my mouth. "Tell me it's real, Nicco."

"It's real, Bambolina." I smoothed a hand over her head, pressing a final kiss to her forehead. Arianne watched as I climbed out of the window, the longing in her eyes matching my own as we silently said everything we hadn't been brave enough to say out loud.

I had to force myself to break the connection, hopping over the balcony and dropping onto the fire escape ladder. It groaned with my weight, the sound piercing the air. I held my breath, tucking my body against the wall. But nobody came.

Once my feet were firmly back on the ground, I jogged over to Bailey and Matteo, disappearing into the shadows.

"Thank fuck it wasn't a trap," Matteo said. "What happened?"

Bailey snickered. "Take a good guess."

"Hey." I gave him a pointed look. "We're... okay."

"Okay? You just risked everything to know the two of you are... *okay*?" Matteo smirked.

"Fuck off." This was awkward. How did I even begin to explain what I felt for her? That already, I felt like a part of me was missing.

"Relax," my cousin said after a beat. "I'm just busting your balls. I'm happy for you, cous." He clapped me on the back. "What's the plan now?"

"I don't know, but I found out something else."

"Yeah?"

"Yeah." Anger boiled beneath my skin. "My father tried to have her killed."

"What the fuck?" Even in the darkness, I could see the blood drain from Matteo's face.

"And that's not all," I said, my fists clenched at my sides. "I think that's why my mom left."

Chapter 15

Arianne

"Is this really necessary?" I levelled Luis with a frustrated look.

"It's Mr. Capizola's orders I'm afraid."

"And what about if she has to pee?" Nora smothered a snicker.

"One of us must be with you at all times."

My brow rose and Luis shook his head. "Of course, you can visit the bathroom on your own. But make no mistake, Miss Capizola, we will be right outside."

"This is ridiculous." I grabbed Nora's hand and yanked her down the hall.

"It's not his fault, Ari," she said, shooting him an apologetic glance.

"I know, I'm just so... so annoyed."

"What did you really expect? He let you return after telling you that Antonio Marchetti,"—she stopped herself, waiting for a couple of girls to pass—"tried to, you know."

"But do they have to be so obvious?" Nixon was waiting at the end of the hall while Luis trailed behind us. There was no mistaking they were here to protect me. I'd heard the whispers as we made our way out of Donatello House, and I knew it wouldn't take long for the entire campus to learn that Arianne Capizola was in fact... me.

Over the weekend, it had seemed like a small price to pay to return here and be closer to Nicco. But in the harsh light of day, I'd realized the life of secrecy I once resented so much, was now looking like a walk in the park compared to this. People stopped in their tracks as we passed them. Gawking at me like I'd grown a second head. A faint rumble of whispers followed us, their speculations brushing up against me, making me bristle.

"Everyone's looking," I breathed, clutching Nora's hand tighter.

"You need to own this, Ari. You're Arianne freakin' Capizola for Christ's sake. Don't you dare cower."

Her words sank into me, making me stand taller. I *was* Arianne Capizola, and I could do this. Until Tristan and Scott swaggered over to us.

"Ladies," Scott said around a smug grin.

"What is this?" I refused to look at him, focusing only on my cousin.

"Your father didn't tell you?" There was a brief flash of guilt in his eyes. "We're here to chaperone you to class."

"Hate to break it to you," Nora said. "But I think you're two bodyguards too late."

Tristan gave Luis a sharp nod and they dropped back

"What the hell is going on?" I leaned in closer to Tristan, my teeth clenched behind my lips.

"Relax, cous. I thought you'd prefer it this way. Luis and Nixon will be around, but at least this way you won't feel so suffocated."

"Don't be so sure about that," I grumbled.

"Arianne," he let out a heavy sigh. "Work with me here."

"Work with you?" I seethed. "You expect me to—"

"Ari." Nora squeezed my hand. "He's right. Let's get to class and figure the rest out later."

"That's the most sensible thing ever to come out of your mouth, Abato." Scott grinned.

"Fuck you, Fascini." She mouthed back.

"Okay, okay, this isn't doing anything but drawing more attention." Tristan ran a hand over his mouth. "The cat is out of the bag now. Soon everyone will know Arianne Capizola is on campus and your life will be—"

"Save me the lecture." I barged past Tristan and took off toward the building.

"Ari, wait." He snagged my wrist, catching up to me. "I'm sorry, okay? I was just following orders."

"Like you were just following orders when you failed to tell me the real truth of our family's legacy?"

His lips pressed into a thin line, his silence all the admission of guilt I needed.

"Whatever, *cousin*. You hurt him, Tristan. You hurt someone I—" I swallowed the words.

"Hurt someone you what?" His eyes narrowed at me.

"It doesn't matter. It's over." My stomach knotted. "Nicco is—"

"The enemy. He's the *enemy*, Ari. You need to remember that."

"I get it. My life has been flipped sideways; I don't need you making it worse."

"Jesus..." He blew out an exasperated breath. "Come here." Tristan pulled me into his arms and I went willingly. He had to believe Nicco was no one to me. Even if it did physically hurt me to pretend.

"I know you probably don't believe me, but I am sorry," he whispered into my hair.

I pulled back and gave him a weak smile. "Yeah," I sighed. "Me too."

His smile grew, and I knew then that my cousin didn't really know me at all. He didn't hear the lie behind my words. See the guilt glitter in my eyes. He truly believed I was the dutiful, docile daughter I had always been.

And that was something I could never forgive.

∞∞∞

It didn't take long for news to travel. By the time lunchtime rolled around and we headed for the food court, people had begun to step aside to let me pass them. It was disconcerting to say the least.

"It's like you're freaking Moses or something."

"Moses?" I asked.

"Yeah, parting the seas."

I rolled my eyes at that. "Hopefully it'll pass soon."

"Not likely. You just went from being no one to someone..." Nora's voice drowned out when I found Enzo glaring at me. He was standing by the entrance to the food court, his icy stare burning into me.

"Ari, I said what do you... oh. *Oh.*" Nora exhaled, slipping closer to me. "He looks like you just killed his favorite puppy and he's plotting all the ways to get his slow and ever so painful revenge."

She wasn't wrong.

I kept my eyes ahead, ignoring him as we entered the

busy food court. Silence descended over the room. It happened like a wave. Gentle at first, a few people nearest us, and then the table closest to them. But quickly it spilled over to the rest of the tables, until everyone was looking.

"Okay, then. Shall we...?" Nora's hand slid down my arm, grabbing my hand. "Together?"

"Together." Head held high, I tried my best to block it all out as we went to our favorite counter. Luis and Nixon stayed close, failing to blend in at all. Not that two immaculately dressed bodyguards ever could.

"Arianne?"

I turned to find Tristan's friend Sofia hovering. "Yes?"

"I just wanted to say, I didn't know... I mean, I thought I kind of recognized you, but I didn't..." She fumbled over the words and Nora snickered beside me. "Well, I guess what I wanted to say was, I'm sorry. And welcome to MU. If I can help with anything..."

"I think we're good." Nora stepped forward. "But thanks for the offer, Cynthia."

"Uh, Sofia, my name is Sof ... aaaand you already know that. I guess, I'll just be..." She spun on her heel and took off toward her friends. Emilia's mouth hung open as if she couldn't believe what had just happened. But then she trained her eyes on me, narrowing them, her expression drenched with jealousy.

"God, that felt good."

"Really, Nor?"

"What? She deserved it. Now she knows her place and we can move on with life."

It sounded great in principle. But I wasn't sure anything would ever be the same again. Then I felt him.

Nicco.

"What is it?" Nora asked, her brows furrowed with concern as I stood there, holding my tray, frozen in place.

"Nicco," his name left my lips in a single breath. I didn't look over my shoulder. I didn't have to.

"He's sitting with Enzo and their friends."

"What are you getting?" I asked, trying to act normal. Trying to resist the urge to abandon my lunch and run to him and ask him to take me far away from here.

But I'd made him a promise, and I intended on keeping it.

"The Asian noodles look good." Nora played along.

"They do." I gave my order to the server and thanked her. As she handed me the bowl, she said, "Is it true? Are you Roberto Capizola's daughter?"

Even the servers had heard the news? I didn't know what to do with that.

"I am."

Wonder filled her crinkled eyes. "Wow, that's... Sorry, I'm being rude." Her cheeks flamed. "It's just... I always wondered what happened to you."

My brows furrowed. "You know my family?"

"I used to serve your father when he was a student here. Such a wonderful young man, so generous and gracious. I always hoped to meet his daughter one day."

"What's your name?"

"Lili."

"It's nice to meet you, Lili."

The woman smiled at me as if I'd just given her the greatest gift in life. "You ignore the rest of them."

Luis moved closer, his proximity irritating me. "Is there a problem?" I asked.

"Nothing to report." His reply was clipped.

"Please don't tell me you're concerned about Lili being a threat?" I whisper-hissed at him. Thankfully, Nora had engaged the women in which dish to get.

"Miss Capi—"

"Arianne. My name is Arianne, and I get it, you're here on my father's orders. But this isn't working for me, Luis. It's college, my life. You need to back off."

"Yes, Mis..." He cleared his throat. "Arianne. I'll be right over there." He joined Nixon, the two of them talking in their usual hushed tones.

"Ready?" I asked Nora, and she nodded.

"Don't be a stranger, Arianne," Lili said.

"Thank you."

Nora went first, weaving through the tables of curious stares and veiled whispers. She chose the table we'd sat at last week. We had no sooner sat down when Tristan and Scott appeared with even more friends in tow.

"What's good?" My cousin dropped down beside me and slung his arm over the back of my chair.

"You, sitting elsewhere?" Nora snickered.

"I have something you can sit on," one of Tristan's friends jammed his hand under the table, grabbing his crotch. The guys all exploded with laughter, but it quickly died down when Tristan glared at them.

"Don't mind them," he said. "Their default setting is asshole."

"Baciami il culo," one of the guys grumbled, flipping my cousin off.

"So what are your plans tonight?"

"There are no plans. We'll probably just do some reading and hang out at the dorm."

"You should come over to the house and hang out."

"That's a joke, right?"

"Ari, cut me some slack. It isn't party central all the time, and I know Scott would like to—"

"Tristan, how many times do I have to say it? There is no me and Scott."

"Because of him." His eyes slid over to where Nicco was sitting, and I felt the anger radiating off my cousin. Thankfully, Nicco wasn't looking at us, but he had been.

I'd felt him.

"This has nothing to do with Nicco."

"So come over later. We have a movie room. We can watch whatever you want. Most of the guys will be out. It'll be fun."

Panic flooded me. Was this a test? Had my father asked him to watch me? To make sure I didn't try to see Nicco?

My fist clenched against my jeans as I said, "We could come over for a little while."

Nora caught my eye and mouthed, "What the hell?"

"That's great, Ari. You won't regret it, I promise."

"On one condition, Tristan," I added, erasing his smile. "You stop with the me and Scott stuff, okay?"

"Sure, I can do that. I'm just happy we'll get to hang out. It's long overdue."

My cell phone vibrated, startling me. Tristan roped his arm around my neck and pulled me in, kissing my cheek. "I need food." He left and the other guys followed.

"What the hell was that?" Nora wasted no time, but I was too busy digging out my cell phone, my heart catapulting into my mouth when I saw Nicco's number.

What was that about?

God, I wanted so desperately to look at him. To stare into his eyes and tell him it was nothing more than me playing a part.

It's nothing, don't worry.

I will always worry about you. Every second of every day.

"Ari," Nora whispered, and I looked up to find some of the guys returning to our table. Shoving my cell into my lap, I typed as quickly as I could.

I am yours and I will do whatever it takes to keep you safe, okay? But you have to trust me. Trust me, Nicco. No matter what happens: what you hear, what you see, you have to trust that I only do it to protect you.

He'd said something similar to me last night. But his words worked both ways. I wasn't the only one who needed protecting. I didn't doubt Tristan and my father would hurt Nicco again if they believed I was still seeing him. Which is why they needed to believe it was over. That he was no one to me. Which is why I had to play Tristan's games.

Another text came through.

I trust you.

Relief sank into me. I could do this.

We could do this.

Because the alternative, a world where I was forbidden from seeing Nicco, wasn't a world I wanted to live in.

∞∞∞

"At least it's not full of football players," Nora whispered as we stepped into my cousin's house.

"You guys want a beer? Don't feel like you need to stand guard all night." Tristan grinned at Luis and Nixon. "She's safe here."

"You know our orders, Mr. Capizola."

"Yeah, yeah, my uncle is a stickler for orders. But it's my house. No one is getting in or out without me knowing about it. Besides, you can protect her and still relax. Have a beer, grab a seat, fai come se fossi a casa tua. We'll be right down the hall in the movie room. Ladies." Tristan swept his arm in an arc. "This way."

The smell of fresh popcorn drifted down the hall as we followed him. Nora hadn't wanted to come, but she understood why I had to and decided she couldn't let me suffer alone.

"You came," Scott said the second we stepped foot into the room.

"Fascini, I'd say it's a pleasure," Nora quipped. "But it's really not."

"Bite me, Abato."

"Guys," Tristan groaned. "Can we try to not kill each other before the movie starts?"

It seemed like he really was trying. Away from all his friends, out from under the spotlight, Tristan wasn't a bad guy. He just enjoyed playing to a crowd. He liked status and power and money, and somewhere along the way, the cousin I'd grown up with had transformed into a man I barely recognized.

Part of me missed him, but part of me also knew we'd become different people.

"What movie do you want to watch?"

"Anything," I said, taking the seat furthest away from Scott. His heavy gaze lingered on the side of my face, but I refused to look at him. I could do this—sit here and watch a movie with him—but I wasn't about to pretend we were friends.

"Has your father talked to you about the Centennial Gala yet?" he asked.

Tristan clucked his tongue, levelling his best friend with a hard look.

"What?" Scott said. "It was only a question."

"No, he hasn't actually. Why?"

"It doesn't matter," Tristan replied. "The popcorn is getting cold."

He was deflecting, and I didn't like it. I made a mental note to ask my father about it.

Nora snagged a blanket off the back off the couch and shuffled closer to me, throwing it over our laps. "You might have to physically restrain me," she whispered through a tight-lipped smile, and I fought a snicker. Scott deserved her wrath, but he wasn't worth it.

"Get in line," I mouthed and we shared a secret smile.

"What are you two whispering about?" Tristan asked, grabbing the television remote and settling back into one of the chairs.

"Oh, nothing," Nora said. "So what are we watching?"

"I figured we'd stick to something safe. *Avengers Assemble*. Remember, Ari? It was one of your favorites growing up."

"I was ten, Tristan. I had a crazy crush on Chris Hemsworth."

The movie started and silence fell over the four of us. It was strange, sitting here with Tristan and Scott, in their frat house, pretending we were all friends. It felt fake. Like we were all waiting to see who would break out of character first.

Nora leaned over and grabbed one of the bowls of popcorn, shoving a handful in her mouth. "Might as well make the most of it," she grumbled, offering me the bowl.

I wasn't hungry—being around Scott was enough to kill my appetite—but I took a handful. It was a distraction. Something to stop me saying something I might later regret.

Two hours later, the film was finished and Nora didn't wait a second longer to make our excuse to leave.

"This has been nice and all," she gave Tristan a saccharine sweet smile. "But I have a thing and I need Ari's opinion."

"Thing?" Scott drawled. "Is that code for some freaky sex move?"

"Nora's right, we should go. But thanks for... the popcorn."

"Come on, cous, stay, hang out." Tristan leaped up. "I'm pretty sure we have some wine coolers in the refrigerator."

"Maybe another time." When hell froze over.

"Sure, okay. Let me walk you out." Tristan led the way, but the second he stepped into the hall, Luis and Nixon stood to attention. "Arianne and Nora would like to return to their dorm."

"Arianne and Nora can speak for themselves." I reminded my cousin. He ran a brisk hand over his head, amusement dancing in his eyes.

"You've changed," he said.

"So have you."

Something passed between us, but I couldn't quite figure out if it was a mutual feeling of respect or resentment. Maybe a mix of both.

"I need to pee," Nora announced.

"Back down the hall, last door on the left."

"I'll be two minutes," she said to me.

"Go, I'll be fine."

No sooner had she disappeared, did Tristan move toward the door with Luis and Nixon. The three of them were discussing something, talking so quietly I could barely make out anything they were saying.

"This game you're playing is cute." Scott stepped up beside me, his proximity setting my teeth on edge.

"Game?"

"You're not fooling anyone, princess, especially me." His warm breath hit the back of my neck, sending a deep shudder rolling through me.

"I have no idea what you're talking about." I hissed, refusing to look at him. But Scott stepped closer, his hard chest brushing up against my shoulder.

"It's okay," he drawled. "I enjoy the chase."

My body began to tremble. Anger. Fear. It swirled inside me like a vortex.

"Please get away from me," I ground out, keeping my eyes on Tristan, willing him to look over at us. But he and

Luis were deep in conversation.

"Sorry I took so—"

Scott darted away from me and I released the breath I'd been holding. "There you are." I turned to Nora who was looking at me funny. She flicked her eyes to Scott who pretended to be checking his cell phone, and back to me.

"We should go," I said.

Tristan and my bodyguards fell into silence as we reached them. I raised a brow. "Is there a problem?"

"No problem." Tristan slung his arm around my shoulder. "Thank you for coming. I know you're still pissed at me but we're still family, Arianne. Us Capizola need to stick together."

Nora let out an exasperated breath and slipped around us, pulling the door open. "Goodnight, Tristan," I said, following her and Luis outside.

"Okay." Nora shuffled close beside me. "What do you think your cousin is up to?"

"You caught that, huh?" I glanced to Luis, and then Nixon, who was following behind us.

"I know he's family, Ari," she lowered her voice to a whisper, "but I don't trust him."

I didn't either.

Not anymore.

The vibration of my cell phone startled me, and I dug it out of my pocket.

I need to see you.

You can't risk it.

I would risk anything for you.

Nicco...

Bambolina, I need to see you. Don't make me beg...

"Is it...?"

I silenced Nora with a hard look. There were too many people listening. People loyal to my father.

We're just walking back to our dorm.

I know.

My eyes went wide as I searched the surrounding area. It was dark though, long leafy shadows dancing over the sidewalk winding through campus.

I can't see you.

It should have felt all kinds of creepy that Nicco was watching me, but it didn't.

Then you're not looking hard enough.

I smothered a smile, walking taller, knowing that Nicco was out there somewhere.

"Oh, you have it so bad." Nora smirked. "I guess you'll be wanting me to make myself scarce when we get back to the dorm?"

"I don't know, we shouldn't..."

"But we both know you will. Just promise me you'll be careful, okay?"

"Where will you go?" I mouthed, keeping one eye on Luis. But he was too focused on our surroundings.

"I'm not against making a booty call."

"Kaiden?"

She shrugged. "Or Dan."

"Hussy."

"Hey, Lu," she called, and Luis glanced over his shoulder. "I'm going out. Is that a problem?"

"I'll let Maurice know."

"Maurice?"

"He's assigned to you."

"I have my own bodyguard?"

"He's on your assignment, yes."

"Cool. But you should probably tell Maurice he might want to bring earplugs."

I quickly typed out a reply to Nicco.

Nora's going out. I'll be all alone.

His response was instant.

Leave the window open.

Chapter 16

Nicco

I waited.

Almost an hour had passed since I'd seen Arianne enter her building, flanked by her bodyguards. She walked with such poise and grace. Her entire world had been flipped upside down, and yet; my brave, strong girl carried herself with confidence.

She carried herself like her father.

I wondered if she realized how similar they were, minus the fact her father was a scheming traitorous asshole.

Arianne hadn't texted me again. It was possible she had fallen asleep. But then her slender shadow appeared at the window, her eyes searching the tree line below for me. Pulling up my hood, I ducked into the darkness and followed the path to the building. I knew MU campus well enough to know every blackspot in the security cameras, every place to hide and remain out of sight.

Climbing the fire escape with ease, I pulled myself onto her balcony. Arianne had disappeared, but the window was open, the curtains billowing in the gentle breeze.

"You came," she whispered.

"You thought I wouldn't?" Stepping into the room, my

eyes landed on her sitting on the edge of her bed in nothing but an oversized MU t-shirt.

Fuck.

I swallowed.

"It's been an hour." She looked up at me through her thick lashes, a playful smile tipping the corner of her mouth.

"Were you waiting for me?" I dragged a thumb over my bottom lip as I stalked toward her. Dropping to my knees, I ran my hands up her legs, ankles to thighs. A soft moan slipped from her lips.

"Nicco..."

"Does Fascini have a thing for you?"

She reared back, eyes fixed on mine. "Why would you say that?"

"I've seen the way he watches you, Bambolina." And I fucking hated it. "What were you doing at their house?"

"Tristan wanted us to hang out."

"With the football team?" My brow rose, anger simmering in my veins. I'd almost lost it when I'd watched them disappear into the house. I wasn't supposed to be following her, but after her text at lunch, about doing whatever it took to protect me, I found myself texting Bailey. Between us, we'd watched Arianne all day.

"No, it was just me, Nora, Tristan, and..."

Her gaze dropped to the floor. I slid a finger underneath her chin and forced her to look at me.

"And?"

"And Scott."

"He wants you."

"Well, he can't have me," she said with fierce conviction.

"Yeah, and why is that?"

"Because I'm yours."

"Damn right, you are." My hand slid up Ari's body, my fingers splaying across one side of her neck as I kissed her hard. She looped her arms around my neck, her legs hooking around my waist, anchoring us together.

"I want you, Nicco," she murmured against my lips.

Jesus. She was testing my patience.

"Not here, not like this,"—my eyes flicked the door—"with your bodyguard right outside."

"You don't want to?" Arianne's expression fell.

"I do. So much. See what you do to me." Grabbing one of her hands, I pulled it down between us, letting her feel how hard I was. "When I finally make you mine in every way possible, I don't want to worry about who might hear you scream my name".

"Oh." The cutest blush worked its way up her neck and flooded her cheeks.

"I didn't come here for that, not tonight. I came to make sure you were okay." *I needed to see you were okay.*

"Because you were jealous." A faint smirk tugged at her lips.

"I will always be jealous where you're concerned. You think it doesn't kill me knowing I can't be the one to stand at your side?"

"Nicco, I didn't..." She fisted my hoodie, letting out a resigned sigh. "It hurts me too."

"I know, Bambolina, I know." I crushed Arianne into my arms. The sound of her soft sobs gutted me. I wanted to tell her everything would be okay, to reassure her I had a plan.

But the truth was, I had no fucking idea how I was going to fix this. There was too much history between our families, too much hate.

"Come here." I stood up, taking Arianne with me, cradling her body against mine. Walking around to the side of the bed, I managed to pull back the covers and lie her down.

"You're leaving, already?"

"I'm not going anywhere." I kicked off my boots. "Scoot over." I laid down beside her and wrapped my arm around Arianne, pulling her close.

"This is nice," she whispered.

"I've never done this before," I confessed.

"You've never snuggled? That's kind of sad."

"I've snuggled. Alessia and my mom. But I've never snuggled with a girl."

"So I'm your first?" Arianne gazed up at me, a goofy smile plastered on her face. "I like that. I like that I get some of your firsts too."

"Tell me something…"

"Anything," she replied.

"Was it Scott who hurt you?"

"Wh- what? No… no, Nicco."

"You're sure?" I narrowed my eyes. "Because the way he looks at you…"

Ari moved onto her knees, cupping my face in her hands. "It wasn't Scott. It was nobody. Just a guy I stupidly agreed to go out with. Forget about him, Nicco. Please."

"The idea of someone touching you, Arianne, of putting their hands on you. It makes me murderous."

"Ssh." She leaned in, kissing my jaw. "Don't talk like that." Her lips brushed mine, but I curved my hand around the back of her neck, holding her still.

"I would kill for you, Arianne. That's who I am. I might not like everything about my life, my legacy, but this life, the codes I am bound to, run through my blood."

"I... I understand." Her voice quivered.

"This... us, it's not fleeting for me. I'm not going to decide in a week or a month I no longer want you." I smoothed my thumb down her cheek. "If you want out, now is the time to tell me."

"You'd let me walk away?" Surprise clung to her words.

"You could try."

"But you just said..."

"Just because you want to walk away, doesn't mean I won't do everything in my power to win you back. You're mine, Arianne Carmen Lina Capizola. Forever."

"Forever... that's a big promise to make."

"Does it scare you?"

"What?"

"To know that you're mine. To know that I already love you completely. Heart, body, and soul."

"Nicco..." Her eyes fluttered closed as she drew in a shaky breath.

"I don't need to hear it back." I kissed the end of her nose. "Not yet. But you need to know this is not a game to me. It's real, Arianne. And nothing or no one is ever going to take you from me."

Fixing my mouth over hers, I sealed my promise with a kiss. Our tongues met in deep unhurried strokes that reverberated through me. Ari took me by surprise, sliding her leg over mine and settling above me.

"Bambolina, are you trying to kill me?"

"Ssh." She kissed me again. "Stop talking and just let go and feel."

Oh, she was a clever girl, constantly throwing my own words back at me. But I didn't stop her, I couldn't. She felt too fucking good, grinding down on me. Riding me, even if there were layers and layers between us.

My hands dipped under her t-shirt, running over her warm, smooth skin. "We should stop…" The words held no meaning as I slowly dragged the material up her body. Arianne lifted her arms and let me pull it over her head.

"You're right, we should definitely stop." Her hands went to my hoodie, curling around the hem. I sat up, helping her yank it off. Her eyes drank me in, roaming over my tattoos, the tiny white scars littering my skin. Her fingers followed, ghosting over every blemish.

"What's this one?" Her thumb brushed a larger scar running beneath my last rib.

"Stab wound," I admitted. There was so much I couldn't tell her: family business, secrets that I would take to the grave, but I wanted to give her the parts of me I could.

"This one?" She shuffled back, giving her more space to lean down and inspect my chest.

"Brass knuckles, split my skin clean open."

Arianne winced, but didn't stop her exploration. "And this one?" Her fingers hovered precariously close to the button of my jeans.

"What are you doing, Bambolina?"

She worked the button free without hesitation. "I want to touch you."

I hissed as her hand dipped inside, grazing the tip of my dick. "If anyone catches me in here with you…"

"You could be inside me, instead."

"Jesus, Arianne." My heart crashed violently in my chest as she continued stroking me as if she was born to do it.

"This is a bad idea," I rasped. It was pointless though. I was weak against her touch. How good her hand felt wrapped around me.

"I want to taste you," she whispered.

"Ari, you don't have to..." But she was already slipping down the bed, working my jeans off my hips. My fingers slid into her hair, involuntarily guiding her parted lips forward.

"What do I do?" she asked.

"Whatever you want."

Arianne took her time, flicking her tongue over the head and running it down my shaft. She was cautious at first, taking an inch into her mouth, sucking and licking, tasting and teasing. But her confidence grew with my moans of encouragement.

"Jesus, you feel... Fuck." The words got stuck as she took me further into her mouth, her hand pumping me hard and fast.

"Bambolina," I tugged her hair gently. "I'm going to come."

She reached for my hand, tangling our fingers together, keeping her lips firmly around me. My body began to tremble, a familiar tingling building at the bottom of my spine.

"Ari, fuck... that's... Jesus." I clenched down as pleasure shot through me. Arianne's soft laughter filled the air as she sat up, flushed and starry-eyed. "That was fun," she said with a hint of pride as she licked her lips.

"You are amazing." I leaned up to kiss her, but someone banged on the door.

"Arianne?" A deep voice rumbled.

"Crap." She scrambled off the bed. "You should go. He'll want to see me, to know I'm okay."

My hoodie landed on my head as she began pulling her own t-shirt back on. It would have been enough to kill my post-blow job high if it wasn't for the fact she looked so adorable.

"Come here." I stood up, hooking my finger in her belt loop.

"Nicco, this is serious. You need to—"

"Arianne?" Another knock.

"I'm just changing, Luis. I'll be right there."

"You need to go." She gazed up at me.

"And I will. But not before I do this." I claimed her lips in a deep kiss, tasting myself on her tongue. I'd never been into all that before, but with her it was different.

Everything was.

"You taste so fucking good." I buried my hands into her hair, kissing her again. "Maybe I should come all over your body so I can lick it off."

"Nicco, God..." It was a breathy sigh.

I walked us backward to the window, refusing to break the kiss. But eventually, she pressed her hands against my chest and tore away. "I do too, you know."

"Yeah, and what's that?"

"I love you, Niccolò Marchetti." Arianne pressed a single kiss to my lips. "But if Luis storms in here and finds you, I will never forgive you. So please, go."

I smirked, and she frowned. "What?"

"Until next time, Bambolina."

Before she could reply, I ducked out of the window and hurled myself over the balcony. My body slammed against the ladders, but it was nothing I couldn't handle.

Arianne had that effect on me.

She made me feel invincible.

Made me feel like I could fly.

She was everything I never knew I needed.

And she was mine.

∞∞∞

I didn't make it back to my apartment. After I left Arianne, my father had called telling me to get straight over to L'Anello's. You didn't tell the boss no, so that's how I found myself standing outside the club a little after midnight, waiting for Enzo and Matteo to show up.

My cousin's headlights lit up in the distance, and I climbed off my bike, waiting. He pulled up right outside and killed the engine. "What's happening?" he asked the second he climbed out of the car.

"Jimmy called my old man, said some guys were causing trouble."

"So, why couldn't Jimmy's guys handle it?"

"Because it's the guy from the other night, the one I fought at Hard Knocks."

"You're shitting me?" Enzo fell into step beside me as we entered the club.

"Seems he didn't get the message the first time around."

"So what's the plan?"

"The plan is to make sure he leaves here tonight knowing not to come around here again."

Matteo let out a long yawn.

"I'm sorry," I said, "are we keeping you awake?"

"Shit, sorry, Nic. I stayed up to help Arabella with her homework, that shit is enough to send anyone to sleep."

"You know you could hire her a tutor, you have the money," Enzo suggested.

"I know, but she likes me to help her and I don't mind. She's my kid sister. Someone's got to look out for her."

"It's a good thing you do, cous." I clapped him on the back. "Everyone stay cool, okay? I don't want this to become something bigger than it needs to be."

The second we stepped foot into the place, heads turned and a low rumble of whispers followed us as we moved deeper into the club.

"Hey, fellas," one of the servers greeted us. "I think Jimmy's expecting you downstairs."

"Thanks, Cassandra." Matteo flashed her a smile.

"Anytime, baby. You know, you should call me, you have my number."

"Another time," he mumbled. "Duty calls." Matteo ducked ahead of us, and Enzo snickered.

"Don't be a dick," I warned. "And whatever you do down there, do not lose your cool. Capisci?"

We took the dimly lit hall toward the back of the building where Jimmy ran the fight ring. It was a lucrative venture with monthly fight nights bringing in anywhere between ten to twenty-five grand.

Enzo shifted beside me, slipping his hand inside his jacket, and I knew he was either feeling for his pistol or one of his many blades.

"E, chill."

"I'm chill," he mumbled. "I just like to be prepared."

The reinforced steel door loomed up ahead. Matteo banged on it twice and the peephole opened. The guy took one look at us and opened up. "Nicco." He gave me a nod. "Been waiting for you to get here. Guy over there says you owe him."

"I don't owe anyone anything, Bobby, you know that."

"Told him as much. But the asshole refused to leave before he got an audience with you."

"Don't worry, I'll handle it."

Jimmy was busy over near the ring, no doubt taking bets for the next fight. He was a trusted associate; not of the bloodline, but someone who had worked with the family for most of his life. He was as loyal as they came. Killian was at the bar, surrounded by a few guys as big and tatted up as him. A couple of them wore leather cuts depicting a biker gang operating out of Providence.

Just what we needed, a biker gang in Marchetti territory.

"Shit, cous, he brought back up." Enzo was like a livewire beside me, itching for a fight. Matteo was quiet, no doubt contemplating all the ways this could go in our favor, or not.

And me?

I only had eyes for the guy whose face I'd already rearranged once.

He spotted me approaching and pushed his friends aside to stand and greet me. "You owe me, kid," he said.

"I already put you on your ass once, old man. I'm surprised you want to go a second round."

The room had fallen quiet, everyone watching as we went head to head.

"Cazzo sí!" he grunted but I ignored him.

"I see you brought some friends." I looked each of them over. "Did you tell them who I am?"

Confusion crinkled their faces. "What's he talking about, Kill?" one of them asked.

Enzo snorted beside me. "Oh, you didn't, did you? You let them come here without giving them all the information."

"Fuck you," Killian spat, and Enzo lurched forward. My arm flew out, blocking him.

"You want a rematch, is that it?" I narrowed my eyes at Killian.

"I want my pound of flesh, kid, sure."

"Too bad. I'm not looking to break a sweat tonight. Do yourself a favor and go back to whatever hole you crawled out of. You're no longer welcome here. Jimmy, show the guy the door." I spun on my heel but didn't get very far. A heavy hand landed on my shoulder yanking me back. A collective gasp filled the air as my hand went inside my jacket and I pulled out my pistol. Releasing the safety, I whipped around and pointed it straight at Killian.

"You dare to touch me?"

"Whoa." His hands went up, the blood draining from his face. "Easy, kid. I didn't mean no harm."

Stepping forward, I pushed the barrel of the pistol into his forehead, watching as beads of sweat rolled down his face. "Who am I?"

"W- what?" he stuttered.

"Who. Am. I?" I seethed, Matteo and Enzo at my side, staring down Killian's guys. Jimmy's guys had closed in too, forming a semi-circle around us.

"Nic..." his voice quivered. "Niccolò Marchetti."

A couple of his guys grumbled. "You brought us here to start shit with a Marchetti? Antonio Marchetti's son?"

"What the fuck did you think we were coming for?" Killian hissed. "This is La Riva, it's Marchetti territory."

He had a point. I raised a brow at his friends.

"Hey, man, we got no beef with you or your family." One of them stepped forward, hands up in surrender. "Killian said—"

"I think we've all established *Killian* needs to learn to keep his fucking mouth shut," Enzo said.

"Is he a member of your MC?" I asked.

"Hell no, but he is family. I can see we made a bad judgment call coming here. The Providence Phantoms have no beef with you."

"You should probably leave then." My eyes flicked to the door.

"What will you do with him?" They hesitated, glancing between me and their friend.

Killian was still sweating on the end of my pistol.

"Nothing less than he deserves." I pressed the barrel harder, angling it downward so he had no choice but to drop to his knees. "Who am I?" I repeated my question from earlier.

"Niccolò Marchetti," he rushed out.

"Wrong answer. Who am I?"

He began trembling; a grown ass man cowering in front of me like a small child.

"I am your worst fucking nightmare. Step foot in La Riva again and I'll put a bullet between your eyes, you feel me?"

"I- I feel you... please, don't hurt me. Don't—" I smashed the butt of my pistol against his face, sending him flying backward. His friends hauled him up and dragged him out of the room.

"What?" I asked Enzo who was staring at me.

"You should have at least shot him in the kneecap. Fucker deserved it."

"We're not all as trigger happy as you." Besides, I was a capo. A captain. One of my father's third-in-command. I couldn't just shoot a guy in cold blood in front of a room full of people. It wasn't how we operated.

It wasn't how *I* operated.

Fear commanded respect just as much as action when you carried a name like Marchetti. Hopefully Killian would heed my warning and never set foot in La Riva again.

Because if he did, I'd have to make good on my promise.

"Nicely handled." Jimmy came over and clapped me on the shoulder.

"Yeah, well, we'll see." I tucked my pistol back in its holster. "Hopefully he won't come sniffing around here again."

Jimmy led us over to the bar. "Three of our finest, Darla. You boys okay if I go take care of business?"

"Sure thing, Jimmy." Enzo shook his hand, and the old man disappeared.

"Here you go, on the house." The server placed down three glasses of Bourbon. "Nice to see you again, Enzo." She let her heavily made up eyes rake over his body, earning her a wicked smirk from my cousin.

"Looking good, Darl," he drawled.

Matteo rolled his eyes, leaning back against the bar,

watching as Jimmy got the next fight underway.

"Hey, Nicco."

My eyes shuttered as I rubbed my temples. "Rayna," I said, slowly turning to find her standing there.

"It's been a while." She smiled coyly.

"Yeah."

"You didn't call." A crestfallen expression slid over her face.

"What was the point?"

She inhaled a shaky breath. "Can we maybe go somewhere and talk?"

Rayna looked good in tight-fitting jeans and a black oversized sweater that hung off one shoulder. Her dark hair hung in waves down her back framing her face. But she no longer set my body on fire the way she once had.

"I don't think so, Ray," I said. "Not tonight."

"So that's it? You're really throwing away everything —"

I stepped into her personal space, narrowing my eyes. "This is not the time or the place."

"So come, talk with me". She curled her hand around my arm as if she owned me. "I missed you, Nicco. I missed us."

There had been a time when I saw myself and Rayna being more than bed partners. She'd grown up in the life. Knew more than most girls. Knew what it meant for someone like me.

Rayna made it easy. She didn't ask questions or dig for dirt. But I never fell hard for her. Not the way I had for Arianne. Being with Rayna had been like a warm, spring day; comfortable and easy, requiring little effort. But being with

Arianne was like the sun. Intense and hot and if you got too close you were bound to get burned. But it was a risk you would gladly take just to say you'd been in its orbit.

I removed Rayna's hand, dropping it at her side. "It's done," I said, devoid of emotion. "We're done."

Surprise flashed in her eyes, but she didn't stick around, storming off in a huff.

"Have you lost your damn mind?" Enzo grumbled. "Rayna just offered it up to you on a silver platter and you turned her down?"

"Have you forgotten, she slept with some coglione while I was seeing her?"

"You weren't exclusive though."

"It doesn't matter," I replied, not wanting to get into it with him. "It's done."

"She's got you all tied up in knots, cous; it's not healthy."

"What did you just say?" My hand clenched into a fist. Surely, he didn't mean...

"Now that the Capizola princess is walking around campus like she owns the fucking place. I can't say that I blame you."

"Oh... that. Yeah, it's a problem." I ran a hand through my hair, shooting Matteo a silent cry for help.

"If you ask me, she's innocent in all of this," he said. "I mean, he kept her locked away for years. Imagine how she must feel. It doesn't feel right using her as leverage."

"It is what it is." Enzo shrugged. "The way I see it, we're at war, and innocent people always get caught in the crossfire. That's how it goes."

I snatched up my glass and downed it in one. "I need to ride. I'll catch you guys tomorrow."

"But, Nicco, we should talk about—"

Enzo's words melted into silence as I walked away from them.

I needed air, before I said something I would live to regret.

Chapter 17

Arianne

Three days passed.

I didn't see Nicco much. There were no late-night visits, and he didn't appear in Mandrake's class again. Instead, I had to survive on stolen glances across the food court and a few heated text messages. I felt him though. Felt his eyes follow me around campus. Sometimes I was sure I could feel him nearby, but when I searched for him, I never caught so much as a glimpse.

"You're restless," Nora said as we entered the food hall. It was Friday and I was looking forward to the weekend. At least then I could avoid my classmates and their curious stares. It had gotten somewhat easier to walk into a room and have everyone look, whisper, and point, but I was more than ready for a break from feeling like an exhibit at the zoo.

"That's weird," Nora stared at her cell phone. "Mamma said, 'see you over the weekend'. I haven't—"

My cell phone began ringing. I dug it out my purse and sighed. "It's my mother. Hello."

"Arianne, figlia mia, how is it?"

"It's college, Mamma. It has its moments."

"But you're okay?" she went on. "I've been so worried."

"Luis and Nixon never let me out of their sight. And if I'm not being guarded by them, it's Tristan. I'm quite safe."

"Good, that's good. If anything were to happen to you..."

"Nothing is going to happen." I rolled my eyes at Nora who smirked.

"Suzanna is coming over tomorrow and we thought it might be nice if you joined us."

"Me, but why?"

"We're discussing the final preparations of the Centennial Gala, and well, your opinion would mean a great deal to us."

"It would?"

"Of course. Besides, it's time you start embracing your role within the family, Arianne."

"Fine, I'll be there." She let out a small shriek of approval, but I quickly moved on. "There was something I wanted to talk to you about actually. I've signed up to help at the local shelter. But I'm worried father will—"

"Oh what a wonderful idea. I'll handle your father. You should probably talk to the coordinator and shelter staff about your... situation though. If you're going to have Luis and Nixon with you it might be intimidating for some of their clients."

"You're right. I didn't think of that. I'll call them later."

"Oh, I'm so proud of you. You have such a big heart, Arianne. You're going to do wonderful things. I can feel it in my bones."

"We'll see you tomorrow then."

"We?" It was her turn to sound confused.

"Yeah, Nora will be coming with me."

"Oh, yes, of course. I'm sure she'd like to see her parents. Until tomorrow."

"So I gather we're going home for the weekend?" Nora asked the second I hung up.

"She wants me to help her and Suzanna Fascini with the final preparations for the Gala."

"Oh fun... not." Nora piled some salad onto her plate. "Have you spoken to him?"

I glanced around to check for eavesdroppers. "Only through text. After the other night..."

"Yeah, that was a close call. You can't be reckless, Ari. Not with the Muscle Twins watching your every move."

"I know." I hadn't intended to let things go so far the other night with Nicco. But every moment with him felt finite, like we were racing against the clock. I wanted to soak up every second, experience everything I could before things came crashing down around us.

We paid for our lunch and headed for our usual table. Tristan, Scott, and their friends were already there. Sofia was too but without her usual group of girlfriends. *Thank God.* I wasn't in the mood to deal with Emilia's death stare.

"Cous," Tristan pulled a chair free for me. I dropped onto it, smothering a chuckle when Nora made a big scene of pulling out her own chair.

"And they say chivalry is dead." She glared at my cousin.

"Act like a woman and maybe you'll be treated like one." Scott grinned across the table, high fiving his friend.

"Don't be such a dick, Scott," Sofia scolded him. "It's the twenty-first century. If a girl wants to enjoy sex, she should damn well be entitled to."

Nora frowned at me, and I shrugged. "Thanks," she said

to Sofia. "I think."

"I'm not a total bitch. Besides, Scott thinks he can do or say whatever he wants and I'm tired of his shit."

Suddenly, I saw Sofia in a whole new light. "Something we can agree on," I whispered.

"Hey, I heard that," Scott protested.

"Good, maybe you'll heed our words." My eyes locked on his, saying all the things I wish I had the freedom to say aloud.

"Yeah, whatever. I'm going to get some more dessert." He stalked off and the tension lifted.

"Babe," Tristan said to Sofia. "Must you poke the bear?"

"Oh, come on, Tristan, you know he's a liability. He practically forced himself on Emil—" My cousin cut her dead, kissing her hard. Sofia melted against him, letting out a little sigh.

"Eww, gross," Nora exclaimed but I was replaying Sofia's words over in my head. Had he tried to hurt Emilia the way he'd tried to hurt me?

Someone needed to know about him, but like my own, the Fascini were a powerful family.

Frustration welled inside me. What was the point of being Arianne Capizola, heir to the Capizola fortune, if I couldn't use my voice for good? To bring entitled rich assholes like Scott to justice. Of course I wasn't the first girl he'd hurt. Guys like him took what they wanted, when they wanted, with little thought to the consequences, because society taught them there were no consequences.

"What are you thinking?" Nora leaned in. "I know that look and you're scheming."

"He can't get away with it," I said feeling a sense of determination wash over me. "I don't know how yet, or even when, but he has to pay, Nor. He has to—"

"Yeah, I think they add an herb or something. It's really tasty. Here." She forked some salad leaves on her fork and offered it to me, discreetly flicking her eyes to where Scott was approaching the table.

"No, I'm good thanks," I mumbled.

I had a fire in my belly.

Scott Fascini would pay.

One way or another, he would pay.

∞∞∞

"Arianne, it's so lovely to see you," Suzanna Fascini embraced me, kissing each cheek before holding me at arm's length. "Such a beautiful girl. Tell me, how is college treating you? I hope that son of mine has made you feel right at home."

"I... uh... Scott has been very... welcoming." I chewed the inside of my cheek.

"Good, that's good to hear. He thinks very highly of you, Arianne."

"Hello, Mrs. Fascini, I'm Nora Abato." She stepped forward. "You probably don't remember me."

"Nora, of course. How rude of me. It's lovely to see you again. Will you be joining us or—"

"Actually," my mother appeared, "Nora is spending the day with her mother."

"I am?" Nora frowned.

"Indeed. I've arranged a day out for the two of you at my favorite spa."

"Oh, wow, Mrs. Capizola, that is... wow." Nora glanced at me, but I had nothing. Suzanna was acting like me and Scott were a couple and my mother seemed off.

And ever since we'd turned into the estate, dread had snaked through me and taken root in my stomach.

"I guess I'll see you later?" Nora's voice pulled me from my thoughts. "You'll be okay?"

"Of course she'll be okay," my mother laughed. "We have quite the day of planning ahead of us."

I gave my best friend a tight-lipped smile and watched as she doubled back and left the house.

"Come, let's sit on the terrace. It's such a lovely morning."

She and Suzanna chatted while we trailed through the house. I noticed Mrs. Abato had prepared quite the spread for us. Fresh fruit and pastries, finger sandwiches and crudités. My stomach grumbled and both women chuckled.

"You need to eat more, mia cara. Italian men like a little something to hold onto. At least, Mike does." Suzanna cackled, the sound like nails down a chalkboard. I shuddered, suppressing the urge to gag.

Mom sat down and opened her planner. "Ah yes, outfits."

"I thought we were here to talk about the final preparations?"

"Choosing the perfect dress *is* the final preparation." Suzanna smiled at me.

I was clearly missing something. I thought they wanted my opinion about decorations and entertainment. Not dresses.

"I'm sorry. I'm not sure I understand."

"The theme is a traditional venetian carnival. So we were thinking something big and bold." My mother pulled out a page and slid it across the table to me.

"Wow, they are... something." The gaudy rococo and baroque inspired gowns were all very *Mary Antoinette* and nothing like the simple dress I'd planned to wear.

"You need to make a statement," Suzanna said.

"I do?"

"Well, of course dear. You and Scott will be the—"

"What Suzanna is trying to say, sweetheart, is that this is a perfect opportunity to make a statement."

I frowned, still not following. "Is there something going on I should know about?" I asked.

Mom let out an exasperated breath, as if my cluelessness frustrated her. "Our families need to show a united front, Arianne, now more than ever."

"And Scott and I figure into that how exactly?"

"You are the future of Capizola Holdings," Suzanna chimed in, "and Scott is set to become a partner in Fascini and Associates as soon as he graduates. Separately we are powerful, but together we could be unstoppable."

"Mamma?" I felt the ground shift beneath my feet.

"Scott is a good man, sweetheart, and he has always had a soft spot for you. Your coupling makes sense."

"Our coupling?" I choked over the words. "You can't actually be serious? You want me to date him because it's good for business?"

"Well, we had hoped you would find your way together naturally once you started MU, but I can see that isn't the case." Her lips thinned with disapproval.

"Unbelievable." I stood up.

"Arianne, what are you—"

"I need a minute. Please excuse me." I made a beeline for the house, anger coursing through me like wildfire.

My mother hadn't summoned me here for a planning meeting.

It was an ambush.

A tag team effort to get me to agree to date Scott.

Luis followed me down the hall, quiet and brooding behind me. "Really, in my own house?" I threw over my shoulder.

"It's for your own—"

"Protection." I sneered. "Wow, just wow." Reaching the staircase, I gripped the rail. "Are you going to stand guard outside my door too?"

His silence told me all I needed to know.

"Very well then." Taking two steps at a time, I stomped up the stairs and hurried down the hall to my door. Slamming the door gave me an ounce of satisfaction but it didn't last. I was furious, anger trembling inside me like a powerful storm. It was bad enough I'd spent five years of my life locked away on the estate, now I was being forced to date Scott, a sexual predator, all because it was good for business.

A frustrated cry spilled from my lips as I ran to the window, curling up on the seat. I pressed my head against the cool glass. Retrieving my cell phone from my pocket, I texted Nicco.

How do you do it?

He texted straight back.

Do what?

Carry the burden of your family legacy? Be who they expect you to be?

Nicco's number flashed across the screen, and I hit answer. "Did something happen?" he asked, his words a low rumble that reverberated deep inside me.

"It's nothing..." The sound of his voice settled me. "I just hate this. All the lies and secrets. I don't know who or what to believe. Nothing makes sense anymore."

"Bambolina," he sighed, so guttural and full of emotion. I pressed my palm against the glass and closed my eyes, imagining he was right there. "Talk to me, Arianne."

"I'm fine. Just my mother and her friend and their meddling ways. It's been an overwhelming morning."

"I wish I could take you away from there; just you, me, and the open road."

"Where would we go?" My lips curved.

"Anywhere. Maybe drive down the coast to New York, head to Long Island. Somewhere no one will find us."

"I like the sound of that."

The silence was deafening as we both allowed ourselves to fall into the dream. Me and Nicco and a world that didn't want to tear us apart.

"I should go," he finally said. Three little words that yanked me back to reality with a resounding *thud*.

"Okay," I whispered.

"You'll be okay?"

"I will."

"I love you, Arianne Carmen Lina Capizola. Don't ever forget that." He hung up abruptly and part of me wondered where he was and who he was with.

Calling me was a risk. Texting each other was too. But I couldn't not speak to him. Not when our messages back and forth made the days bearable until the next time we got to see each other.

A knock at my door startled me from my thoughts. "Hello?" I called out.

"Arianne, it's me."

"Come in."

My mother slipped into the room, closing the door behind her. "Figlia mia, is everything okay?"

"Really, Mamma?"

"I'm sorry, okay. I didn't mean for this morning to feel like an ambush."

"Well, it did. You know I don't like Scott in that way, and yet, you're still pushing for me to give him a chance. He's not the golden boy everyone makes him out to be, you know?"

"Oh, I don't doubt that." She gave me a wistful smile. "Scott is entitled and power hungry and used to getting what he wants. Men like that aren't used to being told no."

"Well, perhaps he should get used to it."

"In an ideal world, you're right. But this isn't the real world."

"So that excuses his behavior?"

"Oh, Arianne. You are so wise beyond your years." She moved closer, leaning over to brush a stray hair from my face. "But you also have so much to learn about the world. A man like Scott needs a good woman by his side. Someone strong and good, to whisper in his ear and keep him on the right track."

"And you want that person to be me?"

Her expression turned sad. "It is not my decision to make."

"You mean Papá—"

"Your father only wants what is best for you."

"Did he tell you?"

"Tell me what?" A frown crinkled my mother's eyes.

"That I know the truth about our family. Our legacy."

She sucked in a harsh breath, mumbling, "Porco miseria! He didn't, no."

"I didn't think so." She'd said nothing to me of it. Part of me even wondered if she knew the whole story, but sitting here, listening to her talking about a woman's duty and how men like Scott needed a strong woman by their side, it occurred to me that perhaps she wasn't as clued in as she considered herself to be.

Tears pricked my eyes as everything came crashing down on top of me.

"What is it, figlia mia? What's wrong?"

Mashing my lips together, I shook my head gently.

"Arianne, sweetheart. Whatever it is, whatever is wrong, you can tell me."

I wanted so badly to tell her. To offload my secret on someone. But I couldn't risk it.

Could I?

"Talk to me. I'm your mother. You can trust me, whatever it is."

"I love another, Mamma." The words poured out, tears rolling down my cheeks.

"W- what?" Fear simmered in her eyes. "But who?"

"Niccolò Marchetti."

All the blood drained from her face. "M- Marchetti? No, no, Arianne, it cannot be..."

"It's true, Mamma. I love him and he loves me."

"Does your father know?"

"He knew I was seeing him, yes."

"And now?"

"He thinks it's over."

"Good, this is good." She grabbed my hands in hers. "You must never see that boy again. Do you understand? If your father ever found out..."

"Why are you saying this, Mamma? I love him. I thought you'd understand."

It was a mistake telling her. I realized that now. She didn't look happy or relieved or even surprised. She wore a mask of terror.

"It must end. Immediately. There is too much blood, too much pain between our families to repair history. What is done is done. Promise me you will end it. Promise me, Arianne."

"I promise." The words killed a tiny piece of my heart. But only for the lie I'd told. For nothing would keep me from Nicco. Not my father, nor my mother's fearful expression. Not Tristan, or Scott's interest in me.

Nothing.

People had spent my entire life lying to me.

Maybe it was my turn to repay the favor.

∞∞∞

The Verona County Transitions Initiative was based in Romany Square. It was technically Marchetti territory, but the director, Manny, had reassured my father personally that I would be safe. I didn't know the details of their conversation; I didn't want to. I was just relieved to be here, helping.

Having my best friend by my side only made it better.

"You know, this is pretty awesome," Nora said, as she laid out another tray of biscuits. Manny had set us up at the tea and coffee table. On Sunday's the center provided people all over Verona County the chance to get a warm meal and hot drink with a side of non-judgmental conversation. Permanent staff were trained in a broad spectrum of skills including: advice and guidance, counselling, therapy, and crisis management, and all volunteers had to undergo an induction session, which we'd completed before our shift started this morning, and then had access to a rolling program of training sessions.

"So you didn't tell him yet?" Nora asked as we waited for Manny to open the doors. It was almost twelve and they expected a full house. Luis and Nixon had strict orders to stay outside of the building unless absolutely necessary. I knew my mother probably had a hand in making it happen.

I tried not to think about whether it was because she genuinely wanted me to experience life, or because she felt guilty after yesterday.

"It doesn't feel right telling him over text message."

My father expected me to attend the Centennial Gala whether I wanted to or not. If I didn't go, I risked him growing suspicious over Nicco; and if I did go, I risked hurting the guy who had stolen my heart.

The answer, no matter how hard, was simple.

I had to protect Nicco.

"You should just rip that Band-Aid clean off. Text him, let him cool down, then try to see him. He's going to lose his —"

"Nor," I hissed, shooting a smile at one of the other volunteers.

Manny had agreed it was safer for everyone if I was here under a false identity. So once again, I was Lina Rossi; not that I expected anyone to ask my name. By all accounts, people came for the free food and company.

The doors opened and people began flooding in. Nora stood beside me, wearing an eager smile. I didn't realize how fulfilling serving strangers tea and coffee could be until I'd gotten through fifty cups and endless carafes of tea and coffee. Some people made small talk, commenting on how refreshing it was to see two new faces, while others offered only a meek smile before they swiped a biscuit or two and moved on.

"That was fun," Nora exclaimed, wiping her hands on a VCTI-branded towel.

"Don't get too excited just yet," a volunteer named Brent said. "The rush doesn't really start until later."

"R- rush?" Nora choked out. "You mean that *wasn't* the rush."

Brent chuckled. "Welcome to Sunday's at the VCTI. You might want to restock those trays while it's quiet." He nodded to the empty silver trays laid out in front of Nora.

"I can go," I said. "I need to use the bathroom anyway."

I left Nora and Brent talking while I made my way into the back. There was a small staff room with a bathroom attached. I quickly grabbed my purse and slipped inside, locking the door behind me.

I had two texts. One from my mother, checking to see

how it was going; and one from Nicco.

How is it?

I typed a reply, unable to fight the smile forming on my lips.

Great. I feel so... useful. Is that silly?

Of course not. I'm proud of you.

Guilt flashed through me. Nora was right. I needed to tell him. I needed to rip off the Band-Aid and just tell him. He would understand.

Actually, there's something I need to talk to you about...

Why do I not like the sound of this?

I'd barely started to type a reply when my phone blared to life. "Hey," I whispered.

"What's wrong?" His words were clipped, only tightening the knot in my stomach.

"I... uh, well you know it's the Centennial Gala in a couple of weeks? My mamma and her friend are on the planning committee and they thought it would be nice if I went with Scott Fascini... as his date." The words spilled out in a single breath.

"What the fuck did you just say?"

"Nicco, please, you have to understand. If I say no—"

"Meet me out back in ten minutes."

"Nicco, I can't just sneak off. I'm at work." It might have been voluntary work, but it was still important to me, and I wanted to do a good job. "Besides, Luis and Nixon are here. If they see—"

"Out back in ten, Arianne. I mean it." The anger in his voice startled me. I knew Nicco had a darker side, one he rarely let me see.

"I'm only doing this for—" The line went dead. I quickly typed another message.

I know you hate him. I'm not particularly fond of him either, but if I don't do this, my father will only get suspicious. You have to understand the predicament I'm in, Nicco. It's just a stupid gala. A few hours. I'll probably barely see Scott. He'll get drunk and find some poor unassuming girl to hit on. You have nothing to worry about. Nothing. I promise.

The lies were piling up around me. But I had to try to reassure him. Because if Nicco ever found out the truth... a deep shudder rolled through me. It didn't bear thinking about.

He didn't text back, but I couldn't stay locked in the bathroom forever. So I brushed myself off, and went in search of more biscuits, hoping Nicco would read my text and trust that I knew what I was doing.

Even if I barely knew myself.

Chapter 18

Nicco

Scott fucking Fascini.

The second Arianne had said his name, I saw red. It was a good thing I was in my Uncle Joe's garage and not with the guys, because there would have been no disguising my anger.

I think the fact that, deep down, I knew she was right only made it ten times worse.

She had to go as his date.

His girl.

When every single piece of her belonged to me.

Just the idea of him putting his hands on her made me murderous. I'd seen the way he watched her around campus, like a predator stalking its prey. It gave me the creeps, not to mention made me want to rearrange his face.

I'd stormed out of the garage, climbed on my bike, and spun out of there before I could even consider the consequences. I needed to see her, now. Luckily for me, we did business with a few places on the same block as the VCTI, so I knew the building well. Well enough, I was aware of the back entrance used for deliveries. I parked down the street, careful not to draw too much attention to myself, pulled up my hood, and headed for the VCTI. I spotted one of Capizola's men standing point outside. Ducking into the alley between the building and the adjoining store, I followed it around back and hid behind two dumpsters, waiting. Arianne had sent me a long-ass message trying to explain, but I didn't need words, I needed to look into her eyes and know this was nothing more than another one of her father's attempts to control her.

Time ticked by. I counted the seconds and then the minutes. I counted the number of bricks on the wall, the number of places I'd kissed Arianne, and all the places I was yet to kiss. I counted anything to stop me from storming into the VCTI and forcing her to leave with me. Despite every cell in my body wanting to do things my way, I knew Arianne already had enough people trying to control her. She didn't need me to become another.

Another five minutes went by and there was still no sign of her. Maybe I'd been too harsh, too quick to lose my temper. I dug my cell phone out, ready to text her again, when the big steel door swung open. Arianne stood there, two huge trash bags slung behind her. She stepped gingerly out of the door and headed straight for the dumpsters. I allowed myself a minute to look at her. She looked so focused, so determined. The corner of my mouth lifted. She was fucking beautiful, even taking out the trash.

"I know you're out here," she said. "I felt you the second I opened the door."

Stepping out from my hiding spot, I held up my hands. "You got me."

She dropped the bags and ran at me, slamming her hands into my chest. "Don't ever hang up on me again." Her eyes were wild as she glared up at me.

"Jesus, Bambolina." I rubbed my breastbone. She was feisty when she was angry, but she was also a lot stronger than I gave her credit for. "Let me guess, your old man had you take self-defense lessons?"

"Something like that," she mumbled, stepping back to put some distance between us. "I'm sorry I hit you."

"I'm sorry I hung up on you. Was that our first fight?" She didn't answer so I crooked my finger at her. "Come here."

Arianne fell into my arms, and I pulled us behind the dumpster, giving us a sliver of privacy. "Look at me," I said, gliding my hand to her jaw. She looked up through damp lashes.

"I know you don't want me to go, but I have no choice, Nicco. Not if I want to protect you."

"You have a choice, Arianne; you always have a choice."

"You think I want to go with him? I can't stand him." Her expression darkened. "But my father has it into his head that it's good for business, whatever the hell that means."

"And you're okay with that? You're okay with being his pawn?" The words came out harsher than I intended and I immediately regretted it when Arianne flinched.

"We're all pawns really." She gave a small shrug. "This is no different."

I hooked my arm around her waist and spun us around so I could crowd her against the wall. My hand pressed the brick beside her head as I leaned in. "You can't seriously expect me to stand by and do nothing while you're out there, on a date, with him?"

"Nicco, please..."

"Please what? Give you my blessing that I'm okay with this? I will *never* be okay with this." My voice shook. "What if he wants to dance? To touch you right here." I smoothed my hand over the curve of her hip, and her breath hitched.

"What if he leans in to kiss you, right here." My lips gently sucked the skin beneath her ear. "What if, at the end of the night, he expects more than just a kiss? What then?"

"What would you have me do?" Arianne fisted my hoodie, her big honey eyes pleading with me. "If I don't go, it looks suspicious."

"Fake a stomach flu. Say you have to study. Say *anything*. But don't go." *I'm begging you.*

Arianne's eyes squeezed shut, a rogue tear slipping down her cheek. I swiped it away, feeling like a royal dick. But I couldn't bear it. I couldn't bear the thought of her on his arm, laughing and smiling at him.

Even if it was all an act.

She opened her eyes, staring at me with such intensity I felt it all the way down to my soul. "It's all pretend, Nicco. An act. I feel nothing for Scott, *nothing*."

"You're going to do it, aren't you?" Disbelief coated my words. "Regardless of what I say, you've already made your decision?" I staggered back, pain crushing my chest.

"Nicco, please. It's the only way to appease my father."

"And if our roles were reversed? If it was me about to take out another girl. To make her believe my act? You'd be okay with that?"

Her eyes flared with jealousy. "I'd trust you knew what you were doing. Even if I didn't like it."

"I see." A wall slammed up between us. I was too pissed to listen to any more. Even though part of me knew she had no choice; the other part, the dominant possessive alpha inside me, refused to accept it. Refused to understand why she wasn't going to stand her ground on this, why she was going to be the good little princess and do what daddy dearest said.

It was fucking bullshit.

Heavy silence hung over us. Thick and suffocating.

"Say something," she whispered.

"There's nothing left to say, we're done here."

"D- done?" That single word gutted me. I should have corrected her. Right then, I should have told her I just needed time to process everything; that once I'd cooled off, we'd talk.

But I didn't.

Instead, I left her standing there, wondering if we were over before we ever got started, and walked away.

∞∞∞

"Nicco." Alessia ran toward me, her long hair cascading over her shoulders like a golden river. "I didn't know you were stopping by."

"Can't I come see my sister on a whim?" I hooked my arm around her waist, guiding her back toward the house. I was here on business, after being summoned by my father. But Alessia didn't need to know that. Besides, after leaving things so shitty with Arianne, some quality time with my sister was exactly what I needed.

"I've been helping Genevieve prepare dinner. Will you stay?"

"Sure, kid."

She rolled her eyes at me. "You're like three years older than me, Nicco."

"Yeah, but I'm a guy, and you'll always be my *baby* sister."

"Bite me." Alessia poked out her tongue and took off down the hall toward the smell of rich tomato sauce.

"Nicco," Genevieve greeted me, giving me a tentative smile. "We weren't expecting you. I'll set an extra place."

"Don't go to any trouble," I said.

"Oh, it's no trouble. I'm sure your father will be happy you're joining us." My brow quirked up and heat flooded her cheeks. "I'm sorry. I didn't mean—"

"Relax, it's all good." Her position within the house was blurred. She cared about my father, that much was obvious, and I was pretty certain he cared too. He just didn't care enough to promote her from housekeeper to lady of the house. I think, deep down, he still hoped that one day Mom would return. When we all knew she wouldn't.

She had escaped a life I never would.

"It smells good, Sia."

"Genevieve has been teaching me."

"You're too kind, mia cara." They shared a warm smile.

It hadn't been easy leaving Alessia here, with my father. But she adored him, and he doted on her. Besides, it wasn't like I could take her with me. So it made me breathe a little easier knowing she had Genevieve. Matteo's mom also came over a lot, and although they were in different grades; Arabella, his sister, and Alessia went to the same school.

My sister had people. She was surrounded by family who loved her. Aunts and uncles and cousins. So even though it brought back too many bad memories being in this house, I knew it was the right place for her to be.

"Is he around?" I asked Genevieve but it was my sister who answered.

"He's in his study... waiting for you." She cut me with a

knowing look.

"Busted." My lip curved.

"You're lucky I love you, Niccolò." Alessia smiled, before turning her attention to the pan of bubbling sauce.

I grabbed a beer from the refrigerator before heading down the hall to find my father. "Come in," he called before I'd even rapped my knuckles against the door.

I ducked inside, taking a seat on the long couch pushed up against the wall. He was busy at his desk.

"What's eating you?" he grumbled.

"Nothing."

"Don't give me that bullshit." He clicked his tongue. "I can feel the tension rolling off you. What did Enzo do to piss you off this time?"

I chuckled. "You're barking up the wrong tree, old man."

"Hey, less of the 'old man' talk, kid. I've still got some good years left in me yet." One of his thick dark brows rose as he looked over at me. "You're dragging on this job; why?"

Jesus. Trust my father to cut straight to the point.

"It's complicated."

"Did you go after the cousin?"

I nodded. "Tristan confirmed she was on campus. Of course he didn't say anything else."

"So..."

"He went running back to his uncle and told him we knew."

"Fuck, Niccolò." He slammed his hand down.

"She's still on campus but she has protection. Around the clock bodyguards. They never let her out of their sight.

I'm not sure she's the—"

"She's the key, Son. It has to be her." Relaxing back in his chair, my father ran a hand down his face.

"You'd really hurt an innocent girl to get leverage over Capizola?"

His expression darkened. "Don't tell me you're turning soft like Matteo? She's a means to an end, Niccolò. I'm not expecting you to seriously harm her, just scare her a little. Enough to make Roberto know we're serious."

My hand curled against my thigh as I searched his face for any hint of the truth. I wanted so badly to ask him about five years ago. To confront him about what Arianne had told me. But if I did, it would out us, and possibly put her in more danger.

So I pressed my lips together, forcing the question down.

"Is there something you need to tell me, Son?"

Yes, I wanted to yell.

"You need to trust me to handle this," I said. "It's going to take time—"

"We don't have time. Capizola has issued another petition to the court. He's obsessed with tearing down La Riva and replacing it with some fancy mall and expensive housing. He wants to turn it into a replica of Roccaforte. This is my home, Son. *Our* home. Our great-grandfathers shook on it and now he wants to piss all over that."

"What does Stefan say?"

Stefan was my father's consigliere, his advisor and trusted friend. He was out of town right now, helping Alonso up in Boston deal with something.

"He thinks we should start paying off the right people."

"He really thinks the court will rule in Roberto's favor?"

"Capizola has as many officials on his books as we do." A guttural growl tore from my father's throat. "He can't take La Riva. If he does, we might as well give him Romany Square because it'll only be time before he comes for that too. The girl is the lucky break we need. Don't fuck this up, Niccolò. I'm counting on you."

I gave him a curt nod. What else could I do? My father believed I would do whatever it took to protect the family, and Arianne believed I would do whatever it took to protect her. And I was in the middle wondering how the fuck to make both happen without everything imploding.

"You staying to eat?" My father asked, changing the subject.

"I told Alessia I would."

"Good, it's about time you came around more. I know things have been hard on you, Niccolò. But you're a capo now. You need to start—"

"Spare me the lecture. I know what my responsibilities are."

"Son, please..." He let out a weary sigh. "I can't change the past, but I'm here, and I'm trying to be better. Alessia is —"

"My sister needs her father, I know that." But I hadn't needed him in a long time.

"You remind me so much of her." Sadness filled his eyes. "Her tenacity—"

"Don't," I said quietly, my body vibrating with frustration. "I'm going to call the guys, see if they want to come over." Rising from the couch, I walked toward the door.

"Niccolò, one day this will all be yours. Whether you

want it or not, it will be yours. Just remember, Son, heavy is the head that wears the crown."

I glanced back at my father, his eyes saying all the things he would probably never say. There was so much pain and regret and shame in his wistful stare. I knew what he meant; I knew he was trying to tell me that sometimes the life was too much. It was too easy for a man, despite all his honor and good intentions, to get pulled into the less honorable side of the life. He became quick tempered with those he loved, those he had to continually keep secrets from. He found comfort in the arms of countless goomars, women who were not his wife. And above all, he lost a part of himself.

All in the name of Dominion.

Dominion flowed through our blood, and he was right.

One day, it would be mine.

Chapter 19

Arianne

"I think I'm going to throw up." I pressed a hand to my stomach, trying to ease the ball of nerves.

"Well, you sure look the part." Nora let out a low whistle as she appraised my dress. It had taken us almost thirty minutes to get me into the damn thing. But even I couldn't deny the handiwork was stunning. The emerald green rococo style gown cinched impossibly tight at my waist, the bodice embroidered with fine gold lace detailing. It flowed over my hips into a full skirt that kissed the floor.

"I look ridiculous." I picked up the layers of material and swished them around my legs.

"You look stunning. Me on the other hand…" Nora glanced down at her own dress, her lip curling. "I look like your much poorer, much uglier cousin."

"Oh hush, you look beautiful." Her dress was simpler in style, one panel of black velvet fitted and flared around her curves with long sleeves that billowed around her wrists. Nora had taken her time curling her hair before styling mine into an intricate updo woven through with diamantes. Suzanna had sent me a necklace she requested I wear, a family heirloom apparently. It was a big gaudy black onyx teardrop pendant that hung in between my ample cleavage, all thanks to the corset bodice. I didn't want to wear it, but I knew better than to risk offending her.

Tonight was about playing a part and appeasing the parents.

"Any word from Nicco?"

"A couple of texts here and there." My chest constricted, and, this time, it wasn't the corset's fault.

Ever since that day, almost two weeks ago outside the VCTI, when Nicco walked away from me, things had been different between us. He'd texted me an apology, reassuring me he understood. But part of him had withdrawn. I felt it, felt the tether between us fade a little.

He was hurting and there was nothing I could do to fix it. Because I had to do this. If I wanted to keep our secret, I had to attend the gala with Scott.

"He'll come around," my best friend said, squeezing my arm.

"I have to get through tonight, then I'll worry about Nicco."

When he'd uttered the words, 'we're done here' my mind had instantly gone to a bad place. A place where Nicco was no longer mine. But I'd quickly realized it was nothing more than his defense mechanism. Nicco liked to be in control, but he couldn't control this.

We were puppets in a game with rules and expectations we couldn't just ignore.

"Okay." Nora leaned in, swiping some gloss over my lips. I blotted them together and forced a smile. "Ready?" she asked.

"As I'll ever be."

The sooner we left, the sooner the night would be over.

Nora opened the door, helping me navigate my dress

through the narrow opening. Luis and Nixon stood to attention, and I was sure I caught a flash of emotion in Luis' expression. "Arianne," he said, stepping forward and crooking his elbow. "Mr. Fascini is waiting downstairs with the car. May I?"

I slid my arm through his, letting him escort me down the hall. We took the elevator as it was a little tricky to navigate the stairs in my dress, but there wasn't room for Nora and Nixon, so they took the stairs.

Heavy silence hung over us, the seconds ticking by painfully slowly. Luis shifted beside me, clearing his throat. "Is there something you want to say?" I asked, craning my neck to look at him.

"I serve your father, but as my mark, my loyalty is with you." I was about to ask what he meant when the doors pinged open. "Ready?" he asked, and I nodded.

But the second my eyes landed on Scott, smirking at me through the glass doors like the cat who got the cream, I wanted to turn around and run back inside.

You can do this. I rolled back my shoulders, steeling myself. Nora clutched my hand, squeezing gently, offering me her strength. Which was good because something told me I was going to need all the strength I could get if I was going to survive the night ahead.

∞∞∞

The Montague Auditorium had been transformed into an exuberant Venetian Carnival. Masked dancers and acrobats greeted us, some eating fire, others hanging from silk ropes suspended from the ceiling. I had no idea how my mother and Suzanna, and the rest of the planning committee, had pulled off something like this, but when money was no object, the sky was the limit.

Scott kept his hand on my arm, leading me through the arch of gold and black balloons. He'd showered me with compliments on the short ride over. We could have just as easily walked, but Scott demanded an entrance, and so an entrance he got. Nora's date Dan, a guy from one of her classes, had greeted her at the steps, looking drool worthy in his tuxedo and plain black Columbine mask. Nora had opted for no mask after my mother and Suzanna requested I didn't conceal myself. I was to be visible—on display.

The noise crescendoed as we entered the inner auditorium. The seats had been cleared to make room for huge circular tables laid out in two sweeping arcs around the stage and dance floor.

"Wow," I breathed, my heart pounding in my chest. I'd never seen anything quite like it.

"This is just the beginning," Scott said, finally unhooking my arm from his. "I'll get us some drinks. Don't go anywhere."

"I wouldn't dream of it." It came out saccharine sweet.

Nora joined me as I stood taking it all in. People glanced my way, doing a double take when they realized it was me. The Capizola heir. But their stares no longer concerned me.

"Your mom sure knows how to throw a party."

"Just a shame she has terrible choice in dates."

We shared a snicker, falling silent as the woman in question breezed over to us. "Girls, aren't you a sight for sore eyes. Bellissima, you look stunning."

"Thank you, Mamma."

"And Scott? He liked the dress?"

I ignored that. "Is Papá here?"

"He's working the room. You know your father, always on the clock." She smiled brightly. "He's hoping to raise a substantial amount for the trust with the silent auction."

The Capizola Charities Trust, was one of my father's many passion projects, bettering the lives of those less fortunate.

"Oh my, Scott, look at you, so handsome."

"Mrs. Capizola." He turned on the charm, taking her hand and kissing it. "It's good to see you again."

She giggled. My mother actually giggled. Nora fake-gagged quietly beside me. "Please, call me Gabriella." She patted his cheek like they were old friends.

I didn't like it. I didn't like it at all.

I was beginning to think Scott possessed some magical qualities that blinded people to his creeper status.

"Well, enjoy the party, won't you?" She brushed a curl from my face. "So beautiful. I'll see you later, okay?"

"Goodbye, Mamma." I watched her walk away, a strange tugging sensation in my stomach.

I put it down to the guy beside me. Scott was oblivious to my disdain at being here with him; that or he just didn't care.

"To us." He lifted his glass and waited. Reluctantly, I clinked my champagne flute against his. "To friends," I enunciated, holding his stare.

"We'll see about that." He winked.

"Excuse me, I need to visit the ladies' room."

"Do you want me to come with?" Nora asked, but I shook my head. "You should stay with Dan." He looked a little out of his depth. "I'll only be a few minutes."

Luis followed me as I wove through the sea of bodies. Some girls wore dresses like mine: big, ostentatious gowns that blended in with the decor. Others had opted for sexy and seductive over authenticity and style. I spotted Sofia and my cousin. She made a beeline for me, her lips parted as her wide-eyed gaze swept down my dress.

"Holy shit, Ari, you look... wow." She leaned in to kiss my cheeks. Somewhere over the last two weeks we had become friends. Or at least, she no longer treated me like a social leper. I still wasn't entirely comfortable with her touchy-feely approach, but her dislike of Scott made her an ally in my eyes. Unfortunately, Sofia's change of attitude hadn't extended to Emilia, who still looked at me like I was the competition. I wanted to talk to her, to ask if Scott had tried to hurt her too, but I didn't know how to approach someone who spent most of their time burning holes into the side of my face.

"Cousin." Tristan kissed my cheeks. "You look amazing."

"Thanks. I'm actually trying to find the bathroom. Do you know—"

"See those doors over there." Sofia pointed across the room. "Straight through there. It's like maze back there so don't get lost."

"I'm sure I can manage. See you both later." I grabbed my skirt and took off. Luis kept close behind me, but I didn't mind. Not when there were so many people.

I burst through the doors, relieved to find the hall empty. "I'll wait right here," Luis declared. "The ladies' restroom is down the hall on the right. There's only one way in and out, so you'll be safe."

I gave him an appreciative nod, hardly surprised he knew the layout of the place. "I won't be long."

"Take all the time you need."

My brows crinkled. Luis seemed different. I didn't want to make assumptions, but he seemed concerned. Obviously not concerned about my safety, because I knew he and his partners working the Gala tonight wouldn't let anything happen to me. But he was acting fatherly, almost like he cared about me.

I moved down the hall, slipping through the archway marked 'Ladies restrooms' and went inside a stall. It wasn't easy navigating through the many layers of skirts, but I eventually managed. After flushing, I headed back out to wash my hands, almost jumping out of my skin when I came face to face with a figure all in black wearing a Pierrot mask.

"You didn't reply to my text," Nicco said.

"What are you doing here?" I didn't know whether to throw my arms around his neck or slap him upside the head. "You can't be here, Nicco."

He snagged my wrist, pushing off his mask, and pulled me into him. "I missed you too, Bambolina." His words settled the fire inside my tummy, and I melted against him.

I'd been so dead set on seeing tonight through, I hadn't allowed myself time to think about the consequences. About how Nicco must be feeling about me being here with Scott.

"Tell me you're still mine," he whispered against my ear, nibbling the skin there. Desire shot through me as I clung onto him.

"Nicco, you have to go before someone sees—"

"Ssh, amore mio. I needed to see you. I needed to know we were okay."

"Where have you been?" I slammed my hands into

his chest, my resolve slowly cracking and crumbling. "Two weeks, Nicco; it's been two weeks."

"It's complicated. But I'm trying to figure it out, I promise." He curved his hand around my neck and drew me closer, fixing his mouth over mine. Nicco kissed me with such intensity I couldn't breathe. I couldn't do anything except give in to him.

"Jesus, Arianne," he breathed against my lips. "You look incredible."

"I feel completely ridiculous." My eyes dropped down, but I noticed he wasn't looking at my dress, he was staring right at my chest.

I cleared my throat, smirking when he looked at me and swallowed hard. "If he so much as lays a single finger on —"

"It's not going to happen, I promise. I'm here for my mother and father, that's it."

Nicco's jaw clenched as he warred with himself. I knew he probably wanted to confront Scott, to stake his claim on me. But his hands were tied, just as mine were.

"You really should go."

"Okay." He let out a resigned sigh. "Just promise me you'll stick close to Nora and your bodyguard, okay?"

"Is something going on?" I frowned. There was something in his voice, an urgency that had alarm bells ringing.

"Everything is fine." He kissed my head again, lingering. "You should go first."

"Wait, how did you know I was here?"

"I am always watching you, Bambolina, even when you think I'm not. Now go."

We shared a last look as Nicco backed away, breaking our physical connection.

"I love you," I mouthed, before slipping out of the restroom. I couldn't stay to hear him say it back, because although I was trying so hard to be strong, inside I felt weak.

Inside, I felt on the verge of begging him to get me out of here.

∞∞∞

"Ladies and gentlemen, alumni, and friends," my father's voice rang out across the room. "It is my honor to welcome you here tonight, in the stunning Montague Auditorium, to celebrate the University's Centennial. My family has a deep history with our great county and it is thanks to my forefathers that you stand here now, in this institution of such academic greatness and achievement, shaping the lives and minds of so many of our children."

A chorus of applause filled the room. Scott stood beside me, nodding and clapping much like every other person gathered here. I couldn't help but feel betrayed. My father presented an air of such integrity and humility, but it was all a front. Hiding a history he'd worked hard to keep buried.

It was bullshit, and I was so over it.

"You need to smile," Nora whispered through gritted teeth, nodding to where my mother stood at my father's side, frowning in my direction. Suzanna and Mike Fascini flanked his other side, the four of them donning nothing but smiles and solidarity as my father held the audience in the palm of his hand.

"You need to relax, babe," Scott leaned in, his lips almost brushing my ear. I jerked away, swishing the loose curls around my face at him.

"Behave," Nora mouthed. Her date, Dan, had relaxed somewhat since Scott had been keeping his drink full. No one seemed to mind that a lot of the people here were under twenty-one. Champagne flowed freely and there was a bar for beer and other drinks. I, on the other hand, had refused his last three attempts to get me a refill.

My father's voice became a monotonous drone as he talked about regeneration and building a secure future for all of Verona County. My thoughts drifted to Nicco and the future. I wanted to believe we had one, but standing here, at Scott's side, with our parents watching on, it was hard to see a way over the obstacles stacked in front of us.

I searched the crowd for any signs of his familiar Pierrot mask, but it was impossible to see in the sea of faceless bodies.

Suddenly, a wave of exhaustion rolled through me and I swayed on my feet, grabbing Scott's arm. He glanced down at me, frowning. I forced a smile, waving him off.

"Hey, are you okay?" Nora asked me.

"Just tired and I can barely breathe in this dress."

Thankfully, my father chose that moment to wrap up his speech. The crowd broke into another round of raucous applause.

"What's wrong?" Scott asked.

"I just felt a little light-headed, I'm fine now."

His eyes narrowed. "You sure?"

But there wasn't time to answer as our parents swooped in on us, showering us with affection and compliments. "Arianne, mia cara, whatever is the matter?"

"She's feeling a little overwhelmed." Scott addressed the four of them, answering for me as if it was his God-given right.

"Is this true, mio tesoro?" My father stepped forward to inspect me.

"I'm fine." I pushed his hand away. "I think the dress is a little too tight."

"You should get some fresh air," Suzanna suggested. "Scott, why don't you take—"

"Actually, Mamma, Papá," I said feeling another strange wave of exhaustion crash over me. "I don't feel so well." My eyes fluttered closed as I reached out to steady myself.

"Ari," Nora's voice edged into my thoughts as I blinked at the six pairs of concerned eyes watching me.

"I think I should take her home," Nora said.

"I've got it, Aba... Nora," Scott interjected, wrapping an arm around me.

"Sweetheart," my mother pressed her hand against my cheek. "Scott will take good care of you; isn't that right?"

"Of course, Gabriella. I'll see to it that she gets back to her dorm room."

"I'm fine." I tried to brush him off, but Scott was already leading me away from them. "Scott," I hissed but it came out more of a pleading cry. "Just stop for a second."

I needed to catch my breath.

Thankfully, as we exited the main auditoria, Luis caught up with us. "Arianne?" He silently asked me what was wrong.

"I- I don't feel so good." My limbs were getting heavier. "Can you please take me back to Donatello House?"

Scott didn't protest but he didn't release me either, keeping his arm wrapped firmly around me. People were looking, their curious stares no doubt working overtime. I'd arrived with Scott, now I was leaving with him. I could only imagine what conclusions they were drawing, ready to spread around the gossip mill on Monday morning.

I just hoped Nicco wasn't out there, watching this.

Watching me.

Luis moved away, whispering into his radio.

"Arianne?" Nora called after me and I turned to see my friend come running through the doors. "Are you okay?"

"I'm fine." I pursed my lips. "I think I just needed some air."

"You're sure?" Concern glittered in her eyes. "I left Dan chatting to your father. He looked terrified."

"You should probably go save him. Luis and Nixon are going to take me back to the dorm. Stay, have fun. One of us should."

"What about..." She glared in Scott's direction.

He flipped her off, chuckling to himself.

"Scott is going to do the right thing. See that I get home okay and then leave," I said loud enough for him and Luis to hear me.

I knew he wouldn't walk away yet, just as I knew my parents had seen a golden opportunity to let him be my knight-in-shining-armor. Just as I also knew I had to find a way to put an end to this charade. For Nicco's sanity, and my own.

Nora hugged me. "Are you sure? I can come back with you?"

"It's fine," I said. "I promise. I have Luis and Nixon with me."

"Okay, don't wait up." She kissed me, before picking up the skirt of her dress and hurrying back inside.

"Alone at last." Scott stepped closer.

"Really?" I quirked a brow.

He smirked but didn't reply as he ushered me toward the main doors. "Nixon is bringing the car around." Luis stepped up beside me, but my father's deep voice said, "Actually, Luis, let Scott take her."

"Of course, sir." Scott stood taller, shooting me a knowing smirk.

"Papá." I turned toward my father, frowning. "I would prefer it if Luis and Nix—"

"Don't make things difficult, mio tesoro." He cupped my face, brushing his thumb over my cheek. "Scott will take good care of you, and who knows, maybe you'll get chance to talk."

"Talk." My brows knitted. "I'm not sure..."

"Come on, Arianne." Scott took my elbow. "We should get going. I'll take good care of her, sir."

"I know you will, Scott."

"Mr. Capizola," Luis cleared his throat. "Perhaps it would better if I drove them—"

"You can follow in a second car," I heard my father say as Scott led me out of the building. "Give the two of them some space. They have much to discuss."

"But, sir..." Luis' voice trailed off as he met my gaze, a flash of concern passing over him. But then the door swung closed and he was gone.

At least the fresh air cleared some of the fogginess in my head.

"Miss Capizola," Nixon said, approaching me as I made my way down the steps. I had been relieved to be heading back to the dorm, wanting nothing more than to get out of this dress and into something more comfortable. Something that didn't make it feel like I was fighting for every breath. But now, it was turning into a nightmare. I didn't want Scott to accompany me, not without Luis or Nixon.

"Where's Luis?" Nixon asked.

"He's—"

"Inside, talking to the boss." Scott held out his palm. "You can hand over the keys and go bring the second car around. I've got this."

Storming off toward the car, I clenched my teeth, anger and frustration rippling through me. I climbed inside, pulling my skirt in behind me, and slammed the door. Scott climbed in a few seconds later. "Shall we?"

"You're enjoying this, aren't you?" My head spun again and I sucked in a harsh breath.

"Everything okay over there?"

"It's this dress, it's… it doesn't matter." I looked out of the window, relieved when I saw Luis and Nixon on the steps, watching after our car. They would follow behind us and they would make sure Scott left after walking me to my room.

"You need to learn how to relax, princess."

"Can we *not* do this?" I snapped, rubbing my head as another wave of exhaustion crashed over me. It was more intense this time, a heaviness pulling me down. "I think something is wrong." I cried, my body and mind splintering apart as I began to fall. Strong arms caught me, "Just let go," a voice said. "I've got you."

"Nicco?" My lips formed his name, hoping, *praying*, he was here to fix this. Something was wrong. I didn't feel right. Locked away in my own thoughts, unable to move.

"I've got you," someone whispered as the world shifted again.

I felt weightless.

Free.

And then I felt nothing.

∞∞∞

"N- Nicco?" I peeked an eye open, wincing as I waited for everything to stop spinning. "What are you—"

"I knew it," Scott growled, roughly grabbing my hair. My head snapped backward, a garbled cry spilling from my lips as I tried to make sense of my surroundings. It was dark. So dark I could barely see him. But a sliver of moonlight shone down on the devil, illuminating his features—monstrous eyes, evil smirk—as he moved above me. Fear pinned me in place, dropping to the bulge in his slacks.

No.

Oh God no.

I willed myself to move, to do something, *anything*, but I was paralyzed.

"Have you given it up to him? Did you let him fuck you like a little whore?" He backhanded me so hard my teeth clattered. Pain exploded along my cheekbone, tears burning the backs of my eyes.

"W- why are you doing this?" Everything still felt hazy as if I hadn't quite woken up, frozen somewhere between a nightmare and reality. "What did you do to me?"

"Such a good little princess, only drinking one glass of champagne. I wanted to do this the good old-fashioned way. Get you wasted and then fuck the daddy's little princess right out of you, but I had to get... creative."

"D- drugged me..." My head rolled back as I fought against whatever sedative he'd given me. "Where's... Luis?

Nixon?"

"No one's coming." He trailed a finger down my neck, toying with the sweetheart neckline of the corset. "We're all alone and I can take what's mine, finally."

"Stop, p- please stop."

He backhanded me again, pain exploding behind my eyes. I cried out, the sound drowned out by his maniacal laughter. "I'm going to have so much fun with you. I had hoped you'd be more... willing but this will work just as well." Scott cocked his head, staring down at me like I was a science project he couldn't quite figure out, as he ground himself against me. "I've never had a girl tell me no before. Well, not after enough drinks."

Bile rushed up my throat.

"My father will—"

"What?" Scott leaned down, pressing his lips to the corner of my mouth. "What will good old Roberto do? He practically handed you over on a silver platter. You think he's going to believe anything you say? He needs me. He needs my family. This, you and me, it *is* happening. The sooner you get on board with that, the better." His fingers dipped into the tight corset and he began clawing at my breasts.

"Stop, you're hurting me." I tried to lift a hand to fight him off, but my muscles were heavy like lead.

"Let's see what you're hiding up here shall we?" He yanked up the skirt before shoving his hand into the layers of material. It was foolish to think they would provide any protection against him, but I couldn't help the pang of disappointment that hit me when his greedy fingers met the soft flesh of my thighs.

"Bingo." He chuckled darkly, pinching and pawing at my legs, moving higher and higher until he grazed my panties. "Lace," he crooned. "For me? You shouldn't have."

"D- don't, please." I tried to force my knees together, to do anything to keep him out. But Scott was strong, his careless touch like sandpaper against my skin. Tears began leaking from my eyes.

"Beg me to stop," he taunted against my lips. "Go on. Beg."

I pressed my lips together in defiance. He could hurt me, touch me against my will, but he would not break me. I refused to give him that power.

"Oh, you want to play it like that? We'll see how long you last." He bit down on my lip, splitting the skin. Blood trickled into my mouth, painting his lips red as he grinned at me. "By the time I'm done with you, that fucker Marchetti won't ever want to touch you again."

I tried to turn away from him, to smother my tears as his fingers tore through the last of my defenses and pushed inside me. A pained cry bubbled up my throat, but I refused to give him the satisfaction. Scott could take everything from me, but I would give him nothing in return.

"I'll make you want it," he drawled, licking my face, tonguing my mouth.

I went into myself, deep into a place where Scott couldn't reach me, until my body became nothing more than an empty vessel. He felt the shift, grew frustrated at my unresponsiveness. He rubbed harder, kissed me deeper. Yanking down the corset, ripping the material wide open, he bit my breasts, desperately trying to elicit a response.

But I gave him nothing.

"Fucking bitch," he spat at me, wrapping his fingers around my neck and squeezing until I thought I might pass out. "I'm going to fucking destroy you, and when I'm done, when he no longer wants you and you come crawling back to me, I'll make you beg for more."

He snapped open his belt and shoved down his slacks over his hips. I knew then; I wasn't going to make it out of this unscathed. Scott intended on taking everything from me.

My body.

A piece of my soul.

And my virginity.

It was the one thing I'd been determined to give on my terms, and he was going to take that away from me.

Something in me snapped.

I couldn't do it.

I couldn't *not* fight.

With everything I had left, an almighty roar tore from my throat as I thrashed against him, trying desperately to gain leverage. Scott was stronger than me, but he wasn't expecting me to fight. He lost his footing and slipped off the bed, "Cazzo!"

I tried to pull myself up, but he was too quick, too overpowering. I bucked and kicked, screamed until my lungs burned and blood pounded between my ears. But in the end, I failed.

Scott backhanded me so hard, my vision blurred and I felt myself slip under again.

But not before I felt him move above me.

Not before I felt him tear through my innocence and rip out a piece of my soul in the process.

Not before I cried, "Nicco, forgive me."

∞∞∞

I dreamed of voices. Angry voices arguing about a girl.

"She needs a hospital. I'm taking her—"

"N- Nicco?" the girl cried out.

"She needs him. I don't care what you say. I'm taking her to him."

"Now you hang on a second, kid. She's my responsibility. I should never have let her—"

"What... what did you do?"

"Nothing, I... fuck. We should call her parents."

"We both know that isn't going to help her. Not tonight. Something about all this doesn't add up."

"Nicco, where are you?" the girl murmured.

"Shit, she's waking up. Your choice. Are you going to let me help—"

"Fine, *fine!* But so help me God, you better know what you're doing."

Silence followed...

The feeling of weightlessness.

Flashes of pain and agony.

Of complete helplessness.

"Nicco?" the girl cried out again.

"Ssh, Arianne. I got you. I got you."

Arianne?

That couldn't be right.

I was Arianne.

Which meant this wasn't a dream at all.

It was my worst nightmare come true.

Chapter 20

Nicco

The loud knock startled me. I jumped off the couch and hurried to the door, yanking it open. "Bailey?"

He looked pale, eyes wild and lip quivering as he croaked out, "It's Arianne."

My spine stiffened. "What happened?"

He tipped his head to his car and I saw her. Shoving past him, I jogged down the stairs and pulled open the door. "No," the single word cracked open my chest. "No, no, no..." Pain like I'd never experienced welled in my chest, clenching my heart like a fucking vice.

Arianne, my sweet innocent Arianne, was lying across the back seat, her dress torn, blood dried on her lip and down her chin. A red welt was streaked across her cheek, the skin sore and tender. Her dress was all wrong, the material ripped and twisted at her thighs, stained with patches of red.

No.

No!

I squeezed my eyes shut, trying to swallow down the acid rushing up my throat.

"N- Nicco," she murmured, barely conscious, her eyes closed as she hugged something.

Fuck.

It was a hoodie.

One of *my* hoodies.

I felt Bailey step up beside me. "What the fuck happened?" I growled, feeling myself unravel.

It was obvious what had gone down, but I needed to hear him say the words. I needed confirmation before I drove back to MU and put a bullet through Fascini's skull.

"After we got rumbled and you and the guys split, I stayed around."

"You were watching her?" My eyes slid to his, although it physically pained me to take my attention off Arianne.

"Yeah. I couldn't just leave her, ya know?"

I don't know what I'd done to deserve this kid, but he was as loyal as fuck. Even if he did have a serious issue with following orders.

"She left with him. Her security detail followed behind, but when I got to the dorm something didn't feel right. One of her bodyguards was standing guard outside the building, but he looked... I don't know. Pissed. So I stuck around. Douchebag eventually left, and I snuck in through the back door and went up to her room. I can't explain it, Nic, but I just knew something wasn't right. Her bodyguard must have felt it too because when I got there, he was there too. And I took one look at his face and knew... I didn't even have to go inside her room."

My fists clenched at my side, agony and anger swirling inside my chest like a vortex. "And Fascini?" I gritted out.

"He was long gone. The bodyguard wanted to call her parents and we almost got into it, but in the end, he knew I was right. He knew I had to get her out of there."

Clamping my hand on his shoulder, I squeezed. "You

made the right call, thank you."

"She's hurt pretty badly," he whispered. "She might need a doctor."

Fuck, he was right. She needed medical attention, someone to make sure he hadn't done any internal damage. I exhaled a steady breath, trying to rein in the emotion bubbling inside me. "I have to take her to my father."

"But Nicco—"

"I know. I know, Bay, but this changes everything." Arianne needed help. She needed proper care and attention. My father could get her that, off the record. He could also make sure everything was logged appropriately should we need to use it as evidence for the future.

Not that the legal route was an option for a piece of shit like Fascini. He didn't deserve jail time, he deserved a slow and painful death.

And he'd sealed his fate, the second he'd laid a hand on my girl.

"Can you drive?' I asked Bailey, and he nodded, running a hand down his face.

"Let's go, before someone sees us." I closed the back door and went around to the other side, gently easing into the back seat of his Camaro. Careful not to hurt Arianne, I lifted her head, cradling it in my lap and brushed the hair from her face.

"N- Nicco?" Her eyes fluttered open. "Is that you?"

"Ssh, Bambolina. I've got you. Everything is going to be okay now."

Bailey got into the car and fired up the engine. "You sure about this?" His eyes met mine in the rear-view mirror. "We can take her to my mom."

"No, it has to be my father." He was the only one who

could protect her now.

Bailey nodded, reversing out of the parking lot and taking off toward the smaller road out of campus. I dug around in my jean pocket and pulled out my cell phone.

"Niccolò," my father answered on the second ring. "Is it done?"

"We have a problem," I said. "I need you to call Doc and tell him to meet me at the house in fifteen minutes."

"Should I be worried?"

"I'll explain everything when I get there." Hanging up, I dropped my head back against the seat rest. Arianne was out cold, gentle sobs still racking her body. There was every chance she was in shock.

"Bailey," I choked out, feeling my grip on reality waver.

"Yeah, cous?"

"Hurry."

∞∞∞

We beat the doctor. Bailey pulled into the driveway and cut the engine. "What do you need?"

"Go on ahead and make sure my sister stays in her room. She doesn't need to see this."

"And Uncle Toni?"

"Let me deal with him."

"Maybe we should call Matteo, strength in numbers?"

"No," I said. "Not yet." The fewer people who knew for now, the better.

Bailey got out of the car and headed toward the house.

I gingerly ran my fingers through Arianne's hair. "Amore mio," I whispered, "can you hear me?"

"Nicco?" She began to move but cried out. "It... it hurts."

I swallowed down the tears of anger burning my throat and opened the door. "I'm going to carry you inside, okay?"

"D- don't leave me."

"I won't, I promise."

Arianne wasn't only in shock, she was barely conscious. There was a likely explanation. One I didn't want to consider.

That motherfucker had drugged her.

I inched her fragile body out of the car and hoisted her into my arms. The front door swung open and my father came bounding down the steps, his eyes widening at the sight of the lifeless girl in my arms.

"Tell me you didn't—" A feral growl rumbled in my chest, and my father paled. "I'm sorry, Son. I should have known better. Who is she?" he asked, flanking my side as we approached the house.

"Not now, later. Is Doc on his way?"

"Should be here any minute. Want me to have Genevieve prepare the guest room?"

"I'm taking her to my room. When he gets here, send him straight up." Arianne stirred in my arms.

"Niccolò, wait." His hand landed on my shoulder and I paused, glancing back at him. "What happened here, Son? Talk to me?"

"I'll tell you everything once I've made sure she's okay."

Genevieve appeared in the hall, and gasped. "I'm sorry, I didn't—"

"Gen, help my boy, okay?"

"Of course, Anton..." she hesitated. "Mr. Marchetti. I'll get some water and towels."

It wasn't Genevieve's first rodeo. She'd been around my family for long enough to know the drill. Except it wasn't usually half-conscious girls in beautiful ball gowns; it was men in blood-soaked shirts.

"Please bring them to my room," I said, moving toward the stairs.

"Bailey?" my father asked.

"Distracting Alessia."

He nodded. "Go see to her, but then you and I need to sit down."

I didn't stick around, taking the stairs two at a time. It had been almost eighteen months since I'd lived here but my room was the same. Same charcoal bedding and gray curtains. But it didn't *feel* the same.

I lay Arianne down on the middle of my bed, tucking a pillow underneath her head. Her hand reached for me as her eyes flickered open again. "Nicco." It was a whimper.

"I'm right here."

Calm settled over her again, as if my presence soothed her. Genevieve knocked, before peeking inside. "How is she?"

"Honestly, I have no idea."

"She was... attacked?"

I nodded, unable to speak over the lump in my throat.

"What can I do?" she asked.

"Will you stay with her, when the doctor gets here? I'm not sure... I can't be here when he..." Fuck. My vision blurred as a wave of emotion crashed over me.

"Niccolò." Genevieve touched my arm. "You care about her." It wasn't a question, so I didn't offer an answer. "I'll stay with her; you have my word."

"Thank you."

I heard voices downstairs, the familiar Italian lilt of our family doctor. He was used to attending to emergencies; used to patching up stab wounds and bullet holes. He'd stitched nearly every scar on my body. But I doubted he'd ever dealt with something like this.

Footsteps sounded on the stairs and then my father's voice drifted into the room. "Niccolò, Doc's here."

"Come in," I said moving to the door.

Genevieve moved to Arianne's side and I knew she was in safe hands. I wanted to stay, to be right there while the doctor checked her over, but I wasn't sure I was strong enough to see... I pushed the thoughts down.

I greeted my father and Doc. His gaze went over my shoulder and he muttered, "Dio santo! She might need a hospital."

"No," I snapped. "No hospitals. If you need specialist supplies, I'll have someone go get them. But she stays here."

"Okay, Nicco. I'll examine her and see what we're dealing with."

"Thank you." I let him enter, watching as he snapped on some plastic gloves and approached the bed.

"Come on, Son. Come share a drink with me." My father walked off, and I followed, knowing no amount of liquor could fix this.

∞∞∞

"Who is she?"

Three little words I'd dreaded ever since the day I realized I couldn't walk away from Arianne, seemed so insignificant now. She was lying upstairs drugged and beaten, assaulted and broken, and everything else no longer seemed important.

"Arianne Capizola," I said, meeting my father's hard glare with my own.

"I'm sorry, you need to repeat yourself, Niccolò, because it sounded like you just told me the Capizola heir is upstairs in your bed. And I know you're not that fucking stupid, boy."

"It's her."

He flexed his hand, the one curved around his glass of bourbon. I was hardly surprised when the glass whizzed past my face, shattering against the wall behind me. "Tell me you haven't fallen for her? Look me in the eye and tell me, that you haven't gotten into bed with the enemy."

"She is *not* the enemy. I know you think she's the way to Roberto, but she isn't." I kept my voice calm and controlled. "They're using her too. I don't know all the pieces of the puzzle yet, but he's using his own daughter to align himself with Fascini. We're missing something, but I'm telling you, she is not the enemy here."

My father collapsed back in his chair, scrubbing his jaw. Anger simmered in his eyes. He was pissed and I didn't blame him. After all, I'd played him. I'd put Arianne first over the family.

In our line of work, I'd committed the ultimate betrayal.

"What happened, Niccolò? And I want the truth, Son. Not the version of events you want me to know. The truth. Whatever you say in the next five minutes will determine your punishment."

I flinched at the severity in his tone. But as long as Arianne was safe, I could handle whatever he decided.

So I told him.

For the next ten minutes, I told my father everything that had happened over the last few weeks. From finding Arianne that first night, to sneaking her out to the country club, discovering her true identity, right up to the moment Bailey turned up at my door tonight.

"Jesus, Niccolò, of all the girls on campus, it had to be her."

"I know it doesn't matter, but I want you to know I never planned for this to happen."

He regarded me, disappointment clouding his eyes. "Do you love her?"

"More than I have ever loved anything else," I said without hesitation.

"Cazzo, Niccolò! And this Scott Fascini, what do we know about him?"

"I have Tommy looking into it. His family is wealthy. They own several businesses in and around the county. Capizola Holdings, and Fascini and Associates, are set to sign a multi-million deal to support Roberto's redevelopment plans for the west side of the river.

"Arianne's parents have been pushing for her to date Scott. I think they think it's good for business. But the guy is a real piece of work. I'm almost certain it was him who attacked her the first night I met her. If I'm right, Arianne was adamant she didn't want to go to security, and I'm betting she never told her parents. Which means she must know they'd have a hard time believing her." It was the only thing that made sense.

"Jesus Christ," my father let out a low whistle.

"You saw what he did to her." I clenched my fist against my thigh. "I had to bring her here. I had to."

"We'll deal with that later. Who knows she's here?"

"Me, Bailey, you, Genevieve, and Doc."

"Okay, let's keep it that way. See what Doc has to say. I'll make a few calls, see what I can find out about the name Fascini."

"Shit, the bodyguard; he knows Bailey took her."

"You think he'll tell Capizola?"

"I'm not sure. Bailey seemed to think he's on her side..."

"Which might mean we can use him. If Roberto finds out his daughter is missing, the clock starts ticking before he points his finger in our direction."

"Bailey can get to her friend. Maybe she can buy us some time?"

"Set it up. But for the love of God, Niccolò, make sure that kid doesn't end up in the wrong hands."

"He can handle it." I knew he'd do it if I asked him.

"Get out of here." My father grabbed the telephone. But I paused at the door and glanced back at him.

"Why are you doing this? Helping her?"

"Because despite what you think of me, Son, I took one look at that girl in your arms and saw Alessia. The thought of someone ever doing that to my little girl..." Pain filled his expression. "And because maybe this can benefit both of us."

"What do you mean?" I wasn't sure I liked where this was heading.

"I take it you've already decided you'll do whatever it takes to protect her?"

I nodded.

"Maybe there's a way for you to keep the girl and for us to use her as leverage over Roberto."

Of course he would see it like that. I should have known.

My jaw ticked.

"Don't look at me like that, Niccolò. You brought this upon us. *You*. You had to know the second you decided to bring her here that you were hand delivering me the leverage we need to get Roberto to back off."

He was right.

Of course he was fucking right.

Still, it made it no easier to swallow.

"I won't let you hurt her," I said defiantly.

"And I would expect no less. She is your woman, your heart, you should protect her with your life. But do not forget, love blinds us. It makes us weak. There will come a day when you have to make a choice; the family or your heart, and it is a choice I do not envy."

Arianne.

My choice would always be Arianne.

But could I really sacrifice everything? My family. Alessia and Bailey. Matteo and Enzo. My aunts and uncles.

Even my father.

Could I condemn Arianne to a life bound to a mafioso who had broken the cardinal code of honor?

"I can see you have a lot to consider. Go be with your girl. I'll make some calls."

"Thank you." I left his study and closed the door, dropping my head against the wood. When Bailey had turned up at my door and said Arianne's name, all I could think about was getting to her, protecting her. I didn't stop to consider the consequences because all I saw was her.

But my father was right. I had set into motion a chain of events there was no stopping now.

A chain of events I didn't know if either of us was ready for.

A chain of events, we might not survive.

∞∞∞

I quietly knocked on the door. It cracked open and Genevieve smiled at me. "She's been asking for you." She pulled open the door to reveal Arianne propped up in my bed, talking in hushed tones to the doctor.

"Nicco," she breathed, tears pricking her eyes.

I went to her side, sitting on the edge and taking her hand in mine. "How are you feeling?

"A little groggy and sore." Her gaze dropped, but I gently tipped her chin back.

"You're safe now."

"Niccolò, if I might have a word outside?"

"Sure, Doc. I'll be right back, okay?"

"Promise?" Fear clouded Arianne's eyes.

"I promise. Genevieve will be right here."

"Of course." She nodded, moving to the other side of the bed.

"I'll stop by tomorrow to check on you, okay, Arianne?" Doc said.

"Thank you, for everything."

He gave her a warm smile before leaving the room. I followed him into the hall, closing the door behind me. "How is she?"

"Miss Rossi," his brow rose with doubt. But he knew the drill; he wouldn't ask questions. "Is strong. It's likely she was given a sedative leading up to the assault. I have given her fluids and treated several minor cuts. She informed me that she was a virgin so I have also taken blood samples to run a full work up as she can't remember if her attacker wore a condom."

My eyes shuttered, my fist barreling toward the wall. Pain splintered through my wrist and up my arm.

"Nicco..."

"Sorry, Doc," I drew in a sharp breath, cradling my hand against my body. "Carry on."

"Very well. Since Miss Rossi is not on birth control, I have also issued her with the emergency contraceptive pill. I would like to stop by tomorrow and document any new bruises. She has some faint bruising around her throat which suggests—"

"I don't need the specifics," I ground out, "I just need to know if she's going to be okay."

"Like I said, she's strong. After some fluids and pain-killers she already seemed much brighter. But Niccolò, this type of thing affects everyone differently. The physical scars will heal, but the emotional scars may take more time." His expression turned grim. "I have taken photographic evidence and swabs. I assume you'll want me to analyze and record those?"

I nodded, too choked up to reply.

"Go be with her, the rest can wait until tomorrow." He squeezed my shoulder.

"Thanks, Doc, I appreciate it."

He took off down the hall, and I went back into my bedroom. Arianne and Genevieve were talking but her eyes immediately locked on mine.

"I'll leave you both. If you need anything..."

"Thank you." I offered Genevieve a weak smile, and she left us, tension filling the room.

"I'm sorry," Arianne sobbed. "I'm so, so sorry."

I rushed to her side, dropping to the side of the bed and gathering her in my arms. "You have nothing to be sorry for, amore mio."

"B- but I wanted it to be you. I wanted to give you all my firsts, Nicco. Every single one."

My heart stopped as pain obliterated me. "*Never* think like that." I cupped Arianne's face gently in my hands and gazed down at her. "You're safe and you're here, it's enough."

"But—"

"Ssh." I kissed the corner of her mouth, careful not to touch the split in the pillow of her bottom lip.

"It feels like a dream, like I wasn't really there."

"Do you want to talk about it?"

"Not yet." Her lips quivered but she didn't cry. "I would like a bath though. The doctor said that would be okay if I felt up to it."

"A bath? I think I can do that." Dropping a kiss on Arianne's head, I stood up. "Will you be okay if I..." I flicked my head to the adjoining bathroom door.

"I'll be okay." She gave me a small smile. My strong girl putting on a brave face even in the direst of circumstances. Being around Arianne grounded me, forced the beast living inside me back into its cage.

"Give me five minutes, okay?"

She nodded, and I disappeared into the bathroom, turning on the faucets of the corner tub before searching for some bath salts. Or maybe salt wasn't a good idea. Shit, I didn't know the first thing about any of this crap.

Searching through the cabinet, I settled on a bottle of lavender and chamomile bath soak, adding a couple of drops to the water. Bubbles began to froth, a floral aroma filling the air. I grabbed some towels from the rack and hooked them beside the tub.

When I went back into the room, Arianne was already trying to get out of bed. I went to her side, wrapping my arm around her waist and taking her weight. "Okay?" I asked and she nodded, pain etched into her expression.

She was wrapped in a fluffy robe, but I could see the faint bruises Doc had told me about. "Don't look at me like that, please," Arianne's voice cracked.

"Sorry." I swallowed. "It's just hard seeing you like this."

"I'm still the same person, Nicco."

Jesus. My body trembled, white hot fury pulsing through me, as I led her into the bathroom. But I knew I needed to be strong for her.

"Can you get undressed if I give you some privacy?"

"No," she blurted out. "Stay, please." Arianne reached for me, threading our fingers together. "I need you."

Slowly, I pushed the robe off her shoulders, gently inching down her arms. Her breath hitched a couple of times, but Arianne was otherwise quiet. She wore nothing underneath, the doctor no doubt collected her underwear and dress for evidence, or as we usually called it, leverage.

I tried to keep my eyes on her face, to ignore the bite

mark on the curve of her breast, or the one further down.

"Nicco," she whispered, palming my cheek. "Don't let him in here with us."

"How do you do it?" I asked, feeling so far out of my depth I was drowning.

"You're here. With you by my side, I can do anything." She leaned in, touching her head to mine. I breathed her in, letting her words sink into me.

"I'm so sorry," I whispered. "I should have never left the gala." Not that I'd had much choice with her father's security men breathing down our necks all night.

"Stop," Arianne brushed her lips over mine, but I pulled away.

"Come on, I'll help you in." I took her elbow, guiding her into the tub. Arianne let out a little hiss as her body disappeared under the water. "Too hot?" I asked.

"It's nice. Soothing. I'm just a little... sore."

The word was like a glacier between us. I didn't want this to be about me, about how it affected me, but I didn't know how to control all the thoughts slamming into me.

I leaned down, turning off the faucets and perched on the edge of the tub. "Do you want me to go?"

"Do you want to go?"

"You know I don't."

"Good." She smiled, relaxing back against the tub. "So this is where you grew up? You know, I've thought a lot about seeing this side of your life. I hoped it would be under different circumstances." A beat passed as she swished the water around her body. "Your father knows I'm here?"

"He does. But don't worry about that right now. You're safe, and that's all that matters. Bailey has gone back to MU to find Nora. He's going to buy us some time while we figure out what to do."

"I'm not going back," she said with an air of defiance.

"We'll talk about that later."

Arianne pressed her lips together, silence settling over us. When she was done soaking, I helped her out of the tub and wrapped her in a fluffy white towel. Scooping her up against my chest, I walked into the bedroom and laid her on the bed.

"You should get some rest," I said.

"Lie with me."

My body went rigid.

"Nicco, please..."

Kicking off my boots, I went around and lay on the other side of the bed. Arianne nestled into my side, slipping her hand under my hoodie. "Bambolina, stop." I gently pushed her away. She stared up at me with those big honey eyes of hers, cheeks flushed and lips parted.

"I want this, Nicco. I *need* this." It wasn't the pain in her voice that surprised me, it was the strength. The conviction.

Arianne truly believed she wanted this.

Wanted me.

After everything she'd been through.

"You don't know what you're saying," I whispered, the words raw against my throat.

"I do." She wiggled closer, kissing my neck, dragging her tongue up my neck. Jesus, it felt so good.

But it was wrong.

Everything about this was fucking wrong.

"Amore mio, stop. *Stop.*" This time she jerked back of

her own volition.

"You don't want me?" Hurt flashed across her expression. "But I thought—"

"I want you," I admitted. I wanted her more than my next breath. But not here, not like this. "You're hurting and you're confused..."

"Confused?" She gasped, inching away from me. "I'm not confused. Nothing about what he did to me is confusing. I remember it, you know? It's hazy but it's there. His weight pressed against me. The feeling of the air being squeezed from my lungs while he..."

Anger radiated through me. Unbridled blistering anger. Scott Fascini was a dead man. Maybe not tomorrow or the day after that. But he would pay. I wanted to watch him bleed. I wanted to stand over him while he begged for his life.

Anything else was simply not an option.

"Ari—" I reached for her, but her hand shot out, keeping me at a distance.

"He raped me, Nicco. He took the one thing I promised myself would be given to the person of my choosing, on my terms. He took that from me." Tears streamed down her face, but I'd never seen Arianne look fiercer. "And I can never get it back. But I can do this. I can choose to give myself to you, Nicco. I choose *you*."

Her resolve began to slip, desperation clinging to every word. "I choose you, so please, *please* don't take this away from me too. I want you. I want you to show me how it's supposed to be. I want you to make me feel good."

I ran a hand down my face. I'd wanted Arianne ever since I'd laid eyes on her and fighting the urge to make her mine hadn't been easy. But I'd done it. I'd done it because I knew giving in would only complicate things in a way she wasn't ready for.

Yet here she was, offering herself to me. Begging for me to erase her memory of that sick fuck Fascini.

"Nicco." Arianne pressed closer, her hands going to my chest again. Her touch was corrosive, slowly decimating my walls. Walls I'd spent my whole life building. She leaned over, her lips ghosting over my jaw, the corner of my mouth. My body trembled with need. To take what she was offering. To do the right thing.

To be the better man.

But I wasn't a good man. I was Niccolò Marchetti, son of the devil, prince of hell.

Ari though, she was an angel. Pure and good. She was everything I wasn't. Everything I could never be.

Yet, she wanted me.

She'd *chosen* me.

Or maybe it was never a choice. I'd never much believed in fate or destiny. My family, like most Italian-American families living in Verona County, were Catholic. But I'd seen too much, experienced too much to have the unwavering faith so many of my elders had.

"I want you to do this, please." Her voice smashed through the last line of my defenses.

How could I deny this girl?

This strong courageous woman before me, with nothing but hope in her heart and desire in her eyes.

The answer was, I couldn't.

But tonight, I would.

I had to.

Because she needed me to make that decision for her.

"Sleep, Bambolina." I pulled her into my side, feeling

the fight leave her fragile body. "We have time. We have all the time in the world."

Arianne didn't answer and I knew she'd fallen asleep.

And I hoped peace would find her there.

Chapter 21

Arianne

I woke with a start, memories of the night before slamming into me one after another. I sat up, wincing in agony.

"Can I get you anything?"

My eyes darted to the corner of the room, landing on a petite girl with familiar eyes. "Oh, I'm sorry. I'm Alessia."

"Nicco's sister," I breathed.

"One and the same." She gave me a warm smile. "You must be the other important woman in his life."

My brows bunched together. "Arianne. My name is Arianne."

"I'm sorry... for what happened to you."

"He told you?" I pulled the covers higher, feeling the need to shield myself. I wasn't offended he'd told her, just surprised.

"Oh no, he doesn't think I'm old enough or strong enough to know stuff like that... whatever." She shrugged. "I'm pretty good at finding my way into places I shouldn't. Is it true, you're Roberto Capizola's daughter?"

I nodded. What did it matter who knew my true identity now?

Everything was different this morning.

I was different.

Scott had taken something from me, something I wouldn't ever get back. But it was more than that—he'd killed a part of me.

The truth was, Scott had changed me.

In ways I knew I didn't fully understand yet.

Tears pricked my eyes, but I would not cry. Not in front of this sweet girl trying to... distract me?

The sound of raised voices drifted into the room. "What is that?" I asked.

"That would be the aftermath of you." Alessia smiled again but this time it was sad and full of sympathy. "My cousins, Enzo and Matteo, got here a while ago. They've been like this ever since."

Enzo.

If he was here, he knew about me. It was the only explanation for all the yelling.

"I have to go down there," I said, throwing back the cover. Every muscle in my body protested, pain radiating in places I didn't even know could hurt.

"You should probably stay here," Nicco's sister warned. "He wouldn't want you to witness..." she paused, "*that*."

"It sounds like they're going to kill each other."

"It wouldn't be the first time. You have met my brother and his friends, right?"

"I..." Had no idea how to answer that. The Nicco I had fallen in love with was kind and attentive, but I knew he had another, darker side. One he'd tried to conceal from me.

Someone yelled a string of Italian cuss words. It was

quickly followed by a loud crashing noise.

"And I'm supposed to pretend none of this happens." Alessia curled a strand of hair around her finger.

"I don't suppose you have any clothes I could borrow?" We looked to be similar sizes.

"For real, you're going down there?"

"I need to see Nicco."

"Okay, then. But don't say I didn't warn you." Alessia got up. "I'll get you something to wear. And while we're at it, you might want to do something with your hair."

I touched a hand to the untamed curls. "That bad, huh?" Laughter bubbled out of me, and it felt good, and strangely cathartic.

Last night had been the single worst night of my life. But then Nicco had taken care of me and I'd fallen to sleep wrapped in his arms, and I knew I would be okay. Because while Scott had taken something from me, he hadn't managed to touch the most important thing—my heart.

That belonged to Nicco.

Always.

"For the record," Alessia paused at the door, "Nicco has never brought a girl home before." She walked away as if her words meant nothing. When in fact, they meant everything.

I smiled to myself.

Scott might have left me bruised and bitten and bloody. But he had failed to break my spirit, and that felt like a small victory.

∞∞∞

"Do I pass?" I asked Alessia twenty minutes later. She'd had to help me get dressed in the end. It had been an awkward moment I didn't want to relive anytime soon, but I'd never felt so grateful to have a stranger around to help me.

"You'll do." Her lips curved. "I should probably warn you; it isn't looking great down there. Enzo looks murderous and Nicco is like a caged animal."

"Not quite the Sunday morning I had planned..."

"Life has a funny way of playing with us."

"Thank you, Alessia. I don't know what I would have done this morning if I'd have woken up alone."

"My brother would have turned up eventually."

I didn't doubt it, but in a way, I was glad it had been Alessia and not Nicco. I could still remember the way he had rejected me last night. My head knew he was only doing the right and honorable thing, but my heart didn't quite agree. And part of me couldn't help but worry if he would see me differently in the harsh light of day.

I forced down the thoughts. There were more pressing issues. Like stopping him and Enzo from killing one another.

"Ready?" Alessia held out her hand and I slid my palm against hers. With every step, the voices grew louder, until we were standing outside a door downstairs. "You don't have to do this." She whispered, squeezing my hand. "No one expects you to get involved."

"I need to see him." I nodded resolutely, despite the band of wild horses galloping in my chest.

"Here goes nothing." Alessia let out a little sigh as she opened the door and stepped inside. I followed her, waiting for the men to notice me. But they were too busy arguing. Nicco and Matteo sat on the couch, while the man I presumed to be his father sat behind the desk, and Enzo paced. There was no sign of Bailey.

"This is bullshit," Enzo ground out. "We need to hand her back to—"

"Arianne." Nicco leaped up, staring at me with surprise. "What are you—"

"Did you honestly think she'd sleep through this?" Alessia raised a brow.

"I... shit, I'm sorry." He slowly approached me, his concerned gaze running over my face. "Bambolina..." It was a pained whisper.

"I'm okay," I said, answering his silent question.

He reached for me, brushing the hair from my face. "You need to rest."

"I slept for hours. I needed to see you."

"Niccolò," his father commanded, and I moved around Nicco to come face to face with Antonio Marchetti.

"Thank you," I said without hesitation. "For letting me stay here."

He nodded, his cool expression giving nothing away. "I'm afraid you caught us at a bad moment, Miss Capizola."

"I didn't mean to interrupt. But I had to see Nicco."

"You have got to be fucking kidding me," Enzo spat, disdain rolling off him. "Are we really going to sit here and act like this is okay? She's the Capizola heir, for fuck's sake. If he gets even so much as a scent of her being here, we might as well leave town now."

"Lorenzo," Antonio warned. "Miss Capizola is our guest. It would do you well to remember your manners."

"Uncle, I mean no disrespect, but only a few weeks ago, we were planning—"

"Enzo, *enough!*" He slammed down his hand against the polished wood. "Alessia, go and find Genevieve please. Make yourself useful."

"But, Papá—"

"Alessia..."

"Fine." She huffed. "But one day, you're going to have to accept I'm old enough to understand what this life means." Alessia fled from the room, slamming the door behind her.

"Please, sit," Antonio said, motioning to the couch. Matteo shuffled along, giving me a tentative smile as Nicco guided me over to it. We sat down.

"You've landed us in quite the predicament, Miss Capizola. I would like to hear your version of events, if that's not too much to ask?"

Nicco started to protest, but I covered his knee with my hand, squeezing gently. "I know you hate my family, sir," my voice quivered. "But I am not my father. In fact, I'm not sure I even want to call him my father right now."

"Arianne, you don't have to do this," Nicco whispered.

"Yes, I do." I met Antonio's heavy stare again. "Until recently, I wasn't even aware of our families' history. I knew nothing of my father trying to acquire La Riva for redevelopment. And I knew nothing of the Marchetti."

"Impossible," Enzo gritted out.

"It's the truth. I have spent the last five years of my life sheltered from the truth, from the world beyond my family's estate. I never questioned it, until now." My gaze slid to Nicco.

"What happened last night?" his father asked.

"No," Nicco went as white as a sheet.

My body was trembling, the memories demanding attention. The feel of his hands around my throat. His weight above me. The way he clawed at my skin. I suppressed a shudder and forced myself to take a calming breath. "Scott Fascini, the son of my father's prospective business partner, drugged and raped me."

Matteo sucked in a sharp breath beside me while Antonio looked on, his lips twisting in disgust. But it was Enzo who surprised me the most.

"Porca troia," he mumbled under his breath, clenching a fist against his thigh. "He did that?" He flicked his head to my face. I knew I looked a mess; the red welts although faded some, still visible. Not to mention the finger marks around my throat and the cut in my bottom lip.

"And worse," I confessed.

It was Nicco's turn to cuss. "Enough. That's enough. She's not on trial here."

"You're right, Son, she isn't. But if we are going to help Miss Capizola, we need to know the full story."

Just then, there was a knock at the door. "Come in," Antonio called, and the woman from last night slipped inside. She wore a simple white blouse and black pants.

"Genevieve," he said curtly.

"I'm sorry to interrupt, but Bailey just arrived and he's not alone."

"What the hell has he gone and done now?" Enzo grumbled.

"Nicco, go deal with him please."

"Me, but—"

"Now, Niccolò."

"I'll be right back, okay." He brushed his hand over mine before taking off after Genevieve.

The tension in the room doubled. Enzo was glaring at

me, his cold assessing gaze like razorblades across my skin. Antonio let out a breath as if he was about to speak, but instead settled back in his chair again.

The silence stretched on.

My heart beat like a drum against my rib cage.

So when the door swung open and I saw Nora and Luis standing behind Nicco, I almost cried out in relief. "Thank God." My best friend rushed over to me, wrapping me into her arms. I winced and she immediately withdrew "Crap, I'm sorry."

"It's fine."

"Nothing about this is fine. I'll kill him. I'll skin him alive, chop off his dick, and feed it to him, that disgusting piece of—"

Antonio cleared his throat and Nora slowly peeked over at him. "Hmm, sorry."

Enzo snorted, and the tension in the room ebbed away.

"Arianne." Luis stepped forward and I went to him. "I am so sorry. I will never forgive myself."

"It's not your fault." I hugged him tight.

"And you are?" Antonio's voice rang out.

"Luis, sir. Luis Vitelli, Arianne's bodyguard."

"I see. You were there last night?"

Luis' expression turned dark as he nodded. "I was at the building, but Mr. Capizola had requested that I give Arianne and Mr. Fascini space to... *talk*."

"Talk?" Enzo sneered. "Seems that fuck Fascini is unaware of the meaning of the word talk."

"Enzo," Nicco sighed.

"You're lucky I'm still standing here. All this time you've been seeing her, a Capizola. The enemy." He pushed off the wall and stalked closer. "You lied to me, cous, over a fucking girl."

"We've been over this." Nicco put himself between me and Enzo. Luis tried to move around me too, but I stood my ground. Refusing to be pushed aside by these men.

"I am not my father," I repeated, locking my eyes on Enzo. His nostrils flared, anger and betrayal swirling around him like a vortex.

"This isn't a game, little girl. It's a fucking war. We make a wrong move and people get hurt. People die. Are you ready for that? Are you ready to watch the people you care about get hurt? Are you ready to—"

"You need to back off, Enzo. I'm warning you." Nicco growled the words, the air shifting around us, crackling with anticipation.

"Uncle Toni," Matteo interjected. "Maybe you should —"

"Leave them be." He dismissed him. "She needs to see this."

"You betrayed me." Enzo lunged for Nicco, clipping his face with a resounding crack. Nicco managed to elbow his best friend and the two them circled each other.

"You need to stand down. I'm warning you, E."

"Stand down? I need to knock some fucking sense into your thick skull, cous. She's the enemy. You're in bed with the enemy."

"Vaffanculo!" Nicco ground out, throwing up his hands in surrender.

"She is in the middle of this, Niccolò," Antonio interjected. "Whether you like it or not. The question is, is she strong enough to handle it?"

Everyone looked at me. I felt their stares burning into

my face as I looked ahead. I didn't have all the answers. I was barely holding myself together, my body broken and sore. But if I showed even an ounce of weakness, I knew Nicco's father would use it against me.

Maybe even send me back into the arms of my father.

Stepping around Nicco, I looked to Enzo and then Antonio. "I am not my father," I said again. "He betrayed me. He lied and kept his secrets to protect me, but then handed me over to Scott Fascini like I was nothing but a prize to be coveted. I am not going back there. I- I can't. I'd rather die." The words echoed around my skull. I hadn't intended to say them, wasn't sure I even meant them, but I needed Nicco's father to understand I wasn't just a pawn in this game.

"I love your son, Mr. Marchetti. I choose him. Always."

What was I saying?

Antonio Marchetti didn't care about me; he'd tried to have me killed when I was just a young girl.

He probably couldn't wait to dangle me in front of my father as leverage.

Oh God...

Nora rushed to my side as I swayed on my feet. "Ari," she cried.

But it was too late.

Everything was crashing down around me. The temporary strength I'd found, crumbling like sand beneath rain. Nicco flanked my other side, his arm wrapping around my waist, taking my weight. Luis moved up behind me.

We'd drawn an invisible line in the sand. But I didn't expect Matteo to cross it and stand beside Nicco.

"Well, well, isn't this interesting." Antonio folded his hands on the desk and leaned forward. "Lorenzo, care to throw in your position?"

"I'm still deciding." He'd moved back to the far wall, arms folded over his chest, a purple shadow forming around his eye. Nicco hadn't come off unscathed either, a small cut along his brow and some swelling around his lip.

"I'm taking Arianne back up to my room." he said quietly. "And then we will settle this." Nicco cut Enzo with an icy look, before scooping me into his arms and carrying me out of the room.

∞∞∞

"How are you feeling?" Nicco stroked my hand. He'd carried me back to his room and insisted I stay put until the doctor arrived to check on me.

"A little tired."

"What were you thinking, coming down there and confronting my father?"

"I wanted to see you."

He inhaled a harsh breath. "This is a delicate situation. If anything happened to you... because of me, I would never forgive myself." Pain edged into his expression.

I sat up, cupping his face. "I meant everything I said. I choose you, Nicco."

"You do not know what you're saying."

"How can you say that to me, after everything?" Tears pooled in my eyes. "I love you. It doesn't even begin to come close to how I feel about you. You are my life."

"Ti voglio sempre al mio fianco," he whispered. "Do you know what it means?"

I could pick out a word or two, but I hadn't grown up speaking fluent Italian like a lot of Italian-American families living in Verona County.

Nicco leaned in, brushing his nose over mine. "It means, I want you by my side, always. Sei tutto per me, Arianne Carmen Lina Capizola."

"You're everything to me too." Our lips met in a gentle caress. "I was so worried you might feel... differently about me."

"Bambolina, I love you. You are my life. Nothing will ever change that." His eyes burned with a fierce possessiveness. It wrapped around me like a warm blanket. "But the road ahead of us is not simple, you have to know that. This life, the family, it isn't a choice. I can't walk away, Arianne. If we do this, if you meant what you said, by choosing me, it means you're choosing this life. And I should be a better man, I shouldn't let you make that choice."

"It's done," I said. "I won't take it back, Nicco. Not now, not ever. I wasn't sure I meant it downstairs, but I know I did. I don't want to live in a world without you, Niccolò Marchetti. I won't."

A knock at the door broke our connection. Nicco let out a weary sigh. "Yes?"

It opened and Antonio appeared. "Niccolò, I would like to speak with Miss Capizola, alone. If that's okay?"

"Arianne?" Nicco asked me and I nodded.

"Come in, Mr. Marchetti."

"I'll be right outside, okay?" Nicco dropped a kiss on my head, moving past his father.

"The guys are waiting for you. I think Miss Abato would also like to talk to you. She's an interesting one, isn't she?"

I smothered a chuckle, dreading to think what Nora had possibly been saying to Antonio. Nicco left us, and Antonio took the chair beside the bed. The family resemblance was stark: same dark eyes and strong jaw. The Marchetti men had eyes that could look straight through you.

"It would seem you have bewitched my son, Miss—"

"Please, call me Arianne."

"Very well". He gave me a small nod. "I haven't seen Nicco care the way he cares for you with anyone except Alessia. When his mother left, it affected him far more than he has ever acknowledged. This life, it demands a man to harden his heart, Arianne. It doesn't mean we don't feel; quite the contrary. Sometimes we feel so deeply that it can be suffocating. But it's different for mafioso. We are men of honor, bound to the code of omertà. Do you know what that means?"

"Yes, sir. It's a code of silence."

"At its most basic definition, yes. But it is so much more than that. It means family first. And I'm not talking about family in the traditional sense." He gave me a pointed look. "Life with Niccolò will be difficult. There will be times he cannot talk to you, times when he disappears and he cannot tell you where he is. You will read things in the papers, see things on the news. But you can never ask. That is the code of omertà and I have seen it ruin more relationships than you can count."

He glanced away, lost in his own thoughts. "It cost me my wife, Arianne. The love of my life. So you see, while I commend your unwavering faith to stand at my son's side, you should know that loving Niccolò is a life sentence your heart probably won't survive."

"And if I still choose Nicco? If I choose to stand at his side?"

"Then I hope you are ready for hellfire to rain down on you both. Because your father won't just roll over and accept this. He will fight, Arianne. He might have renounced his roots, his blood, but it is still inside him. And when he does come, we will have no choice but to retaliate. It will be war."

"You know," I said. "You're not at all what I expected."

"No?" His brow rose. "And what did you expect?"

"Well, for someone who gave the order to have a young girl murdered, I expected someone more... monstrous."

Antonio's eyes clouded with surprise, but he didn't flinch. "A monster has many disguises, Arianne. You would do well to remember that."

"So you're not denying it? You did order a hit on me?"

"Does Nicco know about this?" He ignored my question.

"I told him what my father told me, yes."

"Very well. I need to speak with my son. Please excuse me."

"That's it? No apology? No explanation? I spent five years of my life in solitude because of you, Mr. Marchetti, I think I deserve to know why."

"And you will, all in good time." He rose, smoothing down his jacket. "Doc should be here soon. If you need anything, I'll have Genevieve see to you."

I dropped my head back on the pillow. If I thought Nicco was a lot, his father was something else entirely.

And I couldn't help but think there were still pieces of the puzzle yet to reveal themselves.

Chapter 22

Nicco

"You really love her?" Enzo looked at me like he no longer recognized me. It stung but I knew I deserved it.

"I do, cous. I know it's not what you want to hear, but she's it for me."

"Jesus," he let out a low whistle. "The Capizola heir. I knew there was something about her. I just didn't realize it was because you were bang—"

I levelled him with a hard look, and he threw up his hands. "My bad. I'm still pissed at you, probably will be for a good while yet, but even I can't deny what that fucker did to her makes my blood boil."

"Is she okay, really?" Matteo asked. He was still sitting on the couch. Luis and Nora had gone up to say goodbye to Arianne. They were going to buy us some time until we figured out what the fuck to do next.

"I think she's holding on by a thread."

"She's strong," he said. "I've never seen anyone stand up to a roomful of guys like that before. Let alone Marchetti men."

He had a point. She had been fierce if not a little reckless.

There was a knock at the door and Luis poked his head inside. "She's sleeping."

Thank fuck. At least if she was asleep, she wasn't causing trouble.

"I thought you should know her mother called Nora while we were up there."

"Did Arianne talk to her?"

He nodded, slipping further into the room. "Turns out Fascini went back to the party last night after..." Luis drew in a harsh breath. "He told them Arianne had gotten sick on him and was so embarrassed she kicked him out. He reassured them he would check on her today."

"Motherfucker," I roared, my jaw clenched impossibly tight.

"Easy, cous." Matteo stood up. "What else did the mom say?"

"She asked Ari if she needed anything. Nora grabbed the phone at that point and said Arianne had made a dash for the bathroom, adding it was probably best she stayed away until whatever it was had passed. It should buy you some time."

I gave him an appreciative nod. "What about Roberto? Has he been in touch?"

"He texted me earlier requesting I stay put until anything changes."

"And what about your partner? Is he going to be a problem?"

"I'll handle Nixon."

"Okay, so we have the rest of the day and tonight if we're lucky. But we need to figure out what happens next. Arianne has already said she won't go back to the dorm." Not that I wanted her anywhere near that place. Not after what he did to her there, in her own goddamn room.

Anger flared inside me and I rubbed my temples, trying to rein in the urge to go after him.

"Hey, you okay?" Enzo asked me with a concerned expression. I gave him a tight nod, forcing myself to take a deep breath.

"I'll speak to Nora," Luis said. "We may have an idea."

"Can we trust her?"

"Who, Nora?" Luis balked. "She loves Arianne more than anything. You don't need to doubt that girl's loyalty one bit."

"Okay," I said, "and thank you. For everything. It makes things a little easier knowing she has someone on their side watching over her."

Luis held my stare with his own. My father had already ordered his tech guy to run a background check on Luis Vitelli. He was squeaky clean, except for his current employer being Roberto Capizola. But Luis wasn't mafioso, he didn't operate under the same codes as we did. He was hired help. And hired help usually had a price. Turns out, finding Arianne after Scott's attack was enough to turn him.

"You have my number," I said. "If anything changes, use it."

With a final nod, Luis disappeared out of the room.

"I like him," Matteo declared.

"You like everyone."

"I only like you sometimes."

Enzo flipped him off, then his expression darkened. "So what the fuck do we do now?"

"You two go find Alessia and try to smooth things over. I need to speak with my father."

"Babysit? You want us to baby—"

"Come on, E." Matteo fought a grin. "We can put an ice pack on your face. It might improve things a little."

The two of them jostled each other out of the study. I dropped onto the couch and let out a long breath. Things were moving too fast; the pieces of the puzzle multiplying by the second. Arianne was safe, for now. But it still left the issue of what we were going to do when tomorrow rolled around.

"Niccolò." My father entered their room, closing the door behind him. "I learned some interesting things after speaking to Arianne."

Shit.

His eyes fixed on me, dark and assessing.

"She told you," I breathed.

"And yet, you said nothing. Why?"

"Because I knew it would reveal our secret and I didn't want to put her in harm's way."

"That must have been very difficult for you."

"Finding out my father, a man I thought I could trust, ordered a hit on a *child* and subsequently drove my mother away, was fucking difficult. But I managed." Bitterness coated my words.

"Watch your tongue, boy." His tone was scathing. Antonio Marchetti might have been my father, but he was still the boss. And you never disrespected the boss. "You know," he went on, "I always wondered what drove Roberto to hide his heir away." His fingers tapped the desk.

"Wait a minute." I digested his words. "You mean you didn't order the hit?"

"Niccolò," he sighed. "I am many things, but I am not a child murderer. You believed her? You really thought I could—"

"The timelines fit." Confusion and guilt slithered through me. "Mom left right after it happened."

"I see." He was quiet for a second, contemplative. "It would appear there are things happening not even I understand. But I promise you, Niccolò, I did not order that hit on Arianne."

"But if you didn't, who did?"

"That is what I intend on finding out."

Jesus, we couldn't catch a break. The revelations just kept on coming.

"But Mom—"

"Coincidence, or there might be another explanation." His brows furrowed. "We have more pressing issues to deal with right now though."

"Like how we keep Arianne safe without starting a war?"

His lips pressed into a grim line. "Exactly. Go be with your girl, she needs you. I'll consult Vincenzo and Michele, get their input."

"Do you think that's a good idea?"

"Niccolò, they are your uncles. My capos. I trust them with my life. And now, we must trust them with Arianne's life. I suspect Vincenzo won't like it. But Michele will be on our side."

"So *we're* on the same side?" I wanted to be one hundred percent sure.

"Son, even if you tried to walk away from that girl, something tells me she would find a way to glue herself to your side. She has made her choice. And you made yours the second you brought her here. Whether I like it or not, she's one of us now."

"Thank you." Relief sank into me. I hadn't realized how much I needed him to say the words until they were out there, hanging between us.

He gave me a tight nod. "We still need a plan. And you should prepare yourself for the fact that she might have to return to her family, at least until we can figure out our next move. But Arianne has my protection, I give you my word."

I got up, going to the door, but his voice gave me pause. "There's still the issue of Scott Fascini. He'll get what's coming to him, Niccolò, but until we know more about his family, you are to stay away from him. That's an order. Understand?"

I pressed my lips together, anger vibrating through me.

"Niccolò, you are not to go anywhere near Fascini, do you understand?"

"I'll try." It wasn't what he wanted to hear, but it was the best I could do for now.

Fascini had hurt Arianne. Stolen her innocence. He deserved nothing less than my hands around his throat squeezing the air from his lungs.

I would have my pound of flesh.

It was only a matter of time.

∞∞∞

"This all looks amazing," Arianne said. The second she'd smelled Genevieve's cooking, she had wanted to come downstairs. I couldn't deny her. She seemed lighter somehow. Like a weight had been lifted since our conversation this morning. Doc had stopped by to see her again and was happy with her progress.

"Alessia made pie," Genevieve said over her shoulder. "I have a feeling it's going to be her best yet."

My sister beamed, standing two inches taller, and guilt coiled around my heart. I'd left her. As soon as I'd been able to, I'd moved out and abandoned her. Yet, she'd never blamed me. She never made me feel anything less than her brother, her protector.

It was more than I deserved.

"Nicco?" Arianne's hand curled into my sweater. "What's wrong?"

"Nothing." I dropped a kiss on the end of her nose. "Everything's fine."

Alessia caught my eye and frowned. She was too perceptive for a sixteen-year-old. I should have known she wouldn't stay put last night, or this morning. She was a perpetual thorn in my side, but I loved her dearly. Everything I did, everything I would do in the future was to secure her future. To make life safe for her.

Only now I had two lives to think about.

Sliding my arm around Arianne's chest, I pulled her back against me. She let out a soft sigh, completely at ease in my family's kitchen. Alessia had already taken to her, eager to know everything there was to know about Arianne and her life at MU. Matteo, although quiet, had sided with her without question. Even Enzo was slowly coming around to her. She'd completely bewitched my friends and family. And more and more, it was beginning to feel like Arianne Capizola belonged here, at my side.

"You two are so adorable," my sister crooned.

Enzo snorted, rolling his eyes at us.

"Maybe you and Nora could finish what you started?"

Arianne said, smothering a giggle.

He stood up and glared at her. "I need some air."

Me and Matteo chuckled. Enzo didn't date. He barely talked to the girls he hooked up with. He and Nora were complete opposites, but then I knew first-hand that sometimes opposites attracted.

"You shouldn't push his buttons." I whispered against the shell of Arianne's ear. She shivered, tilting her head to one side. I couldn't resist flicking my tongue over her pulse point, pressing my lips there.

"You should probably close your eyes, Sia."

"Screw you, Matteo," Alessia shrieked. "I'm sixteen. I know what sex is. I'm practically the only junior *not* doing it."

My head whipped up as I stared at her. "What did you just say?"

"Nicco." Arianne squeezed my arm.

"She's sixteen." I protested. "She shouldn't be talking about sex."

"Almost seventeen." Alessia glared back, and Genevieve laughed.

"This is nice," she said wistfully.

"It won't be nice when I lock my sister in her room for the next year."

Arianne stiffened and I cussed under my breath. "Sorry, that was insensitive."

"It's okay. Nicco's right though, Alessia. You should wait. So many girls rush to have sex and they regret it. Wait for someone who deserves you, someone who will treat you right." There was no missing the sadness in her voice.

Pain flashed through me.

"Crap, Ari," my sister rushed out. "I'm sorry. I didn't..."

"It's fine, I'm okay."

"You're nothing short of amazing, Bambolina," I breathed against her neck.

"That," Alessia added, a goofy smile plastered on her face. "I want what you guys have."

"I can't argue with that." If Alessia found someone who loved her even half as much as I loved Arianne, she would be a lucky girl. But he'd still have to pass the brother-test first.

My father joined us and the six of us ate. He even hooked his arm around Genevieve and pulled her down onto his lap, feeding her generous amounts of chicken. Her laughter filled the kitchen, but she quickly grew quiet, blushing profusely, when they realized we were all watching. "I should go check the pie," she said, excusing herself.

"What?" my father barked, smoothing a hand over his hair.

"Nothing, old man." I smirked.

Something was changing between us. He'd sided with me and Arianne, it was more than I could have hoped for.

My cell phone vibrated, and I dug it out of my pocket. "What is it?" Arianne asked as I read the incoming message.

"Nothing," I tried to school my expression. "I need to go make a call."

"Nicco..."

"Welcome to my world," Alessia grumbled, shoveling another piece of chicken into her mouth.

"Be right back."

Enzo caught my eye, but I shook my head. Until I knew more, there was no use in causing a panic. As soon as I was out of earshot, I called Luis.

"Nicco?"

"Yeah. What's going on?"

"He's here. Turned up about five minutes ago. Strolled into the building like he owned the damn place. He's demanding to see Arianne."

"Fuck." I pressed the heel of my palm against my head. "Is Nora..."

"She's in their room, packing some stuff. She doesn't want to stay here either."

"Can you get rid of him?"

"I can try but he's going to ask questions if he realizes she's not here. Leave it with me. I'll see what I can do."

"Keep me updated." I hung up and let out a weary sigh. This was a problem. If Scott learned Arianne wasn't in her dorm room, he would sound the alarm and our temporary cover would be blown.

I walked back into the kitchen, but Arianne wasn't in her seat. Matteo flicked his head to the back door, where I found my girl on her cell phone. She looked over at me, her face as white as a sheet and nodded. "Tomorrow, yes, Papá. I'll see you then."

So much for buying us time.

The clock had officially run out.

∞∞∞

"Hey," Arianne smiled over at me. "It's going to be okay." I didn't respond and she pressed closer to me, sliding her palm along my face. We were sitting in the yard with

Alessia and the guys, drinking beers and listening to Enzo and Matteo's stories about growing up in La Riva. The stories we could tell the girls anyway. I'd wanted to take her up to my room but Arianne wanted to hang. So here we were... hanging.

"Nicco," she smiled up at me, "we knew this might happen."

She was right.

Fuck. Of course she was right. Roberto would want to see his daughter eventually. I just thought we had more time. I thought we would have a plan in place before she had to go anywhere near MU again.

As it was Roberto had summoned her to his estate. It was a small mercy he hadn't wanted to visit her at the dorm, but it meant we couldn't tail her past his estate's perimeter.

"Tell me again," I said.

"Cous, we've been over this—"

"Tell me again." I touched my head to Arianne's, ignoring Matteo's heavy stare. "Please."

"We'll meet Luis and Nora just outside University Hill. Then he'll drive us to my father's estate. I'm going to tell him that a guy Nora has been seeing is starting to get a little intense and that we want to move out of Donatello House." Her eyes shuttered as she drew in a shaky breath.

"Hey," I said, brushing my thumb over hers. "I'm right here."

"I know." Two dark pools of honey settled on me.

"And if your father pushes to know who the guy is?"

"Nora will get upset and say she let it go too far. I'll add that since everyone knows who I am now, I would prefer to live off campus anyway."

"You think he'll buy it?"

"We'd be living in one of his buildings with round the clock security. Of course he'll buy it." She smiled weakly.

"Okay... and if he brings up the gala?"

"I'll affirm Scott's story. He drove me back to the dorm, walked me to the door and I got sick. I was embarrassed and told him to leave."

My jaw muscle flexed. "Okay. Luis will be there, and we'll be close by. If you need me—"

"Nicco." Arianne ghosted her fingers over my face, lingering on my lips. She leaned in, almost kissing me. "We knew our fairytale wouldn't last."

"Our fairytale?"

"Yeah, my prince whisking me off to his castle to protect me."

"Prince, huh?" I chuckled at the irony. She still didn't know everything about me. She didn't know what they called me at L'Anello's. I'd tell her.

I'd tell her everything one day.

Once we got through this.

∞∞∞

The next morning rolled around too quickly. I'd barely slept, unable to take my eyes off the sleeping angel beside me. It had been torture being so close to Arianne and not being able to touch her. Thankfully, she was exhausted and was out like a light the second her head hit the pillow. She needed to rest, to heal. She needed all her strength for whatever today would bring.

We met Luis and Nora in a parking lot just outside University Hill. Arianne dashed from the car, running straight to Nora, the two of them hugging. I caught Enzo watching, a strange expression on his face. He saw me and I smirked, earning me a, "fuck off."

Luis strolled over, offering me his hand. "How is she?"

"She's strong but I'm worried about what will happen."

"I won't leave her side, you have my word. It's likely Scott tipped off Roberto. There's no way he could know Arianne wasn't in her room, but he wasn't happy Nora wouldn't let him see her. Told me to 'go fuck myself' on his way out. The kid is unhinged." His eyes flicked over to the girls. "I wouldn't put it past him to try to hurt her again."

"He's a problem," I said. "But don't worry about Fascini. Your job here is to keep eyes on Arianne. Always her, okay?"

Luis nodded. "Do you think Roberto will buy their story?"

"It could work. I know Mrs. Capizola had to push hard to get him to agree to let her live on campus. He would have preferred her to commute or stay in one of his buildings."

"Any idea which one he'll put them in?" The more we could anticipate, the better.

"La Stella is a real possibility. It's close to the campus and smaller than some of his other buildings. La Luna or L'Aquila are both in that vicinity, but L'Aquila is popular with young single professionals working in the city. I don't think he'd put the girls there."

"Okay. E." I beckoned him over. "I want you to find out everything you can about two of Capizola's buildings: La Stella and La Luna."

"Seriously?" His brow shot up. "You're putting me on research duty?"

"Do I need to repeat myself?"

"No, *boss*." Sarcasm dripped from his words.

"Is he going to be a problem?" Luis whispered as Enzo walked away.

"You worry about Capizola and let me handle my guys. Did you sort things with your partner?"

"He wasn't looking to get on the wrong side of Capizola, so with my advice he's taking an extended leave of absence. Roberto trusts me with Arianne. He trusts that I'll call for back up if I think we need it. I have a couple of other guys on the team I trust, if it comes to that."

"What do you think Capizola's end game is, with Arianne and Fascini?"

"It's hard to tell. Mike Fascini is an elusive man, I can't get a good read on him, but the pressure seems to be coming from him for the relationship to move forward between his son and Ari."

"Okay, I've got my guy looking into them. The second he finds anything, he'll let me know. Arianne," I called over to her. She untangled herself from Nora's arms and came to me without hesitation. I pulled her into my chest, burying my hand deep into her hair. "Luis will be right there, okay? If something doesn't feel right, excuse yourself, find Luis and he'll bring you straight to me."

She eased back to gaze up at me, tears glossing her eyes. "Don't cry." My voice cracked. "I couldn't bear it."

"I'm so angry at him, Nicco. He might as well have given Scott permission to..." Arianne swallowed, her eyes fluttering closed.

"Bambolina, look at me." My thumb smoothed over her cheek. "I won't let him hurt you again, I promise."

Her resolve began to crack so I kissed her, pouring everything I felt into each touch, every stroke of my tongue, until her gentle sobs subsided turning into soft moans.

"Niccolò," she breathed.

Someone cleared their throat, probably Enzo, the cocky fucker.

"You should go. Remember, stick to the story, and I'll talk to you later, okay?"

Arianne nodded, drying her eyes. My cousins flanked my side as Luis led her over to Nora and guided them both into his SUV.

"She's strong," Matteo said. "She'll be okay."

"And if she isn't?" Enzo had to say the one thing I didn't want to think about. I glared hard at him, but I found no malice there. In fact, if anything, he looked as worried as I felt.

"She's strong enough," I said through clenched teeth.

She had to be.

Chapter 23

Arianne

"Mia cara, are you feeling better?"

"I'm okay." I clutched the scarf around my neck. Alessia had thought it would be a good idea to conceal the faint bruises around my throat. Thankfully, with a little concealer and make up, the marks on my face and the split in my lip were barely visible now.

"Where is Nora?"

"She headed to the cottage to see her parents. Actually, I was hoping to talk to you and Papá about something."

"It would seem we all have much to discuss then." My father appeared at the end of the hall. "Come, let us move to the sitting room."

"Scott was really quite worried about you," my mother started as we followed my father down the hall. "Did he stop by to check on you earlier?"

"Gabriella," my father grunted, and she fell silent.

I hated this.

Hated that I no longer trusted my father or his motivations. He'd always been so dead set on protecting me, on keeping me safe, but now when I looked at him all I felt was betrayal.

We sat around the ornate coffee table while my

mother poured us some tea. My father had taken the chair opposite me so there was no avoiding his sharp, assessing eyes.

"I spoke to Scott earlier, mio tesoro. He seemed concerned that you wouldn't let him in to see you."

"Papá, he told you what happened last night? I was so embarrassed, and I still felt a little unwell. I asked Nora to tell him I wasn't feeling up to visitors."

"Arianne, must you make it so difficult for him? He cares about you."

"I am sorry, Papá. His affections are too much. I'm not ready for..."

"Roberto". My mother laid a hand on his thigh. "This is all new to her. We are perhaps rushing something that needs more time. A more subtle approach."

"What do you mean, rushing something? What something, Mamma?"

"Oh, Arianne, my sweet girl. You are a young woman now. You must have... desires. Scott can show you the world. He will court you, woo you to your heart's content."

"Woo me? Really, Mamma?" I balked. If only she knew what Scott liked to do to innocent girls in the dark, I'm sure she would be horrified. But I couldn't risk telling them. Not yet. Not when my father seemed so set on making it work between us.

"Arianne," my father clipped out. "He is not an ogre. He will cherish you, mio tesoro. That is all a father wants for his daughter."

"What about what I want?" Tears pricked my eyes as I tried desperately to stay strong. "I feel nothing with Scott. It isn't romantic, it's hard work. We have nothing in common, and he..."

"He what, Arianne? Tell us?" Concern flashed in my mother's gaze.

"He is much more experienced than I am. He expects things... things I am not ready for."

My mother glanced at my father, and a seed of hope unfurled in my stomach. Maybe she would understand. Maybe she would tell my father it was too much to expect me to be with someone I didn't love.

But a mask of indifference slid over my father's face, as he let out an exasperated breath. "He is good stock, Arianne; everything you could hope to find in a partner. Scott is a man of honor, of traditions. He would never seek to harm you."

But he already has, I wanted to scream. Instead, I steeled myself, biting back the tears threatening to fall.

"It is too much, Papá," I croaked.

"You just need to give him a chance, Arianne. Spend time together, get to know each other. I'm sure you will see you have much in common. These things don't come overnight, they take time and effort. You'll see."

He was wrong though.

When it was right, when someone was meant to be yours, it did happen fast. It happened so fast you didn't see it coming. Before you knew it, your life was entwined with theirs, the fabric of your souls inexplicably woven together. As if Fate herself had willed it.

"Scott would like to take you out tomorrow night. I've told him you are looking forward to it."

"I see." Anger vibrated inside me. So much so, my hands began to tremble. I stuffed them under my thighs and took a calming breath. "Is that all?"

"You had something you wished to discuss with us?"

"I did." I inhaled a deep breath. It was now or never. "Nora has found herself in a difficult situation. There is a guy... he hasn't hurt her or anything like that, but he's becoming a bit of nuisance—"

"Give me his name and I'll have security deal with him."

"Nora doesn't want that, Papá. You see she feels responsible. She gave him the wrong impression and now he's infatuated with her. It's quite sad really. He's always hanging around the dorm building though. So we were thinking, we'd like to move off-campus."

"Off-campus?" My father sounded suspicious.

I nodded. "Honestly, now everyone knows who I am, the attention is stifling. We spend all our free time in the dorm, like prisoners. And now Nora has gained an unwanted admirer, it just all feels like too much."

"Sweetheart," my mother said. "Did something else happen? That's a big request, Arianne. You know how hard I worked to get your father to agree to let you live on campus."

"I know, I do, and I'm so thankful for the experience. But honestly, it's not all I thought it would be. I think we'd be much happier in an apartment off-campus. Just the two of us." I glanced at my father, trying to read his expression. "I think I'd feel safer too."

His eyes softened and I knew I had him. My father, despite some of his decisions of late, still wanted me safe. "Arianne, I would feel much more comfortable talking to campus security about this and smoothing this—"

"I'll give Scott a chance," I blurted out. "If you let us move off-campus, I'll try and be more open minded to the idea of us."

His shoulders sagged as he regarded me with a mix of

uncertainty and pride. "You are more like me than I give you credit for."

"So is that a yes, can we leave the dorm?"

"I'll need a little time to sort—"

"No," I said a little too hastily. Shifting on the couch, I smoothed out my blouse and smiled at my parents. "Nora doesn't want to stay there anymore... there's a little more to it. But that is her story to tell, not mine, and I'd appreciate it if you didn't railroad her into telling you."

My father shot forward. "Arianne, if Nora was hurt—"

"She wasn't, I promise. But we'd prefer to be out of there sooner rather than later."

"When did you get so grown up?" He grumbled. "Okay, I can make some calls. There are a couple of apartment buildings near the campus that could work. If I can't set it up today, you can stay here tonight." He gave me a look that said it wasn't up for discussion. "Are you certain you don't want to tell me what really happened?"

Even if I did, you wouldn't believe me.

"Like I said, it's not my story to tell." The lies came easier now. I barely felt even a sliver of guilt.

My father was wrong though, I hadn't grown up.

I'd changed.

I no longer looked to my parents for approval or validation, and I wasn't happy living a life with my wings clipped.

I wanted more.

I *deserved* more.

I deserved once in a lifetime, fated-in-the-stars, love.

The kind of love I'd found with Nicco.

He might have been my enemy by name, but our souls

were the same.

And I would tell a thousand lies if it meant protecting him and the love we shared.

"Very well, I'll make some calls. You and your mother should spend some time together. She can perhaps regale you with stories of how I won her heart. It wasn't an easy task."

"Ruffiano!" My mother waved him off, smiling at him with such adoration it made my heart ache.

My father left, closing the door behind him. I released a garbled breath.

"Oh, mia cara, come here." She patted the couch and I went to her. The second she wrapped her arm around me, I crumbled. "Oh, sweetheart. What is it? What's wrong?"

The tears wouldn't stop. I'd tried so hard to remain impassive during the conversation with my father. I'd underestimated how hard it would be to keep up the façade with my mother. The woman who was supposed to love me unconditionally.

She cupped my face gently in her hands, coaxing me to look at her. "Arianne, I am your mother. You can tell me anything."

"Can I?"

She blanched, pain glittering in her eyes. "You think you cannot trust me?"

"I- I don't know what to think any more."

"Sweetheart, you are my flesh and blood. Is this about Scott?"

I nodded.

"Did something happen? Earlier, when you were talking to your father, I sensed..." she trailed off.

Slowly I unknotted the scarf at my neck and eased it off. My mother gasped, her eyes homing in on the bruises. "I didn't get sick on Scott, Mamma. He... he drugged me, and he forced himself on me."

"No, no, no. What are you saying, Arianne?"

"He raped me." The word came out a garbled cry as my mother wrapped me into her arms again, crying with me.

"What am I going to do, Mamma? You heard Papá. He is determined that I give Scott a chance. Should I tell—"

"No, Arianne," she rushed out. "You cannot tell him. No good can come from him knowing. He will not..." My mother cussed, something she rarely did.

"He won't change his mind," I finished, my worst nightmare coming true. "He'll still make me go along with this, won't he?"

"Oh, sweetheart. This is not what I wanted for you. But I don't know how to protect you from this."

"Nicco," I whispered. "Nicco will protect me."

"You're still seeing the Marchetti boy...? Of course you are." She gave me a weak smile. "Arianne, do you understand what will happen if your father finds out?"

"I don't care, Mamma. I love him. We have a plan."

Her eyes shuttered as she murmured something under her breath again. She looked so defeated, so helpless. But then her expression hardened, and she nodded. "Okay, okay. Tell me what I can do."

∞∞∞

We ended up staying the night. By the time my father came to find me it was late and Nora was already asleep.

I hadn't wanted to spend a second longer than necessary there, but I couldn't give my father any more reasons to be suspicious than he already had. The good news was he had found an empty two-bed apartment in one of his developments in University Hill. We could move in immediately.

"I can't believe he bought it," Nora whispered as Luis drove us back to the dorm. I didn't want to ever return there but we needed to pack up our things. My mother had begged me to consider staying at the house, but the truth was, I wanted space from my father.

"Have you texted Nicco?" she asked, and I nodded.

"This is him now." I scanned his reply.

I'll be watching. Stay safe. I love you.

I showed Nora and she swooned, sinking against the seat. "He's so alpha; it's a total turn on."

"Nora..." My cheeks flamed.

"You know," her expression turned serious, "We haven't really talked about what happened, with you know who."

"I refuse to let what he did define me," I said.

"And that's commendable, it is. But maybe you should talk to someone about it, a professional."

"Like a shrink?"

"Or a therapist, yes. Someone who can give you a safe space to come to terms with it."

"I don't want to keep reliving it." I folded in on myself, as if wrapping my arms around my waist would keep out the memories.

"And I get that, I do. But you need to deal with it, especially if you're going to have to see him again."

I didn't want to think about what I'd promised my father, not now. I'd said the words to appease him, to get what I needed from him. I hadn't considered what would happen when I actually had to go out with Scott.

I'd done what needed to be done at that precise moment.

"I'll figure it out."

"Nicco is going to lose his shit," she whispered.

"Which is why we're not going to mention it yet." I gave her a pointed look.

"My lips are sealed." She mimicked throwing away a key.

I love you too xo

I hit send and pocketed my cell phone. Nicco would be close by. It wasn't ideal, but it was enough.

It had to be.

We pulled into campus less than ten minutes later, the knot in my stomach so tight I wasn't sure I could do this.

"Hey," Nora said, noticing how quiet I'd become. "You don't have to come inside. Me and Luis can get everything."

"No," I said. "I need to do this. I need to..." Silent tears flowed down my face. "I just need a minute. You two make a start. I'll wait here."

"I can call someone to come and take care of it," Luis said. "We have enough guys—"

"No, no more security."

He nodded as I clutched my cell phone to my chest. I needed Nicco. But I couldn't ask that of him. Not here, where people might see us.

"Go. I'm fine."

Luis looked uncertain but I gave him a weak smile. "Nothing is going to happen to me." He knew the threat from the Marchetti no longer existed. I was one of them now. Not by blood or name, but because the boss' son loved me. Besides, Nicco would be close by. I knew he wouldn't be able to let me out of his sight, not even now.

Reluctantly, Luis and Nora climbed out of the SUV and disappeared inside the building. Less than five minutes later, they reappeared with more bags than they could carry. Luis loaded them in the truck while Nora yanked open the door. "I can get your things. You don't have to do this."

"I do," I said, sliding out of the SUV.

Nora linked her arm with mine as we walked inside. A few girls were hanging around the common room but paid us little attention. Of course, I knew they were probably texting their friends a blow by blow account of our visit. I wondered if they would believe my story if I told them —if they would side with the mysterious Capizola heir, or believe the football playing, rich, entitled guy who had hurt me? He was one of MU's most eligible bachelors. Girls wanted to date him and guys wanted to be him. Would they turn on their prince or believe his lies?

I knew the answer.

It's the very reason I hadn't told my father. He was too blinded by Scott's shiny reputation, by his stupid business deal with Mike Fascini, to see the truth. Even if he saw the truth, I wasn't sure he wanted to hear it.

My heart sank.

With every step, my body began to tremble. Details of that night were hazy like a dream. But you didn't wake up from a dream with bruises littered over your body and dried blood staining your skin.

"Are you sure you're up to this?" Nora whispered.

"I'm fine." I swallowed the lie.

We reached the door to our room. Luis opened it and went first. I took a deep breath and stepped inside. It looked the same, but it didn't feel the same. A deep shudder rolled through me. Nora stayed glued to my side as I stood there, letting the memories of that night wash over me.

"I have most of my stuff. I'll make a start on yours." Nora squeezed my hand before leaving my side and making a start on gathering up my belongings. Luis helped her fill the small suitcase and the couple of duffel bags they had brought up. But I was paralyzed.

A knock at the window startled me and Luis grumbled beneath his breath. "What in the hell?" He stalked over to the window, pulling back the curtain, but I already knew who he'd find.

"Nicco," I breathed, inching forward. He climbed inside, his eyes landing on mine. I ran to him, flinging myself into his arms. He caught me, pressing one hand against the small of my back, fitting us together like two pieces of a puzzle.

"You're here, you're here," I cried, locking my arms around his neck.

"Ssh, Bambolina. Don't cry."

"Marchetti," Luis said, his tone full of warning.

"I had to," Nicco replied over my shoulder.

"I can't say I blame you."

"We'll give the two of you some space," Nora said.

I felt them leave, heard the door click shut behind them, but I didn't leave the comfort of Nicco's arms. I couldn't.

"Shit, Arianne," it was a low grumble. "You shouldn't be here."

"I had to." I fisted his hoodie. "I had to show myself he doesn't have power over me."

I knew it didn't really make sense, but by coming back here, it felt like I was sticking it to Scott.

"He'll pay, amore mio." Nicco slid his fingers under my jaw and tilted my face. "One day, he will pay, I promise."

He kissed me, his tongue licking the seam of my mouth, demanding entrance. It wasn't a hot intense kiss like so many of them were. It was a gentle caress, full of healing and acceptance. It was Nicco's way of telling me that no matter what Scott had done to me, I was still his.

Irrevocably and inexplicably his.

He tucked a strand of hair behind my ear, touching his lips to my forehead. "You okay?" I nodded. "Good. I already have Enzo working on La Stella. Your father has it locked down pretty tight, but we might have something."

"Okay." I hesitated. Now was as good a time as any to tell him about the trade-off I'd made with my father. But as I stared into his dark eyes, shining with so much love and possessiveness, I couldn't do it.

I couldn't ruin this perfectly imperfect moment.

There was a gentle knock at the door and Nora stuck her head inside. "We should probably go."

"She's right." Nicco kissed my hair. "We'll follow behind, okay?"

"I'll see you soon?"

"Nothing will keep me away, not even one of your father's fortified buildings." Nicco smirked. "Now go." He released me, inching back into the shadows. Luis and Nora grabbed the final bags. There were still some things we hadn't packed, but nothing that couldn't wait. I glanced one last time at my bed, suppressing a violent shudder.

"Arianne?" Nora said quietly. "Are you ready?"

"I am." I followed her out of the room.

What had started as my freedom had slowly unraveled into a nightmare. But in the midst of all the pain and confusion, I had found Nicco.

And for that, I would never be sorry.

∞∞∞

"All set?" Luis glanced at me through the rear-view mirror, and I nodded. But he had barely fired up the engine when Scott appeared, his eyes narrowed with anger.

"Get out of the car, Arianne." He slammed his hands on the hood of the car. Luis climbed out to confront him.

"He's crazy," Nora said, hitting the lock on the door. "Batshit crazy".

"Arianne," he yelled around Luis who was trying to calm him down. "We need to speak, baby. Just get out of the car and we can talk."

Lights went on in windows as people began to look outside and see what all the commotion was.

"Is he trying to cause a scene?"

"Touch me again, Vitelli," Scott growled, "and you and me will have a problem."

Without thinking, my hand curled around the handle.

"Oh, hell no," Nora mumbled. "You are not seriously considering going out there?"

"What choice do I have? If Nicco sees him..."

"Crap." She unbuckled herself. "I'm coming too."

"Just try and keep calm, okay?"

"Calm? If he so much as touches you, I'm calling the cops."

"Nora..."

"Fine. But I don't like this, Ari. I don't like it one bit."

Steeling myself, I climbed out of the SUV and marched around to Scott and Luis. He instantly stepped away from my bodyguard, focusing solely on me. "What is this bullshit, Ari? You're moving out?"

"There was an incident," I said, schooling my expression.

"An incident?" he sneered.

"Yes, a guy Nora has been seeing became a little too interested. Turns out he couldn't take no for an answer."

"Is that right?" Scott's eyes flared as he scrubbed his jaw. He took a step toward me and I inched back. "You think you can run from me, is that it?"

"I'm not running from anyone." I rolled my shoulders back, refusing to show even an ounce of fear. "We'll be staying at one of my father's buildings. I'm sure he already gave you the details."

"What game are you playing, Arianne?" His voice was a low growl as he stalked closer.

"I have no idea what you're talking about. Now if you'll excuse me, we need to get going." I began to shuffle away but his voice gave me pause.

"Does he know?" Scott called after me. My muscles locked up, my breathing ragged. "Does Marchetti know how I took the one thing he wanted but can never have?"

I turned slowly, unable to fight the tears any longer.

"Why are you doing this?"

He stalked toward me again, caging me against the SUV, his nostrils flared, eyes narrowed dangerously. "Because you're mine. Because that tight little body of yours is mine. You think you're too good for me? Better than me?" Spittle flew everywhere. "I'm going to enjoy watching you break."

Nora gasped somewhere to the side of me and then I saw him. Nicco standing over by the tree line. He looked deadly, his eyes trained right on Scott.

Scott glanced over his shoulder and snarled, "You shouldn't be here." He grabbed me, his hand digging roughly into my hip as he pulled me around to face Nicco.

"Take your hands off Arianne," he said.

"Excuse me? Didn't you get the memo, Marchetti? She's mine. Her pussy... Fuck, man, she was so tight. So—"

"I'm not going to tell you again, Fascini. Get your hands off her." Dark energy rolled off Nicco, his pupils blown and jaw clenched so tight it looked painful.

"Nicco..." I begged, silently trying to tell him to go. To leave before this got any worse.

I felt Luis approach. Nicco glanced at me. Telling me something.

And then all hell broke loose.

Luis grabbed my hand, yanking me free of Scott just as Nicco crashed into him. The two of them began fighting, fists flying and bone crunching. Nora rushed to my side, pulling me clear of them.

"Do something," I cried. "Someone do something." But Luis didn't move, staying by our side while he let Nicco and Scott battle for dominance. Scott was big, broad, and muscular from hours of conditioning on the football field, but

Nicco was quick and deadly.

"You're a dead man, Marchetti," Scott grunted, throwing his fist straight into Nicco's face. But it only spurred Nicco on. He slammed his body into Scott's, the two of them falling hard to the ground. Nicco dived on top of him, raining his fists down blow after blow, sickening crack after sickening crack.

"Luis," I yelled but Tristan appeared out of nowhere, diving for Nicco.

"Fuck, man, you're going to kill him. Stop, Marchetti, just—" Nicco slammed his elbow into my cousin's face and Tristan staggered back. He lost his footing and fell backward, cracking his head on the asphalt.

Nora rushed to his side. People had begun to swarm around the building now. "Ari," fear clung to every syllable, the world going from underneath my feet as she pulled her hand from beneath my cousin's head, her fingers coated with sticky red blood.

"Oh God, Luis."

Luis jumped into action, hauling Nicco off Scott. He was like a wild thing, fist clenched and bloody, eyes blacker than the depths of hell. "You need to go. Get the fuck out of here before the authorities show up."

Nicco's eyes finally found mine, my Nicco slowly resurfacing. "Arianne?" he choked out.

"Go," I mouthed. "Please, go."

Sirens wailed in the distance, the reality of what had just happened crashing down around me.

Scott lay groaning, his face a mangled mess, while Tristan's body was still and unmoving, a pool of dark red blood spreading around him.

"Go," I whispered, pain splintering my soul apart.

Nicco's gaze lingered, saying everything he couldn't say.

He was sorry.

He loved me.

He didn't know how to fix this.

And as quickly as he'd appeared, he was gone.

Chapter 24

Nicco

"What the fuck were you thinking?" Enzo growled as we tore out of the campus via the back road.

"I wasn't thinking." Flexing my knuckles, pain zipped up my hand and into my wrist. I was pretty sure I'd broken something, maybe a metacarpal or two. But it was worth it.

Worth it to feel Fascini's bone smash under my fist, hear him cuss in agony.

But I hadn't meant to hurt Tristan. Fuck. He hadn't looked good lying there, blood surrounding him like a red halo.

Fuck. Fuck. Fuck.

I slammed my good hand against the dash. I'd screwed up. I should never have gone after Fascini, but the second he'd crowded Arianne against the side of the SUV, I saw red.

"Uncle Toni is going to shit a brick when he finds out."

"I'll deal with him. It's Arianne I'm worried about. She shouldn't have to go anywhere near that piece of shit."

"I know, cous. But you know it's not that simple."

"Motherfucker," I roared, emotion spilling out of me. I slumped back against the leather seat, Arianne's broken expression imprinted on my mind as she'd told me to go.

She knew.

Arianne knew I'd fucked up, and yet, she'd still tried to protect me.

Jesus. There was no coming back from this.

Just then, my cell phone vibrated. "Luis?" I barked.

"It's not good news. Tristan is unresponsive. They're taking him to Verona County Hospital. Roberto is meeting us there. I have orders to take Arianne and Nora straight there. Fascini is being taken in for monitoring, but by the time the EMT's got done with him, he was up and cussing me out, so I think he'll live."

I murmured under my breath.

"How is she?"

"How do you think she is?" His tone was harsh.

"I deserve that."

"Nicco, I didn't mean... Arianne is strong," he whispered, and I knew she must be within earshot. "But she's not strong enough for the hellfire her father is about to rain down. You just changed the game, Marchetti. I hope you realize that." Luis drew in a harsh breath. "But honestly, I can't say that I blame you. I wanted to kill him with my bare hands too."

"I didn't know it was Tristan until it was too late. It was an accident," I said, knowing it wouldn't matter. Roberto's nephew was being whizzed to the hospital because of me. Because I'd let Fascini get the better of me.

Because I'd fucked up.

"Tell her I'm sorry."

"You should probably tell her yourself. I'll keep you updated." He ended the call, but he might as well have shot me at point blank range.

Because he was right.

The game had just changed again.

And I only had myself to blame.

∞∞∞

"Nicco, what happened?" Alessia ran down the drive, smothering me with attention. "I heard Daddy yelling and then he smashed something."

"Guess the cat is out the bag," Enzo grumbled, heading for the house. "It was nice knowing you, cous," he called over his shoulder, before disappearing inside.

"Is Arianne okay? Where is she?"

"She's fine. I could do with some TLC though." I held up my busted hand.

"Oh, brother, tell me you didn't do anything stupid."

"I messed up, Sia. I really messed up."

"Was it because of Arianne?"

I nodded, and my sister touched my cheek. "Then it was worth it."

I only wished my father would see it like that.

We entered the house and Alessia went to grab the supplies. I knew I probably needed an X-ray but it would have to wait.

"Niccolò," the anger in my father's voice shook the house.

"Good luck with that," Enzo said.

Alessia reappeared with the first aid kit, but I waved her off. "It can wait. Go find Enzo something to eat or drink."

"But..."

"Sia," I warned, and she skulked off.

I made my way to my father's study. He was sitting behind his desk, his hand curled into a tight fist. "Tell me you didn't nearly kill Fascini when I ordered you not to go anywhere near him."

"How did you find out?"

"One of your Uncle Vincenzo's guys picked up the call when it came in over the scanner."

"I fucked up. I know that. But you didn't hear what he was saying about her, the way he was intimidating her."

"Damn it, Niccolò. Do you have any idea what you've done?"

"I didn't mean to hurt Tristan. He took me by surprise and I elbow—"

"Tristan? What the fuck does he have to do with this?"

"He got hurt," I said. "It was an accident but it's bad. They're blue-lighting him to County Hospital."

"Maledizione! This is all we need." My father breathed heavily through his nose. "I found out something about Fascini."

"You did?"

"Tommy called."

My spine stiffened. Tommy was supposed to call me with any updates, which meant if he'd gone around me and straight to my father, it was bad.

Real fucking bad.

"Tommy couldn't turn anything up on Mike Fascini. His businesses seemed kosher, his investment portfolio all above board. So he started digging deeper and found something interesting."

"What?" I raked a hand through my hair, wondering how much more bad news I could take.

"You ever heard me mention the name Ricci growing up?"

"It doesn't ring a bell."

"That's because it isn't a name we talk about much anymore." He let out a heavy sigh, leaning back in his chair. "Remember the stories I used to tell you about why there is so much bad blood between us and the Capizola?"

I nodded. We all knew the story. It was ingrained into us from a young age. My father's great-grandfather, and Roberto's great-grandfather, had wanted to unite our families and make them strong. But Luca Marchetti's son, Emilio, didn't fulfil his promise to marry Tommaso Capizola's daughter. Instead, he ran off into the sunset with her brother's fiancée, setting off a chain of events which tore the families apart.

"When Emilio ran off with Elena, it didn't only end the union of the Marchetti and Capizola. It severed our ties to the Ricci too."

"Ricci?"

"Emilio ran off with Elena Ricci. She was promised to Alfredo Capizola. It wasn't just a union of love, it was union of strength, arranged by their fathers, to bring the Ricci family into the fold."

"Okay, but what does any of this have to do with Fascini?"

"Turns out Mike Fascini hasn't always been a Fascini. It is, in fact, his mother's surname. His father took her name when they married. His father's actual name is Ricci."

"So you're saying the Fascini aren't Fascini at all?

They're Ricci? I don't understand."

"Me neither, Son. Me neither. It could be pure coincidence, but instinct tells me it's not. The Fascini have positioned themselves right in the center of Robert Capizola's business. Which puts them right at the center of our business. I've been around long enough to know if something seems off then it probably is. Tommy's going to dig deeper, let me know what he finds. But this shit you pulled tonight, that is a big fucking problem, Niccolò."

"I'll make it right." I didn't know how yet, but I would.

"I'm sending you to Boston."

"What?" I shot forward. "You can't—"

He slammed his hand down, making the table shake. "I can, goddamn it, and I will. I might be your father, Niccolò, but I'm still the boss, and you will follow me on this. Go to Boston, lay low, and let me figure out how to smooth this over. When Capizola finds out you're responsible for this, he's going to want your head on a silver fucking platter."

"But Ari—"

"Arianne got you into this mess. Jesus, Niccolò, you need to think with your head here. You can't protect her if you're locked away or pushing up daisies. Go to Boston, let me see what Tommy can dig up. And trust me to try and clean up this mess you've made."

"If anything happens to her..." Fuck, I couldn't bear it.

"She's under my protection. I gave you my word. I'll figure it out."

"I love her. I love her so fucking much."

"I know you do, Son. But look at your ancestors, learn from them. Love almost destroyed this family once before. Don't let it destroy you too. Go to Boston and lay low until I can get a handle on this thing."

"I won't lose her," I said with absolute conviction. Losing Arianne was not an option, in this lifetime or the next.

My father leaned forward, levelling me with a hard look, but I was certain I saw a flash of regret there too. "Let's hope you don't have to."

∞∞∞

He wanted me to leave first thing. But there was no way I was leaving without seeing Arianne first. She'd spent all night at the hospital, waiting for news of Tristan. He'd suffered a traumatic brain injury, and doctors had induced a coma due to swelling around his brain. There was a certain irony in the fact that I'd wanted to kill Scott, to watch his life drain from his eyes with my bare hands tight around his neck, but Tristan was the one lying in a hospital bed.

Even though I didn't like the guy, I knew if I could take back that moment, I would. I'd played it over and over in my head, but I couldn't rewrite history. If he didn't wake up or the damage to his brain turned out to be too extensive, that was all on me.

It was my elbow.

My blow to his face.

My. Fucking. Fault.

Sure, I couldn't have known he would fall and crack his head, but if I'd have only reacted differently.

Arianne didn't blame me. She'd told me again and again over text. It didn't ease the guilt snaking through my chest though. I'd spent all night awake in my childhood bedroom at the request of my father. I think he expected the police to show up and wanted me close by just in case they did. But no one came. Dawn broke and with it the reality that, by dusk, I would be gone.

I hadn't plucked up the courage to tell Arianne yet. Her world had been obliterated again, and I didn't want to add to her worries. But I had to tell her eventually. Instead, I called Luis and asked him to have Nora call me. There was something I needed from her, from them both.

It was my last request before I left Verona County.

Before I left Arianne.

"You look like shit," Enzo said as I dragged my sorry ass into the kitchen. "It's true then, you're leaving?"

"Leaving?" Alessia gasped.

I shot Enzo an irritated look before turning to find my sister standing there, her eyes full of worry and betrayal. "It's only temporary," I said.

"You can't leave." Her lip quivered. "I need you. Ari needs you."

Inching forward, I opened my arms. But she jerked back. "You can't go, Nicco. I don't care what happened last night. We need you." Big fat tears began to trickle down her face. I pulled her into my arms and held her tight.

"Enzo and Matteo will look out for you. Bailey too. And I'll be back before you know it." I hated lying to her, but it was better than admitting the truth.

I had no idea when it would be safe for me to return. If Roberto and Fascini pressed charges, I would be a wanted man. And if they didn't, it would be because they intended on dealing with me in a different way entirely. Roberto Capizola might have been a straitlaced, law abiding citizen, but he had enough money to make things happen and then make the paper trail disappear. And if Fascini was somehow related to the original Ricci, who knew what his family's real motivation was for being here.

The thought of leaving my sister and Arianne was almost too much to bear. I was supposed to be here to protect them.

"What will I do without you?" She sobbed into my chest, the sound gutting me.

"Ssh, Sia. You have to be strong, okay? You're a Marchetti, and it's time to act like one."

"You're right." My sister eased away, steeling her expression. "If you let anything happen to you,"—she slammed her hands into my chest—"I swear to God, Nicco. I will never forgive you."

Enzo chuckled. "You have nothing to worry about. We'll look out for her."

"Like you aren't going to miss me." I tried to lighten the mood, but his expression darkened.

"Nothing about this is right, you know?"

"My father is right. If I stay... I can't do that to you all. If I go, at least you stand a shot of figuring out a way to take Roberto and Fascini down."

Then I could return. I could be with Arianne and we could get a shot at our happily-ever-after.

Who the fuck was I kidding?

Happy endings didn't exist in my world.

But she deserved one.

Arianne deserved the sun, the moon, and all the stars. And I was determined to try to figure out a way to give them to her.

Even if it killed me.

Chapter 25

Arianne

"Ari," Nora nudged my side and I jerked awake. Not that I was really sleeping. Exhaustion weighed heavily in my bones, but true sleep wouldn't come. I was too plagued with nightmares. Scott's breath as he taunted me and Nicco, the feel of his fingers splayed possessively on my hip. The way Nicco had unleashed his darker side, the side I'd been sheltered from, to rain fire and fury down on Scott's face. Tristan's lifeless body, his blood smeared on Nora's hands.

Oh God, the blood.

For a split second, I had thought he was dead. Killed by the one I loved more than anything else in the world.

It was an accident. I knew that. A tragic turn of events. But I also knew it wouldn't matter to my father. He'd raised Tristan as good as his own. My Aunt Miriam was a single mother, Tristan's father long gone before she ever gave birth.

Nicco might as well have hurt me, that's how hard it had hit my father.

He stood in the door, his expression cold, grief seeping from every inch of him. "I'd like to speak to my daughter alone," he said.

Nora got up and squeezed my hand. "I'll be right outside."

At least twelve hours had passed since they brought Tristan to the hospital. A sleepless night of waiting and worrying. Even the first light of morning had brought no solace. Tristan was stable but he was in a coma while they gave his brain time to heal. Until they woke him, doctors were unable to comment on the severity of his injuries.

"You have created quite the mess, mia cara."

Not 'mio tesoro'.

His voice sounded so cold, so clinical.

"It was an accident, Papá. You have to believe me. Nicco never meant—"

"*Do not* speak his name in front of me. That boy is nothing but trouble. I told you to stay away from him. I told you and yet you disobeyed me, and now Tristan is..." He swallowed, his Adam's apple pressing roughly against his throat.

"It was accident," I repeated, as if it mattered. As if the fact Nicco hadn't meant to hurt Tristan changed anything.

"And what about Scott? Was he an accident too? He's black and blue, Arianne. Did your boyfriend's fist just slip into Scott's face?" He was furious, his anger permeating the air like a dark storm on the horizon. "What on earth were you thinking?"

"I love him, Papá. I love Nicco," I cried.

"Love?" He sneered. "That monster cannot love; his blood does not allow it. Scott is—"

"Scott is a monster." My body shook with the force of my words. "He hurt me, Papá. He... he forced himself on me."

"Don't be ridiculous, Arianne. Scott told me what

really happened the night of the gala. He told me things moved too fast for you and you lashed out."

"He said that?" Of course he had. Why did I expect anything less? "I told him no, Papá. I told him no and he still —"

"*Basta!*" The vein in his neck throbbed. "You will not speak ill of Scott again. Do you understand me? He is a good man from a good family."

"But, Papá..." Tears streaked down my cheeks, my eyes sore and puffy.

"Niccolò Marchetti is done. His father might have friends in high places, but I am Roberto Capizola. I'll throw everything I have at him to make sure he never sees the light of day again."

"You wouldn't..." Fear gripped me like a vice.

"When will you learn, Arianne. I will always do what is best for you. Always."

"You mean you'll always do what is best for you and your business!" I spat the words, but my father had already turned on his heel, reaching for the door handle.

"If you do this," I said quietly. "I'll expose Scott for what he really is. A sexual predator who can't take no for an answer."

My father turned slowly, his expression darkening. "Are you threatening me, figlia mia?"

"I have proof. Evidence of what he did to me. If you press charges against Nicco, I'll release it to the police. I'm pretty sure I'm not the first girl on campus he's attacked. I could persuade others to testify." I narrowed my eyes, nervous energy vibrating through me. "It'll be a huge scandal. It'll ruin their family name. Their reputation."

"Evidence?" He choked over the word. "But he said it

was a misunderstanding."

"He lied. I have the bruises to prove it."

"Are you saying that he... he *raped* you?"

"Did you not hear anything I just told you?" I shrieked. "You chose to put your business deal first. Nothing you do is to protect me; it's all to progress the company. To better you."

"Arianne, mio tesoro." The blood drained from his face. "That is not—"

"Don't." I stabbed my finger into the air. "Don't you dare backtrack. You weren't interested in hearing my side of the story until I told you I had evidence. So here's my deal, *father*. Drop the charges against Nicco, and I won't release the evidence to the police or go public with my story."

"Scott and his father will never agree to those terms. They want blood, Arianne. Nicco's blood."

"Well you need to convince them then, because I'm not playing around. If Nicco isn't cleared of all charges, then you'll find out exactly the lengths I'm prepared to go to for the people I love."

My father stared at me as if he no longer recognized me. It was fitting really. The man I once worshipped had turned out to be a man I didn't know, and the daughter he adored had turned out to be a girl he didn't know at all.

"Who are you, mio tesoro?" Sadness edged into his expression as he stared at me.

"You mean you don't recognize me, Papá?" I stood taller, knowing there was no going back now. I'd made my choice, picked my side. "I am Arianne Capizola. I am my father's daughter."

∞∞∞

Our new apartment was a small two-bed in one of my father's buildings situated in the heart of University Hill. La Stella boasted a fully equipped gym and heated swimming pool and was located on a busy block that had a coffee shop, Chinese takeout, general store, and laundromat.

"Ooh, fancy," Nora said dropping her bags on the floor and scanning the room.

"I just want to sleep," I groaned. My father had finally given us permission to leave the hospital.

"At least we don't have to go to class today. I might go see my parents later." Nora glanced at Luis who was busy checking the place over. "After what happened to Tristan, I feel like I need to hug them, ya know?"

"I'm not sure I want to go back home yet." I'd had enough of my father for one day.

"I can arrange to have Maurice take Nora to the estate. I will stay here with you."

"Thank you, Luis," I said. "For everything."

He gave me a swift nod. "I'm going to introduce myself to security and check in with the team. If you need me just buzz." He stepped out of the apartment, leaving us to it.

"How are you feeling?" Nora asked.

"Like my head went through a meat grinder."

"Tristan will come out of this okay. He's too big and annoying to let something as little as a bump to the head keep him down."

I forced a weak smile. I knew she meant well, but the joke was lost on me. "I'm not sure me and my father can come back from this," I whispered, dropping onto the couch.

"But you said he seemed shocked when you said there was evidence."

"If anything, that only makes it worse. Like my word wasn't enough." I swallowed down the tears burning my throat. "I'm not sure I can ever forgive him, Nor."

"And that's okay. He hurt you, Ari. It's understandable. But maybe he can come through for you when he talks to Scott and his dad?"

"Yeah, maybe."

"Have you spoken to Nicco?"

"He's making arrangements in case my father can't talk Scott and his dad out of dropping the charges. Whatever that means."

"Does it bother you that he's got this whole other life that you'll never truly be a part of?"

"It should," I confessed. "But if you love someone, really love them, you have to accept all the little parts of them, don't you? Even the ones you might not fully understand."

"What do you think about Enzo?" Nora changed the subject. "I can't figure him out. I mean he's so freakin' hot and he's big... *down there.*"

"Nora!" I covered my ears, smothering a giggle.

"Oh come on, we're freshman at college. This is what life is supposed to be about. I came eye-to-eye with that thing and let me tell you, it's a monster."

"Stop. Oh God, make it stop." I tried to slap my hand over her mouth, but she peeled my fingers away.

"At least ten inches. Can you imagine? And he's so muscled and angry. I bet he's a real—"

"You can't go there, not with him."

"What, why? You've got yourself your very own mafioso, seems only fair I get one too." She smirked.

"He's not like Nicco, Nor. Enzo is... well, he's something else entirely."

"Yeah." She sighed, flouncing back against the couch. "You're probably right. I always pick the jerks."

"You'll find someone, just give it time."

"Made you laugh though, didn't I?" She peeked over at me and we shared a smile.

"I don't know what I'd have done without you through all this."

"Probably something very stupid. Now let's go take the tour of our new place. I think we deserve it." Nora grabbed my hand and pulled me up. "Ready?"

I wasn't, but what choice did I have? Life went on whether you wanted it to or not. You just had to figure out how to put one foot in front of the other and keep going.

∞∞∞

"Ari." Someone gently shook me, but the pull of sleep was too much to resist. "Ari, I'm leaving. Maurice is here to drive me home. I'll call you later to let you know when I'll be back. Enjoy your evening." Nora's voice grew louder, the hint of amusement in her words rousing me awake.

"Nor, what's going on?" I murmured.

"Nothing." She smothered a snicker.

My eyes flew open. "Nora Hildi Abato, what did you do?"

"Me? Nothing. I've got to go, love you." She moved to the door. We'd finally chosen our rooms after pulling straws earlier. I drew the smaller room at the end of the hall with its own bathroom, while she drew the bigger one next to the master bathroom. I'd barely gotten fresh sheets on the bed when I'd fallen on top of it and succumbed to sleep.

"See you later." I waved her off, snuggling back down under the covers.

"Oh, and Ari," she called. "You might want to wear something less... bed chic." The door clicked shut and I bolted upright. What the hell did she mean? Unless...

I scrambled off the bed to check my cell phone, and sure enough there was a text from Nicco.

Six thirty. Be ready xo

My heart swelled. He was coming here. I don't know how he'd found a way inside, but I didn't care. Until I checked the time and realized I only had forty-five minutes to get ready.

I leaped into action, stumbling against the dresser, cussing under my breath as pain shot through me.

"Arianne?" Luis called.

"I'm okay," I replied, rubbing my hipbone. "I'm going to take a shower."

A deep rumble of laughter drifted down the hall, but there was no time to dwell. Nicco was coming here, and I looked like I'd been dragged through a hedge backward.

Thirty-minutes later, I had scrubbed and primped, cleansed and styled to within an inch of my life. I'd opted to wear a floaty dress that scooped low at the chest and hit just above the knee. It was feminine and light and clung to my curves when I walked. My makeup was subtle, and my hair fell into thick waves around my face. The girl in the mirror looked lovesick; her eyes glittering and skin radiant. But it was more than that. I just needed to see him, to know we were okay.

I needed Nicco in a way that terrified me.

When I entered the living room, Luis cleared his throat, sitting straighter. "Arianne, you look... beautiful."

"Thank you."

"Nicco is a very lucky man."

"Thank you for everything that you've done for us. I'll never forget it."

He stood up, nodding. "I'll go and make the arrangements."

"He's not putting you or himself at risk, coming here?"

"Let us handle all that. You just enjoy your evening. Lord only knows, you've earned it."

The butterflies in my stomach multiplied and I gently pressed a hand there, trying to calm myself. Luis disappeared out of the apartment leaving me alone. I checked my cell phone, hoping to see a message from my father. There was nothing, so I typed out a quick message to him.

Anything?

He replied straight away.

These things take time, Arianne.

Nicco doesn't have time.

Be patient, mio tesoro, please.

Make this right, Papá. I'm begging you.

I will do my best.

It would have to do for now. It was almost six thirty. I hovered nervously by the counter, waiting. After what seemed like a lifetime, the door swung open and Nicco was standing there looking every bit the dark and dangerous mafioso I knew him to be.

Our eyes met, relief and possessiveness swirling in his depths.

My breath caught as I drank him in. It was like seeing him for the first time all over again. Without a second thought, I ran to him, flinging my arms around his shoulders. "Nicco," My resolve cracked with that single word, all the pain, confusion, and anger of the last few days spilling out of me.

"I'm so fucking sorry," he said, cupping the back of my neck and holding me.

"Sorry?" I eased back to look at him. "But what are you —"

"For Tristan. I never meant to hurt him." His eyes shuttered, pain rippling off him.

"Ssh." I pressed a finger to his lips. "It was an accident, and maybe it makes me a selfish, horrible person, but I don't want to think about Scott or Tristan or my father right now." Something stirred inside me.

Nicco was here.

He was here, for me.

"Say something," I said, feeling the heat of Nicco's gaze drift over me.

"You look... Fuck, Bambolina. I had every intention of coming here and doing this right. But all I can think about is carrying you into your bedroom and undressing you."

Desire flooded me, my stomach coiling tight. "Yes, please," I whispered.

God, I wanted this man.

I wanted him more than I'd ever wanted anything in life.

More than freedom.

More than the truth.

More than I needed my next breath.

"I brought dinner." He held up a brown bag, a rich aroma filling the apartment.

"Dinner can wait," I took it from his hands and placed it on the counter. "I need you, Nicco."

I need to know this is real.

"Amore mio, there is no rush. We have time." Nicco stared down at me with such love and affection I could hardly breathe.

I ran my hands up his black shirt. He'd rolled the sleeves up at the elbows and left it tucked out of his black dress slacks. I'd never seen Nicco look so smart. So devastatingly handsome.

"See something you like?" He lowered his face to mine, a faint smirk tugging at the corner of his mouth.

"You are so handsome." My fingers drifted over the profile of his face, lingering on his lips. Nicco's eyes shuttered as he inhaled deeply, the air crackling around us. "Do you feel that?" I asked.

"I feel it." He gulped, sliding one of his hands against mine, interlocking our fingers. "God, Arianne, the things I want to do to you."

"I want it all. Every single thing."

"You don't know what you're asking." He touched his head to mine, his breaths coming in ragged bursts.

"You. That's all I want." My mouth chased my fingers away, kissing him softly. But then Nicco scooped me up in his arms, making me shriek in surprise. He carried me down the hall, pausing at Nora's bedroom door.

"Next one," I smiled, wrapping my arms around his neck.

Nicco kicked open the door and entered my room. "I haven't had time to decorate yet," I said, "but the bed is pretty comfortable."

His eyes darkened with lust as he stalked over to the bed, lowering me down like I was precious goods. "Are you sure?" he asked.

I pressed a hand to Nicco's cheek, my skin tingling with anticipation. "I have never been more certain of anything."

I'd gone to so much effort to look pretty for him, taken my time choosing the perfect dress. But it didn't matter. Nicco always looked at me like I was the most beautiful girl on the planet. It was both exhilarating and intimidating, knowing that he—Niccolò Marchetti, mafia prince—wanted me.

He straightened, letting his hands fall to his shirt, slowly unbuttoning it. I watched with rapt fascination as more of his skin was revealed. My eyes greedily tracing over the planes of his abs, lingering on the perfect V disappearing into his slacks.

"Hungry, love?" he whispered, letting his shirt fall to the floor.

I wasn't hungry, I was ravenous. Confidence stirred inside me, and I rose onto my knees, sliding my hands down my body, curling my fingers around the hem of my dress. Nicco was as still as a statue, the rise and fall of his chest quickening, as he watched me drag the material slowly up my waist.

"Sei bellissima." It was a low growl in his throat as he took a step forward. "May I?" He finally reached me, dropping to his knees at the end of the bed. I nodded, removing my hands, shivering when Nicco's fingers replaced them, brushing my thighs. He grabbed the material, working the dress up my body, stealing my breath as he pressed his lips to my navel.

My hands slid into his hair as he travelled up my stomach, kissing and licking. Nicco broke away to pull the dress over my head, and then he was kissing me, sweeping me up in his storm. I clung to him, breathless and quivering, and he'd barely even touched me yet.

"Nicco," it was a breathy moan. A plea.

I needed more.

So. Much. More.

He changed direction, trailing his lips up the slope of my neck, nipping the skin beneath my ear. In one swift motion, he picked me up, hitching my legs around his waist, and lay me down. His eyes darkened as they found the faint bruises still tarnishing my breasts and the swell of my hips. My breath hitched, waiting to see what he would do. Whether it would be too much for him. But they didn't deter Nicco.

Dipping his head, Nicco took his time kissing each one, replacing every lingering memory of pain with nothing but pure pleasure. When he reached my thighs, he pulled my body to the edge of the bed and removed my panties. A shiver rolled up my spine as he flattened his tongue against me, sucking my clit into his mouth. I bucked beneath him, pulling on his hair as he worshipped me.

Feasted on me.

"You taste like heaven," he drawled, slipping a finger inside me. "Okay?" Nicco asked, and I nodded, waiting for the discomfort to pass. He kissed my inner thigh, sucking gently, turning the lingering pain to sheer pleasure as he curled his finger enough to hit the spot deep inside me that made me shatter into a thousand pieces.

I was soaring, floating away on a cloud of ecstasy.

But then Nicco climbed my body, staring down at me with nothing but hunger. His hooded gaze grounded me. Anchored me to the moment. "Voglio fare l'amore con te," he leaned in, whispering the words against my lips.

"My Italian is a little rusty," I admitted.

Nicco smiled, giving me a little shake of his head. "I said, I want to make love to you, Arianne. So much..." He brushed the hair from my face, staring right into my soul.

"Yes."

I was stripped bare to him, but it was so much more than skin on skin.

It was two hearts beating as one.

Two souls uniting.

Swallowing, Nicco stood up, digging his wallet out of his pocket. He pulled out a foil wrapper and placed it down on the bed beside me, before unbuttoning his slacks and pushing them and his boxer briefs clean off. My tongue darted out, licking my lips. His body was a sculpted piece of art. All hard lines and carved muscle. But it was his scars that made him beautiful; a permanent reminder of how fragile life was. Of how important it was to make the most of moments like this.

Intense. Overwhelming. Magical moments.

"If I do anything you don't like, anything that hurts, I need you to tell me, okay?" He kneeled on the bed, wrapping a hand around his hard length and stroking himself. I wanted to lean up and taste him again, but I couldn't move. Frozen in place by the nervous energy zipping through me.

Nicco covered my body with his, careful not to put his full weight on me. Dipping his hand between us, he gently worked a finger inside me.

"Oh…" I gasped, trembling at the intimate position. It felt so much more than before, his dark gaze pinning me in place, unyielding. I was lost to him, completely at his mercy as he touched me, his thumb circling my clit in slow motion. It was too much, too sensitive.

Yet, at the same time, it wasn't enough.

"Nicco," I breathed. "You, I need you."

His eyes turned as black as night. Nicco kissed me, easing off me to roll on the condom. Then he was there, nudged up against me. "I love you, Arianne. Never forget that." With one smooth glide, Nicco was inside me.

"Okay?" he asked, brushing his nose over mine, giving my body a chance to adjust.

I nodded, too overcome with emotion to speak. He was everywhere. Inside my body, my heart, my soul.

"I'll take it slow."

"No." I gripped his arm, arching my back. It made him slip deeper, and we both groaned. He buried his face in my neck, and I knew he was holding back. "I don't want you to treat me like glass, Nicco."

After a second, he began to move. Slow at first. Nicco kissed me deeply, mirroring the way his hips rolled against mine in measured torturous strokes. My fingers curled into the sheets as sensation hit me from every direction. I'd always known being with Nicco would be everything. But I hadn't expected to be so consumed by him. Every thrust, every dig of his fingers, the graze of his teeth against my collarbone. I felt it all.

Interlinking our fingers, Nicco pressed our hands beside my head as he rocked harder, deeper. His kisses grew hungry, dirty. He licked and nipped and gently bit my breasts, flicking his tongue over my nipple, chasing away the sting with tender kisses. My hips began to rock, desperate and searching.

"More," I panted. "I need more."

"You feel so good," Nicco rasped against the hollow of my throat, my body stretched out beneath him. He flattened himself to me, changing the angle, reaching some place deep inside that made my breath catch. "I don't ever want this to end, amore mio."

I didn't either.

I wanted to lose myself in him, to drown in his dark waters and never come up for air.

"Arianne..." Nicco was drowning too. I felt it. Felt him ready to shatter. "Fuck, I can't..."

"It's okay," I murmured against his lips, kissing him as hard as I could, lifting my hips to meet his. My body began to tremble as intense waves of pleasure crashed over me. "Oh God..." I cried, clinging to Nicco's body as he stilled above me, groaning my name.

Silence wrapped around us like a bubble as Nicco stared down at me with so much love and longing in his eyes, I felt weightless. "You are everything to me, Arianne. Sei la mia metá. No matter what happens, I will love you until the day I die."

Brushing my fingers against his jaw, I smiled. "Everything is going to work out, Nicco, you'll see."

It had to.

Because Nicco was right.

What we had wasn't fleeting. It was soul deep.

Written in the stars.

It was the kind of love they told stories about.

∞∞∞

I woke with a smile, reaching out to feel the hard planes of Nicco's body. Only to be met with cold silken sheets.

"Nicco?" His name was like a prayer on my lips. Everything about last night had been perfect. From the way he'd dressed up smart for me, to the delicious meal we'd had to reheat and eat wrapped in bed sheets, to the way he'd worshipped every inch of my skin throughout the night.

I'd never wanted it to end—desperately fought sleep as my sated body slowly succumbed to the pull of exhaustion. The only thing that could have made it any better was waking in his arms, safe and cherished and loved.

"Nicco?" I called again as if I expected him to materialize in front of my eyes. There was no sign of him. No clothes strewn over the floor or sound of running water to signify he was taking a shower.

Nothing.

I swung my legs over the edge of the bed and sat up, rubbing the sleep from my eyes. He wouldn't have just left me. Not without an explanation.

Then I caught it.

A note.

A small scrap of paper propped up against a glass on my dresser. Dread filled me, every step toward it like wading through quicksand.

Bambolina,

I love you more than words can say.
Wait for me, please.
Until we meet again,
Nicco xo

"What the...?" I hurriedly read the words again, trying to understand their meaning, trying to read between the lines of a note that otherwise sounded a lot like goodbye. I rushed over to the nightstand and snatched up my cell phone, dialing my father's number.

"Arianne." That one word told me all I needed to know.

Something had happened.

"What did you do?" I ground out, my hands trembling with anger.

"Luis will drive you to the house. I'll see you soon." Then he whispered, "Perdonami, figlia mia."

I hung up, collapsing on the bed in a heap of frustration. Grabbing my pillow, I screamed.

"Ari?" Nora rushed into my room. "What is it? What happened?"

"He's gone," I cried. "Nicco is gone."

"Oh, Ari." She sat by my side, wrapping an arm around me. "I'm sure there's a good explanation."

"Did you know?"

"That he planned to leave? Of course I didn't. I'd hoped everything would work out, just like you." She squeezed me tighter.

"I'm going to call him." I called Nicco's number, but it rang out.

"Try texting him."

My fingers flew over the screen as I typed a message. But no reply came. Nicco wasn't answering. That, or he was ignoring me.

"I need to go to see my father." I shrugged out of Nora's hold and began pulling on clean clothes.

"Maybe we should think this through. I'm sure there's an explanation—"

"He's behind this," I snapped. "When I called him just now it was like he was expecting my call and he'd said something... Perdonami, figlia mia."

"Forgive me? He said that?" she asked, and I nodded.

"He promised me he would try to fix this. He promised."

"Well then," Nora said, standing. "Let's go get you some answers."

∞∞∞

In the end, I told Nora to go to class. She'd wanted to come with me, but I needed to do this alone. Well, I wasn't totally alone. Luis was with me.

We entered the house together, the quiet bang of the door closing behind us like gunfire echoing through me. Nora's mom greeted us. "Oh, mia cara, come." She enveloped me in her arms. "Tristan is a strong boy; he will pull through this."

"Thank you," I said. "Is my father—"

"He and his visitors are waiting in his office."

Visitors?

I frowned, glancing up at Luis. "Will you come with me?"

"Of course." He motioned for me to lead the way.

Something felt off but I couldn't put my finger on it. All I knew was that something had happened between last night and this morning for Nicco to up and leave me.

I knocked gently on my father's office door and he said, "Come in."

The second I stepped inside, the ground went from under me. Luis pressed close behind me, giving me the strength I needed to face Scott Fascini and his father.

"Arianne, how lovely to see you," Mr. Fascini smiled revealing a set of perfectly white teeth.

"What, no greeting for me?" Scott sneered. His face was a mess; a patchwork of cuts and bruises and tender spots.

"Scott," I said politely. "Mr. Fascini. This is a surprise." I turned my attention to my father. "What is this, Papá?"

"Sit, Arianne, we have much to discuss," he commanded. No explanation, no gentle request.

Nothing.

"I think I'll stand." I rolled back my shoulders, facing the three of them. Steeling myself for whatever bomb was about to drop now.

"Very well," my father said, his expression devoid of emotion.

Who was this man?

Because it certainly wasn't my father.

"There is something we need to tell you," he started, shifting uncomfortably in his chair. "Something that may come as quite a shock."

Fear gripped me, my breath catching in my throat as he looked at me with such regret, apology glittering in his eyes. "What did you do?" I asked, my voice quivering.

And then he delivered the words that would flip my world upside down forever.

Chapter 26

Nicco

I waited until I was twenty miles clear of Verona County to pull over. Dust sprayed up around my bike as it came to a halt. Ripping off the helmet, I inhaled a lungful of air, hoping it might ease the tightness in my chest.

I'd done a lot of fucked up things in my lifetime, but none had felt more wrong than leaving Arianne under the cover of darkness. She'd fallen asleep almost immediately after she had given herself to me so completely. It had been the best fucking moment of my life, loving her, being joined as close as two people could possibly get. I'd lain there for hours, stroking her skin, watching her sleep.

It was perfect.

A single moment in time I wanted to freeze-frame in case we never got another moment like it.

It had almost killed me, finally slipping out of the bed and getting dressed. She'd stirred, my name falling from her lips in a soft murmur. She must have been dreaming of me. The thought had made me both smile and die inside. For when she woke and realized I was gone, I knew her love for me would slowly turn to hatred.

One day, I knew she would understand, but in the harsh light of day, Arianne would only see that I had abandoned her after what should have been the best night of her life.

Fuck.

I was a bastard.

Yet, I'd had no choice. To stay and see her this morning would have been torture, and there was only so much pain a man could take before he surrendered. I knew if I told her, if I looked her in the eye and said goodbye, I would never let her go. I would either stay and face the consequences of my actions, or I would risk it all and take her with me.

So I left in the night like the coward I was.

Digging out my cell phone, I expected to see numerous missed calls and text messages from Arianne.

I didn't expect to see Luis' name.

My heart crashed against my rib cage as I opened his message, silently praying that it wasn't about Arianne, that she hadn't done something reckless in the wake of finding me gone. But it was worse.

So much worse.

I stared at the message, reading the words over and over, willing it to be wrong. I had done what he said. I had left Verona County to keep Arianne safe, to protect her.

So Luis' message had to be wrong.

Because there was no way in hell Roberto Capizola would agree for his daughter to marry the piece of shit who stole her innocence and covered her body in bites and bruises.

Yet that's exactly what the message said.

You'd better tell your father to work quickly, because I don't know what game Roberto is playing but I brought Arianne to the house to confront him, and Scott and his father were here. Roberto announced he had agreed

to their engagement... are you hearing this bullshit, Marchetti?!

Your girl is promised to that piece of shit.

I hope you have a plan because come her nineteenth birthday, they are set to be married.

Playlist

Where We Come Alive – Ruelle
I Could Get Used to This – Becky Hill, Weiss
Prism of Love – Blakey, Jones
Mixed Signals – Ruth B
Ocean Eyes – Billie Ellish
All I Want – Echoes
Soldier – Fleurie
Running Up That Hill – Meg Myers
Moments Passed – Dermot Kennedy
Drown – Boy in Space
Own It – Stormzy ft. Ed Sheeran, Burna Boy
I Want to Know What Love Is – Mariah Carey
The Heart Wants What It Wants – Selena Gomez
Can't Help Falling in Love – Kina Grannis
Blinding Lights – The Weeknd
Everything I Wanted – Billie Ellish

Acknowledgement

I have always been a huge fan of Shakespeare, especially Romeo and Juliet. So, it's hardly surprising (to me) that I ended up writing a Romeo and Juliet inspired story. There's just something so tragically beautiful about the idea of star-crossed lovers. Arianne and Nicco's story poured out of me in less than a month. It doesn't happen to me a lot, but when it does, it's really something. I lived, breathed, and dreamed these characters, and I really hope you enjoyed the first part of their story.

As always, there is a long list of people I need to thank for getting me to this point. I want to start with a special shoutout to Nina. She really championed this story—held my hand when I got author's doubt and fell in love with Ari and Nicco as much as I did. Thank you! Next up, is my team of betas who helped iron out the first draft: Bre, Ashley, Priscilla, and Mary, I am so grateful for your feedback and words of encouragement. I am fortunate enough to have an incredible editor who is always a great friend. Andrea, I'm not sure what book this is, but I know there will be many, many more. You're stuck with me for the foreseeable! And to Ginelle, my proofreader rock star; thank you for catching those final errors. Launching a new series is always daunting and I couldn't do it without my promo team. These ladies go above and beyond to spread the word for me, and I would be lost without them. A big thanks also to Give Me

Books Promotions for handling the release events. And my readers group, I am super grateful that you spend your time chatting to me, supporting my releases, and spreading the work about my books.

Last but not least, a shout out to all the bloggers and bookstagrammers (old and new) who signed up to help promote Prince of Hearts, and the readers who took a chance on this story. It is your continued support that make it all worthwhile.

Until next time, L A xo

About the Author

Angsty. Edgy. Addictive Romance

Author of mature young adult and new adult novels, L A is happiest writing the kind of books she loves to read: addictive stories full of teenage angst, tension, twists and turns.

Home is a small town in the middle of England where she currently juggles being a full-time writer with being a mother/referee to two little people. In her spare time (and when she's not camped out in front of the laptop) you'll most likely find L A immersed in a book, escaping the chaos that is life.

L A loves connecting with readers.

The best places to find her are:

www.lacotton.com

Or social media:

/authorlacotton

Printed in Great Britain
by Amazon